THEY DARED CROSS CALIX STAY, THE GREAT WATER GUARDING THE NETHER REALMS.

Otter. Bear. Dwarf. Three wayfarers on a journey to the fabled World Beyond Time, where glowed the ageless Circle of Light.

Little did they dream when they set out of the fair kingdom of Lorini . . . of the chill borders of the Northerland . . . of the perverse Palace of Darkness where green fire grimly glowed . . . of the dread town where the mysterious Humans lived . . .

They had yet to meet such gallant friends as Greyfax Grimwald . . . General Greymouse . . . Froghorn Fairingay . . . Cephus Starkeeper . . . and such fearsome foes as Dorini, sovereign of the sinister . . . and Cakgor, son of Suneater and Fireslayer . . .

Their great adventure had only just begun.

The Circle of Light Series

I Greyfax Grimwald
II Faragon Fairingay
III Calix Stay
IV Squaring The Circle

by Niel Hancock

Available from
WARNER BOOKS

Circle of Light-1
Greyfax Grimwald

by Niel Hancock

A Warner Communications Company

To My Grandparents

WARNER BOOKS EDITION

Warner Books, Inc.,
666 Fifth Avenue,
New York, N.Y. 10103

A Warner Communications Company

Printed in the United States of America

First Warner Books Printing: December, 1982

10 9 8 7 6 5 4 3 2

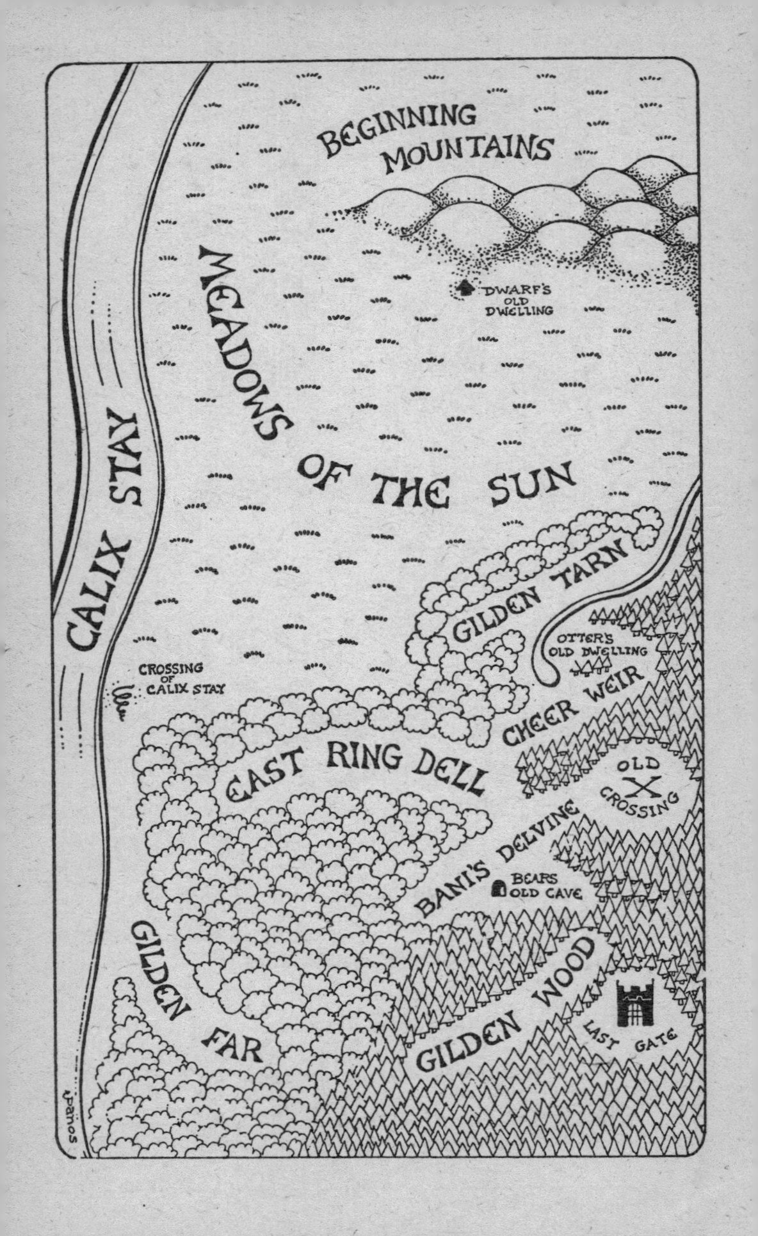
BEGINNING MOUNTAINS
MEADOWS OF THE SUN
DWARF'S OLD DWELLING
CALIX STAY
CROSSING OF CALIX STAY
GILDEN TARN
OTTER'S OLD DWELLING
CHEER WEIR
EAST RING DELL
OLD CROSSING
BANI'S DELVINE
BEARS OLD CAVE
GILDEN FAR
GILDEN WOOD
LAST GATE
Spanos

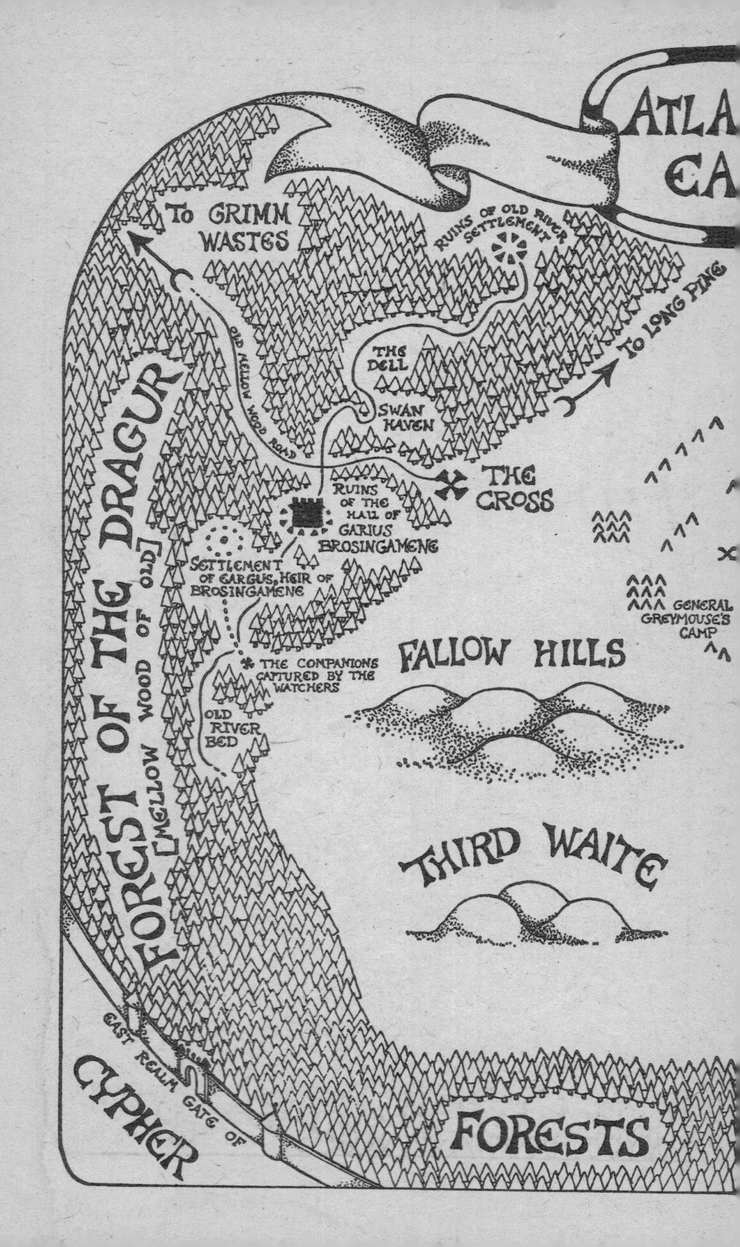
ATLA
CA
TO GRIMM WASTES
RUINS OF OLD RIVER SETTLEMENT
TO LONG PINE
OLD MELLOW WOOD ROAD
THE DELL
SWAN HAVEN
THE CROSS
RUINS OF THE HALL OF GARIUS BROSINGAMENE
SETTLEMENT OF GARGUS, HEIR OF BROSINGAMENE
THE COMPANIONS CAPTURED BY THE WATCHERS
OLD RIVER BED
FOREST OF THE DRAGUR
[MELLOW WOOD OF OLD]
GENERAL GREYMOUSE'S CAMP
FALLOW HILLS
THIRD WAITE
EAST REALM GATE OF
CYPHER
FORESTS

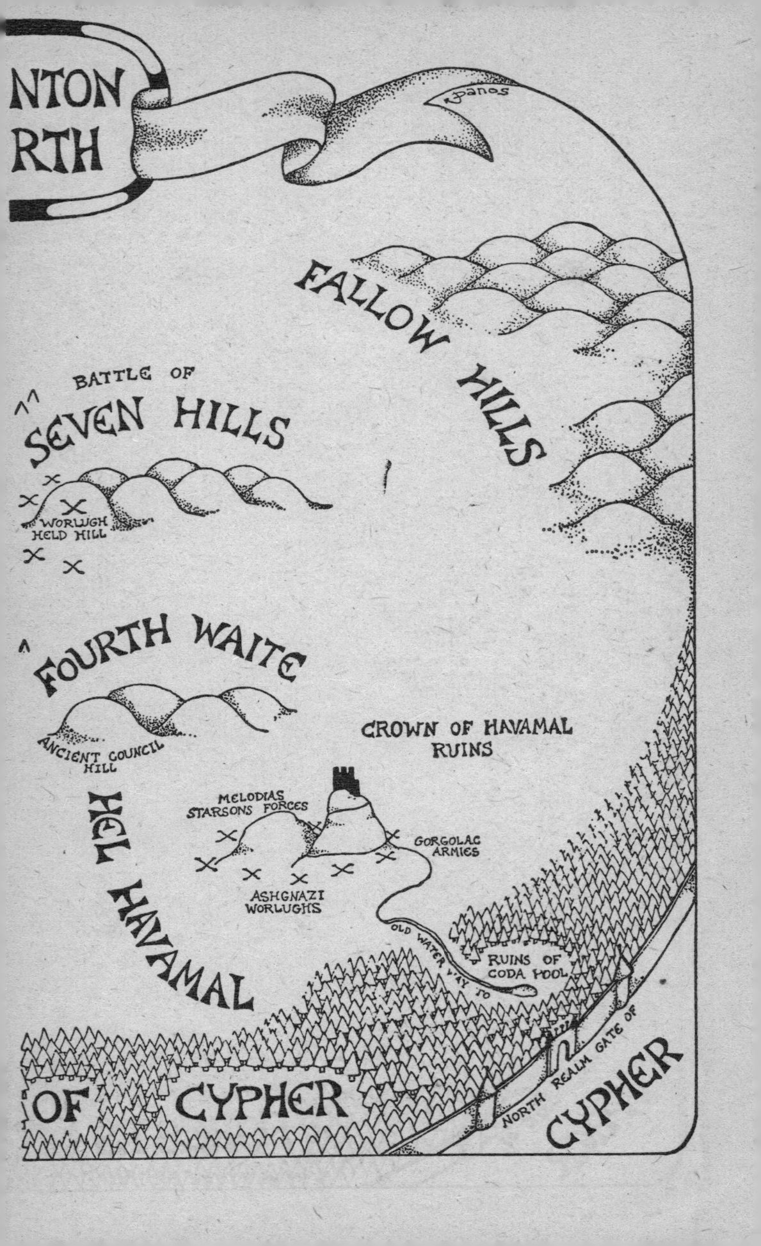

NTON
RTH
Panos
FALLOW HILLS
BATTLE OF
SEVEN HILLS
WORLUGH HELD HILL
FOURTH WAITE
ANCIENT COUNCIL HILL
CROWN OF HAVAMAL RUINS
MELODIAS STARSONS FORCES
GORGOLAC ARMIES
ASHGNAZI WORLUGHS
HEL HAVAMAL
OLD WATER WAY TO
RUINS OF CODA POOL
NORTH REALM GATE OF
CYPHER
OF CYPHER

MEETINGS BEYOND CALIX STAY

BEAR

On the morning of his leaving, he erased all his tracks from that part of heaven, carefully stacked new star branches in a neat pile behind the entrance in the dark mouth of the universe, and sadly began the thousand-year trip down the side of the sky that closely resembled a large mountain. If you looked at it that way. If you didn't, it might seem very much like walking out your own front door and down the steps.

The Bear was leaving in the last part of September, and the wind was still fresh with the old summer, and only the faintest trace of winter was evident. Of course, it was always that time of year in those parts, and he had not seen a winter in many ages, so he decided to travel down to the World Before Time to find out what it was like there now, and to see again the snow they spoke of sometimes when they traveled through. He had crossed many lifetimes before, and was happy with his home. However, he'd promised himself he would go, and the strange unknown feeling that was in him said he must. So he packed a hat of new strawberries, two handkerchiefs, his ancient book of Beardom, and a map of the World Before Time safely in his pockets, and set out to seek the snow kingdom, so far away he could only see the top of its elephant's hat nodding above the cloud fields between. On his way, he began whistling a cheery tune about bears, big and brown and only sometimes gruff, chuckling to himself when he came to those parts that all bears know, and frowning at others when the music described what all his kind knew to be serious business. He smiled more often than he frowned, because all bears are very jolly fellows unless disturbed, and he had not been disturbed in quite a few centuries—except lately, when all the travelers began coming through his side of the woods with distressing tales and sad songs he had never heard before and which made him very sad.

Turning for one last look at his old home, he set off in the direction of the Meadows of the Sun, where he hoped he would be able to rest for a while on his long and weary journey, and perhaps find an acquaintance or two to dance with or sing to. The last time he'd been that way he'd met a querulous old goat from down below the Great Water, and they'd spent many nights telling of green-coated hippogrifs and flying tortagans. He wasn't too sure what the stories would be this time, and an uneasiness stirred briefly, but the day was fine and bright, and he began thinking of other things—cool streams full of salmon, and tingly, frosted bark-brewed tea, or a good glass of blackberry juice, such as his mother used to give him in the days when he was only a cub. Yes, there were too many fine things on this fine day to listen to that small voice inside that would make him forget what a grand day it was, and how nice to be trotting easily along with the sun's golden fingers scratching your back in just the right places.

That was best of all, to feel the warmth touching your fur in delightful, soft glowing movements, and in a little while the thought of a nap occurred to him, beneath some grass green trees grown over with shade.

Only a little nap, for an age or two, before moving on.

DWARF

Broco, the dwarf, lived far under a mountain in a secret place. Only the river ever came near his home, so fast and deep was his dwelling. He'd found his way there after the great time of trouble. He lived alone except for his friend, the river, and never spoke of anything but mending and music. The two friends would often sit together exchanging songs. Broco sang his ancient dwarfish tunes, and the river newer ones, because his tale came down from different parts, bringing some odd bit of new now and then, and he remembered banks from his small beginning high atop another range of mountains miles and miles away to the south. It was in this way that Broco remembered the strange song that was repeated by the river, and it was this strange song that at last brought him forth from under his mountain.

He had hummed it and sung it and played it on one of the fine tiny reed pipes he'd spent hours over—carving minute scenes of woodlawns, or of his old home, with sometimes deer or fauns beneath the perfectly still trees—and it seemed to him a perfectly hummable, singable song, one of the best he'd heard, as far as he could remember. Dwarf memories stretch back to the coming of the First Age, when life once more crept forth from the night into the light of the living.

It was vaguely familiar, the way songs sometimes are, and slowly, so slowly it took what to others might seem years, the song became a sudden memory of his father, bent and old, his beard snow-white and reaching below the ornate gold belt buckle he wore, given to him as a token of affection by the High Master of Lore many ages before.

The memories of that time were unreal, when he had come to make his home under the mountain, with chores and a dozen other things to keep him busy. But on that day the song opened that faraway and long-forgotten door, all the other pleasures he'd so long pursued became empty, wearying tasks he could not keep his mind upon.

A motion had started somewhere, like a ripple far out to sea that slowly builds into a wave, and Broco became more and more restless, unable even to listen to the new songs or stories the river brought him.

As he sat working a molten piece of iron into a broad ax head one particularly long afternoon, with lunch done and supper far away, the thought of remaining longer became so acutely dreary, he huffed a bit, and began packing a traveling kit, not really knowing why, or where he was off to. All he knew was that something was calling him from across Calix Stay, and that for whatever reason, he must obey.

He prepared the last supper he would enjoy in his home under the mountain, and took particular pleasure in it, as a fellow might, not knowing when or if ever he would be back.

A decision had been made, and the restless feeling that had troubled him so long was gone. Only the thoughts of the coming journey filled his head, and the excitement of it all made it hard to sleep because of dreams and visions, until at last he rose, murmuring to himself those words he'd heard his father use when he was going to be away on his travels for a long time: "Well, best be about it now as later. A mile won't wait to be walked, and the road won't nap until my foot is upon it."

And humming the old song once more, it seemed to him it was a traveling song after all.

OTTER

Otter, sleek gray coat covered with mud, peered over the water rushes at the figure that trotted down his riverbank, an odd creature he'd never seen before, curiously dressed in red and green, with pointed-toed shoes and a bright yellow hat with a forest-green brim.

His muzzle barely cleared the rushes, and nothing was visible to Broco but a pair of dark brown eyes and a huge set of whiskers on either side of a shining black nose.

"Hello, friend. I've lost my way. Can you tell me how to get from here to the World before Time?"

Otter stood a little higher until his paws were visible to the stranger, and he pointed in a general direction where he remembered the dwarf's destination to be. Try as he might, he couldn't help asking, "Why are you going there? It's only trouble now. You'd be much better off if you'd stay here with me. We can fish, and swim, and play games."

"I have urgent business there," replied Dwarf, puffing up his chest and standing on his tiptoes. Dwarfs sometimes feel very important, and when they do, they blow up like toads, or balloonfish, or prime ministers, or presidents.

"Begging pardon, but what business, might I ask?"

Otter was terribly curious, and dying to know what made such a stranger travel all the way to *that* place, and what he could possibly do once he got there. He was more than pleased to do his chores, find food to keep him full, and spend his leisure hours constructing mud slides to scamper down, or simply to swim his river from one place to the next collecting stories or exchanging them with whoever might be about.

Then Broco hummed the tune, the song given him a long time before by his father. It stirred all the old feelings his soul remembered from his past. Otter stood suddenly, gray fur hackling all up and down his long back. His eyes were still open, his body still there, but he suddenly felt himself transported back to unordered places in his past, where he tumbled about in some awesome labyrinth full of loud noises and where no river ran. And was he in a different form?

It felt that way. Visions of all this flashed by him like lightning, feelings exploded inside him like thunder. As Broco watched, he turned several shades of gray lighter, his eyes slowly closed, and he trembled violently.

Broco stopped humming and ran over to the small, delirious creature.

"It's all right, little fellow, it's just a song and I'll sing it no more right now. Come on, now, it's all right."

Otter's fur relaxed, his eyes opened, his trembling ceased, and soon he was able to speak with only a little tremor in his voice.

"Where . . . how . . . that song . . . it is so disturbing . . . please go now, I have shown you what direction . . . and leave me here in peace with my river and trees and friends."

Broco stooped, only a little, for he was just slightly taller than Otter, and looked deeply and directly into the gray fellow's eyes. He spoke, quietly and gently.

"They will all be here when you return, and when you return they will all be different. You will really know them for the first time, and speak your first real hello to them. Then you will know, I think."

Dwarf's words trailed off, and he was quite taken by the beatific sound of his own voice.

Starting to protest, Otter looked again at Broco, beginning to understand, knowing that he had been waiting to leave for a long time, and that the time was here. He also knew that if he once left, he would not likely return again to this river.

Otter shuddered, but had to believe the little man.

"But must we leave this moment? Can't I say goodbye to my friends? I could go pick some wild berries, or plums, and we could all sit and eat, and sing, or tell stories."

Dwarf thought of how he had hated leaving his own home after spending such a long time there, and how the feeling of never returning had saddened him. There would be enough time for this simple request, and he wondered, even as he spoke, if it were not truly better simply to stay by Otter's river.

"Of course. You should have a chance to say goodbye, and I've had no fresh plums in ever so long. I'll come along and help you."

"Oh good," said Otter dancing. "There's a big berry bush just across the river there. I'll go get them."

Dwarf and Otter hurried to the river, where the Otter slipped noiselessly under the water. Broco waded in with such a splash that the fish a mile away were filled with terror. Surfacing, Otter raised a pair of angry eyes and twitching whiskers and glared over at Dwarf, whose brightly colored hat from a distance looked like a great yellow river rock.

"I'm a little rusty at my swimming, I guess," He murmured apologetically, feeling a bit guilty at taking the small gray creature from his home.

But they found and picked many dusky blue wild berries, and rich purple plums, and golden peaches heavy with nectar, and a wonderful feast was held, full of great laughter and stories, taller than even the oldest trees, and at dawn, both were fast asleep around the remnants of a fire.

MEADOWS OF THE SUN

It was where the Meadows of the Sun met the Gilden Tarn, right at the outlying edge, that Otter first caught the scent. Looking where he pointed, Broco stared, motionless, at the strange sight several yards in front of them.

They agreed on three things: whatever it was, it was big, it was brown, and it was breathing. And it was dressed most unusually for an animal in this part of the Meadows. A brilliant orange cloak was draped over its back, and a hat of unusual design sat between its ears.

They came even closer.

"It's a bear," said Broco.

"It's sound asleep," said the always curious Otter, who proceeded to crawl up onto the big animal's lap.

"It's been reading," mused Broco, "and gone to sleep."

The snoring of the big animal stopped, and one great red eye opened.

Otter scrambled behind Broco, who immediately let out a startled squeak.

"In the name of the Ancient Oak," boomed the Bear, "I command thee to disappear."

The great animal raised a paw skyward, and the

orange cloak fell askew. The big animal held up his paw until Broco stopped his squeaking and fell into a puzzled silence. The Bear lowered his forepaw, rearranged his cloak, and shut his eye.

Otter moved forward to ask a question.

Bear opened his eyes to a small squint to see if what he had seen had gone away as he had commanded. Seeing Otter and Dwarf still there, he slammed the heavy book shut and flung his hat down before him.

"Drat, and bear curses on it all," he mumbled, and immediately began to snore again.

Otter sat quietly on his haunches, his head turned to a curious angle.

Broco suddenly turned one cartwheel, landing noiselessly beside the great animal. Giving his friend a knowing wink, he began to hum the melody very gently, very soothingly, until the Bear once again opened his eyes.

"Hello," said Dwarf, his eyes dancing.

"Hello," said Bear, remembering.

They all made their way to the stream which marked the boundaries of the Meadows of the Sun. All were thirsty, especially Bear, who completely submerged his head for such a long time it made Otter dive and swim over to see if he was still alive. Bear's eyes blinked underwater at him. Otter blinked back, and returned to the surface. The water felt so good he began to swim and dive and fly out of the water headfirst, then feetfirst, finally giving his companions a display of water acrobatics such as they had never seen.

Later Bear led them into the forest, deep into the darkness, until finally they came upon the entrance to a large cave.

"This is my camp. Come in. You are welcome to

my meager hospitality." Bear entered, then Broco, with Otter dripping and draped on his back recovering from his sudden surge of energy. The cave was very big, with walls that receded past the flickering shadows cast by the huge candle in the center. Along the walls were hundreds of books covered with cobwebs and cave dust, many bearing strange and mysterious titles. Broco studied them for a long time. Bear finally raised himself and came over to stand beside the dwarf, who came barely up to the huge brown animal's knee.

"You've read all of these?" inquired Broco.

"I've either read them or should have read them," he answered, confronting the shelves as one would an old and respected opponent. "Maybe even written a few of them, I don't know."

"All three," mumbled Broco in Dwarfish.

"What's that?" asked Bear, whose ears were very sensitive.

"What I said, as for me, books are not my cup of tea," replied the dwarf quickly.

"Mine either," mused Bear. "When I found this cave, all these were here, and once in a while I pick up one of them and try to read, but either my concentration wanders until I fall asleep, or I stay up all night and read with such feverishness that I don't remember a word." Bear shook his head sadly. "I don't think I used to be like that."

"Most probably not," said Broco in Dwarfish to himself.

"What's that?" asked Bear.

"What's this?" called Otter from across the cave, saving Broco from having to think of another false answer. Otter had recovered, and in his unceasing curiosity was examining a great keg made of old wood, which had a spigot near the bottom of the vessel, and taking the handle in his tiny paws, he struggled to move it, with no success.

"Ah, that, my dear Otter, is the curse of my life, the cause of my ultimate downfall." Bear came over and glared at the keg, which came up to his nose. "This, my friends, is my unfortunate experiment in trying to find something to make me happy. I made it from a recipe which I found in the last book I remember reading. Yesterday I vowed to never drink another drop of the accursed stuff, and in so doing, decided to drink one last mug to celebrate my new resolve. The next thing I remember is opening my eyes and seeing a dwarf and an otter."

Otter, paying no heed to his comrades, was busily engaged in working the huge spigot with his paws, and all at once out came the dark brown bark bear beer, almost as thick as molasses, and emitting a heady aroma of oak bark and clove and new hops.

"My health won't permit such goings-on any longer, and I really am going to start my old exercises again, and begin my running. I used to be the fastest bear in the woods before I fell into this evil habit."

A carry-over from the other place, thought Broco.

Bear entered a deep reverie, and hardly noticed anything at all that went on, so Broco began searching for Otter, and finally found the little animal tucked snugly away in a low sleeping hammock.

Dwarf suddenly realized how tired he was, and yawning once, he crawled into the corner opposite his friend, and before he could even blink an eye, or think twice about all that had happened to him since he had left his dwelling under the mountain, he was fast asleep.

Bear, thinking far into what would have been the night, of other travelers and yarns of his own kind, nodded and loaded his pipe, and agreed or argued with himself, and finally decided that the journey the dwarf was taking was indeed a serious task.

Before Dwarf or Otter had awakened Bear had decided he would travel with them to see what he might and find out what it was in the odd, haunting melody Dwarf sang that made him stir deep within himself.

This occurred in the Twelfth House of the Fourth Rising of the Twin Moons, and already each of the three had been gone from the World Before Time for ten times as long as it takes for a man to be born and die where the sun rises and sets in a single day.

THE GREAT RIVER

"We're approaching Calix Stay now," spoke Dwarf, remembering how with great difficulty he'd crossed it years and years before, after the great battle of the Dragon Wars when the terrible beasts still roamed at will. Broco's mother had been slain in this battle, along with many friends and kin. He had crossed Calix Stay to find his new home under the mountain.

Calix Stay was raging white color, as deep as death's sleep, and swifter than the motion of a striking adder. It was the father of the river that Dwarf knew in his old home, and he hoped he remembered the words of crossing, for if he said the least little thing out of place, or twitched so much as his nose at the wrong time, they would all be plunged into the maelstrom of Calix Stay to be spun away into nothingness once more. There were some few, however, that Dwarf knew could cross or recross at will. His old friend Kilan had been one who had made the journey often in the old days, to mass an army there in the Meadows of the Sun where it would be safe from the prying eyes of the mighty dragon horde that preyed upon their homeland in those times. It was only the best intentions and the stoutest heart that would see man or beast or dwarf or elf pass over safely, and the correct words to hold Calix Stay motionless and still as a backwater of the smallest stream, so that whoever wished passage might go safely into the Meadows of the Sun and beyond, or back into the World Before Time unchanged.

Early into what would be night across Calix Stay, the friends stopped to rest and eat. Dwarf huffed a bit, filled with self-importance, for he was the only one among them who knew the words. He proceeded to give instructions for their crossing.

"Now," he exclaimed, standing before the exhausted animals, "we have before us a most arduous task."

"Scratch my back, Bear, will you? Just there."

Otter shook his fur and let the big brown animal scruff his back coat up in a place where he couldn't reach the itch that had been bothering him all day.

Bear looked away into the near distance to where Calix Stay roared and foamed.

"You silly nits, if you carry on like this, we'll never get across. You must pay close attention to what I say, or we're all lost!"

"How long does it take?" asked Bear, feeling a little distressed at the constant angry sound of the mighty river.

"Take to what?" snapped Dwarf.

"To cross."

A cold seed of mistrust was edging upward somewhere in Bear, although he could not distinguish it from the fear of the noise of the low growl of the water.

"It only takes the blink of an eye, if you know the words. Forever, if you don't. Now if you'll listen for a moment, I'll tell you what we must do, and how we must do it, and then we might get our sleep before doing it."

Dwarf cleared his throat angrily and looked from

one to the other. Finally he was satisfied that the smile on Otter's face was only the one that was normally there, and that Bear, reclining, was not in fact asleep.

"First of all, I must tell you the words to say. O Kale O. This is the ancient name, and as we cross, you must speak the words yourselves. If we had time, we could cross one by one, but the risk of someone forgetting the entire spell would be disastrous." Dwarf paused, glaring at Otter. "So, our only choice is to go all in a bunch. Not that I like it any too much, but that's neither here nor there."

Dwarf pulled out an ancient stone. Dark at first, then catching the sun, it was covered over with many strange glyphs and signs. He rubbed it a few times on his sleeve, breathed on it, spoke softly over it in High Dwarfish, and held it up to the light.

"This is a piece of stone from my old home where I dwelt before. It is a dragon stone, and since I have it, we'll use it to help us along."

Otter's eyes widened, and he poked a flat gray muzzle close up to the object in Dwarf's hand. Bear raised himself a bit, always interested in the lore of others, especially if it was ancient, and grunted.

"A bit moldy, Dwarf. How ever will that stone be of any help?"

"Grimpelty, fie, why am I stuck with such fatheads?" shot back Dwarf, cartwheeling sideways a few steps, then reversing, ending with a thump upon Bear's broad belly. "If you leave matters to someone that knows something about it, you'll find out."

And still standing upon Bear's stomach, he continued. "Next, I shall say the rest of the secret of Calix Stay. At once, the River should quieten, then we must speak the words I told you."

Dwarf's face darkened into a scowl. "Should anyone forget, or misspeak, it could be disastrous for all of us, for crossing all at once as we are, we run the risk of all being dragged along into Calix Stay. And our business doesn't include another tour of that sort."

Otter, fond of any water, asked, "What's so dreadful in a good swim, Dwarf? I've been in and out of and about and around water for quite some time now, and it doesn't seem to have done me any harm."

"Except your silly brain," grumped Dwarf. "I dare say it must have shrunk that a bit." He began spewing and sputtering his anger, but noticed Otter had not even heard, and was staring strangely.

"Otter, are you all right?"

At length Otter, shuddering once, said, "Yes, Dwarf. I suppose so. Just thinking."

"At any rate, this time tomorrow we'll be well on our way, with Calix Stay behind us," said Broco.

"Let's hope so," spoke Otter, so softly no one heard.

Six eyes shut gently after eating dwarf cakes, their magic being to rest the mind and body of even the tiredest travelers on the longest journeys. Soon the three were fast asleep, unworried at even the wild roar of Calix Stay that bellowed and howled before them. The friends were safely away in their homes of old, in dreams engaged with only the most pleasant sort of things.

Dwarf sang and puttered about a shop littered with all types and sizes of machines and tools that always worked, no matter what. Bear was padding down a long cavern hall after having bolted his front door securely against the season, his nightgown warm against his fur, his slippers just the right size, and a huge new barrel of wild clover honey next to his warm bed. Otter slipped into a new river down the longest mudslide he'd ever seen, and contentedly paddled on his back. Only once did he stir uneasily, some dim shape taking hold of him and disturbing even the powerful potion of the dwarf cake, but he soon slipped from the highest edge of a rainbow mountain into his holt, which is a snug otter den, and began thinking of sleep, deep and untroubled, even in his dream.

THE CROSSING

After an ample breakfast of honey and dwarf cakes, the friends set out to cross Calix Stay. It was hidden by a high curtain of silver mist that rose into the farthest regions of the sky.

Bear's heart had been drumming for quite some time, and he frequently twitched his tail, or bared his teeth, or simply reared up on his hind paws to try to get a better look at what they were approaching. Dwarf's own heart was pounding, and he was beginning to fear he would become flustered and misspeak the words, sending them all down into Calix Stay for who knows how long, only to have to begin over again with the entire business. Otter, walking on Dwarf's left, whistled and chirped low in his throat, and at last reached up a paw and clasped Dwarf's hand firmly. Dwarf looked down sharply, intending to scold the little gray fellow, but upon seeing the complete trust, and that it was meant to reassure, Dwarf, too, gave a friendly squeeze and began concentrating on the words.

From the last hills that skirted the Meadows of the Sun, they paused to look at the mighty spectacle before them. The low hills ran to left and right of them, covered with oak and elm and berry thickets, all in a perfect summer coat of deep green. The trees were tall and stout. A great, lush carpet of grass lay at their feet, inviting all who passed to lie down for shade and rest. Berries as big as Otter's paw clung to the low, thick branches of the bushes, giving him no end of temptation, for he began thinking how jolly it would be if they would all sit down in the shade and talk the entire affair out, while of course having their fill of the huge ripe berries, and maybe a short nap before going on, if they did indeed have to go on. Looking away down the slope at the silver mane of angry mist around Calix Stay, Otter whimpered and threw himself to the ground, his small, powerful body convulsed in tremors of fright.

"Oh, Dwarf, this is silly. Whatever are we going *there* for? I haven't been afraid in ages, and I'm all upset and tingly, and I'm sure we could have a much better time staying on here."

"I'm afraid I have to agree with the dear fellow, Dwarf," said Bear, sitting down beside Otter, crossing one great hind leg over the other, and glad Otter had spoken first.

"There's no real sense in all this hurry." Bear looked back toward the forest where he'd camped, thinking of the honey tree he'd found there, with almost all the sweet nectar still in it.

Dwarf sat dejected beside Bear and Otter, taking out his dragon stone and rubbing it with almost one motion.

"I know how you feel, dear friends. I'm not so sure myself now that we're actually here, but something tells me we're doing the right thing, and that we must cross."

Otter, turned on his back in the grass with his paws in the air, raised his head to look at Dwarf.

"It might be, Dwarf, that we were a little overanxious to be on our way. Don't you think we could stay just a while longer? I'm sure we must go and all, but won't tomorrow or the next day do just as well?" The little gray form had found a small rock, smooth and white and round, and began rolling it across his broad velvet stomach, moving it from paw to paw, then dribbling it up deftly to balance it on the end of his nose.

Dwarf sighed and looked away toward the Great River. He could barely remember his crossing. All the time before that was faint and dim—the dragons, and moving about in the time of trouble, when the World Before Time was filled with armies, men and elves, and dwarfs, and animals warring against the dragon hordes. Those memories drifted on in their cloaks, lingering only long enough to dim Dwarf's vision for a moment or two, then passing into the light of the Meadows of the Sun.

Bear broke the silence that had fallen over the friends with a slight hissing snarl. His ears were straight back, his hackles rising and his great body raised to strike.

"What is it, Bear?" cried Dwarf.

"I'm not sure. Something has been here before us. I thought I picked up the scent before, but I wasn't sure. Now I know something crossed, went a little way, then returned, or was destroyed."

"Whatever was it, I wonder? Man?" asked Otter.

"This was nothing from Mankind. I don't know what, but it stinks of something that means danger."

Otter picked up his nose to the wind, shuffled and searched, but could only barely pick up the faintest trace of anything out of the ordinary. He had long been in the Meadows of the Sun, and nothing there had ever had the least unpleasant thing about it, so quite naturally he was the longest in finding truth to what Bear had scented out.

Finally Bear lowered himself to all fours, shuffled

this way and that over the ground where he'd found the scent, laid back one ear, then the other, wagged his tail once, raised himself to his full height, lowered himself again in confusion, and announced, "I think I'm right, but I can't say as I've ever run across this particular scent."

"It's not man," affirmed Otter, poking his head up suddenly from a nearby patch of wild flowers. Poof, the little gray head with its twitching whiskers was gone.

"No, it's certainly not man," said Bear, looking to where Otter had been.

"And it's nothing else I've ever known," came the voice again, this time from a berry patch. Otter scampered out with fresh blueberry juice dripping from his chin. Carefully wiping it with his tongue, he went on. "What do you think, Dwarf?"

"I'm not sure what to make of it, but whatever it was was bad. Most unusual for this part of the world. It reminds me of before, when the stench of the dragon was heavy on us, even to the very edge of the River. If that's so, we have no time to lose."

"I think you're right, friend Dwarf, and I think we'd best move on now."

Bear looked to his friends for consent. All agreed they might as well go on now as not, and Dwarf led the way to the raging flow of Calix Stay. They went single file, in animal fashion. Dwarf gave his last instructions, repeated the words they were to say twice, and cautioned them into silence. Then he twirled thrice about himself, rubbed the dragon stone, and called the words forth. The rampaging torrents and tides of Calix Stay held their breath the barest moment, and Otter and Bear called out the words Dwarf had told them. The silver mist receded, the bright fields of the Meadows of the Sun darkened, a great whooshing darkness engulfed the friends, and after a ray of brilliant light broke over the waters, all was silence and dark, and they had entered once more the World Before Time. The stillness of their passage echoed in their ears, and the strange new surroundings loomed ominously before them, dark and cold. It took another long space of silence to discover that Otter was not with them.

Dwarf's heart grew bitter and impatient to think that Otter had forgotten the words, and that they might very easily have been with him as he was sucked into Calix Stay's depths, but that feeling soon passed, and he lamented the little fellow's disappearance, for that's all it was. Bear sat staring in stunned disbelief.

"Whatever could have happened, Dwarf? He was right beside me when we left," whimpered Bear, chilly now and lost.

"I'm not sure, Bear. It may have had something to do with whatever it was you caught scent of there. I'm just not sure."

"Isn't there anything to be done?" asked Bear, as perplexed as his friend.

"Nothing, I'm afraid. Calix Stay is powerful, and once there, you're there. If it was something else, then that's another question."

Dwarf paced out into the darkness a few feet, and called Otter's name softly. Only silence and the distant, almost inaudible rumble of Calix Stay answered.

"Just as I thought," muttered Dwarf.

"What are we to do now?" groaned Bear, thinking again of his new honey tree, and facing a growing hunger that rumbled in his huge, cavernous belly.

"First we must find shelter, then food, then we'll make our plans for tomorrow." Dwarf strode away.

"What if he comes and finds us gone?" pleaded Bear. "Can't we wait until light just to make sure?"

"Not here," snapped Dwarf. "If it's anything at

all besides Calix Stay, we won't be safe here a moment longer. We'll wait somewhere downriver, where we can hide if need be."

The two friends made their way slowly toward the edge of a woods that bordered the other side of Calix Stay, hearts heavy and exhausted, missing greatly the small animal's companionship and lighthearted chatter.

Bear had just begun to make himself a bed of moss and fir when a tiny voice behind him squeaked,

"Would you like a few berries before you turn in, Bear?"

"Aiiii," wailed Dwarf, as Bear suddenly held him clasped in a strong bear hug.

"A ghost," moaned Bear. "I hear his voice."

Broco spluttered and struggled vainly to free himself.

"It's only me, Bear," came Otter's small voice, chittering from the darkness.

Bear groaned softly, hugging the helpless Dwarf closer.

"Go away, we've no use here for spirits."

His big teeth began to rattle so loudly he imagined dry bones clacking in an invisible wind.

Otter scampered into sight, chin stained bright purple, his paws full of the huge, ripe berries from the bushes across Calix Stay.

"I must say, you two gave me a fright," he scolded. "I wanted to take just a few more of these wonderful berries with me, when all of a sudden I was in the middle of something I couldn't make up from down of, and Dwarf was shouting, and there was so much noise, and then I remembered to say the words, and when it all went away, I was tangled all up in a thorn patch. I called and called, but no one answered, so I got out, but there was no one about. And what's all this about ghosts and such?" Otter crept nearer to Bear, looking over his shoulder. "Are there those kinds of things on this side?"

"Grumplety garrumph," roared Broco, and managed to free his head from beneath Bear's great forepaw. "There's going to be if this fur rug doesn't let me down."

Dwarf coughed loudly, then sighed as Bear remembered his prisoner and released him.

"I'm sorry, Dwarf. It was so frightening, losing him, then hearing him again that way."

"Losing who?" chimed in Otter, unable to see the dark scowl on Broco's face.

"You, you witless water dog. Picking berries," bellowed Dwarf, "while we're stuck in the middle of Calix Stay. You might just as well have brought along a flower or two, since we're just out for a friendly walk."

Bear reached down and patted Broco gently. "But he's not lost after all, Dwarf. And now we're all together again, and they do look like tasty berries."

Dwarf started to bluster again, then thought better of it, feeling again the sharp pain he'd felt when he'd thought their little companion lost.

"Well, hurrumph, just be more careful about how you gather your supper in the future," he said, only half huffed, and he gravely walked over to the little gray fellow and gave him a quick pat.

And Otter, always polite where it concerned someone's feelings, pretended not to see the two small tears rolling down Dwarf's cheek.

"But whatever do we do now?" asked Bear, looking about him at the dark, forbidding woods.

Broco studied the gloomy clearing, then spoke.

"First we'll have that supper Otter brought, then we'll sleep."

Bear woefully eyed the few small berries in Otter's paw.

"Is this the usual fare this side of the River?"

"Better than nothing, my friend, and unless I'm far wrong, more than we'll have until I can get my bearings and find help."

Bear took one of the purple berries and sucked it ruefully.

"I suppose it's meant to be, but I can't help wondering what the rest of this dreary place is like if a fellow can't get a decent supper or a bed for himself."

He munched silently for a while, trying to make his meager supper last, then looked to his two companions, both fallen exhausted and sleeping by his side.

Bear forgot his supper then, remembering how tired he was, and the weariness of crossing Calix Stay descended upon him, and he, too, fell finally asleep, on this, the first night again in the World Before Time.

AT JOURNEY'S DOOR

ARRIVAL

From the south a damp wind blew, bringing with it many strange, old, disturbing scents, smells not quite so fresh as even a bright autumn morning could make things, but filled with unknown terrors and sudden danger. There was a strong odor of man, which pulled Bear from his fretful sleep. He became alert, rising up on his haunches to test the direction and rumbling deep in his throat to warn his friends. Otter slept on, turning one ear back at the big animal's note of caution, then twisting more closely into a ball of gray fur, falling back into the soft, running tug of clear water where he darted in his dream. Dwarf peeped out from beneath his hat, squinting to see the position of the sun, looking at Bear, back to the overcast sky, then to Otter, now diving deep into a school of trout and almost on the point of racing a large, dark-brown-colored tarnfin.

Dwarf kicked Otter hurriedly in rising, and stood close to Bear, who had tested all four directions and could make nothing out of the man scent except that they were surrounded, for the lingering wind told him the message from all sides. It was not immediately near them, but it was not so far away.

"What is it, Bear?"

"Man."

"Are they near us?"

"I shouldn't say too far. I can't hear anything, though."

Otter, sullenly rubbing his eyes and trying his whiskers, grumped, "I knew I should have listened to my own better judgment. Not only am I dragged bodily away from my river by an overpuffed knot of a lumpheaded dwarf, carted across all sorts of boundaries that should better be left uncrossed, plumped down square in the middle of a nest of men, but I get kicked for my breakfast." Otter toppled backward, covering his eyes with his paws.

"Shhhh," hissed Bear, rising up to his full height, ears back, nose searching, great brown hackles bristling upon his neck.

Seeing Bear upright and aroused, Otter forgot all else and darted beneath the huge animal's shadow, crouched and whistling low in his throat. Dwarf brandished his rune-covered walking stick, but also moved closer to Bear.

"The scent is growing stronger. There are many of them."

Otter caught the strong man scent now, powerful and disgusting, and every time the wind caught its breath it grew stronger, as if a great horde of Mankind was approaching.

Dwarf carefully studied the countryside in the growing gray light, and exclaimed, "This is a piece of luck I hadn't counted on. Quickly, you two. We're not far from friends and food, and a place where we may make what plans we must."

Broco moved quickly out of the alder thicket where they had passed the night, out and down the riverbed for a few minutes, until they came to a broad meadow that seemed to make a wide roadway toward the rising sun.

"We'll follow along the edge of the trees there to avoid anyone who might be about until we reach the Galant Road. That was built in my time here. We've landed only a few leagues from where some of my kin dwell. Hurry along now. I have no desire at the moment to explain to anyone the presence of a dwarf and his traveling companions."

The three friends moved silently off and were quickly swallowed by the shadows of the trees, passing quietly, almost no more than the wind rustling across the sun.

A DISCOVERY

"It's long since I've dwelt here, and long since I've had news, but Tubal, great Dwarf Elder, settled here many ages before the World Before Time was peopled with all those kind that move in it now. My cousin, Bani, had a great hall here in the years before I left, and it's to Bani we go to seek counsel now. Another hour's walk should see us safely with him."

"I don't like the feel of this place, Dwarf. There's something that doesn't sit right. I can't begin to tell you why, but I feel afraid now."

Bear walked warily along, massive head raised, complete halt.

"I think we'd better scout ahead first, Dwarf, be-sniffing, testing, shuffling, and finally coming to a fore we go any farther. Otter is small and clever, he can creep ahead and see if this is all my nose playing me tricks, or whether there is real danger."

Otter agreed, and almost before their eyes, he was gone, slipped into shadow of tree and grass, so swiftly they were startled, and indeed wondered if he had vanished into thin air. Before they had settled themselves comfortably down to wait beneath a great weatherworn old oak, Otter had returned, eyes wide, small paws motioning them to follow him deeper into the woods. At last, after walking quite a long way into the thickening trees, and turning every few steps with a stern concerned look every time a twig cracked or a branch snapped, he stopped, and in the lowest of whispers, he spoke.

"A bit farther up the road there's what's left of a man camp of some sort. Still fresh enough to worry you, Bear. I guess that's the man scent. There were two men there, beside a fire, making a meal, I guess, and talking pretty loudly to each other. I'm surprised you both didn't hear it, they were carrying on so."

"We heard nothing," said Dwarf, feeling his ears.

"I heard something, but it didn't sound like man. More a rumble like trees at night, or rock secrets."

Bear shifted his great weight from hind paws to forequarters as he eased himself down to a sitting position, looking away in the direction they had come, and secretly straining to pick up man voices.

"The strange thing, Dwarf, is that I could understand them perfectly well."

"That's nothing to fret your whiskers over, dear Otter. You've lived long on the other side of the River, but there was a time before, I think, when you went about here, long ago. Who knows how many times, or in what forms? Crossing Calix Stay again simply awakened those times, so it's natural you should understand their tongue. I fancy it hasn't changed so much in all these years."

"I rather like to think there would be more civil tongues to discourse in," mumbled Bear, raising a paw to tug at his chin. "I find keeping my own hasn't led me wrong all these years. Nothing ever came of meddling about in tongues." Bear looked up to see Dwarf's eyes resting on his own, deep and thoughtful, and slightly amused.

"No offense, Dwarf. Besides, you're different. Everyone has his tasks and chores, and I guess that must be yours and your kind's." Bear trailed off. "Of course, I haven't known many dwarfs before, but I imagine that's what they're like."

"You're not far amiss there, dear fellow," laughed Dwarf. "For the most part we're builders and delvers, but certain of the clans keep lore masters and such, and it was from a family of those that I sprang. Where others learned the older skills of metal and stone, I was taught songs and stories, and as a gatherer and keeper I traveled far and long to take up the other tongues of the world. All that was ages ago, when I was a spanner, as dwarf young are known, but I've long been under a mountain, away across the River, and have forgotten much I have known, or misplaced it somewhere under my hat."

Dwarf took off the bright yellow head cover with the green brim and twirled it on his right hand. The late morning sun caught and held its spiraling motion, and for a moment it seemed to take flight, the fine gold and silver stitchwork catching fire with light. It began to sing in a low, croaking voice, and as Bear and Otter watched, it began to fashion a series of images, pale and misty, as though they were watching a sunrise through silver-gray mists from a hole in the earth. There were trees in this vision, and a blue sky, sunless, but lighted by some brilliance that seemed to have no center. Then fair, sparkling towers in the form of cloverleaf and rose bloom, dazzling to look upon, and tall. A sound arose from somewhere, everywhere, and it grew until it was music, pure and joyful. Otter rose up to his full height and began to sway from side to side in an old form of dance of his sires, and Bear hummed along, patting a big hind paw and smiling. The hat spun slowly down into Dwarf's hand, and he replaced it quickly on his head, pulling it firmly down until it touched his ears and his eyes were fairly hidden behind the rich green brim. With that, the vision and music vanished, and Bear and Otter slowly returned from where they had taken them, awed and saddened at once.

"There's more to a good hat than to keep the sun off your skull, or a hard rain from slipping down the back of your collar. But continue, Otter. I'm afraid I've misguided your story."

"I've forgotten where I was," he said, blinking and stammering, "I mean, if . . ."

"You were wondering how it is you understood the tongue of man, and I told you, although we haven't heard yet what it was they were saying."

Otter knitted his whiskers into a scowl, twitched an ear, and blushed. "I was so struck with understanding them I've clear forgotten what they said."

"Then perhaps the three of us should take a peep, and see and hear what we can. Not all men even in my last time here were to be trusted, although I'll dare say more were then than now."

"Shouldn't we be getting on to your kin's house instead of dallying about in business that's not our own?"

"My dear shambling old hearthrug, all business here may concern us, and it's always wise to pick up a bit of news when traveling in unfamiliar times. Best armed, best warned, or so it goes in some tongues."

"I hope they're not discussing hides," said Otter.

"I doubt if they're hunters, Otter. What you said of a large camp speaks against that."

"All the more reason to worry, so many mouths to feed," grumped Bear.

"Being thick-skinned, I don't worry as much about that as most might, although bear stew might appeal to some."

Otter giggled into his whiskers.

"There would be a bit left over for supper, too."

Bear's huge paw reached out to swipe his flanks, but Otter had scampered ahead, suddenly alert.

"Shush, they'll hear us," he warned, but too late, for the two men in the clearing of the camp had heard, and both now stood upright, staring straight into the thickets that concealed the companions.

TWO MAGICIANS

"Stand ye, who trespass the two Voices of the Circle. Be ye fair or foul, stand forth for your judgment."

It was more than a voice, and the clear sky filled with frightful figures of riders, cloaked in terrible white robes and gilded helms that did not sparkle but burned deep within themselves, as if the flaming light was far away beneath their smooth, terrible surface. The horses were mighty beasts that straddled mountains, and nearer, rising tall, a shimmering pale-ivory-colored tower that rose upward and into the farthest visions, and near its top, it curled into the shape of a flaming turtle with a pointed shell of brilliant silver.

Bear and Otter were lying flat on the ground, dumb terror so heavy upon them they helplessly awaited their doom without even being able to so much as whimper. Dwarf's hat had been blown off his head by the mighty rush of the voice wind, and he now clutched it, trying to straighten it on his head with shaking hands.

"By the great dwarf's beard," he exclaimed breathlessly, more shaken than really afraid, "I think we've two wizards here to deal with, and of the right sort, if I can go by their words." Dwarf advanced out of the thicket, into plain sight of the two wizards.

"Hail, O wisest and fairest of the Circle. My service and my friends' service are yours, to your bidding."

The first man, who seemed to be the older, made a circle in the air with his staff, and the spell he had woven turned scarlet upon the trees and began to flow back to the earth, and the skies cleared, and once more the peaceful warmth of the sun shone clearly and a cool breeze sprang up from the west, as if it, too, had held its breath before this power.

"And what makes you think we need the services of a dwarf and his kind, good spanner? And be so kind as to ask your companions to step out into the open so that we may see them. I have not much liking for those who would lurk about before the powers of the Circle, for it speaks of a cowardly heart or an evil purpose." So saying, the gray-clad figure moved his left hand in the direction of the sweet briar bushes, and a brilliant blue-green light darted hissing toward the two friends, who quaked and trembled, almost fainting with fright as they saw the ghostly huge hand groping toward them.

Otter leapt up, his dignity overcoming his fear, for the two men were obviously not of a mind to stew them, and he could not imagine a wizard doing any evil to animals of any sort, or at least not any wizards of the nature he had heard of in any song or river story.

"There's neither coward's heart nor evil here," he cried, then added, "Beg pardon, sir, but as you can see, we've only just crossed the River, and are trying to set our course for the house of the kin of Dwarf. We mean no harm to any business of yours, and I ask you leave ours in peace and let us depart."

The taller and younger of the two men stepped forward, looking long and carefully at Otter.

"Step nearer, Olther, Merry Waterfolk of Old. You need fear no harm, nor you, Bruinlth."

The man spoke in an old, familiar tongue, common to all wild things. His voice was clear and reassuring, and Otter knew there was nothing to fear.

"It seems you keep strange companions, Dwarf. Or else you must be one of the lore masters of old. I've not seen friendships between Animalkind and dwarfs, nor any other kind in many passings, except across the River," he added, nodding away in the direction from where they had come. "Still, it is strange and warrants the telling of it, and if you'll forgive my hasty temper, come now and join us in a bite, and perhaps we can exchange news. I am called Greyfax, elder of Grimwald, and my companion here is the eldest son of the ancient Fairingays, in the speech of Windameir, Faragon, in common tongue, Froghorn, heir and lord now of ancient lore, and Third Keeper of the Light."

Greyfax spoke more softly, and the sound of his voice was as pleasant to hear now as it had been terrible before. A great peace descended about the company, and a fresh wind rose up, full of flowers and perfumed with the promise of rain, although the sky stood still bright blue and empty of shadow or cloud.

"I am called Broco, the Younger, of a clan who have all gone beyond the River or into the darkness under the earth. My friends are Otter and Bear, nobles of Animalkind, and lords of the Realm of the Sun."

"Ill fortune awaits those who have dealings with the River. I have crossed it many times in days long past, but have not journeyed beyond its fastness in these later years. There must be a great need for you to venture here now in these times. Atlanton Earth is perilous and troubled, and I regret to say, not as hospitable as of old. A great crisis is, I'm afraid, closer to hand than one would like to say."

"But we may still trade news of a nature more cheery than that. And enjoy our meal as we may," broke in Froghorn. "Ill tidings only give me terrible heartburn."

"A man following my own thought on the matter," replied Bear, eyeing hungrily the slices of fruits and bread that lay beside the small, neat fire. "A little honey would go a long league now in brightening my breakfast, but since I'm here, I might as well take a taste or two to keep my strength." He eagerly sat down between Dwarf and Greyfax, took up a half loaf of tuck, or so the two called their travel fare, and began spreading it with butter from the pot near the fire.

Greyfax withdrew from his long gray riding cloak a small round box, covered with what first appeared to be dents and scratches but upon closer inspection was carved figures and script. He spoke three words slowly, moved his right hand above it, and there beside Bear was a small tote keg of rich clover honey, so fragrant and pure, Bear rolled his eyes and began to stroke it with one huge paw, stirring and feeling the texture of it, and finally bringing a sticky sweet finger to his mouth to taste it.

"Now this is what I call magic," he said, between smacking lips and satisfied grunts. "Truly an art to be looked into." And his voice was lost in low, contented rumbles as he set to work on the honey, drooling and slurping as much as even good bear manners allowed, nodding his approval every few bites.

To Otter's delight, a burnished copper plate appeared before him through a haze of white smoke, laden with plump wild berries, apples, and last, in the center, fat golden fruit that shimmered in a deep silvery light.

For Dwarf there was a large assortment of cakes, prepared as of old, thin and well baked, in the usual dwarf way, in the shape of the head of a hammer.

"Our gossip can wait until we fill ourselves," said Greyfax, settling down to his own fare, which seemed to consist of a cup of some misty liquid he took from a bright gold flagon inscribed with silver. Its edges caught the sunlight and danced merrily each time the wizard lifted it, and to Otter, each time he glanced at it, there seemed to come a gladness in his heart. Bear ate noisily and Dwarf studied the two men quietly as he ate, noticing and making note of each thing about them. Of the younger, he could detect nothing familiar, and decided their paths had never crossed before this moment. Yet the other, Greyfax, seemed to recall to him someone of old, and a waking dream enveloped him. In it he saw a long, warm room, with a glowing fireplace, and snow outside from deep midwinter, and a figure that looked like his father sitting in a low, comfortable green chair across from another figure, a man figure, yet also of other forms, a Master, one who changed shape as the fancy moved him, or necessity, or time, and then he looked closer at that dreamlike face, old and ageless at once, and found himself staring deeply into the living, waking eyes of Greyfax, elder of Grimwald, who smiled mysteriously, then turned back to a question that Otter had asked and Dwarf had not heard.

WIZARD'S FIRE

"Its quite simple, Master Otter, for one to create anything he likes by imagining it so hard that in truth it's hard to tell what's real from what's not. You saw only what I was imagining," said Greyfax, returning his cup to its case and placing it deep within the folds of his cloak.

"Well, it's beyond me," grumped Bear, "but that honey didn't taste anything at all like a wisp of fancy, or any sort of imagining that I could do."

"It was there. All I had to do was suggest it." Greyfax stood and walked over to where Froghorn was packing their saddlebags, and the two spoke in a language Dwarf could not make out, then turned.

"Come now, friend Dwarf, how was it you left the mountain and risked the perilous crossing of Calix Stay? Surely you're not simply out for a walk."

"I really can't say, Master. It came over me one day as I listened to the river that flows in those deep parts where I lived long and alone. Something told me it was time to move, and it seemed that my feet rather than my sense led me here. As for the rest, I haven't the inkling of a feather cap what to do, or where I'm to go, but I thought now, since we've crossed in a place known to me long ago, that I would make to my cousin's house and seek advice there."

Greyfax and Froghorn exchanged troubled glances, and Broco thought he saw sadness lingering there in the eyes of the two Masters.

"Dear friend Dwarf, I must, I'm afraid, be the bearer of ill tidings at the very hour that has seen fit to have us meet once more."

Before Dwarf could think about that, Greyfax went on, his face slightly shrunken and older-looking now, the deep gray eyes darker, and seemingly tired. "Not two days ago, Froghorn and I first entered this country, and found to our great dismay that all of our friends here of old have long been slain or fled away. Your cousin's house is in ruins, the anvils stilled, and the mines filled with the dust of years. All there is now is old Creddin, who is only waiting his time to run out so he may return to where he began. Of the facts, I know none, but from what we could make out, a great battle was waged here close to twenty years ago, in Man's reckoning, and all your kin were slain, or taken by the darkness. We have been on the road long now, trying to see as best we can what's to be done, and I'm sorry to report that this has been much the same in every land we've traveled. Wars between all kinds, famines, plagues, great fires. Evil times indeed are these."

Dwarf coughed, got up, paced a few steps, clearing his throat loudly to cover his soft weeping at the news of the dark fate of his kin. "I'm afraid I've really led you both into evil fortunes, dear friends," he spoke to Bear and Otter, who were sitting uneasily, looking from Greyfax to Froghorn, to the countryside surrounding them, as if at any minute they expected to see dark hoards sweep down upon them from the edge of the forest. "I had counted on the aid of my cousin, and perhaps to have tarried there until I could decide what further to do. Now I hear that he and his house are destroyed and in ruin, and I've no other plan to serve in its stead."

Froghorn spoke now, standing and looking deeply into the fire. "Try not to be without hope or plan, friend Dwarf. As dark as it may seem now, shadows have a way of passing if one holds true."

"He speaks wisely," said Greyfax, "and I think the thing for you to do now is to try to make a plan that will hold you until more is brought to light. I would, in other times, counsel you to recross Calix Stay, but now it is most difficult, and I do not think the River would allow you over again. Many things have changed, and it guards its dominion ever more closely. It would be difficult even for me to venture a crossing, and I know it as well as any who have ever mastered its timeless flow." Greyfax broke off, his eyes filling with time and dimming until he was far away, withdrawn, looking to the others as any old man, drawn and bent with age. Froghorn watched him worriedly, a frown of concern spreading across his fair features. After what seemed centuries, Greyfax spoke again. The light had returned to his face, and age and care passed, and once more he was commanding and firm in his stance, his voice bell-clear. "Friend Dwarf, I think you and your companions must find a safe haven here, even upon this country, and stay out of reach of either men or other kind, until I return. This may be, even in its ill timing, a far better stroke than any of the wise could have struck." He chuckled, a rippling flight of laughter, his eyes twinkling and flashing. "How well-laid plans play upon fate, like harpstring and lute. This, indeed, may have been even more than we could have ever hoped for."

Greyfax chuckled again, sitting down by the small lap of flames, and in a thrice the bright orange and red lips of the fire had leapt up and touched the wizard's brow, then opened in a great wave of white foam that roared like the distant Sea of Farcrossing. In it, as they all gazed upon it, great histories began repeating themselves in blue and green and bright white pillars of fire, huge hosts of men and elfin kind, and dwarfs and animal kingdoms that made Otter and Bear gasp, for there among them were Othlinden, king ruler of otters, and Bruinthor, great lord of bears. Then shadows passed over each, until there were many forms lying slain, and towers cast down, and the great kingdoms fell one by one into ruin and passed away slowly, sadly, on the black smoke born of war. Otter wept openly as the animal kingdoms waxed, then waned, and flowed away across the River, past and forgotten in their glory. Bear clenched his great bear fists and gnashed his teeth in savage anger as he watched the traitorous defeat of Bruinthor, who vanished in the battle, never to appear again to living soul.

Dwarf gasped as he saw plainly before him the sitting room of his ancient home, a room both homely and comfortable, low green chairs of ancient make that removed all weariness when you sat in them, a fire dog that spoke rhymes when asked, a pewter cup that filled itself with clear springwater, cold and pure, from the Endin River that ran deep among the dwarfhalls of old. As he watched, the music began, the songs, and his eyes widened as he saw the gray figure sitting across the years by his father, looking exactly as he did now, unchanged; then there came a small spanner into his sight, and he knew it was himself. This vision lasted long, then the flames darkened again, and a great, vile winged form swept over the light of the fire, darkening all about it and bringing a pall even over the sunlight of the clearing where they now sat, at so great a distance in time and space, as if the presence of its evil memory yet held powers over those of the light. The animals shuddered and whined, and Dwarf covered his eyes.

When they looked again, it was gone, but it had gone deep into them, and although dismissed, was not forgotten. There were visions then of fair kings, handsome and heartening to look upon, but without all the majesty of those that were before, although they were still fairer than the fairest now. Through their hair a silver light shimmered, making their brows aflame with what appeared to be sunlight dancing on clear, untroubled water. Their queens were of such beauty the heart quailed to look upon them full, and were all come of the line of elfin elders, wise and kind. After these, another shadow fell. Otter and Bear found the visions of the fair kings and ladies disquieting, as if there was something there they were trying to remember, although they could not find what, and forgot once more as the darkness crossed the flames. The fire seemed to burn less fiercely now, and Dwarf saw a small, lonely figure kneeling by flowing water in a deep dwelling. He raised himself to cry out, but the picture faded and passed, and there were the three of them, trotting along through Gilden Far, by Gilden Tarn. At once, they were at Calix Stay, and passing through that roar and mighty mist again, they saw themselves land upon the far side, the World Before Time, and a great shadow again appeared. Then there was a brief flash of fire, and the three friends saw only a cold, pale light, frozen as if in some great sheet of ice. This last vision awakened a terror in them, so cold and cruel was the sight, and the sun glimmered faint and far away, and their bones turned to hardened stone, the breath left them, their eyes filled with the stillness that is death, and all thought left their numbed minds except the cold, piercing them like shafts of icy steel and holding them forever in its grim, terrible hand. Greyfax moved his eyes, and the fire billowed and raged, shot up great sparks, whirling and spewing, and a cyclone of sun and stars whirled mightily all about them, grim white flames rode down the wind, and a towering fall of sparkling geysers erupted into bursts of gold and crimson stairways, at the top of which stood forth a light, so terrible and white it threatened to release them from all form and substance and draw them into its brilliance forever. With another flash and roar, all was gone, and there sat Greyfax before them once more, small and drawn, smiling slightly, as an old man by a fire might smile after retelling an old but particularly good story.

Froghorn sighed and touched Greyfax lightly on the shoulder. "I guess that saves us a lot of useless words when there is no time."

Greyfax smiled up at his friend. "No words are useless, Fairingay, except those spent in praise of foolishness." He then turned to Dwarf. "Heed my counsel, old friend, and take up roof where you may here, but let none know of your coming, and conceal yourself well until I return."

"When will that be, sir?" asked Otter, shaking his head and trying to get rid of the bright tower of light that still lingered in his eyes, making the sunlight seem dull.

"Not long, by my reckoning. By yours, maybe something longer. My absence, unless something unforeseen occurs, shall be counted in days, I think."

Otter was not pleased at the thought of taking up abode in a country with no river close at hand, but resigned himself wearily. Bear merely grunted his disapproval of so unlikely a wood for housing, and set about making himself one last sandwich.

As the company made ready to part, Greyfax drew

Dwarf aside, and the two held a hasty conference out of earshot of the others.

"Whatever could be so interesting?" said Bear, through a mouthful of tuck.

Otter made no reply, but felt that no good would come of it, whatever it was.

Froghorn held up his hand after their own fashion in parting, and the three friends watched the two disappear into the waning sun.

"Let's get to our own travels quickly, before it's too dark to steer," said Dwarf, and they turned their backs on the now fading shadows of the riders as they passed on into the forest and out of sight.

"Where shall we make for?" asked Bear, grumbling and already hungry again, his mind running over distasteful images of lying starved under a breakthorn patch. The prospects, it seemed to him, did not look very cheering, and his mind ran ahead to the morning. "Gnawing old bark, and drinking rainwater, I should say," and after a pause, looking at a distant gray haze growing near across the horizon, "That what's not soaked us to the bone."

"We'll at least stop the night with Creddin. A roof, but not much more, from what Greyfax said."

"Better that than nothing," chimed in Otter, looking back wistfully over his shoulder at the invisible river away beyond the forest's end.

After an hour's walk, they reached what was left of old Tubal Hall, its gates now broken and rusted in the fading gray light of dusk, its once wide paved road cracked with tree roots and disuse, and the many aboveground windows of the hall itself darkened and lifeless. A deep, open well lay in the courtyard, many fathoms to its near-empty bottom, and Bear, looking up at the dismal dark form of the building, knocked a rock over its edge, and it echoed hollow and distant for a long time before they heard the almost inaudible splash.

"A good thing it was a rock and not you," scolded Dwarf. "I thought bears had night sight."

"Enough to know a dwarf when they see one," said Bear. "Especially one that has a wagging tongue."

Bear had been badly frightened by his near escape.

"Stop this silly nonsense, you two," admonished Otter, tugging Dwarf by his coat sleeve. "A light just came on there."

At one dark end of the north side of the hall, a flickering light now glowed dimly from a lower-story window, and a creaking voice called anxiously out of the shadows, "Is that you?"

"It is I, Broco, Dwarf, lore master, cousin to the late and glorious owners of these halls, Tubal, sire, Bani, son, come to seek shelter for myself and friends, two animal lords from beyond Calix Stay."

Darkness fell thick and heavier than before as the light was extinguished. All closed into silence. Bear's great hackles raised, his eyes flamed, and he bared tooth and claw and began his war rumble deep in his throat.

"Here you, you lowly thief, speak out your name and business where you have none. These halls stand no dishonor, even in ruins. Come forth, or feel the wrath of Bruinlth, bear lord and stout heart," cried Dwarf. "Speak."

Creaking, old, and breaking, the voice called back, "If you be who you say, step forward that I may see you."

Fearing ambush, from they knew not what, the three friends cautiously advanced. Bear was raised to his full height, and alert, expectant.

"Hold, that's close enough," croaked the voice.

Suddenly a blaze of light drowned them, blinding their dark-seeing eyes.

"Well, upon my beard, it's as you say." The voice had lightened. "Come in, come in, old Creddin speaks, Cousin." And a shuffling, knobby figure advanced out to meet them, head bowed, shaking paw and hand alike.

"I fear any who go about these parts, day or night," he explained. "And one can never be too careful who he lets through the door. I've got this part of the hall bolted and airtight, so nothing save an army could batter it down once I'm locked in. Come, there's mulberry tea and a loaf or two if you're hungry."

Creddin led them into his fortress, bare and stark with but a table and chair before the fireplace, but farther down the room they saw broken and tattered pieces of the old furnishings stacked neatly. The rooms were actually larger than they appeared; a doorway opened off to the right onto what turned out to be the galley where Creddin prepared his simple meals, and another door to the left stood closed. "My sleeping quarters," he explained, bobbing back and forth, bringing up three more chairs and placing them by the fire.

They sat long, eating and talking, refilling their cups with the slightly tart mulled drink, exchanging what news they had, omitting only the part of seeing Greyfax and Froghorn, for all the three friends knew better than to speak of wizards' journeys.

"And you, Master Otter? How come you to be traveling with my illustrious cousin?" Creddin's eyes narrowed suspiciously, although he spoke in an oily, kind voice.

Otter, his mouth full of buttered bread, had to chew quickly before answering. "I'm not at all sure why, although it seemed the thing to do when Dwarf was talking. And then he sang that song, and it seemed as if I was remembering something. I can't remember what, but it was beautiful, yet scary at the same time, if you know what I mean."

"Exactly, old fellow," agreed Bear. "That's what I've been trying to say myself. It seems as if I'd been waiting across the River for something, and then you and Dwarf came by my camp, and all of a sudden here I am."

Bear fell silent, a slightly concerned look creeping across his broad muzzle, and he repeated the last words.

"And all of a sudden here I am."

"It goes deeper than that, I'm sure," encouraged Creddin, refilling the tea mugs all around.

"Not really," went on Otter. "I only know that I spent quite some time in the Meadows of the Sun. I know I have a mother and father somewhere, or many of them, but that was all long ago, and I barely recall them."

"Crossing the River often does that, according to Greyfax," put in Dwarf, then hastily corrected himself. "At least that's what it says in any of the lore I ever read."

"I guess it must," Bear grunted. "I can't for the life of me tell you about anything except the time I spent across the River. But those things I saw in the fire, about all those things, they made me feel all funny inside, like I was watching things happen to me in a dream."

"That's what I felt, Bear. Like it was me, but me a long way away," chittered Otter.

"And you, dear Coz? These are terrible times to be out upon these roads."

Creddin refilled their mugs as he spoke, and his old eyes glistened in the cheerful firelight.

"I'm not sure, yet I do feel as if there is a reason.

It's like trying to remember something that's right on the tip of your tongue. It's all right there, but it's as far away as last spring's pancakes." Dwarf was feeling ill at ease as he spoke.

"Well, enough for now. Let's have a cheery note to go on. Master Bear, how was it in the Meadows, or wherever it is you say you hail from?"

Creddin's old hand shook nervously as he lit a blackened stump of a pipe from a blazing coal he had taken from the fire with a pair of tongs.

Bear knitted his brow, and sought to recall the place the old dwarf asked of.

"It seems I've forgotten much of it," began Bear, "although it hasn't been even a full day since we crossed."

"Then you've only just crossed?" asked Creddin quickly.

"Well, so to speak. Yes and no. I mean it's all confused."

"It feels that way, doesn't it, Bear?" chittered Otter, rolling his empty mug about on his smooth gray stomach. "I can hardly recall how those berries we had for breakfast tasted. But I remember perfectly well how the travel tuck tasted."

"Travel tuck?" queried Creddin suspiciously.

"Some we'd baked for the journey," put in Broco. "But come, tell us of how you've come along these past years."

"It's a sad lot, that tale," croaked Creddin, "and one that hardly bears the telling."

"Were they slain in battle?" chirruped Otter, holding his mug out to be refilled again by Bear.

"No in one case and aye in another, Master Otter. Cousin Bani was killed by the Dragon Hordes at Last Battle. Cousin Tubal lived on for a great many years, prospering in many ways, and building up a great commerce with all kind in these realms. There was lumber to be traded with Mankind, and ores to swap for the fine jewelry and cloaks from the elfin hosts who dwelled in these parts."

Creddin's old eyes sparkled as he spoke, and his voice grew stronger as he told of the years of plenty.

"But then began our fall," he snapped, and the light went out in his eyes. "Dealing with men and elves soon led to trouble, and one after another, wars broke out on our boundaries. Small at first, but leading to longer sieges."

The old dwarf banged his mug on the arm of his chair.

"And that's what led to this," he said in a wheezing voice, throwing his other arm wide to indicate what was left of the ruined hall. "When the darkness began to move, the end wasn't far beyond."

"The darkness?" echoed Bear, his heart frozen, remembering for some reason the vision in the wizard's fire, the icy emptiness he had felt. Yet as soon as he'd thought it, the other vision of the dazzling white flame drove out the chilling memory of that vast white frozen abyss.

Creddin closed his story abruptly, and simply said he now stayed on in hopes of better days. He made no mention of how he had come to be spared while the rest perished, nor said anything of who it was he had been expecting when he first called out to them in the darkness of the courtyard.

When at last they went to the beds Creddin had prepared, Bear decided that he would pass the night on watch, although he said nothing to the others. Something, he could not say exactly what, kept making his hackles tingle, and if there was no clear, definite scent of danger, there was another, deep and disturbing, as formless as the terror they had seen in the wizard's fire.

The night passed, and nothing happened, but

toward the first gray streak of dawn, Bear thought he heard voices far off in the hall somewhere, but when he'd cleared his ears of drowsiness, all was a deep, foreboding quiet. As the sun rose, red and dim through the window of sky above him, he fell after a time into a troubled sleep, resting more easily when he at last heard Otter snort-snuffle and begin stirring about, and Dwarf clearing his throat on his way out from under his covers. When they asked if he weren't ready for a bit of breakfast, he replied he would rather get a little more sleep, which struck them as odd, but they left him there, beginning to snore, sliding off again into the unknown dangers of his dreams.

THE MASTER OF TUBAL HALL

Below the great hall of Tubal, deep in shafts that wound away, reaching out for the roots of darkness, walked Creddin. His gnarled old body moved with amazing speed, stooped and shuttling, not with the speed of sturdy dwarf legs, but with spider agility. His old joints creaked as he moved farther and farther into the mines of old, where once gold ore glittered like fingers of light run through dark, deep, unstirring thought. Creddin's dim lamp smoked and cast long shadows on the grim walls, barren now of all save the tombs of its masters of old. At intervals, the tunnel branched into other chambers, soundless rooms filled with the dread of those long dead, treasure troves and burial vaults together, now plundered and broken by invading soldiers, themselves long since perished.

His old, bleary eyes caught sight of bones, stark white in the surrounding blackness, a man skeleton, face down in a crosspath of shafts, lost in death as in life, perished in the unknown depths in greed and horror. Creddin chuckled sourly, muttering, "Dwarf gold, eh, a glittery seal of doom for the likes of you." So saying, he went down along the tunnel from which the man long ago had crawled up, hopelessly lost in the dark labyrinths of the mines, starved to death, his eyes filled with the sight of immeasurable wealth that could never be squandered.

Coming to the end of this tunnel, Creddin raised his stooped frame, reached out a bony hand, spoke two words in ancient Dwarfish, and touched a spot on the higher part of the wall. The huge rock that stood before him rolled back slowly on the stone hinges wrought in forgotten ages, and the shadowed light of his small lamp leapt into dazzling brightness, spun and whirled in that chamber in a dull, golden explosion. The chamber was immense, rising to a height that devoured the light, leaving the tops of the carved pillars that ran in twos down the center in dark shadow, and the walls, at the farther edges, darker than if no light had wakened their slumbering gray-black forms. He lit three torches that stood on the near wall, and turned, eyes glittering with the fire of aging madness. Before him stood row on row of casks filled with gold bar and coin, diamonds set and unset, in platinum or silver, or other precious metals. Each was wrought as thin and fine as a gauzed web, sparkling stones set to enhance their brilliant beauty. There were arms and scepters brought from ancient kings and forefathers, the treasures outlasting their owners. At long last, the might and fortune of forgotten kings and halls belonged to him, Creddin the Old, Creddin the Wise, Master Creddin of Tubal Hall, wielder of such wealth as no man had ever beheld before, and few dwarfs; Creddin, who all had laughed at or pitied, scorned or shunned, he who was waited upon to die. Now he alone remained, outliving the lot of them.

"This pleases you, Creddin, this pile of trinkets?" A thin, cold voice echoed through the chamber, dimming the light.

Creddin turned. A heavily cloaked dark form

stood against the door, a shadow upon the deeper blackness behind.

"You seem to have forgotten our appointed hour."

Creddin's eyes fell from the unseen gaze, and he trembled before this awful presence.

"No, Master, I did not forget. Unlooked-for company held me past the hour. I thought it was you when they came."

"I've seen your guests, and can think of no useful purpose they might serve. Still, even I don't know all, so I shall have to report their presence here. Whence came they, and where bound?"

"From the River. I know no more. They seem to have close tongues. I couldn't get them to speak their errand."

"I have ways," came the voice, like an icy wind and Creddin's face paled, and his old limbs trembled. "But then you well remember, don't you, miserable shaft rat." Harsh laughter rang through the chamber. "If your bedraggled guests are no more sport than you, it wouldn't be worth our time questioning them. The Queen may be bored, and wish them for games." Piercing, mirthless laughter stabbed cruelly into Creddin's heart. "Now, about the other two strangers. What have you learned?"

"I was not able to gather, Master, except that they were lords of some nature. They only watered their horses, and came not to my house. There was no chance to slip them the potion you have given me." Creddin withdrew a step, trembling.

"Imbecile. Miserable wretch. They were from the cursed Circle."

A long, curled whip lashed out from beneath the dark cloak, whining and cracking across Creddin's bent form. He cried out, cringing. The lash devoured him again.

"No, Master, no. It was not Creddin's fault. I

thought they were magicians and the potion would have done naught save deliver their anger upon me."

"Now mine is upon you, wretched filth of a dwarf. I shall punish you no more at the moment, but my wrath is upon you if these worms upstairs are of no worth to Her Darkness. Now off with you. No more of your trinkets tonight. Begone."

The ebony finger of the whip cut deeply into Creddin's legs as he fled the chamber. In his pain and haste he left the entrance open, and heard, as he hurried from that coil of searing heat, dark laughter echoing across the mounds of glittering, precious gold and casks of jewels. He turned, filled with desire to return, to fill his eyes once again with the treasure's beauty, to run the heavy golden shapes through his fingers. But the great stone rumbled and darkness fell upon the chamber, darker than no light, deeper than stillness, and the laughter rang cold upon the still gray-black walls. Shadows from his flickering lantern played about him in the shapes of winged beasts, filling him with renewed terrors. He scuttled down the long tunnels, over the stark white bones of the lost plunderer, up the long flight of stone stairs, and into the upper hall, lighted with a pale orange glow from the eastern windows. Sunrise once more, and he had much to do.

He quickly closed and locked the tall ironbound doors to the tunnels below, crossed the huge chamber, dusty and unused, and safely back in his own bedroom, he locked the outer door. Creeping to the only piece of furniture in the room other than his bed, he took from it a flask, black and foul-smelling. As his bony hands clutched it to him, his eyes filled with a wild despair. His sight dimmed for a moment, and his mind retraced the long, bitter loneliness of his years. He heard laughter from the outer room, where Dwarf and Otter were searching for him, calling his name as he had not heard it since before he'd discovered the treasure chamber, before his heart had turned in him and he'd desired its consuming beauty. He had paid dearly for it, kin and friend alike, and the dark shadow that dwelt upon his soul lifted at hearing Dwarf calling gaily and good-humoredly from the galley.

"Creddin, Creddin, where are you, old fellow? You've got two unquenchable appetites to deal with here. Come along now like a good chap."

Otter's long lilt of laughter followed, and his words were lost in the confines of the kitchen.

Another voice filled Creddin with trembling and fear again.

"Give it to them, stench of Dwarfdom, give it to them."

A struggle took him, and at last, hand trembling and eyes closed, Creddin replaced the flask in its hiding place. He would find out what he could by his own skill, but that was as far as he would go, no matter what. More than that, he would try to warn Dwarf of his danger without exposing himself. He knew he would be watched, but not so closely in the sunlight. He must at least try, or the pleasure of the hall below would be useless. His conscience, which he had buried long ago, demanded this token of remembrance, and until he satisfied this small kindness, it would be dark indeed, and not even the sight of the vast treasure would ease him. They had promised him wealth and long life when they first came, and the sight of all Tubal's hoard had consoled him for his treachery. Again when Bani was taken, gold filled his heart with a hard, remorseless light, and all the others seemed only leaves at the end of a long summer. One by one they passed, in wars and famines, until he alone was left, untroubled and content to find friendship deep in the old mines, where golden eyes lulled him to a waking sleep and silver hands touched his brow at night, turning away all thoughts but of their beauty. At times, when Doraki, the dark lieutenant of the Queen, came, his existence was miserable and he was taunted with the memory of his friends and his treachery, and filled with a grief almost more than he could bear. But then they increased the treasure store with some bauble or other, taken from other men or elves, or dwarfs, or other kinds, and left him once more helpless. But their promise of long life was failing, and day by day he watched his limbs wither, and he knew then that long life meant only the mind, for his body was aging. Soon all that would be left would be his unsleeping mind, tortured in that poisoned darkness, unable to move, or die, and he would be kept forever like that. He must save at least something against that time, dwarf or animals, so that the darkness would not be quite complete.

"Coming, coming," he answered their calls, and leaving, shut the door resolutely on the dark, frightening voice.

ESCAPE

Under a bright field of stars, Greyfax and Froghorn made their supper beside the green lawn that ran down into the mists that covered Calix Stay. Their horses, enchanted bearers from the great rolling lands of far Windameir, had carried them the two long miles since their parting with the three comrades. Against the dark mirror of night, a dim luminous glow covered the vale, and dew began to decorate the turf and low scarletberry bushes that covered the sides of the hills. As midnight approached, the stars seemed farther away, and began to dim. Over the distant mountains, a thin wisp of a trine moon began to rise, shimmering in thick mists of whitish silver guaze, looking like a half-drawn scimitar hung suspended over the lands.

"I don't like the looks of her tonight," said Froghorn, looking away toward the mountains. "Her beauty wanes most as our need greatens."

Greyfax studied the moon in silence. A nightcaw spoke in hushed flutterings somewhere off in the thickets. Another answered, far away, barely a swishing wind over the dark silence. Greyfax looked quickly from the mountains into the near darkness, and held up his hand for silence as Froghorn began to speak again. The pale glow that had illuminated the ground around the two stilled and disappeared, and all fell into a tense silence, a quietness choked with some presence that Greyfax now detected. It was still far off, but searching, and he did not like the sound of the birds' cry. There was something about it that struck him as harsh, more menacing than a lover calling to his dark mate somewhere in the deep folds of thickets. It came again, and the answer was closer now, and a distant, faint murmur of padded footsteps could be heard by his keen ears. An'yim, Greyfax's steed, started, raising his head, snorting and pawing the grass with his powerful forehoofs. Soon Pe'lon neighed softly and drew closer to his master, Froghorn. The stars had gone, and the only light came from the splinter of moon, a deadly gray glow that seemed to darken even more all the shadows as they waited breathlessly, listening, in the clearing. Hastily Greyfax drew Froghorn near him, and spoke so softly into his ear Froghorn was not sure he had heard him.

"We must fly now, quickly. Our ways part here for a time. We must not be snared like rabbits. Away. I shall find you next where I can. Fly, old fellow, and use all speed."

Even as he spoke, Greyfax was astride An'yim, and lightly the two, horse and rider, moved away into the darkness without so much as a blade of grass disturbed to mark their fleet passing. Pe'lon trembled eagerly to be gone, and had barely given Froghorn time to mount before he, too, had climbed the wind and bore away his master with an ease of speed that brushed the treetops silently into a faint tremor of leaves. The only evidence that they had been discovered was a last, long, angry cry of the night bird's voice, its wail of defeat echoing emptily above the vale, and something else joined, not bird nor beast, a scream that turned Froghorn's heart cold, and Pe'lon, at hearing it, lowered his great head.

"Snared like rabbits in a trap, indeed," Froghorn thought, then remembered a time, beyond all years or measurement, when Greyfax and he had been exactly that, snared rabbits in an evil web of the spider-cold heart of the grim Queen. They had grown strong again over the ages of time, but even now could not withstand her forces alone. With a word he turned Pe'lon toward the south, where lay the house of Lorini, sister of the Dark Queen, whose halls were always golden. Lorini, holder of the Sacred Fire, wisest of all save Melodias, now second master of the Circle, would perhaps have news that would aid him in these dark times. And Greyfax, too, might at the very moment be making his way to her halls. There was much he had not asked, and much he desired to know, and the closeness of the elder of Grimwald irked him into touching Pe'lon's neck, urging yet more speed.

There was a shadow of light, so swift and bright in passing over the lowering shoulders of the mountains, the hollows of their deep hearts trembled in its wake. Far ahead, the moon seemed to shrink from the swiftness of Pe'lon, now only a motion of stillness across the hidden faces of the stars in the silent heavens.

CREDDIN

"So there you are at last. We thought you'd disappeared, without so much as breakfast." Dwarf poked his head out of the galley door upon hearing Creddin's call. "Come along, your guests have helped themselves. There's enough here to satisfy our host, too."

"Can you hand me down that larder, Dwarf, there on the buttery? I simply must have something to go with this loaf."

Dwarf stretched far up on the sideboard to remove the tin, but to his surprise, Creddin almost bowled him over with a darting hand that snaked past him and clutched the canister.

"No, no, you mustn't use this, friends. It's spoiled, I'm afraid. I've been meaning to throw it out this past fortnight, but it's always slipping my mind. And being here all alone, you know, I guess my old head begins to let things slide." Creddin looked up between half-lidded eyes to see what effect this explanation had. Dwarf stood wide-eyed, staring, and Otter, paw still poised in midair to reach for the can, hesitated, then chittered cheerfully, "Oh, never mind, Dwarf, thank you. I've taken a fancy for some jam. There's a jar there where I can reach it myself."

Otter stretched up to his full three feet, and shuffled the jar from the counter.

"That's excellent good, Master Otter, raspberry from last year's stock. I pride myself on my jams. Sweet tooth, it seems, is ever my failing."

Otter spread the jam on the thick slices of bread, and contented himself filling his cheeks with it, tasting the full round berries, tart and still juicy. A trickle of scarlet crept past his mouth onto his whiskers, and he quickly licked it back.

"Excellent, most delightful, sir."

Dwarf now covered his own bread with the jam. Creddin eyed them for a moment longer, then excused himself to throw away the spoiled larder tin.

"Awfully jumpy about his kitchen," whispered Otter when Creddin had gone and his footsteps had faded away toward the back of the house.

"It seems so. Still, he's old, and I imagine living alone all these years has affected him." Dwarf put a finger to his temple, making a circular motion.

"I wonder what was really in it?" muttered Otter, mouth full of thick red jam bread. "Some of your old cousins' jewels or gold, I expect."

"Nonsence. From the looks of the place, the only thing worth having around here would be the dwarf cakes, and that's not much better than gnawing my hat." Dwarf went to the small keg of tea set out upon the stone floor, and drew a short cup.

Otter, having finished, began poking his small head into cabinets and drawers, pawing and whistling occasionally, leaving Dwarf talking to a gray twitching tail or back as he came in and out of spaces, nose dusty, ears covered with ancient cobwebs.

"Stop it, Otter. That's not polite, nosing around

someone's kitchen. He'll think us horrible guests. I'm sure there's nothing better than what he gave us."

"I'm not looking for anything to eat, you thick-headed dwarf. I'm looking for some more of what he's got in that larder tin. Priceless, no doubt, and I'm curious as to why he thinks we shouldn't see it."

"Leave off, I hear him coming."

Otter quickly straightened up at the approaching footsteps, bumping his head on a low shelf he had slipped beneath.

"Oooooh."

The contents of the shelf spilled noisily onto the floor, clattering and ringing through the empty halls.

"Now you've done it. He'll think we were snooping." Dwarf glared angrily at Otter. "And he is, after all, a cousin of mine, loony or no, and I won't have you behave like this."

Creddin's large, round head peered in the door, eyes drawn to slits.

"Still hungry, are you? You won't find anything worth having in that lot. Old pans and scrub pots and such. I'm afraid I haven't more to offer for a breakfast than what you have."

"No, no, dear fellow, we're quite satisfied, and I'm afraid we must be pushing on today." Dwarf knelt, helping Otter pick up the upset pots and pans.

"Oh. Where might you be bound in these troubled times, Coz?"

Creddin's face clouded, his heart beginning to darken within him. Perhaps they were after his treasure. He forgot his promise to himself.

Muffled footpads reached them, hesitant, dragging, something sinister and forbidding filling their gait with dread. Creddin's eyes widened with delight as Dwarf and Otter moved nearer together, seeking shelter from that deadly-sounding approach. Otter slipped under the table, ears back, ready to attack anything from a man's knee level.

Dwarf quickly looked to Creddin. "Are we the only visitors here, Cousin? Some later arrival last night, perhaps?" Dwarf's eyes filled with stunned wonder when his eyes met Creddin's. Almost, he would have sworn, they were filled with an ugly light, devouring him. The murderous glare took in Otter's small gray form under the table, then quickly extinguished itself. An oily kindness crept into his voice as he spoke.

"No, you're the only ones here, to my knowledge, or by my leave. Perhaps it is your friend, coming down to breakfast." Creddin's broken smile revealed yellowed teeth.

Nearer came the steps now, almost to the galley door. At last Dwarf screwed up his face into a hideous dwarf scowl, and stalked as angrily as he could to the door.

"Hello there."

The footsteps fell into silence.

"Dwarf?"

"Bear?"

"I changed my mind about breakfast. I kept tossing and turning, so I decided I might as well come down and have a small something to ease my stomach."

Bear tumbled backward in surprise as Dwarf fell on him, small arms flailing. Otter ran out to join them and try to make peace.

A low moan halted their scuffle.

"It's Creddin," said Dwarf.

"I hope our mischief hasn't harmed him," said Otter.

The three companions hastened back into the kitchen to find Creddin in a faint upon the floor, hands clutching air, as if he were struggling with an unseen assailant.

Bear ran to the well outside to fill a water jar while Dwarf and Otter tried to make the old dwarf comfortable. Creddin's mouth worked wordlessly, then suddenly whispered loudly. "They can't have it, it's mine, the thieves. It's mine, all mine, old Creddin's." Dwarf looked blankly at Otter, then to the gnarled old figure.

"He must have struck his head when he fell," said Dwarf.

"What's all his?" asked Otter.

"He's ranting," replied Dwarf. "Poor old fellow's probably remembering the Tubal Hall of old."

Otter, still suspicious, looked at the old dwarf's face. "Then why didn't he want us to see what he had in that old tin? I wager on the whiskers of my gray muzzle, he's got some ill-bought treasure hereabouts. He's still not told us how he was the only one to escape unharmed from all that's gone on. Or who he was expecting in the night when we showed up instead. I know he's your kin, Dwarf, but something rings false here, as sure as I've drawn a breath. And that look that took him just before Bear came down. Brrr. It chills me to remember it."

Dwarf remained silent a moment watching the feeble old hands knot and twist.

"Gold, more gold than kings, heh, heh, heh, and the fools will never find it, not while old Creddin guards it." His crackling laughter filled the room with a cloud that darkened the bright sunshine for a moment.

"But," and eyes bulging, Creddin started up, seeing nothing about him but the dim, forgotten places of his mind, "But I won't, I won't tell them." He fell back, struggling, and as if a younger Creddin of long ago still lived within him, another voice crossed the old man's lips, clear and strong, although softer. "You must warn them of their danger. They've done you no harm, and seek not your precious worthless treasure."

The old voice croaked its reply. "I won't. They've come to murder me in my sleep and steal the treasure. I should have turned them over to him. I should."

"You're lost, Creddin. They'll come for you soon, and then you'll be taken down forever to your treasure and starved like a rat in a vault."

Creddin's wrinkled old face drew into a terrible, tormented mask. "No, no," he shrieked. "They won't kill old Creddin, not old Creddin. He's given them everything they asked. They won't take old Creddin."

Across his face now crept a shadow as Dwarf and Otter watched, numb and helpless, and it grew until the room was darker than the deepest night, and Creddin's grew still, and the shadow of his soul stood upon his heart, seeking the consuming blackness.

"Open the door," cried Dwarf. "Light, quickly."

Bear, returning just as Dwarf cried out, flung open the big kitchen entrance, flooding the room with a dazzling light that made Dwarf and Otter flinch. A hush fell over the three friends for a moment, and the dark shadow on Creddin's breast sensed the light, absorbed it, and fled away into the brilliant rays of sun that filled the room. Bear and Otter whimpered softly in the passing of life, rocking slowly from side to side and calling in their secret tongues, and Dwarf, in a voice he did not recognize as his own, hummed softly part of one of the old songs. For a moment, he thought it might have been his father, so deep and pure it was, but it passed, too, and silence returned.

Deep below them, in ancient caverns and tunnels, where no sunlight ever delved, the ancient stones of Tubal Hall shuddered and moaned, and with the passing of their last master, a tremor shook the hall, grew into a long, shuddering roar, and the burial vaults and chambers of gold crumbled and fell, tunnels long unused collapsed, and as the three friends raced into the courtyard flooded with morning, great beams and rafters crashed down with plumes of dust and masonry, the four massive outer walls shivered as the ribs of the hall faded, and in a final, thundering noise, Tubal Hall crashed into a heap of stone and wood, treasure and treachery sleeping side by side in the dark past, now gone and sealed forever.

Dwarf looked on the settling ruin in silence. Otter and Bear stood quietly a little way from him, and finally as it all grew clear in Dwarf's mind, his small shoulders trembled and he let out a small sob of anguish and despair, and wept into his hands.

After a time, the tears and grief left him, and he placed his torn hat firmly upon his head. The two animals thought he had grown older in the short space of time, and there was something different in his voice when he spoke.

"Well, we've brought ruin and death here, but perhaps we can be forgiven in the end. I think Creddin has found his peace at any rate, and now my kindred can rest in their tombs avenged."

Dwarf looked back at the warm sun falling on the stark, broken hall, the cracked doorways and arches opening only onto the bright, clear sky beyond.

"Now we must find a place that we may pass unnoticed, I fear. I don't know what I've led you into, but I feel somehow that today was only the beginning." Dwarf turned to his two friends. "And now Greyfax says that the River has closed and there would be no chance for you to return, at least not yet."

"I've seemed to remember something, Dwarf," said Bear. "Not about anything here, but something in the fire that the wizard showed us. Exactly what keeps escaping me, but I'm sure it had something to do with why we came."

"Besides," broke in Otter, "it's plain we can't go anywhere but on. I don't much like these parts, and I'm afraid, but we're simply in a tail-chasing circle, so let's make the best of it we can."

"And it's not your fault anyway, dear Dwarf. If it hadn't been you, it would have been something else that brought us here. I'd already left my home when you found me. It's almost as if we were waiting for you."

"My old river was far away north, and I'd come that far alone," added Otter. "So you see, all the animals and others were already moving, Dwarf. We couldn't leave you alone now. Why, that would make us worse than old Creddin." Catching himself, Otter continued. "I mean even the really good sometimes get into things that they can't handle, and he's all right now, I know. I wish we knew what we were supposed to do." Otter sat down heavily at Bear's great hindpaws.

"I guess we must first find shelter, and carry on like before," Dwarf declared, standing a little straighter. "I don't know what we're to do, but anything is a start." And turning away from the fallen hall, he added, "Let's move from here. It makes my heart too heavy to see it."

And Dwarf moved off toward the great tall shadows of the forest, away from Tubal Hall and its ruins, away from the River. That crossing seemed miles away, and buried with time, and Otter and

Bear followed along after, single file, their hearts saddened yet determined.

At sunset, the three comrades halted at the top of a long green ridge sprinkled with mulberry thickets and great, tall oaks that towered above the mossy floor below. There was almost no light left, but the tail of the sun's eye covered the valley below them in an orange fire, setting the swift stream there aflame with changing light. And far off, near where the hills covered the last light in a deep black blanket, a rainbow glistened and danced above a small waterfall that flamed from the darkness into the last veil of the crimson day, fading quickly over the woods and distant mountains, and they watched long as at last, like a quiet flow of deep, blue-black water, night came softly down. Stars appeared, flickering on as dark unveiled its curling robes, first two or three, then the sky was filled with their distant lamps, lighting their way almost as surely as if it were midmorning, and the three friends walked onward into the deep smell of wood and stream, and a wind came gently up from the mountains, bringing new hope, and a new home.

They built no fire that night, for it was warm, and they lay down to sleep close together, speaking their goodnights in low, tired voices, and the valley, sensing its new inhabitants, smiled in a renewed flow of pine scent and flowers, and lulled them quickly to a deep, peaceful sleep.

Otter listened to the laughing voice of the stream calling, but he was too weary to heed it, so he played and swam in his dreaming mind. Bear sat down to a table filled with ten huge kegs of new honey from a secret sweet gum tree, and Dwarf, mind filled with sorrow and past, at last gave up and heard the deep voices of the oaks calling out to each other and the rocks chuckling and rumbling deep in their gray beards, and at last, he, too, dreamed, or dreamed he dreamed, of the morrow, when he could start his new dwelling, and do whatever else he knew must be done.

As the dawn lightened the chambers of night, the new morning brought the beauty of Dwarf's new home to him in the first yellow gleam of sun, winking over the far hills. His limbs were strengthened and his mind at ease as he hurried to wake Otter and Bear to see this first sunrise in a place where they would long and safely dwell.

IN LORINI'S HALLS

In the time it took Froghorn, elder of Fairingay, to reach the halls of Lorini, golden lady of the Light, sister of Dorini, Dark Queen of the World Between Time, many months, as counted in the world of ordinary men, passed. The swiftness of Pe'lon was great, and no lapse occurred from the moment Froghorn left Greyfax until he was standing in the great white-towered courtyards of Cypher, where many-colored trees of all kinds bloomed in forever spring and all things never withered or grew old as long as they stayed within the mystical realm of Lorini's powers. She had dwelled many lifetimes here, lighting the four borders of Atlanton Earth against the darkness of Dorini. In Origin, the many-petaled Lotus world, she kept her court, until Suneater and Fireslayer had escaped their prisons and devoured the light, leaving all that world frozen by the cold ice night of Dorini's dominion. When Lorini fled to Maldan, she was closely pursued by those great beasts, and before she could move against them, they had brought the darkness into that world, too.

After Melodias, of the Circle, and other powerful Masters took up the fray, many long years of weary struggle followed, but the Dark Queen and all her servants were imprisoned in the World Before Time and safely contained there with the help of the White Light of the Star Keeper, mightiest King of Windameir, next servant to the King of All, and Bearer of the Golden Book in which all things that were or are or will be are written in a golden print that is in the eye of the beholder rather than on the page itself. This Master lived in regions far above, and distant, and the journey there was indeed long, immeasurable in years or space, and although each living thing in the Nine Fields of Windameir had been in the presence of this sovereign lord at one time, few remembered it. Only the oldest and wisest remembered his name, and Lorini and all the other Masters only referred to him as the Starkeeper. Melodias, as well as all the rest, including Dorini, were sons and daughters of this sacred King, and spoke the true name of this King only in the mother tongue of Windameir, and none but the enlightened understood its difficult and ancient manner.

These thoughts ran through Froghorn's head as he allowed Pe'lon to be taken to one of the many airy stables built for just such bearers as this. The young elf who led Pe'lon away immediately began a conversation with the horse, and the two, laughing and touching many subjects, disappeared into a high arched doorway, into a cool stable that smelled of lilac and fresh-mown hay, and Froghorn parted with his faithful companion for so long with a call of thanks in Pe'lon's own speech.

"Good rest, my faithful Pe'lon, and even the best cannot reward you rightfully."

Pe'lon lifted a forehoof slightly and bowed graciously.

"And to you, lightkeeper, deep sleep and a healing heart."

The elf, amazed at such talk, turned to Froghorn.

"You speak very courteously, Master. It's rare to find horse and rider so closely bound."

"It's rare to find such a horse, or such a rider," laughed Froghorn, and was gone, changed into the form of a sleek falconhawk, soaring up into the deep azure of the sun-bronzed sky. Higher and higher still he roamed, riding down the back of clouds and up light beams until he perched atop the crease of horizon that enveloped all the fair kingdom of Lorini and beyond into the already dimming borders about it, until his sharp sight was clouded by the half darkness that covered that portion of the world. Looking down, and hearing a small, faraway voice, he saw a tiny white-clad figure waving to him from the turret of a tower shaped in the fashion of an immense white turtle. Down he plunged, the soft wind against his wings, faster still, until the wind eased, and light and speed melted him into a beam of gentle sunlight. The figure lost sight of him, and cried aloud.

"Oh, he's gone."

No sooner had she spoken than a tall, handsome courtier, in fine silks and velvet, with a splash of lace at his throat, approached her from behind.

"My lady Cybelle, fairest sight that eyes might hold, dearest heart of all that yet live," and the grand vision of the courtier took the shape of a shining silver dove. "Your most faithful servant, Faragon Fairingay, begs your command."

The dove flew to a perch beside the young woman. Her hair was of a yellow gold mist, burnished like finespun copper, and her face was fairer than Froghorn remembered. He had seen her last quite a long time ago, but she seemed not to age, nor to change. Her blue-gray eyes still laughed gaily, and her mouth formed an almost eternal readiness of a smile that revealed straight, even, white teeth. The smile broke now, followed by a lilting laugh.

"My dearest Fairingay, you are come, after all. I've been so frightfully bored lately. I do hope you have some new fun for me."

"Dear lady, I've traveled far and wide searching for tricks to amuse and bewilder you, but first I must see your mother, if that be possible."

"Mother always looks forward to your coming. She's downstairs now awaiting you. We saw you cross our borders ages ago."

"Then I must go to her at once."

He turned to leave, then looked again at her shining form. "I promise to show you my travels later. Don't be saddened if I'm in such haste to leave you. There is much I must disclose to the lady Lorini, and much counsel to seek."

"You'll be locked away with her for hours, I know it. But I shall wait upon myself until you come back." Her smile darkened, and her eyes glistened. "First Greyfax, and now you. There must be much afoot in Atlanton."

"He's here then," cried Froghorn, and leapt away down the tower steps, not heeding her small cry.

"Oh, go and take the lot of them," she said sadly to the carved statue of a wood stag, and clasped her arms tightly to her sides. She turned and followed Froghorn down the long stairway that led to the lower floors.

Another elf had gone into the stables, and now led Pe'lon out to the silver flowing fountain in the forecourt, and she decided to go and seek conversation with them, and to admire the beautiful horse.

"At least the elves aren't too busy to see me," she said, leaving the tower and winding her way down the outside stairway that led onto the large paths to the gardens and stable quarters.

Below, in the large, comfortable study, Greyfax sat deep in his own thoughts in one of the high-backed, finely carved chairs, and Lorini, also turned inward to herself, stood before the hearth, fireless in the warmth, tapping a slender finger to her chin, one arm resting upon the elbow of the other.

Froghorn knocked softly.

"What took you so long, dragleg? I've been waiting for days," called Greyfax, looking up, and reaching out for a small silver goblet before him.

"Come in, dear Fairingay. We've not been waiting days, but it might seem so. "I've been hearing all the news, and I'm afraid all of it's distressing. I hope you've not come bearing more ill tidings."

Froghorn bowed low, kissing the lady's hand.

"No more than Grimwald has already related."

Froghorn cast a searing glance at Greyfax, who simply laughed soundlessly into his wine.

"Well, come then, and tell me again, then we shall have a nap, and time for you to wash the journey away, and to dine tonight with light heart. I'm sure we may come up with some plan that will check my sister's mischief."

"I'm afraid time is rather pressing, my lady," said Greyfax, rising and walking to a window that overlooked the eastern grounds. Below, he saw Pe'lon standing, an elf on either side, in deep talk. Occasionally the large head of the horse would nod, or his tail would twitch, and the two elves would double over with tinkling, light laughter. As he gazed downward, Cybelle joined the three, and she stroked the mist-silver neck of the great horse, and spoke unheard words.

"We shall rest here and take our dinner, but we must be away soon after. If matters weren't so grave, this fair house would keep me long and pleasurably."

"We've hardly just arrived, we can't go barging

off like that, bolting our dinner and saying our goodbyes from stirrups," shot Froghorn.

"You really must tarry awhile, dear Grimwald. We haven't had a good visit since she started this dreadful business again. And it would be nice to have you without worrying about departures before you've hardly arrived."

Greyfax crossed and bowed low before Lorini. "I'm afraid it really is urgent we stay only this short time. There are matters so dire I fear even delaying this long may have grave consequences."

Froghorn looked at Greyfax wide-eyed. "You can't mean that business before we parted. Surely that's no cause for any undue alarm. It's been going on like that for years out there."

"Yes, years, my dear Fairingay, and it wasn't this last adventure that I refer to, but one with far more import."

"And what might that be?" Froghorn stared hard at the older, gray-cloaked figure.

"The appearance of a dwarf," he said softly, meeting Lorini's even gaze.

"The dwarf from the River," she said, drawing up a chair and sitting down, suddenly tired.

"Yes, from the River, and an otter and a bear from there also. There is much movement across Calix Stay, and it seems the time is quickly nearing."

"Does he know anything yet? Have you instructed him?"

"I said nothing. I must have counsel, and our plans must be made. He's safe enough where I left him."

Froghorn looked on blankly.

"Great blade of Arinhod, whatever are you two secreting? What's a dwarf got to do with all this?"

"Much more than you would ever dream, old boy, indeed much more."

Lorini rose and walked to the silver decanter on the table.

"Here, Fairingay, take this to refresh yourself. We'll get to that soon enough."

Froghorn drained the tankard with a gulp.

"Why didn't you say anything then, if it was so important? Why, or what, makes one particular dwarf of any great interest in this business?"

Greyfax settled back into the high-backed chair, refilled his cup, and fell silent a moment.

"When you were first entered into the Circle, whenever that was, time seems to slip by me, you'll remember that soon after, you and I fell into the hands of Dorini." He paused, and took a small sip of his drink. "She had offered to treat with the Circle, and called for representatives to meet with her about the terms of her return to the Fields of Light in Windameir. It fell our lot to go, and of course, it was but a ruse to take one of our number hostage. Yet I don't think she counted on her good fortune at having the two of us show up on the appointed hour, full of good hopes and cheer, and oblivious to the fact she had never planned to come to terms at all and was determined to wrest the reign of these lower worlds from their rightful lords, who serve the One of Windameir." Greyfax scowled at the younger wizard, who went crimson to his ears. "But that is of no importance now. What is of interest is that before we had that fall, I had found out certain pieces of information that led me to believe the Dark Queen was in close pursuit of me, and that she had found out I carried one of the Five with me. This I entrusted to a dear old friend of mine, long since gone over the River, a lore master and keeper of Dwarfkind, very wise and learned, and who at one time served at the court of Melodias in the capacity of adviser. However, as dwarfs and elves disappeared from the coming of the Dark Highness, and men more and more came to power, and the great trouble came, there was no need any longer to have a close spokesman from Dwarfkind or Elfkind or Animalkind. All those who were, passed over, and the Circle had to start anew among men. Dorini and her servants successfully captured two of the lower worlds, and hold half of this one, as you well know. From her mind came the evil that destroyed commerce between the other dwellers of Atlanton Earth and eventually drove men's other allies underground, or across Calix Stay. All this you will find in your children's primer, if you want to refresh your memory of history."

Greyfax took a long sip of the cool drink, then continued. "Just about this time, you were admitted to the Circle. Young, impetuous, conceited, but still eager to serve, you had nothing much to do with me then, as I was often away for long periods, and not inclined when I was about always and forever to be answering your infernal questions."

"Still aren't much inclined, to my way of thinking," broke in Froghorn. "And when you do answer, it's an hour-long tale I can't make head or tail of."

"I neglected your highest quality, dear fellow, which is that of eternal patience."

"Stay your interruptions, Master Fairingay. He's not well-known for directness. Have another cup, and listen."

Froghorn poured out another draft, and sat back, patting his foot anxiously. Cybelle's long, glittering laughter reached him from the open window, and his mind burned with the longing for Greyfax to go on.

"Of the Five Sacred Secrets, you know the story. They were distributed among five of the Circle for safekeeping after it was learned that there was danger and peril and treachery afoot, even among the

Circle. That business was dealt with long since, but Melodias thought it wiser for the holders of these secrets to keep them, until such time they would be reunited in the final stroke. The dwarf I spoke of who kept mine safely from her was the father of the dwarf we met on the road, and he carries it innocently, for his father passed it to him before he crossed the River, and I still had not come for it. And then, after we blundered squarely into the hands of Her of No Light, she thought she had captured one of the Five and had achieved a great victory." Greyfax chuckled to himself as he remembered the fierce, icy wrath when she discovered he did not hold what she most desired. The darkness of that time covered his eyes a moment, and the room suddenly went cold. Froghorn shivered beside him, and Lorini's face saddened, and she reached out and touched Greyfax upon the arm. This seemed to dispel all the gloominess, and Greyfax cheered again, and laughed.

"How well she would have treated us if we hadn't escaped you may well imagine, old chap."

Froghorn shuddered again.

"So we defeated her twice. First, by my having left it with my old friend, and second, by escaping her anger. I fear we don't stand in good stead with our cold Dark Highness."

"Then if you knew this dwarf to be the son of your friend, and that he possessed it, why didn't we bring it here? Why should it be entrusted to a lost dwarf and two animals to keep it safe? She'll find it surely, with only those three to protect it."

"She won't find it, because she won't think of 'those three', as you refer to them, as being even faintly concerned with any such thing. As long as she thinks of us and the rest of the Circle, she won't have time to find out."

"But you also had the Arkenchest. What if someone should see it? Does the dwarf even still have it? I saw nothing."

"I have it still," Greyfax replied, lifting from beneath the deep folds of his cloak a small carved box, ordinary to look upon, but magnificent in its effect upon any who beheld it. Their hearts lifted as he placed it on the table before them. "And soon all shall safely rest again inside, for that, I deem, is our next task, Fairingay, to gather the Nine and set the stage for our last and final move."

Silence fell heavily upon the room. Outside the air stilled and the laughter faded on the shadows that closed over their heads.

Lorini raised her eyes from the box and looked into the distant eyes of Greyfax.

"Then your haste is well founded, my good Greyfax. But these tidings need not spoil our rest for now, nor our dinner. It will wait till then, but no longer, I fear."

She rose and laughed lightly, like a bell sounding the changing of sadness into joy. Greyfax let back his cloak and returned the box. Froghorn heard Cybelle calling to Pe'lon and the great animal answering, and he bowed low, excused himself, and hurried away.

"I'm afraid, old friend, your young charge has fallen under my Cybelle's charm."

"He could do himself no harm there. When his wizard's cloak fits him a bit better, I think you'd best start arranging a betrothal. It seems she finds our petulant Master Fairingay far more to her fancy than any other of your court."

The lady Lorini smiled, but said nothing. They left the study, and she led him down a long, deeply polished corridor, walls ablaze with thousands of finely woven silver flames like tiny suns sparkling in its mirrored glaze, and left him before a large, airy chamber draped in white tapestries, covered with dragons spun of emerald fire and towers and legends that shimmered into life as the wind touched them through the high, brightly lighted, open windows.

Greyfax lay back on the purple and gold bolstered bed, watched the movement, of the long histories of the tapestries for a moment, then gently slid into a long and dreamless sleep. The weariness of long journeys and the dangers behind and those ahead dimmed into nothingness, as his mind turned softly into itself, and Greyfax, elder of Grimwald, holder of the Arkenchest. Bearer of the Light, dropped gently as a stone into a deep, still pond of rest, washed clean of all fatigue.

It was the first real sleep he'd had in an age of Atlanton Earth, as years are counted, and the first chance his mind had found to ponder upon itself in many more than that, and the last he would have, perhaps, before the end.

Outside, a golden dim glow of twilight fell upon his window, as if the sun there were afraid it would disturb his long-awaited, well-earned repose.

FEAST AND FAREWELL

At the great marble and ivory table, covered with the finest linens of her realm, Lorini sat upon a silver-colored chair. Its legs were fashioned after the likeness of pearl-gray clouds, and reached down to globes at the bottom, each a perfect wrought replica of Atlanton Earth in each of its four ages. At the top of this chair was a haze, almost a fine mist, but done by metalsmiths of the elves in a precious, rare metal that looked like silver in some light, gold in another.

On the table, goblets of this same metal stood before each person, and plates of fine china reflected back the light from the huge chandeliers which held no flame but gathered the sunlight outside and brightened it in finely wrought, many-sided surfaces. A great fare was set out, great dishes topped with herbs and fruit, and flower-sweet vessels of honey and bread, and beside each one there, a silver pitcher filled with the wine of Lorini, which washed one clean of illness or age, and gave each one who drank it renewed strength and hope.

Upon Lorini's right hand sat Greyfax, and at her left, Cybelle, arrayed in a glistening, shimmering white gown, tied at the waist with a bolt of ancient pearls. Upon her head was the Trident of Cypher, a plain silver band with a single cluster of five stars, each a different color. Lorini was attired the same, without the belt of pearls. Her gown was adorned only with a brooch, a stone set in the mystery of some unknown frame, and it changed color from time to time, brilliant scarlet to deep, soft blue, or a light shade of pale ivory silkiness. This was the Stone that sang the music of the Fifth Kingdom, the secret from the Arkenchest that she held.

Froghorn was next to Cybelle, and the rest of the long table was lined with many guests, elfinfolk, and a few men.

Cybelle was whispering to Froghorn behind her napkin.

"Why must you part so soon? You promised you would entertain me with your travels, or show me a new magical form or two."

"I'm sorry to disappoint you, my lady, but we really must go. It's something very important, I can assure you, or else nothing in the imagination could separate me from your divine company."

"I accept your polite excuses, but I wish my mother had no sister, and I wish everyone would stop all this nonsense. Why can't everyone just live as we do here? Then we might find time to sit down to a conversation that wouldn't be interrupted by leaping off in who knows what direction."

"My fairest, wonder of beauties, if only that were possible. I would be the most eager and obedient servant of a world given over to those peaceful pursuits."

Greyfax from the corner of his eye saw the crestfallen look that played across his young friend's face.

"Here, here, Master Fairingay, what troubles you so that your mouth tries to touch your toes?"

"Nothing of import. A passing thing, I suppose," Froghorn replied, a little loudly.

"Cybelle, have you done something to discomfort our guest?" Lorini frowned the slightest displeasure as she spoke.

"No, Mother."

"It's my own doing, my lady. I beg your forgiveness." He laughed easily, putting his disappointment aside. "I'm not the one to breach the merriment of this company by sour humor. Let us have a little music, and I'm sure all will be well with me."

Without a word or motion from their mistress, there sprang into the room three elves, instruments readied, who began to weave the air into beautiful, moving patterns of sound and light. Having finished their meal, Froghorn took Cybelle's arm, led her to the large open space in the center of the chamber, and began to dance.

"Come, old graycloak, dance me a stanza," laughed Lorini to Greyfax, and after much grumblings of protest, he gave his arm and the two entered the dance, gliding softly upon the music, away into harmony and peace, and soon others joined and formed a gently moving whirl and circle of fair faces and flowing bodies, and the room filled with the music, and outside the very air moved as if dancing, and joyful laughter rose and fell upon the strings and reeds of the instruments, until at last the farthest corner of Cypher was a pattern work of golden music, sparkling and shining in the bright sun, and light spread from the four corners of Lorini's realm into the darkness beyond, and the winds there carried the music far and wide, gladdening the hearts of all who heard, filling them with deep peace and courage, and wonder.

As the music of Cypher played, and the lady Lorini danced with Greyfax, and Cybelle with Froghorn, and all the others in the hall were woven into its spell, all the lands in Atlanton Earth brightened, the darkness driven away for a short while. A troubled peace fell over the warring armies, of Atlanton Earth, men turned to men as brothers, and for a time, a part of the long-distant past reappeared, and the forces of the Dark Queen retreated into the World Between Time.

Yet as the dancers spun slowly down, and the music stilled itself into echoes, then silence, the darkness came forth once more, and a gray shroud enveloped the world once again.

Greyfax stood ready by An'yim, speaking in a low voice to Froghorn.

"I have a task at hand that will take me still farther, Fairingay, and I can't return as yet with you to my old friend, the Dwarf. But I want you to go to him, in a guise that won't arouse suspicion as to your true identity, and stay with him until I return. You are not to let him out of your sight, understand? And you are not to reveal to him who you are."

"What use can I be if I tell him nothing?" Froghorn was experiencing a touch of misgiving.

"Your use would be of no use at all if it were to be known that the elder of Fairingay were dwelling with a dwarf. We might as well send a message to Her Darkness saying, look, here you are. Take it. Sometimes, Master Fairingay, what little sense you possess could be drawn on the head of a riding quirt and flung to the wind like a feather."

"All right, as you wish, Grimwald. But I still don't fathom the reason behind it, and I wish you'd open your mouth as to what's going on in your head."

Greyfax, mounted and posed to ride, looked kindly down upon Froghorn.

"If I did that, old chap, I'm afraid I'd have less of a feather to throw to the wind than you. But good cheer, and courage, old fellow, and keep the Light.

When next we meet, I'll have much to tell you, and can perhaps bring more clarity to my speech than now." Greyfax paused. "Unless, of course, my hour-long rambling might bore you."

And touching An'yim lightly with a hand, Greyfax disappeared, leaving Froghorn alone in the courtyard. He sighed aloud, called Pe'lon, and quickly mounting, drew under the tower shaped like an ivory form of a great bird in flight and raised his hand to Cybelle, whose fair face was drawn and streaked with tears. The sorrow he saw there bit deeply into his heart, and he resolved to do quickly whatever must be done, to dry forever the tears of Cybelle, and, indeed, remove the reasons for sadness anywhere that now struck at the very heart of gladness and peace. For if even here in Cypher the seeds of the Dark Queen were sown, then the final hour must, as Greyfax and Lorini agreed, be rapidly drawing all into the last, great swirling vortex of destiny. All that remained to be seen was whether the great darkness could swallow them all, fair and foul alike, or whether the Sun of Windameir would once more shine upon all of Atlanton Earth, and all that existed of it, or upon it, or as a part of it.

With a soft promise that stung Cybelle's heart with the dagger of his parting, Froghorn whispered to Pe'lon, and horse and rider disappeared from her sight for a time that might be called a century in the worlds where the passing of time was marked by clock or calendar.

HEARTH FIRE

In the safe confines of the glowing green wooded valley, Dwarf, with the help of Otter and Bear, fashioned himself a snug, small house, half above, half below the fertile earth. Its roof was thatched with the still living boughs of pine, which gave the interior of the dwelling a heavy resin incense. The floor was covered by thick, growing clover, adding its soft, pungent smell to the pine. Dwarf, along with his lore learning, tongues, and history, had been steeped in the most ancient of dwarf skills as a spanner. His stone masonry and woodcarving were fair to middling by old dwarfish standards, but far better than any craftwork of man, and with tools he had journeyed back to the ruins of Tubal Hall to find, along with Bear, he had shaped and built many things.

Otter that day had woven water sprite and pond lilies into long fragrant coils, and hung them as curtains on the outside windows of the house. He had also taken great time and spent much effort making a little finger of the stream run directly by Dwarf's sleeping room, so that at night he could fall asleep to the music of the water, tinkling like a soft, hushed lute in cheerful song.

Dwarf, upon returning with his sack of tools, was so grateful and pleased with Otter's gifts he had set to work that evening and fashioned a living green door for Otter's holt, with dwarf magical runes, and many scenes of Otter's kind swimming, or fishing, or playing upon the bank of a river that seemed to be flowing through the dark wood. Otter's holt was located near Dwarf's home, close under the waterfall, and although dry and warm, its rearward section wound around downward until it was well below the falls, forming a small grotto that Otter used at times for sleep or play or getting away from things. For Bear, Dwarf built a sturdy kitchen table, with places in it to keep utensils and a small keg attached to one end for his honey, and a large drawer in the center for whatever there might be that might need storing out of the way of daily chores. Bear's cave was large and commodious, and needed few comforts to make him right at home.

On other trips to Tubal Hall, rusting quickly into the earth, the three friends rummaged through all the quarters left aboveground, and Bear carried away a great stack of leather-bound volumes of histories and subjects of all sorts, and all the usable cooking ware was salvaged. Dwarf found an old coat of arms of the ancient masters of the hall, and this he mounted above the hearth of his fireplace, polishing and cleaning it until it once more shone in a splendid way. Otter also found a stout dwarfish walking stick, with the head of a swan on its end, and often used it on hikes the friends took to explore further their new homeland.

Days passed into months, and autumn came and went, and winter settled in a pure white blanket on the valley, and still they had no word of Greyfax, or indeed anyone, save the birds and other wild kind that shared the valley with them.

Summer came and passed again, and they still busied themselves with their everyday lives, patching and mending, digging or building other wings, or forming new tunnels, playing or working, and had little time for thought as to what errand or journey either Greyfax or Froghorn might be on.

All this time, and more, was in swift movement while the two servants of the Light were with Lorini in Cypher, for all time there was in a constant flow, touching past, present, and future at once. In this fusion, time, as such, did not exist. There was dimension, but beyond the knowledge of the worlds, dimension as was in Windameir, the very heart of existence, the breath in the eye of the One. While Greyfax and Froghorn talked with Lorini, five years slipped by outside her realm, and five more as they dined. And at last, when Froghorn and Greyfax departed, fifteen years had marked the calendar of Dwarf in his little house with the living roof and floor, and all thought of the wizards had ceased to entertain their minds. Their dwellings had grown into homes to them, and each pursued his original quest as best he could, studying and planning, but Dwarf still had no idea what it was they should do, nor Bear, nor Otter. So each in his own way prepared himself for whatever had called him, and lingered still for it to declare itself as to what was to be done.

The lands beyond the valley grew barren and deserted, old men's dwellings vanished into thick overgrowth, and for years at a time they saw no movements, save once, when a band of swarthy, bearded soldiers went through on their way to a destination beyond the horizon. Bear and Otter had followed them secretly, and tried to gather what news they could, but all the soldiers' talk was of the war, and other topics that bewildered and frightened the animals, but nothing more. Another time, not long after the soldiers' passing, the western skyline was blotted out with great billows of black smoke, and far-distant thunder rolled and curled about the sun. That night, a blood-red glow lighted the distance until dawn. After that, they neither saw nor heard anything of Mankind.

Otter became acquainted with two blue jays that had come long miles from the direction where the smoke and light had been seen, but he could never get them to speak of it, and when pressed they would fly away, giving excuses for their reluctance to talk by saying they had food to seek, or a nest to tend to, and after a while Otter gave up questioning them about it. The only remark he ever heard them say that he imagined might refer to it was once when the husband snapped testily at his wife, "Well, if this tree doesn't suit your nest, think what it would be like *there* now." His mate chattered apologetically, and there was an end of that.

As the years grew on one to another, each of the three contented himself with his books, or river, or cave. Dwarf began polishing up his almost forgotten dwarf magic from a book he had taken from Tubal Hall. It had belonged to Bani, who, like Dwarf, had been a lore master.

Such were the lives of the three comrades during the time it took Greyfax Grimwald and Froghorn Fairingay to seek their counsel of Lorini, and make their plans, and to set out once more from the halls of Light into the darkening world of Atlanton Earth.

THE WORLD BETWEEN TIME

In the World Between Time also, where Dorini, Queen of Darkness and the Frozen Night, ruled, time did not move as in the world. Her great ebony halls glowed with an evil greenish light when she held court or met with her servants to gather news of her progress in her war to capture Atlanton Earth. Doraki, her prince and next-in-command, came and went many times while Greyfax and Froghorn were at their business in Cypher, and Fireslayer and Suneater devoured armies and smote kingdoms with their fierce, frozen breath. All the others, including Cakgor, son of the vile two, Fireslayer and Suneater, chased the stars at night for sport and haunted the places of men by day. Still, there were those upon Atlanton Earth who had mighty powers to resist, and the war had fallen into a stalemate of half light, half darkness.

Dorini called for Doraki. In the throne room, greenish blue shafts of fire cracked upward into the frozen stillness as the two talked and made their schemes. A low rumble fell over the World Between Time as their two cold voices rose and fell, full of violence and destruction, and the icy touch of hopeless, eternal death.

"What have you learned of our accursed meddlers, my repulsive love? What of the Secrets? And that despicable box?"

Anger exploded her words into shards of steely darts that pierced his dark soul.

"Everything possible is being done to find and capture it. Or even if we had only one of the miserable Secrets, we could keep Atlanton Earth forever in the dark." His laughter came, sharp and barbed. "All our reports lead me to believe Greyfilth still holds the box, although he has disappeared since his escape from us, and none of our eyes or ears have spied him out yet."

"What of Foulingray? Anything of that squirming meddler? Oh, how I long to lay my hand just once more on those two."

"We've discovered no sure sign of either of them, Your Darkness. I thought once we might have turned up something, near the stink hole of Tubal Hall, where old Creddin, the imbecile wretch was at watch for us, but it came to naught. I was close at hand at the time, but the fiends, whoever they were, slipped by me with some accursed magical stunt. I have no proof it was our delightful friends, although I am sure it was some of those of that vile Circle of your foul sister."

"Acccccch," came the cold screech of reply, shuddering the dark hall to its cold, deep roots, and setting Fireslayer and Suneater quailing and howling at their chains. "Don't drag the mention of her filthy name before me. I have been tricked and deceived by my sister and that lot she runs with for the last time."

"Forgive me, Your Darkness," trembled Doraki. "I know what grief she has done you, but I only tried to answer your question, Your Darkness."

A fiercely gleaming finger of cold fire blazed from

the Dark Queen's eyes, huge and yellow-glowing in her wrath, but she spoke so softly Doraki had to lean closer to hear the words.

"I am denied my rightful throne beside my witless, spineless sister, and that miserable pack of fools she has thrown her lot with all conspire with her to keep me from what is given me by the High Crown of Windameir. Yet they shall see that it is I, and not she, nor even he who sits on the High Crown, who shall wax more powerful. And the grief, as you call it, that the fools have done me is but a small token of what I have in store for you if you fail to find me Greyfilth and his groveling friend."

Doraki shivered before her.

"No, Your Darkness, there will be no failure."

"My good friend Greyfilth will wish he had taken me up on my offer of half my realm before all is said and done." Dorini suddenly laughed menacingly. "Does that bother you, my sweet, to hear me talk of replacing you with that monster Greyfilth? But you, my lovely, shall share it with me if you complete your errand successfully. And if not, perhaps I shall have my revenge I had planned for them on you."

Shrill, jarring, pleasureless peals of mimicking laughter filled the huge black expanse of the throne chamber.

Doraki bowed low and fled, the darkness of his bitter heart frightened and angry, and he went to the chamber of Cakgor and took the gaunt, huge beast with him, and sped away into Atlanton Earth with vengeance welling inside him. At his heels came Cakgor, great wolflike jaws slavering and evil, vile frozen breath deadening the air, down, ever down into the world of men.

A great, ominous black cloud enveloped the sun with their passing, and all who saw it quivered and shuddered in their hearts and their minds were filled with a dark, unspeakable terror.

Those who served the Dark Queen gladdened at the black immenseness of the cloud, and planned new evils to strike against the light. Their bitter hearts feared the light, but also the darkness, and the icy fingers of the Dark Queen covered their eyes and numbed their minds to all but obeyance of her will, and new strife and crises spread like a raging black fire over the world of Atlanton Earth.

A VALLEY FAIR

MAYFEST

In the month of Mayfest, two strange events occurred in the valley that Broco, Bear, and Otter had dwelt in so long, both unknown to the friends, but which would bring eventual terror and force them once more to their long-neglected journey.

On the day of All Summer, four dim, cunning eyes watched from the hills above Dwarf's now rather large house, for many wings and new windows had been built. He now had room for all the friends to live together under the same roof, but Bear wanted privacy, and apologized to the hurt dwarf that bears really wouldn't feel right even in such a nice home as Dwarf had, and that he liked to ramble around in the little-used tunnels he had dug, then forgotten, then occasionally rediscovered. Otter simply said he'd be lost without the river close to paw, and scampered away, giggling. Dwarf solved the problem of having his roof shared by taking in a smallish, beautifully marked tabby cat that arrived drenched one night in a driving rainstorm. It showed such intelligence and affection for him he couldn't bring himself to part with it, even when they fought, as they did often. They all came to love Froghorn well, which is what Dwarf named him, for he thought the animal's eyes bore a striking resemblance to those of Greyfax Grimwald's friend. The cat knew many strange tales, and often amused the friends after a long late night's supper by reciting old histories or spinning yarns about the ghosts of men who dwelled under the earth, or telling funny little anecdotes about falcon hunting in far-off lands. Even Froghorn was unaware of the spies who watched them steadily on All Summer's Day, hidden in the alder trees away from sight or sound that would give their grim presence away.

"Let's eat them, says I," growled the low voice, harsh as a sticker burr, and menacing. "We ain't had the likes in days, and I'm hungry."

A snarl of protest rumbled in the other huge wolf's throat.

"You know what he said. Any strangers are to be reported, and we're not to touch anything till he says so."

"He says, he says. Bah. His belly's always full. Let's at least have the dwarf, then we can tell him. My stomach don't fancy animal meat, anyways not no more. We haven't had man flesh since the war left these parts, and even a miserable dwarf would make an all-right snack now."

"We leaves 'em, I says. We can come back for 'em if he don't want 'em."

The great grayish-white hackles of the first werewolf rose and bristled, but the other gaunt beast bared his huge throat-tearing fangs. Their dull yellow eyes flashed in the silence, then the first beast retreated, snarling sullenly.

"All right, has it your way. We'll tell him, but mark me, if he don't want them, I gets the dwarf to myself."

"We'll see about that when he gets to it. Come on."

On silent feet the two beasts slipped away, leaving only the foul odor of their filth to stain the earth where they had hidden, and the birds hung to their branches high above, terrified and silent. Soon afterward, a silence fell in the green woods that guarded the valley, for a dark presence was felt to descend into its undisturbed tranquillity, but nothing of what it might be or what end it sought was learned, for it, too, passed away silently, letting the golden shafts of sunlight whirl and dazzle the stream, and the wind crept forth from its hiding and brought back the old, untroubled music and songs of the birds. Peace descended once more, and the three friends found new joy in their companionship, and held a great feast on Midsummer Eve.

Otter danced, and Bear paraded about with a tablecloth over his great head, reciting the tale of a fisherwife, and Froghorn amused them all with a dazzling light display, and at long last, as the night grew old, and all the friends began to turn to thoughts of sleep, the slightest change came riding down the wings of darkness, turning the warm night suddenly cold. It lasted but a few moments, but the friends quickly cleared the table and hurriedly went indoors.

"I don't remember sensing a change of weather," worried Bear. "I've never known it to grow so chilly *this* time of year."

"Must be the passing of the Old Sow," offered Froghorn, outwardly calm, but secretly alarmed. There was nothing definite, but something stirred deep within him, and his sharp green eyes watched the darkness as it turned and rolled, trying to detect anything amiss. Whatever it was was gone, he decided, having seen and heard nothing as he watched intently and listened. It was growing close to moonset, and he suggested they all find their hammocks.

"Tomorrow is Otter's birthday," protested Dwarf,

"and we really should drink him a toast before we retire. So, Otter, dear old companion, I give you a hundred more whiskers to gray your muzzle, and as many more returns."

"Hear, hear," joined in Bear and Froghorn, and they all emptied their cups, and after much paw shaking and well-wishes, Broco and Froghorn stood at the door until Bear and Otter were out of sight, on their way home to their own bed or hammock.

Otter left Bear where the path divided, and gave the big fellow a hardy paw grasp as they parted.

At the edge of the reed bed, a great trampling of shore and stir of water alerted the unwary animal. He quickly slipped into the pool, and glided silently underwater until he saw the flowing wands of reed above him, then rose cautiously to sniff and search. There was nothing, but one large section of his slide had been damaged by hoof or paw or foot, and after carefully assuring himself that whatever or whoever was gone, he hastily repaired it and trotted straight through the long path that led through the stream marsh, testing the wind every few steps as he went. The fragrant perfume of the lilies and a fresh swell of summer from all about him convinced him it must only have been some other large animal traveling through, and nothing more, and his step lightened, and by the time he was tucked into his small rush hammock, only the thought of the morrow filled his head.

He fell into gentle sleep, thinking how honored he was to have two such friends, honored indeed, and he wondered if ever the great King Othlinden had had such companions. The thought of the great king disturbed him for a moment, for a reason he could not sleepily remember, then he was safely slipping away down a slide that ran from a high blue cloud into a silver pond filled with bark eels, and he slid and swam away the remainder of Midsummer Eve happily.

Froghorn stayed awake until the sun began to creep over the edge of the window, its glowing golden finger filling the room. He had followed the rafters of the stars, and glided along the roots of mountain and valley, searching but nothing at all was to be seen or heard that had disturbed him. After a time, there came back to him the familiar sounds of bird and tree and rock, and he decided perhaps, after all, it had been some change of weather to come, an early winter perhaps, no more. He curled comfortably up upon Dwarf's chest, and delighted by Broco's squirm and mutter, fell to musing upon astronomy.

Next morning, a great shout and rapping upon Otter's door knocker aroused him, drowsing along into the fresh-smelling sunlight, and there stood Bear, Dwarf, and Froghorn, all gaily adorned in garlands of mayberry and dew lilies. They placed one upon Otter, and taking him by his paws, they led him down to the reed lawn where the water shone and glistened. Bear and Dwarf were beside themselves with loud congratulations, dancing and giving each other loud thwacks upon back and shoulder, and Otter, caught up in the festivities, spun and whirled with a great sploowhoosh into the stream at a great rate of speed, showering all on shore with a fine mist of cold, clear water. Even this startling setback couldn't dismay the friends, and Bear had soon caught up Dwarf in his great bouncing grasp, and completely out of control of himself, flung Broco into the stream, then followed behind, sitting down with a great geyser of water billowing high over their heads, and even Froghorn, who had retreated to a drier spot farther up the bank, was drenched to his muzzle whiskers, but his heart was light, and he kindly refrained from turning them all into chimney whippets, and good-natured and laughing, raised up instead of whirling, tall waterspout that engulfed Bear, Otter, and Dwarf in a torrent that went on until all three friends scurried spewing and laughing at once to shore. Bear gave Broco a hearty salute for his fine magical rebuke for being dunked, and Dwarf, casting a suspicious glance over his shoulder at Otter, accepted, and all four went to the table Dwarf had laid for the feast and fell upon the delicacies Froghorn had produced from some unnamed source, although all secretly suspected he had found them somewhere in the ruins of Tubal Hall, and far into the night the friends' laughter and songs filled the air with joy and gladness, and they drank many toasts to Otter, and the Midsummer Maiden, and to each other, and the next dawn found the four going still, mellow and full. At last Dwarf rose unsteadily up.

"My good, dear friends, we've been most fortunate and lucky in our lives and fates. I think we should drink a cup to this beautiful valley, our home all these last years."

In the growing red gold mantle of sunrise, the four comrades stood against the light, four tired, sad, happy friends, and they lifted their cups and drained them to the surrounding woods and stream.

"The best water I've swum in or under, in my reckoning," said Otter, bowing low.

"I've certainly had my luck with my cave," answered Bear, raising a great paw in tribute.

"And I," said Dwarf, "have fared far better than most I've ever heard tell of."

Froghorn, green eyes taking in each face, each form, raised his cup and added, "I can't say I've gone so badly myself."

He longed for news of Greyfax, and chafed in impatience every time he thought of being left to dwarf-sit, or watch after a bear and an otter, but now, at this moment, his mind filled with kindness, and for the first time since he had come, he felt how deep his affection was for his three charges.

Another Midsummer Eve passed into light and memory.

A LATE SUPPER

Once, the book had been secret-fed and held all the things no one ever thinks about, except at night, when the sun is tired and rests behind the shoulders of a big mountain down in the regions covered over with the mist tears make when they die on a face. Some tales were about the sun, and all the places Otter had been, in and out of clouds that made maps out of patterns, and dry land out of reflections off the sea. It was this book, much soiled and dusty, and a little sad by long unuse, that Otter now took out of his old knapsack and inspected. He had carried it for years and years. Even before there were bywaters and weirs to mudslide into on frolic-coated mornings when the rain had come and swept everything down, being very careful not to muss the flowers or trees too much, and left a small, faint radiance glowing off the earth's new clothes. Turning through the first few pages, he remembered writing there about the great fun days when he and all his friends scampered about playing wiggles, or the nice feeling of warmth at a kind friend's hearth after a long day sledding on his nose down fresh, soft packed snow.

His father and fathers before him had written in the secret book on back to the king of all otters who now dwelled somewhere in the light regions as a mighty wizard, among the wisest of all the other animal kings. They went about in the world at times, disguised as men, and tried to tidy things up a bit, but that wasn't half as pleasant as rocketing down a new mudslide into your very own pool, or discovering a new spot where you might find a nice bite for a late summer's supper. He returned to his book slowly, feeling the great pull of the sun distracting him, and the slow, warm feeling spreading over him as he thought of sliding noiselessly into the cool green water. But here was the book to be read, and nothing for it but to do it. The quick smile faded with his low laughter, and he rearranged his whiskers into a small, serious otter frown, such as he imagined the king otter might affect when dealing with such arduous matters, and opened the book to the next page, which spelled the ancient words of sadness and death in such a way as not to be really upsetting, but only as they were, simply a page of lessons and stories to be lived and told over again. Settling back with his head resting comfortably on a flat gray stone, he twitched his nose twice as ancient custom demanded, and fell gently into the rising golden words as they came softly up to his eyes, and the gentle pipe music began as it always did when he read from this book. He remembered his youth, and the lives before, and saw a little something of the ones to come. Much of it made his dark brown eyes turn sky gray and his mind move toward the ending of time when all would take their place once more in the shadow of their former lives. Shades of black appeared across the pages in terrifying hours of doom, then dispelled themselves into the bright arms of the sun, turned over, and were gone as easily as they had come. It had been so long since he had read from the book he had almost forgotten, and when he woke from the deep sleep he had fallen into, it was long past dark, and he was much too tired even to think of his dinner or move from the spot.

A sudden footstep nearby startled him into a tiny whistle, but the voice from the darkness was only that of Dwarf, who was out for his evening walk along the river.

"Otter?"

"Dwarf?"

"It's very lovely out tonight. I've just spoken with Froghorn and Bear, and they were wondering where you were for supper."

"Oh, I've just been reading a story and fell asleep. Such a nice evening to spend here by the river."

"Will you come along for some hot soup?" Then thinking better of it, "Or I've got some fresh raspberry dwarf cake, if you're more of a mind."

Otter's small, pointed ears picked up at the mention of raspberry dwarf cake, for it was among his favorite dishes.

"I'd love to, Dwarf. That's very kind."

"Besides, I've been meaning to talk to you about some matters of grave importance, and I'd like to have your ideas on them."

Otter's head cleared, and he remembered their talk on the art of seriousness. Trying to oblige the usually kind dwarf, who only occasionally became irritable and grumpy, Otter pursed his whiskers into a suitable pose of gravity, souring his smile and screwing his eyes up into a most hideous squint. His ears began to burn with the thought of what he must look like, but he mustn't offend the dwarf, or make fun, even when his face began trying to squeeze out a long, tingling laugh that was welling up inside him.

"What was that, dear friend?" asked Dwarf, puzzled and worried at the grave face, its gray and silver edges turned down at the mouth, and only two sloping slits where the usually merry brown eyes should have been.

"Are you feeling up, old fellow? You look a sight."

"Only thinking, Dwarf," hissed Otter, trying to choke back his laughter.

And on their walk, Otter leapt many times to the side of the trail to recompose his face and laugh quietly into his paws so that Dwarf would not hear and become hurt. He really loved Dwarf, and would do anything otterly possible for him, but sometimes he worried about the dwarf's eternal seriousness. Only once in a great while could he get him really to laugh and play on long winter nights such as this. But Dwarf was really upset this night, so he must try his best to be civil and courteous, and to do exactly as Dwarf asked, and to try to help his friend if he could.

When they had reached Dwarf's house, a small but cherry wood fire was started over the old ash for luck, and soon a table set with dwarf tea and cakes was placed before him, and the two sat down for a late snack. The little green clock struck one o'clock, and Otter wondered at how long he had slept and dreamed of that still, clear river that separated all time from pasts and passings. And Dwarf, full and drowsy by the fire, raised a knobby little hand in mock protest when Otter refilled his cup.

"Stay, I've had more than enough, friend. My heart is full of confusion, and I'd want no more spirits to haunt me."

His tone disturbed the gray creature, for in it he heard a page from the book, and when he looked at his friend, his eyes were full of firelight gone, the fires of many nights past, spent here and in other distant places now smoky and dim in the dying fire. Otter threw on two new logs to dispel the gloom, and tried singing one of his river songs to brighten up the morose dwarf.

I've played in rivers made of fire
And swam the sun
In autumns past,
Given magic necklaces to ladies,
But still my paws are fast
And I dart away
Dart away
When the snow flies
Down deep slopes
Dark slopes
To play in the skies
Up the great rivers
Into the tomb
But my heart is full of gladness.

There were others from his book of otter lore, but Dwarf still lolled in his chair, never once helping the song along or moving as Otter danced around the table, bumping into chairs, or falling down in great long gasping giggles.

"Otter, we must find our way again. We're spending time here we no longer have. I've been computing on my calendar, and we should have heard from Greyfax ere now. I'm afraid here, somehow. He spoke to me that day we met near Tubal Hall, and the matters he spoke of were very disturbing."

"Nonsense, nonsense, pure puff talk. We've only just come, Dwarf."

"It's been quite a long time, Otter, and you know how it is out there nowadays. We haven't seen or heard anything in months. No armies, almost no animals, no nothing. And it's the emptiness that frightens me most of all."

His voice trailed away on the blowing of the wind outside, and the two friends watched the white arm of snow beckoning by the frost-fingered windows. They stared and listened for quite some time, until Otter, trying not to think of the consequences should they discover them, walked to the fire and threw another log on, causing a great many sparks to crackle out, spitting and glowing onto the soft clover earth floor.

"No one could have found us this soon, Dwarf. Besides I've only come to know this river, and I really am much too tired to move right now."

"You're always this way, Otter. If you're not too tired, you're too busy playing or swimming."

"Can't we talk about it tomorrow, Dwarf? I'm really so sleepy now I think I won't wake up till noon."

"Ollllllllllerrrrrargrumph. You stupid gray-furred dunce. Can't you see we must do something now? We've been here much too long, and we haven't done a thing but play, or build, or swim. I can't do my dwarf work, and you've certainly not been doing much, skipping around all day beside your dratted pool singing your foolish songs, or sleeping." Dwarf punctuated his anger with a mighty stomp of his pointed foot.

"Now, now, Dwarf, things aren't as bad as all that." But his reluctant reply was not enough to stem Dwarf's reproach.

"And I'm feeling so much confusion I'm not sure anymore why exactly we're here to begin with. Or anywhere, as far as that goes."

Otter had fallen to watching the brilliant reds and oranges of the fire, and only half heard Dwarf's angry voice.

"It's such a nice fire, Dwarf. You really must come and watch it."

"Ohhhhhh, you silly animal. Now he's watching a fire when there are important matters afoot. Sometimes I think you've nothing in your skull but Christmas ribbons and fishtails."

"I guess so," Otter sighed, stirring the fire with the carved iron poker. "I mean I guess you're right, Dwarf. I was reading in the book today, and we've been here forever. Perhaps we should be moving on."

"But there's still work to be done here before that. I've still my spells to work out, and you still must complete your journal. And we can't move without word or sign from Greyfax."

Otter turned upside down on the comfortable leather couch and reached his paws toward the ceiling in a long, leisurely stretch.

"I know, Dwarf. Sometimes I simply think we've lost our way, and at others that we must be mad, carrying on this way. But I was rereading the book again before you found me this afternoon, and there were such lovely things there." He rolled over to face his friend from behind crossed paws. "Truth is, if we don't keep ourselves alert, we are going to get caught, just like I think they caught Creddin, and then it'll be too late for any of us." He paused, then brightening, with a flash and scamper, he was on Dwarf, bowling him over heels up from his chair, leaving two pointed-toed shoes struggling in the air, and gasps of surprise from below. His yellow hat crushed down over his eyes, the dwarf rose strangling back his anger, stuffed and puffed and grabbing blindly for his friend.

"And furthermore, Gnome, we must find something with a bit of humor to it, or we'll all be turned into fancy pickles. This time, perhaps, it's my turn to find it, and you'll never see it with that silly hat over your eyes that way."

Dwarf, shrieking, lunged after the voice, promising the most severe dwarf pummel ever, but stumbled over his foot and fell with a crash into the table.

"You ungrateful beast, you ingrate," howled Dwarf.

"Puffed-up gnome," giggled Otter, saving the pot of good dwarf tea from toppling.

And Dwarf slammed with a vengeance into the chair, spun backward, and landed heavily in the spilled remains of the dwarf cakes, which skidded crazily across the floor.

"You've been working on your formulas so long you're afraid even to laugh anymore, Dwarf. Besides, it might strain your face. But it won't, Dwarf, if you give it a chance."

And the dwarf, striving vainly to get up off the slippery floor, finally succeeded in pulling his hat up from his eyes, and staring dumbly for a moment at the fire, spoke in a much gentler and more hushed tone, as if he had really only seen for the first time again.

"You may be right, old friend. You may be right, this once. For all your foolishness, you sometimes remind me a bit of Greyfax. I only hope he has good reason for leaving us so long unguided."

"He must have, or we would surely have heard something by now."

"I would like to think so. After these past few years, I've begun to wonder if he hasn't forgotten all about us. After all, what's a dwarf and two animals to Greyfax? And he must have more important things to do than worry about the likes of us."

Otter thought quietly a moment before answering.

"It wouldn't seem too likely that Greyfax would tell us to stay and then forget us. Yet I do see your point about him being busy and all. He could well forget us, but I don't feel like he has. There was something more to our meeting him that day at the River than a chance encounter. I've thought and thought about that, and Bear and I have talked about it, too. We both felt something was going on we weren't too sure of, and Bear got quite stuffy about it later, and said we would all be better off if we stuck to our own, and left wizard's chores to those who didn't care a hoot about their own welfare."

"Oh, bother Bear, the dear ass. He's always concerned about something or other which never turns out to be anything more than crabgrass. But I do wonder at the silence, and the fact we haven't heard a word before now."

"Perhaps we're forgetting something, or not remembering all of what Greyfax said," suggested Otter doubtfully, his small muzzle worked into a frown.

"No, we've followed his instructions, insofar as he gave any instructions. But it does wear on my nerves, to be waiting like this."

"Well, I'm sure we'll hear word just as soon as we are supposed to. Now let's have another little bit of this wonderful herb tea, and sleep on tomorrow. I'm sure our heads will be clearer, and we can see what Bear makes of all this. Or perhaps we could make a scouting party to see the countryside hereabout, and find what news, if any, there may be for the having."

"That might answer, my friend. Although one of us should stay here, in case Greyfax or Fairingay should come while we are away."

"Good. Then perhaps you can stay, and Bear and I might just nose about a bit. It's been some months since we've had a look beyond our own front porches. And we're much more able to go about unnoticed."

"Well, a plan is what it took. Now I feel much better. Just to be doing something to fill up the waiting."

"And we can fill up the waiting before our naps by falling to on these household chores."

And Dwarf and Otter, after carefully cleaning the

floor, straightening and rearranging the furniture, washing the dishes and banking the fire, finally finished, and the two friends crept off to the two tiny hammocks hung from the walls, and each dreamed of the day when whatever it was they must do would arrive, and in their dreams, each tried to find new strength to face that inevitable hour. Then the dwarf tea began its magical healing, and the two friends passed out of the heart of that disturbing realm, into peace and harmony once more.

A SCOUTING PARTY

A new layer of snow blanketed the valley as Bear and Otter set out on their errand to see what they might of the surrounding country, and to try to find clues as to what went on in the world that existed beyond their own borders.

Dwarf had furnished them with journey cakes that he had baked especially for this trip, although Bear's own pack bulged with other items he had thought to bring along.

"You never know how long these all-day outings will last," he said sagely, looking a little accusingly at Dwarf, who simply grumped and huffed.

"I'll be surprised if you're able to walk at all, with that load."

Otter giggled.

"Look how he sinks down in the snow."

"We'll see who's laughing when we run out of food, and it will be, 'Oh, Bear, why didn't we think to bring enough?' " snapped the big animal indignantly, tightening the harness on his pack and wriggling it onto his back.

"You'll both be back here long before that happens," shot Broco. "Or at least if you haven't lost all your senses you will. There's no need to stay gone till next Mayfest."

"I'm sure we'll be back long before then," agreed Otter, putting his own pack on. "I'm not too keen on taking longer than I need on this chore. But I will get to find out about that backwater I saw when we were first here. I've just never had the time since to explore it further."

"Hurrrrumph," groaned Bear, "I think if all this trip is for is finding you a new water hole, then if it's all the same, I'll pass. I've just got a new store of firewood laid in, and I need to do a little mending on some of those old sleeping hammocks I've found in the back of my pantry."

"It's far more important than finding Otter someplace new to swim, Bear. We've talked it over, and it's all been decided. If you'd rather stay, then say so, and I'll go in your place, and you stay here in case Greyfax comes."

Dwarf's voice had taken on a worried note that brought Bear to his senses.

"Oh, Dwarf, you know me. I wouldn't be happy if I couldn't complain a bit. Of course, Otter and I are the ones to go. We can travel easier, and quieter, and cover more ground in less time. And if there is anything at all out *there*, it won't seem so strange if they catch sight of an animal or two." Bear paused meaningfully. "But seeing a dwarf abroad might very well turn some heads."

"And anyhow, I've really been wanting to see what's been going on beyond the falls. It's been so quiet lately, you'd wonder if there's anyone at all beyond our settlement," chittered Otter, testing his weight on the walking stick Dwarf had fashioned for him.

Broco's manner grew more serious.

"Do you remember all the signals we've agreed on?"

Bear repeated back the words, his eyes shut, with a slight frown creasing his brow, as he struggled with the detailed instructions Dwarf had given him.

"We're to watch for any sign from you here, in case we're needed to return, or in case Greyfax shows up." Bear paused, the frown growing deeper, then went on. "If we find anything of interest, or that warrants it, we'll signal you."

"Do you think this power will work?" asked Otter. "I mean so that it can be seen for any distance at all? It's fine in the small fires on our hearths, but will it make enough red smoke to carry anything farther than that?"

"It will do," reassured Dwarf. "We used that powder for signals before, during the time of trouble, to gather the dwarf lords to do battle against the dragons."

"Then that's settled. But what I'd like to know is, exactly what are we searching for?" asked Bear. "I mean, Greyfax wouldn't have any trouble finding us if he were interested, I don't think. So are we supposed to be out looking for him? Or what?"

"No, he'll have no trouble finding us," replied Broco. "But what I'm curious to know is if there is anyone, or anything, other than the wizards, who would have any reason to be looking for us too."

Otter's eyes widened.

"You don't think anything is, do you, Dwarf?"

"No, although best warned, best armed, as the saying is. And we've been content here, at our own tasks, minding our own pots, and not knowing what's going on, or gone on, beyond our own noses. Success in matters of hiding are often dependent upon knowing from what you're hiding, or in what way you need to go about the business of hiding at all."

"Well, that's all good and proper, I'm sure," snorted Bear. "The saying goes in bear lore that a sleeping bear is the best bear in winter, and here I am, out traipsing about like a silly goose, looking for I don't know what, and not even sure of what to do if I find it."

Otter tugged at the pack to settle it more securely on his back, and patted his ruffled stomach fur down.

"Oh, we'll know what to do, Bear. I can't imagine not knowing. We'll most likely creep quietly back here, or signal Dwarf, or as likely as not, have a good walk, and maybe exchange news of some sort, if we do chance across any of our own kind anywhere."

"Not likely to meet our sort in these parts," muttered Bear. "And I haven't heard or seen any indications that there *are* many animals left this side of the River. And those there are might be not so much of a mind to have any dealings with us. I'm sure they're all very nice, good sorts, perhaps, but not very much company, I shouldn't imagine."

"Oh, Bear," chirped Otter, "there are good sorts here, I'm sure. Maybe just not as well traveled, or as well read. Things have changed a bit since you and I were new here."

"You two have managed to waste the better part of the morning, and so far as I've seen, not made any real progress at getting down to the job at hand," snapped Dwarf, huffing a bit.

"At least we'll have a mile or so between us and this pesky dwarf," replied Bear shortly. "Come on, Otter, hop up, and I'll give you a ride."

"Thanks, Bear, but I'd just as soon walk awhile. There are some lovely snowbanks I'm dying to sled on. You might try too, if you'd like some fun."

"No thanks, I'll find my fun in front of my fire

when we get this little errand done. It could even be that I may not hear more from a dwarf the rest of the winter."

"And you won't, old fellow, if you'll only be about what you ought to be about. This is for our own protection. And there won't be *any* fire at the hearth if we let ourselves be lulled into a false sense of safety simply because we were too lazy to look to our own defense."

"Come on, Bear. Dwarf's right, and you know it. We'll get this done, and settle it all, so we can have a nice surprise party for ourselves when we get back."

"Otter's right, Bear. Hurry along, and the quicker done, the sooner forgotten. We'll all rest easier, knowing one way or another the lay of the land and who or what's been passing on or around our boundaries."

Otter had scampered ahead of the big animal, and turned to shout over his shoulder in a giggling voice.

"Last one to the marsh pond is a spotted plover."

Without waiting for a reply, Otter was gone, galloping hard in his clumsy-footed manner toward a long, gently sloping rise that ran in a slow, flowing motion down the lower portions of the white-covered valley.

In another instant, Otter was nose-bumping down a long drift, whistling and chirping his high spirits, and the object of his mission forgotten.

Dwarf huffed, and turned angrily to Bear.

"There, if for no other reason, is why you should be going, to keep an eye out on that reckless, irresponsible water dog friend of yours."

Bear was already away without answering, for he'd remembered as they talked that he'd found a honey stump along somewhere down in the area of the marsh pond, and that the tree was more than half full the last time he'd been there, which was beyond the fog of his day-by-day memory, but he'd liked the clover sweet taste of the marsh bees' honey, and if one were forced to be out in the middle of winter, then it was good to have the pleasing prospects of a decent meal to keep one's spirits up.

Bear loped on, the cold snow lying in a fine powder over his back and squeaking beneath his paws.

Ahead he saw Otter, standing to wave his farewell to Dwarf, who stumped forward a few paces, his hands jammed deeply into his cloak, a worried frown playing across the smile he had made himself wear as he was saying goodbye to his friends.

Broco could not put his finger exactly on any one sign or indication, but there was something, some indefinable something that was not right. A raising of the hair at the back of his neck, or an odd sensation in the middle of the night, or passing fancies at different times that someone, or something, had broken their fastness in the beautiful valley, and that they were no longer out of sight or reach of an enemy that Greyfax had warned him of in their meeting, so long ago now that Broco began to wonder if it had taken place at all.

As he watched his two friends scrambling across the wide white expanse before him, out of earshot now, he raised his hand in salute, and rather than let himself go on imagining things, he marched resolutely into his kitchen and began the tedious task of cleaning up after his baking.

GREYFAX RETURNS

Dwarf sat before a late evening fire, reading and making a note or two as he turned through the heavy journal on his lap.

This time, he thought, something must surely come of it. The signs of all the suns were in the right spheres, and the signs of his family lore book spoke of the sameness as there was before, when the lords underground had forged their brilliant wares, and the heavens were only a few billion aeons old in their second birth.

For a relatively young dwarf, he had seen something more than a small part of this world, and had been caught up in the long and weary Wars of the Dragon, in the times of trouble, and gone over Calix Stay at the end of those years, his heart saddened and broken by the death of his mother and the departure of his father for the Delvings. His mother had perished at the Fourth Battle of Endin River, along with many cousins, uncles, great-granduncles, and a host of friends from the multitude of dwarfish clans which flourished in the early beginnings of Atlanton Earth.

He knew of the stories of Bear and Otter, who had so often related tales of their other lives over the comfort of a late fire such as the one he sat before now.

He missed the company of his friends, and he could not keep himself from being concerned about them.

"Stumble into no end of mischief, as like as not," he muttered aloud. "I've always been fortunate enough to be close by to keep them from coming to any real harm, but drat it, I simply had to let them go off alone this once, and we must simply have the lay of the land. Greyfax never said anything more than hole up and wait, and that's twelve winters past."

Froghorn lay curled at the little man's feet, and he opened one eye to listen to Broco.

"It's been two full days now, without a signal or any other sign. I hope they haven't come to grief."

Broco leapt up and began pacing furiously up and down before the fire.

"It really isn't like them to stay away like this. I half suspected they'd come dragging home last night, reporting all's well, and there would have been an end of it."

Froghorn had opened his other eye, and sat up, cleaning his paw.

"I don't suppose you might find them for me?" mused Broco, half to himself. "They probably have lost themselves somehow, and need a guide to find their way back. And it wouldn't hurt anything if you were to take a look around yourself."

Froghorn swallowed a lazy yawn and went to the door.

"That's the spirit, old fellow. We'll both feel better if you take a look. Perhaps it's all unnecessary, but then better safe than sorry. And I'll keep the fort here."

The crisp chill of the night blew into the room as Dwarf opened the door, and Froghorn shot quickly out, and soon was beyond Broco's vision, disappeared into the bright glow of the firelight that glittered merrily on the new powdered white snow on the porch step.

He gazed out into the darkness for a moment longer, then shut the door softly on the doubts and fear that had stolen over him.

And inside, now completely alone, the doubts took on more terrifying possibilities.

Broco stirred up the fire and threw on another log to brighten the dark shadows that seemed to have invaded the cheery little study since Froghorn had gone.

A strange change came over the flames, turning from orange to bright green and purple, and then a series of brilliant white flashes, followed by a beautiful sound of pipe music, soft at first, then louder.

Broco had been lost in thought in his old easy chair, but now jumped to his feet in great alarm.

"Great blades of Co'in," he cried, and dashed for the bucket of water that stood on his sideboard near the sink.

A loud crackling sound exploded with tiny blue stars, and as Broco whirled to douse the runaway flames with the water, he became aware of a figure sitting in the chair he had just vacated. It was an old man, dressed in gray from head to foot, except for his vest, which showed through his open cloak. It was a magnificent brocaded vest of such fine material it sparkled and spun the firelight in dizzy reflections, as if it were water, or glass, or some wonderful stone. Upon his head was the five-pointed star of the Circle of Windameir.

The dwarf stood speechless for a moment.

"Greyfax Grimwald," he at last breathed softly. "I thought you'd never return."

The wizard smiled gently at his small friend.

"I was gone for a time, but the hour has now struck that I have returned."

"But," Dwarf blustered, "I mean just like this?" Broco reddened, then blurted out, "I thought there would be more of a to-do than this."

"Fireworks, or a parade? No, my good spanner, nothing so grand as all that. Enough to be here at all, with all the uproar and turmoil. I'm lucky to have a moment to spare."

"And Bear and Otter will never forgive me, to say nothing of that infernal cat of mine," went on Dwarf, rolling his eyes and clenching his fists. "Or am I just dreaming this?" he cried suddenly, and before Greyfax could move, Broco had sprung at him and clutched the arm of his cloak.

"Here, here, old fellow, this will never do. You may rest assured that if I wanted you to assume you were dreaming, I would arrange it. Now, there's no such thing going on, and I have much to say, and instructions to give, and I must be quick about it. And in order to do that, I think we shall have to return to my own drawing room for a chat, and to take care of the business there that must be taken care of."

With this, he raised a hand and made a secret sign, and to Dwarf's amazement, he was aware of flying beside Greyfax through a dim tube of flashing stars, with glowing crimson and purple lights, somewhat like the lights made by the passing of a loud sound on a dark night.

Presently they were standing in a cozy little sitting room with a bright fire.

Greyfax spoke as if nothing at all had occurred.

"I must tell you, my dear fellow, that what I have to propose to you won't be at all pleasant, but it is a necessity all the same."

Dwarf had stumbled in a daze to the fire, and stood staring at the gray figure before him.

Greyfax hastily poured out a cup of tea for Broco, and handed it to him.

"I will try to explain a bit further, although it may seem a bit confusing at the outset, but perhaps it will make somewhat more sense further on." The wizard paused, and took a sip of the cup he had poured for himself. "This is all a hasty business, and I regret the fact you've been here so long without a sign from me. I had not planned things to keep me away for so long, yet there were other matters that had to be attended to, and events don't always turn out exactly as we would have them. Naturally, it is all his will, but there are still surprises, now and again."

"What's all this?" Dwarf muttered feebly, trying to steady the teacup long enough to take a sip.

"Exactly, old fellow, exactly. What's all this, indeed?" Greyfax chuckled momentarily.

"I'm pleased, by the way, to see you've followed my advice, and kept yourself out of harm's way."

Broco's confusion was diminishing, and he managed to calm his voice long enough to speak.

"I know time isn't much, to your way of thinking, but I've seen twelve winters, counting this one, since I last saw you. There's been no word, no sign, not so much as a hint as to what we should do or not do, and all we've managed to do is exactly whatever it was we were doing before we crossed Calix Stay, although I dare say we did it under more pleasant circumstances there than here. And now you poof yourself back from nowhere, drag me here in the middle of the night, and I can't make head or tail of any of it."

Dwarf's teacup rattled noisily against his saucer, and he had to reach out quickly to keep it from spilling onto the gold and red hearthrug.

"Has it been so bad as that? You sound bitter, friend Broco."

"Not bitter, just confused. I've had no word from beyond our valley in so long that Bear and Otter went off to see what news they could gather, and there was no one to guide us, no advice from any quarter, and then I sent that lump of a cat off to find where Otter and Bear had gotten to, and while they're all away, here you've shown up."

"You have been more closely guarded than you may have been aware of," Greyfax said, smiling slightly.

"Then couldn't I have had some sign or token of it? I feel we've been wasting time, and our journey across Calix Stay of no importance."

"You have been of more use than you imagine. But come, this is our first meeting after a long parting. I'm here now, but rather in a hurry, and must soon leave you again." Greyfax ignored Dwarf's anguished look, and went on. "My instructions to you now are these. This box you will take with you, and keep safe. No one, not even Bear or Otter must know you have it. I can only impress upon you the fate of your journey beyond the River, and all my own, and indeed of all the Circle, depend upon your safekeeping of this box."

Greyfax had become slightly stooped as he spoke, and Dwarf detected a faint edge of fatigue.

"Am I to do nothing more than hold a box? Is this the part I've come so far to play?"

"Yours, my friend, is perhaps the greatest part of all, when it comes to that. When well-laid plans are made, the smallest, as well as the largest, must be perfect."

"Then can you at least tell me something of where you've been, or what news you have gathered?"

Dwarf was recalling the long wait, and determined to pry out what he could of the wizard's news and actions, to make up for the long nights of worry and torment.

"In brief, to answer your reasonable demand, I have been up one side of these worlds, down the other, over, under, and beyond anything that would make any sense to you. I may simply say that the darkness has been gathering since the rebirth of these creations, and now gains strength in these lower worlds. The sister of our lady Lorini waxes strong, and seeks to overcome these lower realms of ours, and to put herself on an even footing with the King. We have the five Secrets to combat her, and the Sacred Arkenchest, which contains the Music. You must watch yourself carefully, and your friends. From now on, you are in the gravest danger you have ever known."

Greyfax paused, patted the stunned dwarf affectionately on the shoulder, and went on.

"Now I really must be off, dear Dwarf. You may look for me at this parting much sooner than last. And remember, you're better guarded than you realize."

Dwarf was in the beginning of a huff to demand more, when Greyfax thrust the tiny box into his hands, murmured his farewell, and without further explanations, the lights inside the spiraling cyclone began again, and Dwarf was returning alone, clutching closely the small object the great Greyfax Grimwald had entrusted to him.

If he had been less upset, and not quite so impatient, and had he but looked into the older man's eyes, he would have seen in that atmosphere of serene quietness, the late sun slanting through the slow, swirling music which danced in the room, and in the middle of it, Greyfax Grimwald, looking at him with an expression of infinite love and patience, marred only by the tiniest fleck of sadness at the slow and painful inevitability of everything, of the unfolding of it all.

But immediately afterward, the golden light came forth once more, and the love in the wizard's eyes flowed forth in unchanging, ever widening circles.

IN THE DRAWING ROOM OF GREYFAX

Greyfax Grimwald had barely conjured the dwarf out the door when into the book-cluttered room came Froghorn Fairingay.

"Don't you ever announce your arrivals, Fairingay? You might have come while I was working, and you know what that would have meant," growled Greyfax, but without real menace.

"I'm sorry, Grimwald, but you know why I'm here. I've just seen Dwarf sitting amid a great heap of leaves where you dropped him, hat askew and grumbling horrible oaths into his hat, and I knew he'd been with you."

The marmalade-colored cat with the distinguished dark blue-black stripes down his back casually transformed himself into a pale halo of light, then with a sudden fiery popping, Froghorn stood before the older wizard in his true form.

"I was hoping, Grimwald, that this trip wouldn't become necessary, but I fear you told Dwarf nothing at all of our plans, and you know how little able he is at dealing with a problem of this nature without guidance. He's been harping at Bear and Otter until they've gone out wandering about all over the valley, and he thinks I am out now looking for them. It's all absolutely absurd. I could well be used elsewhere more effectively. And I find this task you have set more than tiring."

Froghorn glared hard at Greyfax to see if his protest was registering.

"You know how little we have to go upon now, much less having to deal with that bungling gnome not knowing his giblet from his grump, or his bookends from a shield boss. Why, dear Grimwald, didn't you tell him anything of what he was to do? Or at least something that he *wasn't* supposed to do?"

Fairingay had paced down the room until he stood staring out the window into the forever twilight that had fallen while they were talking.

Greyfax sat silently as his friend finished speaking, and stroked the fire absently. The room brightened, turning the bright beige and golden carpet into figures that turned and spun from the light, and the room was like a thousand bright lamps come to life on the face of the moon.

"I told him everything he needs known to him for the moment. If I were to tell him all, it would overpower him. But he knows as much as he need know at this time. And I gave him the Arkenchest to hold."

Grimwald looked closely at his young friend as he said this. Fairingay drew in an involuntary gasp, but said nothing.

"You know it's much safer there, Fairingay. They would know exactly where to find it if I had kept it much longer with me."

Froghorn Fairingay thought a moment, his eyes cast downward, watching the movement of the figures upon the rug as they portrayed the story of their birth and life, the finely woven shadows and patches of light swimming back and fro to the soundless, unceasing Music of the Universes.

"But do you think Melodias will approve? And what of Cairngarme? Is this not a decision for the Circle? To put the Secrets to such peril must surely be the responsibility of Cephus Starkeeper. It carries the fate of our entire mission upon it."

"There was no time to call such a meeting. And I shall go soon to Cephus Starkeeper, to find what I shall find, and give him what bit of news I have that he doesn't already know. I shall be gone perhaps quite some space of time, as this world knows. And if the Darkness thinks I carry the Chest with me yet, perhaps it will keep their interest upon the bait, and away from where the Chest in truth lies."

"This is a serious decision, Grimwald. I only hope it proves you right in the end."

"In the end, my friend, we have no responsibility for anything he does not will, except to ponder whether or not we did anything at all, right or wrong."

Greyfax walked to his minutely carved figure of a sea sprite and withdrew a tiny bottle that was blown in the form of a rose petal, and poured two small cups of its contents.

"Now, dear Fairingay, we've talked much too long, and I fear I've been rather curt. Take this, and let's think no more of it for the moment."

He handed the brass cup to his friend, and the two drank the strong potion, made of snow from the high mountains in Cypher and a deep part of the sea from their first passing.

"But what shall I do in the meanwhile, Greyfax? I mean while you're away?"

Fairingay had begun to suspect that the valley was, as Dwarf dreaded, or felt in his own huffy way, known to some outsider, or worse, real enemies. Froghorn could put a name upon it. He feared the Darkness had stumbled across the quiet valley, and knew of its inhabitants. How much they knew of the nature of those inhabitants, he did not know, but he did not like to think that Greyfax would be unavailable should an emergency arise or events take a general turn for the worse.

"It is not as dire as you think, my friend. After all, you will stay with the Chest. It is extremely dangerous, and very important, so you must, as you already know, keep yourself close to it at all times, and reassume your other guise. I don't really think you shall have much trouble before I return, but if you should," and here Greyfax removed a carved ivory ring with the face of a hippogriff smiling sadly upward. "Place this ring over your head and call three times on the Order of the Ancient Yew. You will then be able to speak to Melodias, or myself."

Froghorn placed the ring in an inside vest pocket, feeling at least a small bit better.

"Thank you, Greyfax. I hope you have a safe journey and good luck."

"With any at all, I shall. I will see you next when it is written."

Froghorn Fairingay turned thrice on the bright carpet and was gone, leaving Greyfax facing away toward the fire, drawing circles across the face of this place where he now stayed. It would be a long space of time before he could relax here in his little room he loved so dearly again, with his books and charts he was forever laboring over.

But then there was the Darkness, and it must be dealt with before either he or anyone else could safely sit before his fire, or doodle, or swim, or anything else one loved to do enough to not do something else in place of it.

He gazed on briefly at the fire, and when he knew Froghorn Fairingay was far enough away for convenience, he showered the room and the sky and the dark wind outside with the sparkling light of his passage, upward and beyond where the sleeping stars napped on in the warm dark arms of the tree called night.

DEPARTURE

As Greyfax Grimwald sped on his way, he sensed the dark and ice-covered world of the realms of Dorini, and although none there could see him, he shivered secretly to himself at the memory of the great frozen palace where he and Froghorn Fairingay had been held captives, and where they had first learned of the creation of the dark hordes of Worlughs and Gorgolacs that Dorini intended to use to overcome the faltering resistance of Atlanton Earth, and to wrest away from the Circle the rightful reign of the lower worlds.

Dorini had fallen quite enamored of Greyfax, and although she recognized him as her enemy, she confided many things to him in her grim chambers, for she was much in his company, and thought it safe to divulge her plots and schemes against the other worlds. She never believed that he or Fairingay would ever escape her. Dorini had tried to enlist Greyfax in her plans for keeping the lower worlds forever under her dominion, going against the natural order of the evolution of the Creation, keeping the lower three spheres in ignorance of themselves, and thereby under the power of the designs of the Dark Queen, and making them unaware of the fact that they were all children of the Light, and that their true home lay in the very Heart of Windameir, and not on these dark and frightening planes where they found themselves imprisoned.

Greyfax was at once repulsed yet oddly drawn to the cold beauty of Dorini. She was a twin to her sister, Lorini, lady of the Light, although there was a harshness, a bitter edge, that flawed the awesome beauty of the Dark Queen.

"I can make you the equal of the arrogant Starkeeper himself," she had said, "if you will but cast your lot with mine. We shall rid these worlds of the imperfect and weak, and create a grand new design to equal that of Windameir itself."

Greyfax, although unafraid, suddenly saw the power and danger of this creature, cruelly beautiful, ambitious, and determined to be on equal footing with the very Creator himself.

Her eyes held him enthralled, and he felt a momentary urge to give in to her and join her dark designs, but the sound and beauty of the Music overcame her clever snare, and he remembered himself. He chided Dorini gently at her outrageous plans, and urged her to return to her former place within the natural creation of the three lower worlds.

Her laughter came, cold and terrifying, and as Greyfax listened, he heard the low, menacing laughter shattering the icy air still, and knew the Queen of Darkness was yet busy planning her siege of these lower universes. The great wolf she kept to slay the suns growled hideously when he sensed Greyfax passing, but sent up a long, high wail of anger and despair when he was unable to follow Greyfax in his swift, invisible flight. The wolf had helped Greyfax and Fairingay to make good their escape from the dark realms, by carrying the two on his back beyond the enchanted gate after they had told him they knew the silent signs to halt the sun long enough for him to devour it. They had kept their word by halting a nearby sun, and the great wolf had gulped it down, only to find it cold to touch, and icy in his great cavern of a stomach. For Grimwald had merely made an illusion, and what he had eaten had been only a long-dead star, and while his attention was diverted, Greyfax had tugged an ancient talisman from his coat pocket and tossed it toward the rising sign of Capernicus, and Fairingay spoke silently in the depths of his deep gray-blue eyes, and the two were far away before the great wolf had realized he had been tricked. It was too late to give chase to the two, who left their laughter lingering on in the silent globe of the star in his stomach, so that forever he heard their laughter ringing quite clearly anytime he became hungry. His hatred of the two friends smoldered constantly in his cold, revengeful heart.

Greyfax looked away from that dark place, into the distance ahead where his mission awaited him, much more important now than giving any thought to the Dark Queen or the great wolf, for he must seek counsel in ways to combat Dorini and her creations, and find means by which the beings of these lower planes might find the Secrets that would free them of her dreadful reign.

Melodias had told him long before that at the appearance of the dwarf he was to seek Cephus Starkeeper, and others of the Circle, to complete their plans and begin the last campaign of the cycle.

It was to this purpose Greyfax journeyed now, to find the assistance of Cephus Starkeeper, along with the others of the Circle, and borrow the unquenchable Fire of Windameir.

CEPHUS STARKEEPER

"Welcome, Greyfax, elder of Grimwald. How come you to venture so far from home?"

The speaker was an identical version of Greyfax, with the exception that he gave the impression of being older.

Greyfax bowed low, then embraced Cephus Starkeeper warmly.

"I come seeking aid and advice, my brother. I had hoped that this visit wouldn't have concerned such weighty matters, but I fear it has to do with our errand upon Atlanton Earth. The Dark Queen has overstepped her realms, and now she holds half of Atlanton. She was given, as you know, the task of keeping those three worlds, of Maldan, and Origin, and Atlanton Earth, and only allowing those to come up who had succeeded in mastering the Secrets. But now she has attacked in force, and begun to use her power to keep all those on those worlds there forever. And she has set out upon the task of capturing the Arkenchest, and thus the Secrets, and thus the power to keep all those there forever ignorant of the Path that leads back Home."

Greyfax had paced to the high windows at the end

of the room which looked out into the pale silver eye of the night of Windameir.

Cephus Starkeeper breathed out a long sigh, and tugged his beard slowly.

"Ah, and so it is that we have the very problem we have been warned of, and the very task before us that we suspected would come to pass."

Greyfax nodded, his back to the older man.

He felt suddenly weary, and for a brief moment, discouraged.

Cephus went to Greyfax and put an arm about his shoulder.

"This means, then, exactly what the Book spoke of. The omen that would signal the last recall of this cycle. It's almost upon us, then, if Dorini has begun her bid to overthrow his natural plan of things."

"And the other omens have all come," said Greyfax softly, "one by one. I hardly noticed at first. There was the failing of the Order of the Circle, when Eiorn refused to give the Secret he held back, and passed it on to his son Tyron instead.

"In the first War of the Dragon, it was decided that the Five Secrets should be distributed to certain elders of the Circle for safekeeping. Eiorn was assigned the task of guarding one of the Secrets, and promptly took it where he thought it would be best kept, which was to his old wood across Calix Stay.

"As time wore on, Eiorn became more and more taken with the beautiful thing he kept, and in the end, he began devising schemes that would enable him to keep it for himself, rather than return it to its rightful place.

"It was in this way that he disclaimed the decision of the Circle to return the Secrets, and said that as long as Lorini was not returned to the Fields of Light, they would never be rid of her dark sister, and as long as she remained free, he could not give over the Secret in his keeping and thereby place it in such grave danger.

"Eiorn, of course, knew that no one would suggest sending Lorini away, and therefore, in his own mind, he had created the perfect reason for keeping the Secret to himself, and at his own passing for turning it over to his son Tyron.

"That Eiorn, a highly respected and honorable member of the elders of the Circle, should fall prey to the great temptation of using the powers of the Secret speaks clearly the dangers of the forces at work in the mighty wonders of the Arkenchest.

"There is that chaos to deal with yet. Then the appearance of the dwarf from beyond Calix Stay with the Secret which I had given to his father to hold, and who had handed it down to his son. He had it with him still, unknowing. And then all the rest, and now Dorini on the march, attempting to put herself on the footing of our Lord."

Cephus Starkeeper chuckled, his clear blue-gray eyes dancing.

"I must admit, this is exciting, Greyfax. I know it is unheard of to allow oneself to feel this way, but I almost certainly do. And I can't say I'll be too sorry to get Home, once this is over." He shook his head. "How long has it been now? A second? A day? An aeon? Or simply beyond measure?"

"It has been long, my dear fellow. I feel it more where I carry on my tasks, for there is where we feel such a thing as marked time."

"And I am sure it is growing tiresome for you?" Cephus smiled gently at his friend before going on. "I know. I spent my time upon a sphere such as that long before you attained the Circle. I know the agony it is."

"Yet I can't complain at all, for it is as it should be," Greyfax hastily corrected. "It's just that I miss talking to you, or Erophin, or any other friends of the Fellowship. It is very lonely, at times, knowing what is to be, and unable to tell anyone."

"All, as you say, to the purpose. It is the way we progress, old fellow. And what of your aide? Faragon is one of the Fairingays, and I should think he would be most suitable for the mission."

"Oh, the lad is more than one could ask for, but you know what it is working with these impetuous young pups. They've not gotten over their somewhat overpowering passions yet. And even the passions of a good nature can complicate one's effectiveness, you know. But he's a good lad, and we get on famously, although he does get miffed at me now and again."

"I'm glad to hear it. I've always thought a lot of Faragon, and his father and brothers, too, for that matter." Cephus paused and glanced at his friend. "Come, we must take some refreshment now. We shall have our chat, then meet with Erophin. He will be with us presently."

"I know this is all highly unusual, but I needed to hear your thoughts and get Erophin to express his views," said Greyfax, sitting down to a long, low table, spread with a faintly glowing silver cloth that shimmered with a fine golden mist deep within its depths.

"Not unusual at all, old fellow," chuckled Cephus, clapping Greyfax heartily on the back, then taking his own seat. "We had been expecting you long before now."

"You mean you've known of Dorini's plan, and all the rest?"

"Oh, ages since. The Book has it all there. It was foretold. But the Circle has met since last you came to us, and all that is known to all now. So perhaps we can be of some help to you on this visit, and fill you in on the things you will need to know."

Greyfax sat back in his chair, shaking his head slowly in amusement.

"I should have guessed this visit of mine wasn't chance happening. Nothing ever really is. But let's see to our supper now. I am anxious to hear the news, and to find out what suggestions I may take back with me to help me carry out my errands successfully."

And so the two began talking low and earnestly, eating from the long table, and laughing in places, or chuckling, or frowning, or pacing up and down the long, comfortable high-raftered room.

This took place in the early afternoon of that realm, and it was a stroke past teatime before Erophin arrived.

TEA WITH OTTER

Otter, at the moment, was pouring out a cup of blueberry tea for Bear, bustling about his shelf trying to find honey, and exclaiming loudly, "Oh, drat and confound it, I never seem to be able to find anything at all here when I want it, or even when I don't want it, for that matter," He slammed another cabinet shut and scampered angrily to a small sideboard next to the fireplace, his gray muzzle whiskers twitching rapidly and his little paws darting here and about in the jumble of stuff and junk on the shelves. Bear had gotten up and was cautiously poking about, for the room was really only meant for animals or elves or dwarfs who measured no taller than three or four feet high, and although Otter considered his kitchen ceiling very high and roomy compared to some holts he had lived in, it forced Bear to walk about on all fours, and even then there would be a grunt or gruff, snort or shuffle, and he would have banged his nose or stubbed a paw. Now the great brown head was lost almost up to the ears in a cupboard, and his rumbling voice sounded far away to Otter, who had to keep saying, "Whater, whater," anytime Bear spoke.

"I said, are you sure you had honey?"

"Oh, bumblebee hickiby, yes, I have honey. It's around here somewhere, and now the tea is cold and nothing ever goes right in this holt. That's the third cup of blueberry tea I've had cold today, and I still can't find honey."

And Bear, who had moved into a still lower shelf, his great, flat brown haunches pointing almost up to the roof, wiggled his brown and white tail in sympathy, but still sorely disappointed at not having his afternoon honey without looking all over Otter's kitchen for it, and bumping his nose or stubbing his paw every so often.

"Well, it's good to be back, anyhow. I've had enough of wandering around beyond our valley," grumped Bear, raising his head in a sudden caught breath. He bumped his nose badly. "Honey," he whispered under his breath. Down lower, until he was flat on Otter's earthen floor, reaching a great paw back and back to the inner depths of Otter's not so neatly arranged staples. He trapped his paw, and backing out too rapidly, put his tail straight into the open fire.

"Eeek, dear me, ohhhh," and moving much too quickly for Otter's small quarters, he bumped his nose hard on a roof beam, and while grabbing for the new hurt, he tipped over the pot of water boiling on the hearth. "Aiiii," moaned Bear, crashing headlong onward.

"Watch out, Bear," cried Otter, too late, and sensing the end, dived headlong under the table to avoid being burned or crushed, and Bear, one paw to his nose and one to his bottom, danced on one back paw that was in the pool of hot water, and crashed and tore his way outside, knocking Otter's small green door off one hinge in the process.

Bear fell down under a pine tree, holding his nose and rump and trying to cover his burned paw with his other, but he at last gave up with a long sigh and wail, and finally simply sat heavily in the soft blanket of snow, moaning from time to time.

Otter, peering out from under his table, rose cautiously and went slowly to his damaged door, looking at his wrecked kitchen, starting to chastise Bear for his clumsiness, but seeing his friend hurt, he darted to the big animal, angry and sorry that he had let himself get upset at the accident to his kitchen.

"Dumb honey, anyhow. If we hadn't been looking for that, this never would have happened. Here, Bear, come on, maybe we'll have our tea straight."

"Grumph," growled Bear. "Thanks, but I'll just sit here a bit."

"We'll have it all put back as nicely as before, Bear, don't worry. That door had a terrible squeak in it anyhow, and I think that top hinge was the one. I've been meaning to do something about it for weeks, even before we went on our little scouting party, but I just never seemed to get around to it." Otter sat down in the snow beside his friend. "It's much nicer out here now to begin with. I don't know why we don't bring the table out under the trees and have our tea here, and watch the sky awhile."

So the two friends brought out the table and tea and sat outside, watching the mountains grow dark as the sun began slowly to lower its light into night.

"My, but sunsets are very nice. I don't see why Dwarf never enjoys things anymore. He's so glum lately, especially after we told him we'd really found nothing at all." Otter paused, then went on in a different tone. "I don't remember ever being anywhere there was no sunset. Do you, Bear?"

"I can't really say. I think maybe when I lived for a time in the far north, we had days and days of light. It was strange, but then I've seen stranger, and I don't remember a lot of things that have happened to me."

The great creature tugged his whiskers, his eyes growing darker, and he left Otter for a while, thinking. "But now I think I remember something, but I can't recall exactly what. It was finding nothing at all that seemed to be the most scary thing."

Otter ignored his friend's reply.

"Do you think I might just have let it slip my mind, Bear?"

The big animal looked startled.

"Let what slip your mind?"

"That jar of honey."

Bear moaned softly, stroked his muzzle, and drank what was left of his bitter tea.

The sun was gone completely now, leaving the animals in the soft twilight, and a cool breeze sprang out of the dim forest, crisp with pine smells, and snowy fir and gorse, and the sweet smell of powdery snow on berry bushes. Otter's ears flattened back and his little body began to shiver, nose up, searching the evening winds, small brown eyes all black now, and wide. He began whistling low in his throat as if in danger, and his forepaws moved quickly to cover his face from whatever he saw or heard or smelled. Bear, seeing his friend, suddenly rose up to his full height, hackles bristling, great paws opened and showing long, sharp claws, huge, powerful mouth drawn back in a menacing, terrifying snarl. He let go one long, rumbling growl that stopped the wind for a moment, and the trees in the forest cowered, and even the distant mountains halted for a breath and echoed back that raw, stark, horrible warning. Then the wind resumed, and everything was as before, and Bear looked around to his small gray friend, who had crept between his back legs, whimpering and whistling, for he had never heard his friend raise his mighty voice before in such a strange, yet familiar rumble.

Bear carefully stepped away and lowered himself to all fours.

"What was it, Otter? What frightened you so?" His hackles began a tentative lowering, and he reached out one huge paw and patted the otter gently on his soft gray back.

"It wasn't anything here, Bear. Just when you were asking me if I remembered anything from before, I did, and I saw what it was for a moment, but it was all dark and I couldn't see it, but I knew it was there. And when I remembered it from before, it was here, too, and then when we didn't find anything on our little trip up the valley, and you said that was what scared you most, it seemed to scare me. It had something to do with the light, but I don't remember what. But I'm frightened now, Bear."

"There, there, old man. There's nothing here now, or at least there shouldn't be," and just to make sure, Bear raised himself to an even greater height, his massive head thrown back, his chest expanded until Otter could no longer see the sky above him. He then let forth such a bellow of rage and danger that the wind quit altogether and turned inside out, rustling the treetops like a cyclone and filling the canyons with a harsh, rasping shriek, and the mountains increased the rumble growl until it shook the distant seas, and the awakening stars hid their eyes for a few moments, leaving the silence that followed as still and dark as a musty, creaking dream of what no sound is like, but is when it throws off its cloak and takes the dreamer into its arms in the deepest stillness of all.

Bear's great ears were laid back, his teeth flashed like dancing white steel fire in the darkness, and he raised his forepaws forward again, showing the dagger-sharp claws that out of old animal habit he always kept trim and properly honed until he could rake the bark off even stout oaks or ironwood trees with a simple swipe. Then there was the moon, and the stars one by one came out again, and the wind caught its breath and resumed its gentle snoring, and brought with it the smell of the sleeping, snow-blanketed forest again, and whatever it had been that was there was gone from Otter's heart, and only a trace of his fear remained. The two friends did not speak for a while longer, for it was only polite not to speak of it, unless absolutely necessary, and even at that one must always be very careful. Finally Otter's gray ears twitched and popped up from flat back, and he shuffled his forepaws a few times in the snow, sniffed, stuck out his tongue, raised up on his hind paws, looked all about him, chuckled low in his throat, coughed and said, "Do you think this has anything at all to do with what Dwarf has been so worried about? Or with anything that he might have been sending us out to look for?"

Bear looked down at his little companion for a long while. "Perhaps so. Somehow I feel it does, but then you know Dwarf, always full of mysterious goings-on, and you never can get him shushed up once you get him onto his gloomy tales and lore books." He stopped to trail his paw across his sore backside awhile. "Except I do remember an awful lot of goings-on from my time, like this, and others, and I think it must all be part of whatever it is Dwarf speaks of. There seems to be a lot more in our crossing Calix Stay than finding a new home in this valley."

"Oh, let's put the door back up. Bear. I don't think I'll be able to sleep unless my door is locked tonight."

Otter looked despairingly at his door, broken and hanging by one small steel finger. And starting to move off, Otter stopped again. "I think we must talk to Dwarf tomorrow, and see what is to be done, or make some sort of plan. Something from a long time ago has come back to me, and I'm sure we must have seen it, or rather felt it tonight."

"Or not seen it," finished Bear, shooting a meaningful glance at his friend. "It's always the things you can't put your paw to that are the most frightening."

After the door was repaired and locked, Bear and Otter talked of going to the river for a late night walk, but the thought of it didn't appeal to the friends, especially the thought of going about in the darkness that now seemed darker than before. The moon slowly slid into a vast gray-black cloud and disappeared, and after Bear had reluctantly gone home to his lair, Otter latched all the shutters, checked the door twice, banked the fire, and laid his stout little walking stick beside his hammock for a cudgel, feeling silly at the thought of it, but somehow it made him feel better that it was near.

While they slept, Otter with his walking stick and Bear with one great dark brown eye open, Dwarf awakened with a scream that he thought was a nightmare.

Froghorn Fairingay, who had been wandering across the star universes of Windameir, knew better, and leapt up in the dark room to work a spell, cursing himself for becoming so secure and not thinking anything would happen until Greyfax returned, but it was too late.

The son of Suneater and Fireslayer had come on a ray of ragged silver-edged mooonlight and taken Dwarf away into the land of cold and darkness.

Froghorn, spinning around and lamenting to himself in his own tongue, felt somewhat better when he saw the Arkenchest was still safe, but it was a bitter consolation for him, and he ground his teeth in anger and frustration, full of despair that his friend had been taken to a place he knew well, and feared.

In the cold, empty room, he sat down at last, to plan and think.

Somehow, he must save Dwarf before Greyfax returned.

CAKGOR

Cakgor, son of Suneater and Fireslayer, had waited for Dwarf's house to darken before he moved, and in the half-light of the moon, his savage dark eyes burned in silent hatred of the warm room and all those who dwelled in light. It was only on the darkest nights one could feel his presence, and that icy finger of fear that comes then is the nearness of Cakgor, whose domain is terror and blackness. He roamed across the world unnoticed by most, until the evil which lived within him was rampant and spread from every corner where there were living things to infect. His special allies in this world were many, some animals, some men, all who fell under his maligned, cancerous spell. And it had been his passing that had frightened Otter, who knew of him from another time, when he was new in the world and went under another name. Cakgor had heard Bear's great defiant war cry, and laughed to himself at the thought of how puny and helpless the bear would find himself should Cakgor reveal to him his presence in any one of his terrible forms. Sometimes he chose the wolf, such as his father Suneater, or the body of a burning wind, a cold blue figure that closely resembled a cloud of snow or sleet, but with a great, yawing mouth with long, jagged teeth that shone a vile greenish glow and eyes that were taller than high mountains and phosphorescent in all their dim depths. His dreadful laughter had rung out over the mountains, and took up the sound of the trees rattling dry leaves, or the grating, harsh sound of sand across parched skin. His business tonight was elsewhere, and he had no time for frivolity, for anyone the Dark Queen should deem important enough to call for must indeed be a powerful enemy. He had crackled silently when he'd seen Dwarf, for surely anyone so small and insignificant could not be so dangerous as the Queen had told him. He stole as silently as a wind into Dwarf's room, froze him immobile with his frigid breath, and hoisted him up in those huge, dripping jaws and was gone, leaving only choking fumes and frozen ice fingers in his wake.

Dwarf, senseless and frozen almost solid, dreamed of disaster and catastrophes far-reaching and dreadful, and nothing would come of the Five Secrets but doom and death for all who believed in their power.

In the Palace of Darkness, great stone Bells rang out, and the great Suneater rattled the dwarf-wrought chains that bound him, made under earth by Broco's forefathers ages before when the Circle had imprisoned Dorini and all her creations in the World Between Time, and Fireslayer, his wife, whirled her thirty heads around her great, oozing body, snarling and spitting her anticipation at such a grand defeat of the Circle. Now all they needed was the Arkenchest, and hope would be destroyed for all those upon Atlanton Earth, bringing total victory for the Darkness, and the light and warmth would be devoured and imprisoned in the cold wastes of Suneater's ravenous hunger. And an evil air of great celebration rang dully through the dark kingdom. Theirs had been a great advance.

DWARF DISAPPEARS

When Otter and Bear reached Dwarf's early on the second morning after their scouting trip, only a deserted house greeted them. Not even Froghorn the cat was anywhere around, and the room stank of sour, foul odors which made the animals' ears lay back and their hackles rise.

"Something very bad has been here, Bear. I smell it in the air."

"I know, I caught its scent when we came in."

"But what would anything like that have to do with Dwarf? He's only a dwarf, and of no importance to anyone."

Then, catching himself quickly when Bear turned to stare at him, he said, "I mean why would anyone bother with a dwarf when there are so many more important men in the world?"

"It may have been something about what we were speaking of last night. It seems he did know more than either of us."

"What shall we do now? Oh, Bear, what can we do? We don't know anything at all, and we're all alone now."

"Just let's think a moment. Things aren't as bad as

all that. He must be somewhere. So what we have to do is get him back."

And Bear, as he spoke, began helping himself to a huge slice of bread and jam from Dwarf's cupboard.

"First let's get our breakfast for strength, then we shall see what's to be done."

"Bear! How can you go fumbling around eating when Dwarf may be in grave danger?"

"We can't do anything at all if we're starved half to death."

Bear made up two giant sandwiches, which Otter could eat only a few bites of, and the two comrades sat down in Dwarf's kitchen, bent low over the table talking in hushed voices and trying to plan what must be done. They got only as far as to decide Dwarf was gone, and quite possibly in danger, and that the best thing that could be done would be to find out how to get him back.

"How shall we do that?" asked Otter, wiping the sandwich crumbs from his whiskers.

"Ask someone," replied Bear shortly, amazed at the little animal's lack of following through on the obvious answer.

"Who?"

"Well, uh, we could, ahem, yes, cough, ahem, well."

"You might try me," broke in Froghorn, striding into the room, disguised in the form of a gypsy peddler.

"A man," gasped Otter, darting under Bear's chair.

"Grrrr," snarled Bear, baring his man-scaring teeth and laying his ears flat back on his huge head.

"Oh, stop it, both of you. I'm well aware of your distress, and am here to help you."

Bear let one stubbv brown ear pop up to hear this strange man, who did, after all, speak their language.

"Now, first off, we must leave this house and find a

better hiding place. It's no longer safe here, and if those powers that took Dwarf happen to return, we'll all be in a fine fix." And Froghorn looked from one to the other. "Well?"

"We could go to my house," offered Otter, "only the ceiling is so low as to always be getting in the way of anyone taller than three or four feet high."

"My cave should be quite secure. We'll go there."

"Fine." And Froghorn followed the two animals out and down through the forest to Bear's great cave, sunk in the side of a mountain near the river and concealed from view by blackberry bushes and rocks.

"This should be safe enough," observed Froghorn, striding into the center of the rather gloomy cavern.

Otter had crawled upon Bear's big table, and now studied the strange man that spoke so well in their language. Their was something different about this man, and Otter thought for some reason he seemed exceedingly familiar. Something in the eyes, but he couldn't recall exactly what.

"Our friend," Froghorn said, "is captured and a prisoner in the palace of Darkness, if you are aware of anything of that nature. The Dark Queen found out somehow that Dwarf had some connection with Greyfax Grimwald, and that he might have some information that would prove valuable to their war on these worlds."

Bear's eyes widened in amazement and wonder to think that he, a simple bear, was caught up in anything so important as all the strange man was saying. Otter flipped backward off the table, and now stood full height, which was only three or four feet from tip to tail.

"Great Weir of Baccu, what on earth could Dwarf be doing fiddling around with anything this Dark Queen could want? I've always thought him a little eccentric, but I never thought he'd gone that far."

Froghorn now removed the Arkenchest from beneath his cloak, and held it up to the two friends. "This box is what they were after." He paused to let that information sink in. "Furthermore, they will stop at nothing to gain it."

Bear padded over and reached out a paw to touch the box.

"May I touch it?" he asked softly.

"Not just yet. First I must have proof of your feelings, for I fear greatly the powers of darkness, and know they work in many guises. If you are true and just, you'll agree to help me without desiring to know the box's contents." Here Froghorn paused again, and returned the Arkenchest to its hiding place in the great folds of his cloak. "They shall, however, if you prove yourself, be revealed completely to you, if you still wish it so."

"The box is of no interest at this moment, Gypsy, for we've still not discovered what you know of where Dwarf is, or if you do know, what there is to be done. I'm sure it's a fine box and all, but don't you think we should be trying to get Dwarf back? He has a lot of puff about him, but he is very clever at some sorts of things, like hiding places and all, and I'm sure he'd be of great help finding a safe place for your box."

"Well said, friend," and Fairingay walked to the table and sat, placing the box before them, and began.

"First, we must give you disguises." And his hand went into his cloak and returned with an object that looked to Bear very much like a honeycomb, although Otter thought it had rather an appearance like a pond lily, but before they could decide, Fairingay ordered them to eat of it and close their eyes, turn around to their left twice, and say after him exactly the words he spoke, which they did.

"Now, Bear and Otter, you both have the power of

one of the small secrets of my trade, which is that you may now move about under the illusion of men. You need only speak those words, and repeat the ritual, and you will be able to change back and forth at will. Later, naturally, you will be able to assume any form you wish, but all that's of no importance."

Bear looked at Otter, and instead of the gray little figure he knew, stood a regular, frightening man with long side-whiskers and rather an otter-like mustache, but a man nonetheless.

"Bear, you look all funny," giggled Otter. "You've certainly changed." And he went to wiggle his tail and cover his nose with his paws, but to his surprise found hands instead, and no tail to wiggle at all.

"You look rather stupid yourself," growled Bear, and felt his new body carefully, running the somewhat awkward hands up and down his sides and over his face. It certainly felt queer to be a man, and he understood that sometimes they must act so strangely, with hands instead of paws, and no fur at all to keep them warm.

"Now you both must go for help from one certain man that is now among the northern folk, in a place near where the two great rivers begin high in the mountains in a country known as Amarigin. This man has powers that will help us, and he must be told what has happened here. He fights the Dark Queen's armies upon those borders, and to some he is known as General Greymouse. He also has many friends among the elvish clan."

"However shall we find such a man, Gypsy? We know nothing of this world, and have never gone about as men." Bear began disliking their mission very much, and was no longer sure what it was that had drawn him on this foolish journey when he could be having a late supper or snoozing comfortably before his fire, without the least thought of any unpleasantries at all.

Otter, feeling much the same way, and not at all comfortable in the form of a man, asked Froghorn rather shortly, "Isn't this whole business rather silly? I mean what can you hope to have but two silly animals walking about on two feet, not even able to get their own supper, much less make some sort of ridiculous journey to someplace they have no idea where it is to begin with, much less find if they did? If there's anything sensible to be done, it's certainly not going around dressed as a man. And what has any of this to do with men, anyhow? Just because Dwarf got himself stolen certainly doesn't concern anyone in the human world."

"There you're wrong, friend Otter. You ask true questions, but there's more here than I can begin to explain to you at the moment. All I can say is that to get Dwarf back, it is necessary to seek the aid of the man I speak of."

Otter, who had repeated the spell, now resumed his true animal form, and stood straightening his fur and wiggling his tail to make sure of its fit.

"And if it's so important, why don't you go, Gypsy? You're a man, and need not go to all the bother of changing shapes whatever. Everyone should stick to his own, anyhow. Never was able to see the sense in pretending you're something you're not. Only leads to the worst sort of trouble," grumped Bear.

A thick blue-green smoke filled the cave, and when it had gone, Froghorn stood revealed to them in his usual form.

"Shame on you, Bear. You don't see sense in anything that doesn't happen to agree with you at the moment."

Bear was taken aback at the changes that had been

occurring and quite confused at the entire proceeding.

"Froghorn Fairingay."

Another flash, and Froghorn returned to the figure of their long-familiar friend, Froghorn the cat.

And leaping upon Bear's shoulders, he said as matter-of-factly as possible, "Sometimes I even turn myself inside out, or upside down, as much as I detest the idea, but what must be done simply must, so there's no two ways about it."

Bear reappeared as Bear, and the three friends began making their plans, and Froghorn showed them the maps of where the Master lived who must help them. Otter was still not convinced that they and not Froghorn should go, until Froghorn showed him a glimpse into a memory from long ago, and his small brown eyes grew hazy at the picture of it and his heart saddened at what he saw.

"I'm truly sorry, Froghorn. I'm only a simple animal, and I suppose it's quite a lot to ask of anyone if they don't know anything much, and I don't claim to be so smart anyhow. If we must do this, then I guess there's simply nothing for it but to do so."

"There's the old fellow. And there's really no one else to do it now but you and Bear. Everything depends upon it."

"What will you do, Froghorn? While we're gone, I mean?" asked Bear, beginning to like the thought of this adventure, since it seemed no more than something that would last for only a few weeks or so, and then the whole business could be put away into some story or other and forgotten about.

"I seek the lady of Cypher, whose sister, the Queen of Darkness, holds our friend Dwarf in her frozen halls."

"Well, if we must go, we must. Now I think I

shall find myself a bite to eat. All this excitement has simply exhausted me, and I'm hungry enough to perish." And Bear began to forage through his larder, laying out a cheese and two good-sized loaves of bread, a bottle of his best honey, and two tall glasses of cider for Froghorn and Otter.

"I shall be gone before long, and it's most likely I shall not see you again until you have found Greymouse. It is a long journey, and hard, but I've been among you for quite enough time to know you will not fail me. Remember all I've told you, travel cautiously, and our next meeting shall be hastened." He whirled, was Froghorn Fairingay the wizard once more, whistled a long high note, and in an instant Pe'lon had sped from his waiting in Cypher to the door of Bear's cave to carry his master away upon his journey.

Froghorn saluted them with a nod and was gone, leaving Otter and Bear perplexed and feeling the least little bit as if they'd been deserted.

"At any rate, Bear, we shall get a chance to see the lady of Cypher when we return. I've always wanted to see her."

Bear, souring on the whole adventure as soon as Froghorn had gone, took another mouthful of cheese, and said grumpily, "When? When? You mean *if* we return. Why couldn't we have gone to fetch the lady, and Mr. Magical Fancy Pants gone off galivanting after this fellow we're supposed to find?"

"It's no use, Bear. You heard him. We're the only ones left to do it."

"I dare say," snapped Bear, "since he's going to be so tied up on that other errand. Then of course there'll be no one left to do it but us."

"I wonder how the water is there?" mused Otter, half aloud, already thinking of a strange new river. "Or if they have any water there at all?"

"I'm simply wondering if we shall ever have any peace and quiet anymore, without all this to do. We must, we absolutely must, get Dwarf back, and interested in some nice tame hobby like gardening or lawn tennis, instead of his infernal obsession with all that philosophy and mystical stuff and poppyrot."

Bear belched a long hiccup, covering it with his paw. "And this all has me upset again, and now I'm going to have a terrible stomachache just thinking about it all."

"I'm off to pack now, Bear. I'll throw together a nice lunch for tomorrow, and perhaps we shall find a new berry spot for dinner, or who knows what might happen? My goodness, Bear, it shall certainly be exciting, no matter what."

"At our expense, no doubt," said Bear dourly. "And I never knew a good thing yet come from any such goings-on as this."

"Oh, Bear, you're much too quick to think the worst. And you know we must get our poor Dwarf back. I shudder to think what they might be doing to him now."

Bear, softening his harsh scowl, looked at Otter a moment before speaking.

"How dreadful of me, Otter. I'd quite forgotten to think about that. Of course, we must go first thing in the morning." And after another moment, "I rather miss his puffing about, you know."

Far into the night the two friends prepared for their impending journey into the world of men.

DORINI RECEIVES DWARF

Deep inside the frozen place, away from all light except the cold fire that burned like a pale yellow coal in the eyes of his guardian, Dwarf trembled and ached over his whole body. His clothes were only those that he'd worn to bed the night he was captured and carried away by Cakgor. Bundled in that great silver-black wolf's jaws, he'd wept and chattered with cold, and looking down and all around him, he saw nothing familiar, but the darkness that grew deeper and stiller, until at last he was dropped at the foot of a huge throne inside a structure that he could not see. His breath came in cold streams, leaving fingers of ice before him. A very small light gave off him, enabling him to see a few feet around him, but all he saw or felt was the icy hall, and silence. After Cakgor left him, he began to feel a little better, and gathering all his dwarfish stubborn courage bred into him over the lives in his home, he puffed up a tiny bit, cleared his throat, patted his foot twice, and was startled at the huge amount of noise these actions produced.

"Ahem," he said softly. The cold echo came back from what seemed a very long distance away. His heart was bursting with the difficulty he was having breathing the frozen air, and to speak seemed almost an impossible chore, but his curiosity began overcoming his fright. When nothing happened he started again.

"Hmmph harrumph."

Still only the frozen silence.

Dwarf, always being a polite person, despite his frequent huffing and cartwheeling when upset, called out in a very small but somewhat reassured voice, since he'd heard nothing since Cakgor left.

"Ahem, excuse me, but could anyone explain to me why I've been carted off in the middle of the night from my warm bed, jawed viciously by some lump of an overgrown dog, and deposited so rudely in the middle of a freezing floor, without even so much as a how-do-you-do?"

His words flowed out into the great, frigid distance, and echoed back, tingling and tinkling as if they, too, had become part of that dark, frozen silence.

"Or," began Dwarf, becoming more and more puffed, "could anyone have the decency to offer me a coat, and slippers? One of mine fell off on the way here, and this floor is like ice. I'll catch my death of cold soon if I'm left standing one-slippered this way."

Only silence, and the echo. Dwarf advanced a few feet forward, groping and feeling slowly with his bare foot, curling his toes and wincing with the cold. A bit farther on he could make out the dark outline of a shape, the barest shadow of a shadow. He went hesitantly foreward, his curiosity growing until he almost forgot his bare foot. With his hands outstretched to keep from bumping his nose into a door or table, he advanced farther toward the dark object. As he moved, he heard the slightest sound, the softest movement, like someone breathing under a cover on a dark night. Thinking of a cover, he began shivering again, remembering the warm quilt and dwarf comforter at home in his warm bed, and the hot-water bottle with its rosy touch next to his feet, and Froghorn curled in a ball at his head. A sudden thought struck him, and he immediately called out in an angrier tone.

"Greyfax, if this is one of your jokes . . ."

And a great frozen wind howled and shrieked, sending pellets of ice and snow like powder into Dwarf's face, entering his body like frozen darts until the only thing not numbed by the great icy finger was his thumping little heart. He had to close his eyes and put a hand to his mouth to keep from suffocating, and the silence grew again so still all he could hear was the terror of his own soul. Slowly, as though a curtain of ice was lifting, a green and pale yellow glimmer began to outline the shadow before him. It grew and grew as Dwarf watched, struck with a fear greater than he'd ever before known possible. He thought the great dragon Beoliel, whom he'd helped slay in the older days of his home, was nothing compared to this shadow form flowing dimly in its green-yellow fire before him. He could not see at first, for even the faint, sickly light hurt his eyes, and when he opened his eyes again, he saw what looked to be a throne, as tall as the chamber itself, which reached away upward until it faded from Dwarf's vision. A phantom of a figure was seated on the throne, glowing green, then yellow, and he could make out yellow hair, and greenish eyes that were so cold he froze at the sight of them.

They rested upon him like a tomb, and his heart gave a sigh and was resigned to its death in the presence of these eyes. All hope left Dwarf, and all he could think of, all that entered his numbed mind was death, an eternal sleep in frozen halls, where even in death the cold would freeze and torture those after death forever.

Great and booming, echoing against the chamber, came the dagger ice voice. "Greyfax Grimwald is dead, you miserable wretch of a dwarf. Soon you, too, will feel my hand extinguish that paltry heart of yours. Isn't it good to be where you're welcome?"

Laughter, cold, malignant, grew like a tumor in Dwarf's ears.

"You are where no one can help you, not even those of the accursed Circle. They shall soon fall to me, and like Greyfax Grimwald, be forever banished into the cold grasp of my breath."

The Dark Queen exhaled a great breath, and there floating before her were crystals of ice, each containing the frozen, slumbering bodies of many forms, of men, and elves, and dwarfs. He saw his old friend Co'in there, who had been slain in the Battle of the Dragon many, many years before Baliel, the father of Beoliel, and son of Braele Faf, who had dwelled long in the homeland of his dwarfish fathers. His eyes welled with tears, which were frozen before they could roll to his nose.

"That's where you, too, shall soon rest, along with the rest of your world."

Another explosion of laughter, vile and bitter, entered Dwarf's ears, turning his brain deaf to any thought except what the Dark Queen spoke.

"But first, I must have the secrets of the box, for without those, you frail beings upon Atlanton Earth will wither and perish like the scourge you are. And you shall never escape me."

Dwarf struggled to speak, but his voice froze in his chest, so he stood transfixed, looking at those pale, glimmering green eyes.

"Where is the box, miserable gnome? Tell me."

Words formed on Dwarf's lips, to speak the betrayal of the Arkenchest, but then something stirred in Dwarf's heart, something he'd forgotten was there. He remembered his father, and dwarfs like Co'in, and his homeland; and pride, aided by his stubborn dwarfish nature, choked the words off.

"Speak."

By a great streak of dwarf huffiness, he was able to remove his eyes from the Dark Queen's face. Looking down at the floor at his own bare foot, anger once more stole through him, and still looking downward, so that the Dark Queen's great power was lessened, his mind began working slowly once more.

"I know of no box. What I do know is I was kidnapped from my house, dragged out here in the middle of the night, and now I'm cold and hungry, and I demand to be taken back immediately." Dwarf's voice cracked as he spoke, and he could barely hear the words himself, but he felt much better, and at once he began thinking that Greyfax was indeed not dead, and would help him get away from this terrible place.

"Indeed, Gnome. You shall not leave my palace, now or ever. The cold will grow in your bones like death. Whether or not you fight, you will tell me where the cursed box is. I have time. Forever."

The green-yellow light flared up briefly, then disappeared as quickly as it had come. Darkness covered Dwarf, and he thought it grew much colder than before. And then the yellow eyes of something approached him, put a rough, scaly hand around his throat, and began dragging him away into the darkness.

He couldn't breathe or struggle, and the thing's breath reeked of decay, but he could not see its face, except for the yellow eyes, and soon after a door was pulled open and the thing flung Dwarf into it and followed him in, bearing dull yellow-glowing teeth when Dwarf picked himself up to a standing position.

Into the darkness, and against the growing panic he felt, he whispered two words, Greyfax Grimwald, over and over.

INTO THE MAELSTROM

OTTER'S DECISION

By the river, Otter's lamps burned far past moonset, and strange noises broke the silver-mist silence that gathered above the shining, flowing water. A cheery travel tune played on a reed pipe, followed by the patter of dancing feet, then silence for a while, while Otter sat dejected and saddened by his own decision to leave Bear behind and to seek the man Froghorn had told them of by himself. "Bear has been so happy here," he thought, "I'll simply scamper out, get this silly fellow, and bring him home. Then Froghorn can get Dwarf back, and we'll all be right back where we were, eating and drinking, or playing and swimming, or telling a good tale or two over a cozy winter fire, as simple as that."

Otter twitched his left muzzle whisker, scratched his back against the chair, and darted off into a dark pantry. He took down the three berry leaves he had planned to have for breakfast, ate them quickly, then had a long drink from his pewter water jug.

"No time for eating tomorrow," he said sternly. Then, brightening a bit, he added, "Unless, of course, I happen to chance onto another good berry patch." He packed his ancient otter book into the open rucksack, then added as many tins of honey extract as he could carry, a candle, an heirloom chain his father had given him when he was a pup, two maps, his favorite water ball for playing, and a cherry pit for luck. He quickly dashed outside for a look at the moon, saw it was an hour down, hurried back, trimmed his lamps one by one, extinguishing them carefully, made sure his cooking fire was banked, secured all his doors but his secret exit, hoisted the well-laden pack onto his small back, and scurried down the long tunnel that opened out onto what appeared from the outside to be a reed bank. He stopped at this entrance, turning.

"Now what have I forgotten?" he sighed, knowing that no matter what or how carefully he planned, he always managed to forget something when he was traveling. He hastily undid the entire pack, rechecked its contents, and tied it all securely up again.

"I should leave him a note," he mused, "or else the silly ass will waste away worrying."

And saying this, he reached into the pack again, took out a small sheaf of parchment, searched angrily for the stub of a pencil Dwarf had given him for writing his poems on deep snowfrozen nights when it was too miserable for visiting, found it, and scribbled in his small, fine hand

Du'nud Bruinlin
An effin man
Huin bo'le leightle sonde
An'lolie
Ot'er

which read, in High Bruinlin,

Dear Bear
Am off to find man
Will be back shortly
Friend
Otter

He silently followed the path that led past Broco's dark, empty house, to where a large, well-paved trail led up through the thickets. That path disappeared into a wild tangle of choke thistle and dewberries, and only those that knew where to look would be able to find the well-concealed dwelling. Otter crept forward, disturbing no leaf or limb, and listening for a moment at the front door heard Bear's low growling noise inside. He laid a rock over the paper at the door where Bear would be sure to find it, returned as quietly as he had come, and cut around the dark side of the hill in the direction of the distant mountains, invisible now in their nightshirts. The moon was gone, but the stars had grown brighter, and to Otter's eyes, it was more than enough light, even for unfamiliar surroundings, and he climbed to the highest point of the hill to look one last time at his valley, where the friends had dwelled so long and happily. The dark water gleamed here and there where stars nested in her hair, and the vague outline of Dwarf's house stood out in the shadows. Farther down, he knew, was the low mound with the green door, full of his life for so long, now dark too, waiting. Otter chittered twice, whistled low, a goodbye tune, raised a paw, and was gone into the darkness.

BEAR'S PLAN

Bear sat long into the night, planning and thinking, his great form sunk low over his table, one huge paw drumming upon the stout oak top, the other idly stirring about a freshly opened cask of new honey from a tree Dwarf had discovered on one of their many explorations. His mind was full of sorrow at the disappearance of Dwarf, and all Froghorn had told him, and having to leave his beloved cave after all the contented years they had spent in the valley. Wars and contagion, man and beast alike slaying each other in wanton fashion, magical boxes, wizards, and all sorts of disturbing memories spun through his troubled mind. Bear lowered his head into his paws, sighing wearily.

"Well," he said aloud to his cave wall, "if anyone should have to go on the errand to find this man Froghorn speaks of, it should be me. No sense taking Otter into heaven knows what danger. Silly old fellow would only be in the way if one was really hard pressed. I may as well get an early start and simply leave him a note explaining it all."

Bear, heart heavy and saddened at the thought of leaving Otter, rose up and began packing what he thought he would need for the journey. Clever dwarf tins of the new honey, full of the comb, and an extra cask of water, maps, and a favorite book or two, and lastly, pulling it out of the other knickknacks upon the high shelf, the dragon stone of Dwarf's, which he had picked up from Broco's floor, where he'd found it lying forgotten when he and Otter had discovered Dwarf gone, and Froghorn full of his incredible tale.

Knapsack bulging, Bear started for his entrance door, then halted. He remembered Otter's odd visiting hours, and as likely as not, he'd run into the little gray fellow capering about for a last swim, or sitting on the rush shore counting ripples, or other such otter nonsense. He decided to use one of his other tunnels, unused until now, which led through the hill to an opening on the other side. He'd dug that long ago, right after they had first settled in the valley, for that spring brought floods and high water, and he'd wanted to have a dry spot to nap in should the water decide to visit him in his lower den. The thought of padding about up to one's hocks in water was a drearier thought than a bit of a dig, so he'd set to work on the project, and after all his fortnight's effort, the river had receded, and spring turned more beautiful than ever, and he'd forgotten the tunnel until now.

"What good sense to have that shaft," he chuckled to himself,' then, recalling that he was leaving his home, and Otter, and all else he had come to hold closely to his heart, he turned, brushed away a single, huge tear, and packed two extra cooking pots that Dwarf had forged for him, with clever folding handles so that when placed atop one another, they slipped into the space of only one.

"Whatever else Dwarf is always meddling with, he certainly is skillful with his hands," he sighed, hoping Broco not too badly off wherever he was. "If only he'd contented himself with making things sensible, we all wouldn't be in this mess. Wizards and wars, bah. A bear pox on the lot of them."

The night outside was folding over its bedding and thinking of waking when Bear poked a cautious nose out of the end of his tunnel. A cricket was singing a very sad song off over the slope toward Otter's house, and a few birds, early risers, chittered staccato greetings when they saw him. A stately ebony raven perched on the low thorn thistles near Bear's exit hole.

"Good morning, Master Bruinlen."

"Greetings, no-sleep."

"Away on a journey so early? What tidings are these? My slow toes out and wandering before the sun shines?"

"I've important matters, chatterbox, ones that would stand your features as straight as quills if I wanted to waste my time talking. But good health and hunting, Raven, if I lay my eyes no more upon you. Goodbye."

Bear grunted and snorted, heaved his large bulk through the rather small opening, and started at a brisk trot away from the river toward the first gleam of morning on the distant, snow-covered peaks.

"The same to you, Bruinlen. I just saw Otter not ten minutes ago, and he told me the same thing. To my reckoning, I haven't seen things so strange since early this summer, when those others were skulking about. My Aunt Caw and Uncle Croak both were eaten in that scare, and I dare say, a lot of others I didn't know about, but I didn't think things were so bad as to drive you big folks off."

Bear jolted to a stop, planting his forepaws sturdily into the dew-wet grass, almost sliding down to his nose. He lifted his pack from where it had tumbled over his ears.

"What? What's that? Otter gone? What others?

Speak, sticktongue, before I send you off to join your Caw and Croak. Why haven't you spoken to us before, you tree duster? If you'd spoken up before, Dwarf might still be about, and all the nasty business avoided. Speak up."

Bear had raised up full height now, in anger and frustration, advancing toward the raven's perch. The bird fluttered and started to fly, but Bear, amazingly quick, caught the black form of the bird and held him fast in his two great forepaws.

"Cawright, cawright," screamed the frightened bird, "I'll tell you. Let me down. You're squashing my pinfeathers."

Bear loosened his grasp a bit. "I'm sorry to have to be so rough, Raven, but it's of dire import you tell me all you know. We'll forget what you didn't tell any of us before, for that's beyond help. I thought you'd be a better friend, after all the meals Dwarf left you and your kind. Speak up, and perhaps it may be some knowledge to undo the wrong of your silence."

The bird was stirred by Bear's speech, and fearing no harm now, and remembering, too, the bread crumbs and dwarf cakes left upon Dwarf's table when the deep winter snow made other food difficult to find, he spoke willingly. His kind, once befriended, were loyal friends, and true, but were cunning and close among themselves, and usually avoided contact with anyone who didn't possess a pair of wings. He was sorry not to have made Bear a friend, and now, it seemed he was leaving .He would tell him all, and perhaps give out a morsel or two of advice to boot.

"Where shall I start, Master Bruinlen?" he asked earnestly.

"With the others you mentioned. Begin with that."

"It started a few days before All Summer's Eve, I

think, or that's when I first came to know about them. They came into these parts foraging for food. That's when they got my Uncle Croak and Aunt Caw."

"Who is they?" queried Bear impatiently.

"Wolves, or they had wolves' bodies, but bigger, and they spoke to each other as men do. I overheard them the day they left, or All Summer's Day, after you had your party. They kept saying something like 'him' and reporting you all to 'him' or something to those likes, and I guess that's what kept them from having you all in a stew." The raven chuckled at his own black humor. "But anyway, they left, and no one heard of them or saw them again, until this very morning. Mrs. Jeffrey Sparrow heard them speaking again last night, and saw them moving down the valley edge toward your settlement."

"Just the two?" asked Bear, growing alarm rising inside him for Otter, helpless ball of fur who hadn't a chance at all against two such adversaries.

Raven nodded.

"And then Otter showed up not ten winks before you, made me a little speech, and darted off down yonder. Pretty silly, an otter out of water. He had a bundle of something wrapped in a rucksack, and was gone before I could say a word."

"I dare say, it must have taken you aback, Raven. But what I said before is now more urgent. You've put yourself aright, friend. I must go now."

As Bear raised his great paw to release the raven, a cry, loud and screeching, followed by two long, hideous howls, broke the stillness of the gathering dawn. Then Otter's war cry, terrified and terrible, tore loose the roots of Bear's paws, and he broke into a thunderous, rumbling run, his great voice angry and deadly, away in the direction where Otter had been set upon by his two dreadful foes.

THREE TOES AND GAGROT

"We don't needs to wait for sunrise for our sweets," growled a low, cruel voice. "We gets them now, I says."

"We waits," snarled Three Toes, great yellow fangs bared, an oozing spittle slipping past his crooked underlip.

"Then we splits the dwarf, says I. I don't want no animal flesh."

"We'll kill 'em all first, then we'll see who eats who. Maybe you should gut the bear, Gagrot, since you seems in such a hurry to eats."

"If we gets them now, they'll all be asleep," protested the first werewolf, Gagrot.

The two lay hidden in a thicket, out of sight of the valley below, evil eyes shining a dull yellowish green light. Far above, in the very top of a great shouldered oak, a small sparrow hung, trembling.

A faint noise of a leaf stir caught Three Toes' attention. He snarled quietly to the other beast. The noise, faint but barely perceptible to their keen, cruel ears, grew closer. An animal, a not very cautious animal, was moving in their direction. The light of their harsh eyes was lidded, and they waited for their unsuspecting victim to deliver himself to hungry fangs. Closer still, until they could distinctly see the dim outline of a small animal with a peculiar hump on its back moving directly toward their hiding place. When Otter was within a paw's length, the two ravenous, growling beasts beset him, without so much as a snarl of warning.

Otter's cry went up, startled and frightened at first, then seeing the great open vises of jaws rowed with cruel, tearing teeth, it turned to terror and his battle cry. As the two dark, scab-covered beasts circled him for the kill, Otter slid out of the heavy pack and turned in a slow circle, warding off bites from those vicious jaws by side leaps or quick, slippery twists. His folds of loose skin saved him from serious harm when the beast behind got his mouth upon what he thought was Otter's neck, but the skin lifted upward with the fierce bite, leaving the beast's mouth filled with gray, twisting fur. Otter was lifted off the ground, whirling and trying to get his powerful jaws onto some part of his attacker's body, and the wolf made the mistake of letting the wriggling form bump against his chest as he tried to find Otter's throat or backbone to snap it. Otter's viselike jaws clamped onto the werewolf's right foreleg, and with all the grinding strength in his small body, he forced his upper and lower teeth deeper and deeper until they met with a rending, crunching sound, and the bone was splintered and split.

A great, deafening howl of misery and pain and hatred rent the peaceful dawn. The other beast jumped quickly to grab Otter's small body, howling fiercely. Gagrot, his leg broken and bleeding badly, dropped the gray thing whose jaws had so cruelly hurt him. All thoughts of breakfast were replaced with the single desire to maim and kill this filthy rodent-like creature.

Next moment, the trees trembled and the earth

shook, followed by the long, angry wail-bellow of a great beast. Otter, fearing help had come to his two assailants, seized the surprised instant when the werewolves turned toward the great bellowing charge, snatched his rucksack, and was safely away into the surrounding dense thickets, running as fast as his short, stubby legs would carry him, heart pounding, out of this terrible wood. As Otter topped the hill, and half slid, half ran down the other side to safe hiding, Bear, hackles bristling, claws and teeth gleaming like steel flames, burst into the clearing where the two startled werewolves stood frozen. Bear's great speed carried him over the two huge forepaws raking the gristly flesh from the side of the injured beast, great jaws snapping closed onto the back of the other, and he flung his head high, clamped his teeth harder, and skidded to a halt, raising his great bulk to an upright fighting bear stance. Three Toes, still in his mouth, was dead, his back broken from the terrible pressure of Bear's huge jaws. He flung the lifeless brute into the thicket with a flick of his head, and advanced upon the other beast, cornered now, and wounded. The werewolf, seeing his death in Bear's flaming red eyes, dragged himself to the foot of a wide-girthed ash tree, fangs bared, waiting. His front leg was dangling uselessly, and his ribs were torn open and bleeding, and all the strength he had left he would use for one last lunge at this fearsome raging giant.

The battle fire that burned Bear's heart subsided a moment, seeing his enemy beaten and dying, the other already dead. He quickly looked about the clearing for what he feared most to find, Otter's small, helpless body torn and bloody, or worse, half eaten. There were no traces of Otter or his knapsack to be seen. Bear halted a paw's swipe from the werewolf, still snarling and dangerous.

"Be quick with your answer, foul breath. What happened to the waterfolks? If your answer is true, I'll give you the mercy of a quick death. If not, I have ways to rend your bones and drain your filthy life slowly enough."

"The gray water filth escaped," growled Gagrot. "A curse on his filthy lot forever. He's escaped *us*. But Doraki still knows. *He'll* have his gray fur rotting on his door before too long." Laughing cruelly, the werewolf coughed blood from the terrible wound Bear had smote him. "And yours, too, scum of a murderer, if I don't sink my fangs through your fat throat." Savagely speaking, the beast leapt feebly at Bear's chest. Lightning-quick and lethal, Bear's great forepaws crushed the werewolf's skull in midflight, and the body of the beast crashed lifeless at Bear's feet.

Bear's booming victory cry shook the woods with a roaring shudder. In another part of the forest, the birds and other animals who had not heard the struggle thought the day brought a thunderstorm, although the dawn was breaking bright and clear.

"May the carrion birds pick your bones," growled Bear. "And if any harm has come to Otter, a curse and bear fangs in the throats of all your vile kindred."

Bear's body began to tremble slightly as the fire burned down, then out, and he sat down wearily at the far end of the clearing, away from the bodies of his two slain foes.

The trembling stopped after a few deep breaths, and the sorrow at having taken life, even as evil as this, set in. He looked away from the clearing, his heart choked with shame, then that, too, passed swiftly, for the thought of Otter, perhaps hurt, or dying off somewhere in the thickets alone, hastened him back to where he'd dropped his knapsack. He placed it quickly on his back and began circling, trying to pick up Otter's trail. There was no blood spoor, which gave Bear hope, but for a great distance all about, the foul scent of the werewolves lay heavily upon the dew-carpeted lawn beneath the wood, and their death smell was so thick and vile, he soon left the clearing and surrounding thicket. At the far side of the hilltop, he picked up a faint trace of Otter, then as he moved more quickly away and down into the small valley beyond, it grew stronger still, and he put all other thoughts aside as he set to work earnestly picking out and following the faint waterfolk smell that led ever downward toward the gorse berry thickets below.

At full light, Bear had covered a league or more in his search, and looking up now and again, he saw the trail was leading him farther and farther from their valley, away from the peaceful life they had carried on for so long, on, ever on, toward the now shining snow crowns of the far mountains.

And on the bright rays of early sun, Bear began reading the story they had long ago begun, across the River, and even beyond that. The difference in this morning was that instead of waking in his pleasant valley and having a rather late breakfast with his friends, Dwarf was a captive of the powers of some great darkness, and Froghorn had revealed himself as none other than Froghorn Fairingay, and Otter was lost, in his own way trying to spare himself, Bear, the weariness and dangers of a journey into the world of men. And now, he, Bear, Bruinthor's far distant decendant, had slain in battle again upon this sunrise, and was upon the journey he had proposed to himself to take alone to spare Otter. Now the two of them were far past returning, bound to the promise to Froghorn to seek the aid of this powerful man at map's end.

All taken carefully into Bear's slow, cautious consideration, it wasn't much of a promising morning at all. Nor would be the mornings ahead, wherever they might find them.

"I knew all this wizard talk and dwarf magic would turn to no good," he muttered to himself, then bent forward and hurried along to catch up to Otter, lost now in his own weary, unpleasant wanderings.

CAKGOR RETURNS

"Fools, all of you," shrieked the icy voice of Dorini, in the Dark Palace in the frozen realm of the World Between Time.

"But Your Darkness," began Doraki, sniveling and frightened by her anger, "we brought you the dwarf. What else could be done? I didn't think those slime crusts would have left such a thing with one miserable runt like that."

"Silence, imbecile. You had best not fail me again. Bring me those other scum breaths here. I would question them also. And if you fail me, you'll pay more than the miserable traitors themselves. I shall rob you of your precious power, and leave you among mankind forever."

Shaken visibly, Doraki bowed low, retreating. "It shall be done, Your Darkness. I shall send Cakgor this moment to bring them."

"I hope for your sake you speak the truth," returned Dorini, the green flames leaping high in the throne room, illuminating her evil, malignant smile.

Soon the great roll of dull stone bells and drums hastened Cakgor upon his way once more, and spiraling into the dark world like a shadow, he silently sped toward the valley where he had stolen Dwarf away in his sleep. He had never known the Queen to be so angry before, not since her last imprisonment by the Circle, and his leaden heart beat faster to think of his doom if he failed her command. He must be quick and deadly to defeat Fairingay, and there would be no element of surprise this time. That hateful beast would be waiting for him, and his heart quailed at that meeting. Cakgor flashed out with his great claws and tore asunder a passing wind, then flaming into the still hour of night, he assumed the form and smell of death, great oozing body showering fear and destruction as he flew, and as he passed over parts where men still dwelt, their hearts turned to icy fear and they fell before his awful presence, and still onward he hastened, the fear of Dorini raging inside of him until the very sunrise of the new day was blotted and dimmed with his coming, ever faster, until great green reddish sparks flew before and behind him, circling closer and closer to the valley of the cursed dwarf.

Otter, far below, saw the dark form showering hideous sparks and hurried on away from its presence, and Bear, close behind Otter, shuddered at seeing the dark shape so harshly glowing as it crossed the sun, darkening it for a moment.

Falling upon the valley shrieking, Cakgor sent out a slimish green-colored breath that deadened wills of man or beast, that drowned them in a waking, nightmare-ridden sleep and made all but the most powerful his prisoner, to do with as he liked. Birds tumbled from their high perches, numbed. Animals stood frozen, helpless before this doom shroud. With a rending, splitting crash, Dwarf's door burst its hinges, and Cakgor leapt inside, breath on fire, scorching wood and earth alike into a black, ashlike heap. This sudden, terrible assault rang like a hollow tomb upon the empty, scarred house. No defense confronted Cakgor, no counterspell to defy him. His black heart grew inside him to think he had slain the hateful Fairingay in his slumber. This would please Dorini. This time there would be no escape for the puny magician, for her power this time would hold him frozen forever in her death breath, imprisoned, alive, helpless, tortured through all time. He burned the bedroom door from its posts and entered. Fire and destruction, they were gone. His breath reeked of ash and scorching, searing icy flames. Great billows of thick, dead smoke rose against the morning. He sought the dwelling places of Bear and Otter. And after a time, he found Bear's cave entrance, enraged and in a great shrieking fury, cast down Bear's door into a thousand pieces, filling the cavern and all the tunnels with the green, nauseous, evil gas. Nothing, no one. Shrill and deadly came his cry of failure, and Otter's river turned to sheets of gray ice as Cakgor crossed it, devouring Otter's green dwarf door as he came. There, too, he found all deserted, just as Otter had left it only hours before. His great dumb brain filled with rage and failure, and he scorched and burned, and broke into a wall of shooting green-yellow flames, leaving Otter's dwelling ravaged and wracked in his fury. His one thought was that they had fled after Dwarf's capture back across the River to safety, where he could not cross, for Klag and Forg had done so, and recrossing, were consumed in a horrible agony of doom. Whirling and spinning, he rose upward, setting green fire to the woods nearby, and the shining river was clogged with debris from falling tree and rock, and all living within Cakgor's fearful passage were burned or suffocated by the fury and death of his anger. Racing away to report these evil tidings to Her Darkness, and to explain away his failure, he crossed a great battle, waged below him in a deep green jungle. He passed close upon the fight, and all there slew themselves with a great fever burning away their minds, and with a greater fear upon him, he sped away to the darkness. He must convince Dorini that the fault lay with her evil prince, Doraki, and that if anyone must be punished, it should be he, not the loyal and trusted Cakgor. If Doraki had been cunning, he would have the lot of them prisoners now. For that mistake he must pay, not the loyal and trusted Cakgor.

The sun burst forth once more behind his passing, and the day breathed its relief. The war went on upon Atlanton Earth, but without purpose, no dark hand close by to guide it, and babies once more nursed from their mothers, and living things yet grew.

The darkness was only half complete, and there still burned the bright rays of sunlight and hope.

MANKIND

Two lonely, smoking lamps marked the town as Otter crept softly forward onto the road that split the green valley in half like a winding white ribbon. Upon both outer walls sentries stood, tall men with strange high helmets upon their heads, and farther up, wild dogs were turned loose at dark to keep anyone, man or beast, from coming on the fortified town without first being announced or eaten. Speaking the words and repeating the ritual, Otter felt himself assume the awkward man shape. He looked down at his new, unfamiliar body and sighed. No trace of fur, no remains of tail could be found. He was of man now, and afraid. Trying to adjust his walk, he held himself from his usual trot, and approached the main gate of the city, hungry and tired, and not knowing what reception his presence would bring at so late an hour. He had moved to within hailing distance when a low, harsh voice rasped out.

"Hold and speak your name and business."

Otter blurted out in his own language, "Peace, friend. I'm of Animalkind and only need a bit of water, and a morsel, if you have it to spare."

"What's that he says?" came another thin voice from behind a dark wall.

Otter realized that in his excitement he'd merely made a series of chitters and whistling sounds that these men were not likely to understand. Struggling, he fell into common speech.

"I'm called Otter, friend, and seek shelter and food for the night. My journey has been long, and I've passed through great danger." Otter stopped, trying to remember what he'd said to see if it were correct.

"Step into the light, stranger. If you have arms, leave them on the road."

"I carry no weapon, friend, but my walking stick."

Otter stepped forward into the lamp's flickering light.

"He looks fishy to me," came a dry voice from a low guard shack. "And what's he doing on this road by night?"

"He's got nothing about him to harm us. Come, stranger, step in and identify yourself and your errand that carries you abroad this road so late at night. There's been no well-meaning traffic upon this road for more than two years now." The first man beckoned toward the guardhouse, and followed behind Otter into a well-lighted, comfortable room.

There were many firearms and other weapons all about the walls, a low, broad table, a cooking fire, and common mess plates for the men who were at duty there.

Otter studied the men figures more closely in the light. He was ill at ease, and his natural distrust held him quiet a moment. All were dressed in a like fashion, a uniform of sorts, with many pockets, and a design of a coat of arms upon their left shoulders. The man who had followed him into the building was tall, but of slight frame, with a steady gaze, and somehow Otter trusted this man. He thought of

Froghorn Fairingay when he looked into his eyes, and it was to this man Otter spoke.

"I'm of waterfolk, mostly a mender by trade. I've journeyed out seeking a powerful man that lives beyond the mountains. I travel so late because the urgency of my errand is great, and all speed needed. I've come quite a long way since early this morning, before sunrise, have been beset by werewolves, and now seek shelter and a bite to eat, if you have it. If not, a corner to sleep in, and I'll be on my way come dawn."

"I suppose you would, taking all our defense plans along, right back to those who sent you." The thin voice came from a dark-faced man who stood against the doorframe, cleaning his nails with a long, evil-looking knife.

"I come from no one, friend. I'm alone, and seek only aid from the man beyond the mountains. If any here be friends of the Circle, you'll know I speak the truth."

"The Circle? What battalion is that? And on whose side?" sneered the thin voice.

"Ease off, Ned, you've had your say." The first man crossed to the cooking fire, took down a mess kit, and spooned a heating ladle of the stew from the pot.

"Friend or foeman, we won't starve an answer out of you. Come eat, and we'll talk when you're refreshed."

Otter gladly accepted the man's kindness, and thanked him. His stomach turned inside him at the first bite of the man food, but his new body accepted it, felt nourished, and he ate the last of it.

"Now tell us more of your strange tale. Were your kin wiped out in the war? Have you a regular sort of home, or is it gone too? You're young and strong; do you serve any general, or army?"

Exhaustion was quickly overtaking him, and the questions came so fast, he hardly had time to make answers, and he began greatly to desire to return to his natural otter form. Men were certainly a suspicious lot, and no amount of talking seemed to satisfy them. Whatever he said, someone questioned it with some silly nonsense, or accused him of deception, which he did not understand, for he never knew anything of speaking what was false, or of making up a reply. By the time an hour had passed, he had been questioned steadily and had answered more questions than he had ever dreamed there were in the entire world of Mankind, and still they went on. He longed for his quiet river and his own snug fire, and no one to talk to at all, unless maybe Bear wanted a short chat before going off to bed. At least there they might talk of something sensible. Then he remembered Bear would have found his note when he awakened, and probably searched a little while for him, then resigned himself to waiting. He would be home safe in his cave, reading a page or two from one of the books that lined his shelves, or just simply having a walk, or perhaps making up a new tune. Otter looked around the room at the unfamiliar shapes and faces, down at his own grotesque man form, and wished with all his heart he were there with Bear. Without thinking, he found his hand-paw reaching into his jacket for his reed pipe, and meaning no offense at all to the thin voice that was droning on in his ear, he began to play a lullaby, one of his favorites, which he always played before crawling into his sleeping hammock in his holt by the soft shoulder of the river. When he had finished, he found, to his amazement, that all the men were fast asleep, one with his head upon his hands at the table, another against the side wall, a firearm clutched close to him, the thin-voiced man called Ned, who had been speaking, still standing against the doorframe. The room was filled with the crackling of the dying fire, broken by intermittent heavy snoring. No one stirred a muscle when Otter got up and went to the door to look outside. Even Ned didn't budge when Otter stepped around him to look at the stars, trying to determine the time. At the gate sentry box, two shadowy forms were propped against their posts.

"Well," sighed Otter aloud, "of all the things I've ever seen or heard tell of!"

He returned to the guardhouse, picked up his knapsack, said a thank-you to the sleeping man who had been kind to him, tweaked the nose of Ned as he crept out, and passed on through the dark streets unseen, until at last he came to the unguarded back gates. This road led away toward allies, and none in that town feared assault from that sector, so no sentinel or beast stood watch from the direction where friendly eyes watched. Walking on as far as he could, Otter felt sleep taking him, so he quickly left the road, entered a thick stand of alders, repeated the ritual to change back into his old form, and found a secure, warm nest of undergrowth for his small body, tried to think out a plan for the morning, grew weary of that, tried to remember all he had learned from his first real encounter with man, giggled quietly into his paws, thought sadly of Bear, all alone now in their safe valley, and fell asleep, dreaming of men with tall helmets, and their endless nightmare of confusing questions.

"They don't even know any games," he told himself in his dream. "Being a man is no fun at all," he concluded, and went back in his mind to the more pleasant pursuit of nose-sliding down a long mudslide, safe by his own holt door.

BEAR TURNS TO WITCHCRAFT

A great commotion stirred Ned Thinvoice from his standing sleep.

"Sentry, sentry, where in blazes are you? Open, curse your eyes, before my feet fall off from standing here."

Ned shook the sleepy web from his eyes to find day faintly rising. All the others still slept.

"Here, hold on. I'm coming."

He quickly shook the others awake, and went out to draw open the crossbar from the gate. By the sound of the voice on the other side, it couldn't be less than a major commander. As the gate swung open, three men strode in.

"It's high time I had you all hided, dolt. Where's the rest of the scurvy crew? Sleeping late? Breakfast served up in their chambers? Get them to stand down now, soldier," bellowed the swarthy, mustachioed man, graying slightly at the temples, face bright crimson, uniform adorned at the collar with two iron eagles.

"Sir," cried Ned, raising one hand in salute, and hurrying off in the direction of the guardhouse.

"And you," said the commander, turning to the man behind him, "your story rings false from the moment you said you'd come from the east. No one has lived in that plague hole for more years now than I can recall. And if you were there, it must have been some business that would turn a decent mind cold with terror. But we shall see." He coughed, bristled, turned a brighter crimson, spun on his heel, and marched into the guardhouse.

The man addressed was stout, taller than the others, dressed in a forest green jacket and trousers, and carried an old, well-used rucksack. He was ill at ease, almost cunning, his large brown eyes going from his guard to the gate, to the door of the guardhouse.

Loud voices erupted from within, followed by the sound of a foot falling on flesh.

"You let him escape, did you. I'll see to it you all are at the front before the week is out. You shirk there like you do here, and you'll all end up on a roasting fork. Now get out there and bring the prisoner in." The commander's voice was the same shade of crimson as his face.

"Sir," blurted Ned, and full of military duty, he marched duly out and grasped Bear by the shoulder.

"In you go, blackguard, double quick." Ned's voice was shrill with fear and his own power over his hapless prisoner.

Bear ambled along in his own time, still unused to this clumsy shape he had taken when the two men had come on him on the road; had he not had his senses about him and remembered Froghorn's words, they would have shot him on the spot. Bears were not well thought of among men, he mused, but then obviously neither were other men.

Commander Crimsonface sat at the table as if it were a desk, waiting impatiently as they stood Bear in a respectful position before him. To Bear's alarm, the commander picked up a short, white object, placed it in his mouth, lit it, and began smoking from his nose.

"Great crown of Bruinthor, another wizard," he said aloud, eyes bulging.

"Speak only when spoken to, prisoner. I want your name, number, and outfit. They'll be pleased to hear we've got you." More smoke, followed by a short coughing spell.

"And if you're from over there," he jerked a thumb in the direction they had just come, "you're in for a jolly surprise." A snarling smile revealed uneven yellow-stained teeth.

"Speak up; name, number, and outfit. Be quick."

"I told you, friend, my name is Bruinlen and I have no number. I'm a stranger to these parts, and to your armies. I seek my comrade, who has lost me, and we're traveling in search of a powerful man beyond the mountains yonder. Our errand is no harm to any of you."

"Liar. Deserter. Sneaking about in the dark to conceal yourself. No one who is true to the flag has need of night to move about."

"I move by night and day, for I have need of great haste. I must find my friend once more, for we are upon a great journey to save our dwarf."

"Dwarf. I saw no dwarf. A half man? Do you expect me to be taken in by this kegtale?"

"Beg pardon, sir," broke in the man who had been kind to Otter, "but the one who escaped us spoke the same. That he was seeking a great general across the frontier, for some purpose or other."

"What general? What purpose? Who was he, another deserter, or a spy?" The commander smashed out the white smoke thing under his heavy bootheel.

"I think they're what they say, sir. I see no evil in them. They carry no arms, and indeed seem stranger to all our ways."

"If I were caught red-handed, I'd play it sweet and innocent, too. Idiots, all of you. You'd hand them all our plans and pat them for it, and sit back and wait for their friends to have us all up like fish on a platter."

Bear's ears picked up at the mention of food, which he thought was the only thing the man had said so far that made sense.

"I wouldn't mind a platter, if it came to that," he said aloud, then blushed when the commander whirled upon him.

"What's that? You wouldn't mind what? I guess you wouldn't, seeing as how you're caught dead center. Guard, take him away. We'll decide what to do with him when the company relief comes down." Another white stick hung from his lips, and Bear was led away to a cell behind the guardhouse, wide-eyed and wondering what sort of magicians he had fallen in with now. Nothing these strange men said seemed to have any sense to it, except when they had spoken of eating. His stomach hounded him unmercifully in this form as much as it did when he was his usual self, and he groaned aloud when they took his rucksack away from him and banged the thick steel door shut upon him.

"A sweet keg of molasses this," he grumbled, alone, imprisoned, hungry, and without the slightest notion as to what he should do. "If only Dwarf had stuck to gardening," he sighed, looking out the barred window, away toward where the sun had risen, vainly trying to see his peaceful valley with its comfortable river, and his cave, stored with new honey, and combs, and a larder full of bread.

Bear decided his first meeting with Mankind left much amiss, and they seemed never to eat at all. He would, he promised himself, if he ever got away with a whole hide, never meddle in another's affairs, especially where it concerned wizards or dwarfs, or an otter's. Somehow, someway, whenever you took up with any but your own, you always suffered.

At dusk, Cranfallow, the man who had spoken up for Bear to the commander, came bringing a tray of food and water. He opened the door wide, and approached Bear in a friendly fashion, setting the food down on the single table before the hard, stiff bed.

"If it's any comfort, I believed your friend, and you. It don't seem right what they're saying. I've been in this army all my life, and I've got eyes on me, and I think I'm sharp enough to knows a soldier when I see one, enemy or friend, and neither of you fellows seems one to me."

Bear had fallen on the tray ravenously, smacking and guzzling the soup, bread dripping, and he drained the water jug in a single draft.

"Ahmm. Well now, you wouldn't have another dish of that handy by any chance, would you, friend? Or my rucksack would do, for I've a few staples in that."

Cranfallow laughed good-naturedly, went out, locking the door after him, and returned a few minutes later with a second helping.

"You've a good enough appetite about you, stranger. But I guess it takes plenty of gruel to full up a big man's hunger."

Bear thanked his deliverer heartily, and finished the bowl and jug. Cranfallow made no motion at leaving, standing idly in the door, studying him.

"Just what exactly are you going to find this fellow across the frontier for? Does he have men, or arms, or wealth? And what help can he be to you there?"

Bear looked long into the man's eyes before answering.

"I see you mean me no harm, friend, so I'll tell

you a little of my long tale, and what my companion and I started out upon," and Bear, half full, and recovering from the slow faint he had almost fallen into from hunger, began relating his story, omitting only Greyfax and Froghorn, for he felt any mention of their names would only bring him fresh disaster, and far into the setting darkness, his voice went on, and Cranfallow fell under his spellbinding, incredible tale. When at last Bear disclosed how he had been captured, the man stood up, shaking his head.

"I think you must be either a witch or a jester, I don't know which, friend, but your story has given me much pleasure. Wait until I tell this to my messmates." He chuckled, picking up the tray, and turning, started to thank Bear once more for his amusing story. The tray clattered loudly to the floor, smashing the jug into tiny white particles, and his eyes went wide with horror and disbelief. There before him was the monstrous huge hulk of a standing bear, reddish brown with gray-white tips at ear and tail, and a great, neat vest of white upon his chest.

"You see, friend, I speak truly," said Bear gently, examining his forepaws, and looking downward to make sure his hind paws were right.

Cranfallow was slowly backing for the door, his speech gone, eyes bursting from their sockets.

"A bloody witch," he gasped, preparing to flee.

"No, friend, a bear, and one who doesn't harm a friend. Come, stay a moment and hear me out." Bear sat down upon his great haunches, and motioned the man back.

Half from fright, half from curiosity, Cranfallow halted where he was, out of reach, and with the safety of flight close at hand.

"My comrade is an otter, a small, gray furry fellow with more fun than sense in his silly head, and that's why it's most important I find him, before he gets himself into something he hasn't the faintest idea how to handle." Bear held up a great paw to a height of about three feet to describe Otter.

"That's somewhere around how high he stands, when he's standing, but most of the time it's more along here," and lowering his paw to a foot above the floor, he halted. "Of course, he probably would have looked like a man when you saw him, if he had his wits about him, and I'm not exactly sure what he would look like then. Rather odd, no doubt," and after a pause he added, "But then so are you all." Bear met the man's numbed glance. "No offense, old fellow. These things are all as queer to me as they are to you, and all I want to do is find this particular man everyone's so taken with, deliver him back to my valley, and take up a nice quiet life of beekeeping."

Cranfallow closed his eyes tightly, then opened them quickly, hoping to startle away whatever vision he was seeing, but Bear's huge form still sat, smiling, before him.

"It's the gourd what's done this," stammered Cranfallow. "It's the bloody barley that's eaten my brain."

Bear, at hearing that, remarked, "I've got a good stock of barley tea at my cave, which I think might please your taste." Then, remembering how far away that was, he placed his muzzle in one great paw.

"A bloody stinking bear witch," groaned Cranfallow, and closed the door frantically behind him, not seeing he had missed the latch in his hurry. The great steel frame remained ajar, and Bear padded over, tested it, looked out over the empty grounds between the cell and the building that housed the guard, listened intently for a moment, then not having any idea what else to do, he reassumed his man shape, opened the cell, and quickly made away toward the center of the town. A nagging doubt kept troubling him at having left his rucksack, and the thought of the dragon stone in the hands of man slowed his pace. Darkness had closed over the world, and the streets were deserted, so he stood inside a shallow doorway, trying to decide what he should do. He had his freedom for the moment, but Cranfallow was sure to have given the alarm, or to spread such wild tales among his comrades they would all be coming to goggle at him. Then a thought suddenly presented itself. Quickly he retraced his steps, hurriedly checked for any signs that they had come looking and found him gone, crossed the short open space that separated the beginning of the town street from the guardhouse and the cells behind, secured the lock, and went behind the cell to where he could look in upon its interior from the barred window. Just as he had tiptoed up high enough to see inside, the sound of footsteps hurrying toward the cell rang dully on the hard-tramped earth. They halted before the steel door, voices muttered, the lock turned, and four men, Cranfallow among them, burst into the room.

"He's bloody disappeared himself," gasped Cranfallow. "He's a bloody witch, I tell you. He sat right there not ten minutes ago as big as life all turned into a bloody bear."

"Cranfallow," boomed Bear's best bass boice, low and rumbling at the edges, "Cranfallow, you have betrayed me, now you and your friends shall be punished."

A creeping white crossed the four faces, eyes shining in fear, and two of the men made for the door, panic heavy in them, turning blood to water.

"Do not move, or I shall pronounce thee stone flies and swat thee dead with my broomtail," threatened Bear, voice deeper, menacing. He almost ruined his whole plan when a snigger stole quietly past his ominous tone, but he contained it in time, and continued.

"Cranfallow, to save thyself, fetch me my rucksack, and say nothing to the other guards. I will send my servant with thee to vouchsafe no betrayal."

"Yes sir, yes sir," moaned Cranfallow, blanched face sweating, trembling.

"Go," commanded Bear, "and your three fellows will stay to make sure you return. Their doom is upon thy head. Do not fail."

"For the sake of the bloody martyrs do what he says, Cranny. Hurry. I don't want to end up swatted to death. Go on." The second man shook heavily about his knees, teeth chattering as he spoke.

Cranfallow darted from the room, his feet barely touching ground as he sped to the guardhouse, blood racing, heart stopped up in his throat. In all his years as a soldier he had never run, and never feared an enemy, but none of them had been witches, or at least if they had, he hadn't known it, and so wasn't frightened of them. But meeting one face to face, who changed form right before him, then vanished into thin air, with nothing left but a voice. No man could stand before that. And the other one, who had hexed them all to sleep, leaving nothing behind him to show he had existed at all. No sergeant, or commander, or even bloody general could order him to fight with witches. It wasn't natural. He'd stand and thrash an enemy bare-handed, and had done so many time, but no witches, no witches for Corporal Cranfallow, none at all, and the sooner they were rid of them, the better off they'd be. He grabbed the heavy rucksack from its peg in the guardhouse, muttered "Orders," to the startled, sleepy sentry there, and raced back to the lockhole, breathless. Just the fact that the two witches had been there meant no good tidings for any of them, and he knew some waiting catastrophe hung over their heads, as heavy as cannon smoke, and only the quick departure of this witch could alter it. He flung the rucksack down into the room, panting.

"There it is, all your kit, sir. Now have mercy on the poor likes of us, and go." Cranfallow fell to his knees, and the others followed.

"You have done fair by me, Cranfallow, and I shall spare you. But hear this. I have placed a spell over all your heads, and if you ever speak of this to anyone, my curse will fall, and indeed you shall all end up stone flies yet. Mark my words well." Bear's voice rumbled lower still. "Now go, Cranfallow, all of you go. Do not stir from your beds tonight, I warn thee."

Eight legs bolted into flight, carrying wildly beating hearts and starting eyes across the yard, into the sleeping quarters, and eight arms pulled up their blankets to cover heads and keep off the horrible curse of this powerful witch. No words from the duty sergeant could rouse them up, and blows from his fist were a small price compared to suddenly waking in the morning to discover yourself conjured into a pesky, noisy stone fly. There would be extra duty, and perhaps a transfer to the front, but a bullet or bomb could only kill, not bewitch.

Bear moved cautiously to the door, went in, hurriedly checked to see if all his belongings were intact, and satisfied, slipped away into the deep shadows of the sleeping streets. After five minutes of a steady trot, he found himself outside the town, upon the road that wound steadily away toward the mountains and the end of his journey, and which Otter was already upon, a good way ahead after this unpleasant delay. But the direction was right, and he knew his friend free and safe from harm, and with a steady march through the night, perhaps closer than he might imagine.

Bear settled his pack, repeated the spell, and on all fours, set off at a rapid pace, determined to travel on in that manner until daybreak. And Otter, farther ahead than Bear's calculations allowed, wakened from a nap, and decided his best plan would be to put as much distance between himself and the town as he could before first light.

EROPHIN OF WINDAMEIR

Erophin, clear blue-gray eyes turned a sea cloud misty, looked long into the mithra goblet before he spoke again. He had sat quietly, listening to Greyfax's long story, nodding occasionally, or shaking his silver-maned head sadly. The only part left out of the tale was Dwarf's capture, which Grimwald knew nothing about, as yet.

"So she has moved, then? We have expected this, but not, I fear, quite so soon." His soft voice held hidden his troubled heart.

"Our hour is indeed near, if things fare so well with Dorini," added the ancient Erophin. "It seems you have come seeking advice, and shall receive more, Grimwald. I shall summon all those of my realm who will be of aid to you this moment. And we shall begin to play out our own parts, as is written."

"A thousand thanks, Master. This is more than I had hoped. I shall set out immediately to hold council with Melodias, and deliver your decision." Greyfax paced toward the table from where he had been standing, relating his news.

"There is no need, my old friend. I shall go myself to Melodias, and I think your wisest path would be to return to your dwarf, and the box. Dorini will be seeking that most precious item, for if in power of that, Atlanton Earth has no hope to withstand her. You did not do as perhaps I might have done, although I'm sure you held your own reasons for your choice of Arkenchest bearer; yet its guardian is far too weak to refuse it to her, should he be taken."

"That was my strongest point, O wisest, for she would never imagine the Arkenchest to be left so open to capture. If I'm not too far wrong, she thinks I still carry it, and has busied herself with the task of pursuing me, thereby blinding her to its whereabouts."

"It feels sound, on the outside of it, yet I would still urge all speed in your return. You will be sorely needed there now."

Erophin looked up from his glass. "My mind unfolds the darkness, and I see now your Arkenchest with another, not Dorini, but yes, it is your Fairingay that holds it. I see only a faint image; a wall of cold mist hides the dwarf from my thought."

Greyfax stiffened, rubbing a hand quickly across his brow.

"Then he is taken." He smashed his fist onto the table. "And it's my own fault, for I thought she would not suspect him."

"Did you speak to him of the thing he carried? Of what his father carried before him?" Erophin asked anxiously.

"He knew nothing of that, although he might have guessed from the things I allowed him to see. But at our last meeting he told me of his confusion, and I don't think he realized the extent of the weight laid upon him."

"She has ways of freeing all things hidden in a mind, whether one is aware of them or not. If she has questioned him closely, we have been struck a sharp blow. Perhaps too sharp a blow for us to realize its consequences yet." Cephus, the King, rang a small, pear-shaped bell, which sounded softly through the throne chamber. Presently a messenger appeared, clad in deep mist-silver livery. Cephus spoke quickly, and the messenger disappeared, footfalls fading gently away into the antechamber.

"We must move swiftly if we are to avoid further defeat on Atlanton Earth. You, Greyfax, must set out at once to do what you can where you're needed most. I shall go to Melodias, and those I have chosen from my realm will seek out the defenders of the Light. All speed will be slow enough to turn this tide," said Erophin, "for I see all heavily sieged upon that sphere. Yet there is still resistance, and all is not dark at this hour. If we but contain her this time, all will be in readiness for the new dawning."

Greyfax, eager to be off, made the sacred sign of the circle, bowed low, and was once more flashing away down the broad highway of stars that whirled and spun in glowing circles about him. His heart was full of the news of Dwarf's capture, and not he, nor Erophin, nor any others of the Circle of Light could offer aid to Dwarf where he now was imprisoned in the frozen palace of Dorini. Heavy was his reproach at his close mouth, and his decision not to tell Dwarf of the Secret he carried innocently, for that, and that alone, could help him now, in his dark, tortured mind. And it was that Secret which Dorini sought, for it was of the Arkenchest, that great symbol of all who opposed her, a sign of light and life that thwarted her cunning designs to darken the universe into eternal frozen wastes.

If Froghorn did indeed hold safe the Chest, then it was beyond harm in Cypher, of that he was sure. But that did not alter Dwarf's imprisonment or lessen the danger of Dorini discovering his Secret. Of Otter and Bear, Erophin had said nothing, so it was to the valley he guided his course, whispering like a flowing river of light through time and space, faster still, until all dimension and light were fused, and he came through that dim corridor out upon the rim of the valley, which now lay buried in ruin before him.

Even his haste could not turn back the months that had slipped by, irretrievably, since Dorini took Dwarf to her poisoned, malignant heart.

THE VALLEY IN RUINS

After carefully studying the ruins of the dwarf house, otter holt, and bear cave, Greyfax Grimwald sat down upon Broco's ruined table to see what he might read from the fire. He laid the small sticks of the sacred trees before him, and they burst into a brilliant white flame as he removed his hand. The white flames bowed, touching the gray figure's brow, and Greyfax looked far and wide over and under earth, past regions of flying maned stars, deeper still into the fire. A high, thin arch of bluish white light spiraled away upward, until it had vanished from sight. Raven saw it from far away, thought it a lightning flash, and turned to the more urgent business of gathering food for his hungry family.

The wizard's eyes reflected back the brilliant light, and there came to him Melodias, and their minds opened to each other. Cephus Starkeeper had reached the king, he learned, and the two were in council when Greyfax called them to the seeing eye of the fire. Greyfax made the seventh sign of the holly and Melodias disappeared, to be replaced by I'one, then En'the. Having gathered all he could, and delivered his intelligence in return, Greyfax bade the fire turn upon itself to reveal the destruction of Dwarf's fair valley. His heart grew heavy as he saw the dark shroud of Cakgor's passing, settling over the house of Dwarf, and the narrow escape of Froghorn, son of Fairenaus Fairingay. He promised himself to lessen his scolding when next he met his impetuous young friend, but even a mild rebuke from the elder of Grimwald was one counted harsh among those who knew him. He watched further, relieved to see what instructions Froghorn had given Otter and Bear, and saw their almost fatal adventure with the two werewolves.

"Well, at least that's done with an inkling of sense, my good Fairingay," he said aloud, reaching out his hands to warm them on the now sleeping flames. He replaced the cooling sticks of the sacred trees back into the folds of his heavy winter cloak, and prepared to leave the valley. He whistled twice in an ancient fashion for An'yim and while waiting for the great steed to reach him, he once more went through the broken ruins of Dwarf's house.

"I suppose I should leave a sign I was here," he mused aloud, "should any of them return," and thus saying, he motioned with his eyes, made a slight movement of his hand, and there appeared upon the frozen air before him a brilliant silver bell shaped in the fashion of a falcon at rest, and upon one of the finely carven wings was his sign, ^{G}G. It was an instrument soundless to all ears except those of the Circle, and he would be able to hear its chime anywhere upon Atlanton Earth if rung by a hand in need of him. He placed the bell upon Dwarf's broken sideboard where any would be sure to find it, and hearing An'yim's neigh of glad greetings, he went out to the noble horse.

"Well met once more, brave An'yim. I seem always to be upon errands these days."

"Well met, Master. My wind is strong, and I await your journey," said An'yim politely.

Greyfax stroked the great silver-maned neck, mounted, and the two were away, leaving a silent breath behind that ruffled the snow's sleep, and the tiny silver bell, all that was left ever to betray his presence there.

Raven, flying high over the ruined forest in search of supper for the nestful of ugly, open black beaks, circled twice over the burned settlement of the three friends. He came this way from long habit, and had rummaged through the three dwellings often, occasionally finding crumbs of long-left dwarf cake or otter tuck, so he swooped down to have one more quick look before returning to the wood where he now rested, away over the valley rim, where living things still grew and one could find a decent tree to build in.

As he glided slowly down to a landing over Dwarf's house, a glittering eye winked up at him through the burned and fallen thatch.

"Now what in Crow's croak could that be?" he muttered, and landing on a broken beam, he saw the tantalizing, shining form of the bell. "Strike my tail-feathers," he cawed, and fluttered down to look more closely at the glittering object.

"A goshawk, if I ever laid eyes on one." He hopped around, carefully inspecting his prize, and put his beak to the small, finely turned handle. "Weighs no more than one of my young uns," he said, surprised. "No good to eat, but it'll make the missus happy, I guess. Fool woman always filling up my bed with rocks and such. 'They're fancy,' she says, while I have to toss around all night without my sleep. Ah well, maybe if I bring her this trinket, she'll get rid of the other stuff. I suppose I could sleep easier on this."

And so saying, Raven hoisted the light, fine bell in his beak and flapped loudly away to show his treasure to his wife.

Greyfax, at the moment leading An'yim to his elfin stable in Cypher, did not hear the chime of the bell as it was dropped down into Raven's soft nest far away, beyond the valley of Dwarf, and beyond all eyes who might have welcomed and been strengthened by its sight.

THE ROAD LEADS EVER ON

CHAOS

Freezing mists surrounded Dwarf, as Erophin had seen. He had remained tormented and tortured for such a length of time he had lost all count, for he did not know that in the Dark Palace where he was imprisoned no time, as he knew it, moved. She had questioned him many times, but always at the moment he was ready to speak, and betray his friends and the Arkenchest, he repeated the name of Greyfax, and thus had defeated her designs upon him. Dorini, after gaining from him other information Dwarf did not know he had given, so powerful was her cunning, began to suspect the box was still in the hands of her hated enemy Greyfax Grimwald, and so she renewed her pursuit of the wizard with all the forces she commanded, the dark powers opposed to the Circle of Light and many men and creatures upon the embattled Atlanton Earth. Her thoughts were bent solely upon capture of the Arkenchest, and her will elsewhere, her servants there were lost and with no definite purpose, but the war still raged on, unabatingly, and from one end of that sphere to the other a poisonous cloud descended, maddening men's minds and slowly eating away their resistance.

Dwarf, in his cold dungeon, wept himself to

sleep daily, for he was slowly coming to believe that what Dorini said was true, that Greyfax was dead, and he would never again feel the warm sun upon his back in his beloved, peaceful, faraway valley. In his frozen tomb, imprisoned forever, Dwarf tried to sing to keep his failing hope from dying. To fill his mind, he began an old song Otter had been fond of, describing snowfall on a reed bank, but cold as he was, he left that tune quickly, and went on trying to remember one about sunrise. His voice broke and cracked with the effort, but he went on, and soon had hummed a few bars of Bear's, then another about hammering, and out of a dusty corner of his memory that held his journey of old he faintly heard the strange song his father had taught him so many dwarf ages ago.

His mind stirring from its frozen sleep a bit, he remembered the warmth of the Meadows of the Sun, and meeting Otter and Bear there. It seemed all a faded dream he had had, then forgotten. Now he dwelt in the deathless, frozen breath of Dorini, and the others were gone, all probably lost now to him forever. His voice strengthened a little in answer to that thought, and he hummed his father's song a little louder. It somehow gave him strength, so he began the first stanza, voice growing, and on through the middle of the second.

A distant tremor shuddered, and low, rumbling sounds erupted, as if huge rocks were shifting upon one another. It grew colder, and a shrieking, biting wind began to howl. Suneater, down in the deepest chambers of the Dark Palace, raised his gaunt frame and let forth a chilling growl-wail, rattling the great chain of mountain roots and wind that bound him. Fireslayer whirled her gruesome heads, beating her oozing body against her prison walls. Dorini was in dark council with Doraki, and the two rose quickly, hearing that faint melody ringing through the frozen halls of the Dark Palace. Never had anything so vile and bitter, or dangerous, sounded through the World Between Time. The foundations cracked, and a deafening, roaring maelstrom engulfed the Dark Queen and her lieutenant. The great stone alarm bells clanged sullenly alive, and her other servants sent up a high, wailing lament.

Destruction and chaos broke forth across the dark realm, and Dwarf, hearing it, grew frightened and sang yet louder, finished the song, then began all over from the start. His gallant little heart beat furiously in his throat, but he sang out in a clear, high voice.

A sudden, rending darkness cloaked him, followed by a bitter, freezing cyclone of wind, then stars whirled dizzily by, and he felt the terrible sensation of falling, on and on, through lifetimes and then beyond those. He thought at once of Calix Stay, of the great River, for it was in this way one returned to begin again, and seized by panic, and breathless, not knowing what else to do, he repeated the spell of the holding of the River, not once, but nine times, for it took him so long to fall. All about him, spinning dark shapes loomed, then disappeared. There were so many, he thought perhaps it was indeed the ending in all, the great intake of the one, but the dark forms vanished one by one, and with a last blinding explosion of light and sound, Dwarf stood, breathless, upon the foot of his fire-scorched bed, in the ruins and waste of his beloved, gutted house in the now barren, snow-locked valley that was his homeland.

His escape had come almost three months after Cakgor had carried him into the dark, malignant reign of Dorini.

OTTER FINDS A NEW COMPANION

Winter grew steadily on as Otter grew nearer the great range of bluish-white-topped mountains that defined the northernmost frontier of the land he traveled. From various men, he had learned it was called Amalnath, but before the invasion it had been known as Amarigin. The regions he sought still were besieged by the invaders, but they had not yet been overrun, as was much of Amalnath. As he came nearer to the borders, he saw great battles raging like wildfire. His caution had kept him safe this far, and he doubled his carefulness, until he journeyed only at night, and in his animal form. There were too many risks and dangers to traveling as a man, a lesson he had learned well, coming upon a day-old battlefield and seeing the rotting corpses turning slowly to worm and dust. Animals were no safer, but still they were more wary and stood a better chance of passing unnoticed than those other folk who went about upon only two feet.

In the early evening sky, the first trine moon of the descent raised her tusk-shaped head and shook out her hair over the snow-covered world. Otter's small calendar was marked the ninth day of the birch, which was upon calendars of Atlanton Earth the ninth of December. He had been upon the road since the fourteenth day of September.

As the night grew older, Otter stopped near the stone ruins of what had once been a farmhouse, and decided to rest inside its shelter and perhaps have a nap and good nose slide or two before he went on. His short legs were aching from his day's march, and he promised himself to resume the trip in man form, perilous or not, to use the fresh muscles of that body to continue. He carefully placed his rucksack beside the broken door, and cautiously began his exploration of the interior. Much of the roof was gone, although the walls still stood, offering at least protection from the cold wind that had risen as the sun went down.

Otter poked his snub nose into the darkness, and tested it. Man scent. He retreated quietly, trying to find the man form in the dim, open-topped room. A deeper black shape than the surrounding darkness revealed where the man lay. Small ears straining, he detected irregular heavy breathing, followed by a low moan. Whoever was there was wounded, or dying, and Otter spoke the words and turned twice, and stood stretching his man limbs to get the fit of them. Then he stole quietly over to where the wounded fellow lay.

"Hullo. What hurt have you taken, friend? Is there something I can do?"

A weak hand struggled feebly toward the ugly firearm that lay propped against the wall. Otter reached out quickly and took it, moving it out of reach. It was the first man weapon he had ever laid a paw upon, and its cold steel barrel made his hand-paw tremble as he touched it.

"I mean no harm, friend. If I may help, I will, if you wish."

"I won't go back. You may as well finish me now.

I won't go back," croaked the dry voice, breaking and catching on burning lips.

"You have to go nowhere, friend. I'm called Otter, and only want to aid you. If you'll show me your hurt, I may be able to mend it."

The sprawling, fevered form of the injured man pulled upright, half sitting, half supported by an elbow.

"You really mean me no harm?" came the hopeful, hoarse voice.

"None, friend. How are you called?"

"Flewingam, recently private in the 12th Battalion of General George Greymouse."

Otter started at the mention of the general's name, for that was how the wizard king he sought called himself among his followers.

"Did you do battle on this side of the border, friend? Or have you come this far alone?"

Otter was tying one of his spare handkerchiefs about Flewingam's hurt arm.

"Ah, go easy there. That hurts." Flewingam moaned between clenched teeth. "We fell upon a rear guard of the enemy not more than five miles from here last night. I was struck by a bomb before I fired a shot, which was well enough by me, so I decided then was as good a time as any to chuck it all. I was a conscript, and never had a heart for fighting anyhow, but you know how it is nowadays. Anyone who can carry a weapon or strike a blow is sucked into the bloody mess."

Otter had finished binding the arm, and now gave Flewingam a drink from his water jug. "Not too much at first, you'll choke on it."

The man gagged once, then greedily took another long pull.

"I've been eating snow to keep me going since this morning. I never thought to find a friend here," he said, falling back against the wall. "What brings you, if you're not a soldier? Most folks have long left this cursed place, since the fighting."

"I seek after the general you just named, Greymouse, although I know him better as Mithramuse. Three moons now I have journeyed from my home to find him."

"You try to find General Greymouse? To what purpose? To turn me in for deserter's fee?" Flewingam laughed bitterly. "I should have known as much. Fifty gold dollars is all a man is worth who has no stomach for fighting."

"Money is of no interest to me, friend," Otter assured him. "I'm waterfolk by trade, and need only a roof and a full river to keep me."

Flewingam stared up at Otter, trying to see his eyes in the dim silver light.

"I think by your voice you must be what you say."

"My errand to your general is to seek his aid to help us get back our dwarf. After that, I plan simply to slide all day, or swim, or whatever. These wars are more than I can fathom."

Otter sat down next to Flewingam, stretching out his awkward legs before him. "Do you have a blanket to cover up with, friend? If not, I have a duster I brought along that you might use."

The injured man's teeth chattered a constant, staccato tattoo. "That's kind, Otter. Is that really what you're called?"

"If it would not be too much of a shock for you, I'd say I am an otter, but then explaining things to a man is a more difficult thing than conversing with, say, a groundhog or a muskrat."

"You lead me in circles. Groundhog? I know groundhog stew, and have trapped muskrats often as a boy."

"Do tell," snapped Otter, a trace of reproach edging into his voice. "That's why I never have much commerce in places infested with you folk."

"Are you a religious hermit, friend?"

"I wouldn't exactly say that, although I do have a chat or two with the great king now and then. Makes more sense than anything I've found in Mankind yet. Now you'd better try to sleep. I'll be gone soon, but I'll give you the cover, since you're hurt, and have none. In return for that favor, you may give me your promise not to trap animals in the future, if you live through the war." Otter lay back, looking up through the open roof at the dim, glimmering triangle of Styphlus.

"Oh, I'll live through this all right, and I haven't trapped an animal, save for food, since I grew into a soldier's size. I have said something to offend you, I fear. If that's so, I'm sorry, friend, for you've shown me more kindness than many I might have chanced upon."

Otter, almost asleep, whistled in his own tongue, forgetting his newly found companion would not understand. He fell into a light doze, wondering if he should trust this man. Just as he was on the very light gray border of slumber, heavy, booted footsteps aroused him from that land. Muffled voices, low and harsh, grated the air like iron bars dragged across stone.

"We'll break here and wait till sunrise to set up the rest. Osglat, you and Prax take first watch. The rest of you sleep while you've got the chance."

Then came noises of many men dropping their burden; the jingle of pack harness and the dull metallic clang of weapon butt or barrel as it touched earth, or other gear was heard, and Otter, fighting the urge to return to his other form, silently crept to the window in time to see two large, uniformed shadows approaching the ruins where he and Flewingam lay hidden. Even with the moon gone, the room was light enough to see distinct shapes by, and there was no immediate place to hide. Flewingam crawled to his firearm, and had it ready when Otter moved quickly back from the window.

"There are too many of them for that," he hissed sharply, remembering at that moment his rucksack, still where he'd left it by the doorway. "I should be captured and roasted alive," he rebuked himself.

A dark shape crossed the dim outline of the entrance.

"Don't has so much as a roof," complained the shadow voice. "But it takes the bite out of that wind, it does."

"We might as well stay here. I doesn't like the looks of it. Too many ghosts around for me," growled the second.

"Is you still full of your balmy stories, Flick? I thought you just got them ghosts on the late watch." A harsh laugh, followed by a grunt.

"You is going to wish you had listened when they is come for you, dunghead. Them as don't believe they eat," snapped the voice called Flick.

"They they is going to have themselfs a sorry feed for that, if they takes us. I hasn't had my stomach full since we stewed that village two days ago. The way these easterns eat, you would thinks they was too weak to carry an ant, much less fight."

"We ain't had nothing but trouble since we crossed borders. I don't see no use in why we is here, except maybe to scare up a few seed planters into thinking about moving on," the second voice added.

"Like this turnip picker here," put in Flick, gesturing at the fallen stone house. "Must be pretty hard farming in the middle of a fight. Thataway, the only thing you might get planted was yourself, if you get my meaning." The voice, harsh and guttural, laughed a short rasping echo of humor.

"Let's see if there's anything worth having left in here," snapped one of the voices. "We might find something to fill our bellies."

Otter's rucksack had not been discovered, but the two soldiers approached the door again, and he was sure they would see it this time.

Flewingam held a long, dull black knife in his hand as Otter turned to warn him.

"Can you take one of them?" he breathed, barely a whisper into Otter's ear.

"I'm not much of a fighter," Otter shot back, but hearing the heavy footsteps almost on them, he slipped behind the doorstone, clutching his thick walking stick after the manner of a cudgel. A gaunt brown form appeared through the dark slit of the ruined entrance. From farther away, the snoring of the other beasts reached Otter's ears.

"Come on, Flick, I smells something in here." The figure crouched, moving into the room. Otter let the shadow go on, and soon Flick's grotesquely shaped head showed itself.

"There's some—" the second man started to say, his speech cut short by the blade in his hairy throat. Flick started to run, but a heavy blow from Otter's stick knocked him senseless to the floor. Flewingam came, and with expert skill dispatched the unconscious Flick with a silent thrust of his knife.

"We must be gone before they're missed," whispered Flewingam. "By their gear, I think we've landed ourselves in the middle of a Gorgolac raiding party."

"Did you have to slay them?" asked Otter, surprised at his new companion's cold actions.

"That's a point, friend, I'm sure they wouldn't

have asked us. Let's get away from this place quickly." Flewingam's voice was as gentle as his hand had been quick. Otter reached around the doorpost cautiously, saw no one, and pulled his rucksack quietly in.

"The general will have to know of this," said Flewingam, turning over some question in his mind.

"I thought you had given up that life," said Otter, slipping into the harness of his pack.

"I still have kinsmen in these parts, or I did if these villains haven't already slain them all. General Greymouse has long protected these regions, and he'll be quick to remove them. They must have crossed far below his borders."

"Then you'll go with me to find him?" Otter brightened at the thought of company.

"Yes, we'll go together. The two of us will have a better chance, at any rate, of getting through. I'm sure there are more of these handsome fellows than our friends outside."

Otter shuddered, thinking of how he would have been caught in his sleep by these new enemies had Flewingam found some other hiding place. He was not entirely trustful of the man, remembering how swiftly he had slain, but then the war changed many men, and Flewingam certainly didn't seem to have taken pleasure in it. Too, Flewingam knew where the man was he had traveled so far to find. This thought decided Otter. The two of them would go on in search of their general, each for his own reasons. The comfort of having a companion again after so long eased Otter's weariness a little, and as they crept hurriedly through the broken back window of the ruins toward the snow-blanketed fields beyond, Otter reached out a hand-paw to Flewingam. The man silently took it, and nodded.

At daybreak, the two had entered the outlying rolling hills, where the cover was heavier, and their journey was hastened on until the third hour of sunrise. They had seen no further signs of raiders, but the two decided that one would sleep and one keep watch, taking turns that way until they were both rested enough to go on.

DWARF'S PROMISE

Dwarf's heart swelled with confusion and sadness. He slowly got down from his broken, fire-torn bed, and began wandering about the room trying to piece together all the black, frightening things that had happened. He had no way of knowing how long he had been gone, nor of what time it was. He stepped past the ruined bedroom door into the charred remnants of his snug sitting room and kitchen. The small ancient green clock was rusting, its case only a blackened pile of sticks. The living thatched roof was burned and dead, and the clover floor was nothing but parched, lifeless earth. He crossed the splintered outer door, and looked with dismay and a growing anger at his valley. The forest was gone, grim black trunks rising out of the snow on the surrounding hills, making it all look full of charred tombstones, and the river was no more than a trickle, what water there was not frozen, being a dirty gray-brown color, and poisoned.

He searched in vain for Froghorn and the box. His heart turned as dark and cold as the ice palace of the evil queen when he realized that both were gone.

He ran to Otter's, wept again when he saw that cheerful little holt burned and falling slowly to dust, and before he reached Bear's den, a vengeance, swift and terrible, had begun growing in his heart, a vengeance more embittered by his helplessness, and more dreadful because of his throwing care for himself aside. All Dwarf sought now was a swift sword, and a reckoning, and if he must perish in the effort, it would be great satisfaction in the empty face of death to know he had at least struck a blow for his companions' foul murder.

Returning to the crumbled dwarf home of all those long, peaceful years, Broco salvaged what little he could that might be of use to him on his journey. Before leaving the valley for the last time, he fashioned three stone markers with the mallet and hand chisel he had found unharmed, one in the high tongue of Bear, another in Otter's language. For Froghorn he fashioned a simple Circle of Life on the smooth surface of the old stone. He placed them down near the remnants of where the reed lawn had once seen the merry All Summer's Day, that midsummer only a burned phantom now in Dwarf's heart, and pausing for one long, lonely last moment, he wept.

"Aieee," he wailed, "and now I've been the curse and murder of my best comrades, stout Bear and gentle Otter, animal kings from beyond the great River, and my loyal Froghorn. I brought them all this way on my mad journey, and here, in the valley we loved so well, I find them slain and perished away, and their footsteps will follow mine where I go no longer. I've failed them all, and broken Greyfax's trust. This then, dearest comrades, is our last farewell. I'll see thy fair faces no more." He could not go on, for his voice failed him, and the tears flowed long from his tightly closed eyes.

"Curse you, filth," he cried at last, brandishing high the short dwarf sword of Tubal Hall he had found safe behind the fallen fireplace of his wrecked house. "The ancient vengeance of all my father's fathers forever on your villainous souls. I shall at least have the pleasure of burying Tubal's blade in your blood, if I never draw a breath after."

And with the echo of his sworn word to avenge his fallen friends still ringing grimly in his ears, Dwarf set out from the valley, not knowing where he was directing his course, so he picked the most obvious path to guide him, the majestic heads of the far, cold blue shoulders of the mountains that shone over the western borders of Atlanton Earth.

AT THE SIGN OF THE SHAMROCK

Over the door hung the sign of the shamrock. Dark lamps burned dimly in the short alleyway that led to the main room, and off the stairs to the right were three rooms to accommodate any travelers that might still be upon their journey of trade or commerce; but for the past year, they were mainly used by officers of the armies that swarmed about the countryside. Jason Wheatflower was therefore greatly surprised when the stout man in forest green appeared rapping upon his window at two strokes past midnight, carrying a common knapsack, and no weapons at all.

"Have you sleeping quarters, my good fellow? And a plate or two for a hungry traveler?" Bear's overpowering thirst for a taste of something sweet had at last driven him from his usual practice of sleeping away from men's settlements and traveling only by night, and that hunger within him grew huskier now as he spoke.

"I have, stranger, for those that can pay," answered Wheatflower. He had had only a precious few soldiers that ever paid for what they took, although upon occasion some powerful general or commander would happen through, leaving gold enough to keep his door open for business.

Bear had forgotten the matter of money. Quickly he thought of anything he might have that would be of worth to this innkeeper. "I can pay," Bear said shortly. "I have precious wares about me that will more than settle you."

"Wait a moment, then," replied Wheatflower. "I'll be down in a moment."

He went to a drawer beside his bed and took out a long-barreled, ugly-looking pistol. One never knew, he told himself, what mischief these night crawlers might be up to. Hastening downstairs, he hid the firearm in the pocket of his robe and opened up the barred front room.

"Welcome, stranger. If you desire food before you sleep, I'll fix something cold in the galley to hold you over until morning."

Bear strode over to the still glowing remains of the fire that burned in the large hearthplace.

"I'd like to warm myself a bit first. Then honey, if you have it, would settle my stomach for eating."

"Certainly, friend. I have good wildflower comb on the premises, stout enough to kill the chill of colder nights than this." Wheatflower disappeared through a door, and Bear heard steps going downward, into a cellar.

He looked about the room, studying his surroundings. The dying fire and the candlelight showed it to be comfortably furnished, two rather large stuffed armchairs before the hearth, two long tables, sideboards, and a bookshelf at the far end that contained a number of well-thumbed volumes. Mulling irons and pokers hung in their proper place, and Bear was already tasting the warm sweetness flowing through his chilled, bone-weary body. He was inspecting the coat of arms above the fireplace when Wheatflower bustled back into the room, bearing three old, dusty brown bottles and a fourth container that looked to be a pot of hot coffee, and a large copper cup.

"These should hold you a moment while I get your food. Nothing fancy, mind you, but it'll stick with you. Bacon, liver pie, and sweet bread my cook makes like no one else. There, sit awhile and stoke up the fire if you wish. By the time you've got the chill off, I'll be back with the supper."

"Thank you kindly, friend, but the sweet bread and butter will do," Bear said, pulling up one of the big comfortable chairs and reaching out a fire poker to stir up the glowing ashes.

Wheatflower paused at the galley door.

"Begging pardon, friend, but I always get my price in advance. A reasonable demand, these days, and if you'll not be offended, I'll ask you now what you plan to settle my bill with. Jewels, or what sort of wares?" Wheatflower looked down at his feet as he spoke.

Bear, flustered by the request, picked up his rucksack and began opening it. The tantalizing, heady aroma of the honey had turned his mind from all other thoughts.

"Ahem," he began, shifting and tumbling through the contents of the pack. "Here," he stammered. "No, now where has it gotten to? Ah, here it is," and his hand fell on the gleaming eye of the dragon stone. He wasn't sure if it was made of stuff men would treasure, but it sparkled and caught the dim light, bursting into a hundred colors at once, filling the room with the glow of an exploding rainbow. Bear had never really looked closely at the stone, and was as dumbfounded as Wheatflower, who stood, eyes starting from his head, at the door. The two figures watched, speechless, as the colors began taking shapes, moving quickly into spinning, glistening patterns upon walls and ceilings. A head, large and bright emerald green, appeared, snake-like, but with long rows of curved, gleaming teeth. Then came a body, serpentine, coiled and covered by a sheen of pale golden skin. As this vision unfolded before them, a distant echo of a deep voice reached through the veiled room.

"What seek ye of the stone, Master?" Vibrations of red and purple-gold sound rang about them, and a faint chime of bells in some faraway citadel sounded.

Wheatflower's jaw dropped, and Bear had sprung for the safety of the underside of the nearby table.

The sound of a great, rushing tide flooded their ears.

"Speak, Oh Master. What task is set for the dwelling within the stone?"

Dwarf had never said anything about the dragon stone, except that it was an heirloom of his family, and Bear trembled to think he had been carrying it about with him like some ordinary piece of common feldspar. Tentatively, voice breaking, he called out.

"I am Bruinlen, descendant of Bruinthor, mighty king of old, keeper of the stone. My dear friend Dwarf has been taken by the Dark Queen, and I now carry you until such time as I may return you to your rightful master."

Two sudden brilliant white flashes lighted the room, and the two men had to cover their eyes with their arms to keep from being blinded.

"I am aware of all you say, Bruinlen. You have carried me well, and I shall serve you as my master for the time it takes to discharge your mission. I would have spoken to you before, but there was no cause to awaken me until now."

From the far corner of the chamber, a great, armored golden fish swam onto the air and passed over their heads, spewing large crystal bubbles that burst and showered the floor at Bear's feet with a dozen or more perfectly shaped stones.

"You may use one of these for payment to the innkeeper. Carry the rest and use them as the need arises."

"I wasn't really going to part with you," stammered Bear, but he was cut short by a loud, popping noise, and a miniature display of fireworks sizzled and whizzed about the floor. As the last rocket burst, the light faltered, flared once more, then went out, leaving Bear staring dumbly down at the dark eye of the stone in his still outstretched hand.

Wheatflower shook his head violently, blinking his eyes twice in rapid succession. He looked quickly at Bear, who was picking up the small, shining stones from the floor.

"I seem to have dropped them," he said, trying to disguise his bewilderment. "Here, friend, here is your price, and more, but it's the smallest I have to offer." He placed the small, round stone in Wheatflower's hand. The man stared in amazement at it, rolling it around with a finger, and at last placed it between his teeth and bit down sharply.

"Aoow," he mumbled, taking it out again, rubbing a hand over his jaw. "Just testing, friend," he explained. "I'm not so dumb as to have never heard of worthless glass being passed off as jewels. This one seems on the straight, though. A pretty thing, too. I accept it, against your bill, and will extend you credit, too, if you travel these parts often."

Bear had drained one of the honey bottles in a swig, and now sat wiping a sleeve across his mouth to clean the comb from his mustache.

"Thank you, friend. I don't expect I'll be in these parts beyond this once, but if you have any more of this, I'll take a few more bottles in place of credit."

"As you wish, sir, there's plenty more where that

came from. You admit it's good then," chuckled Wheatflower, the warmth of his new treasure resting safely in the pocket of his robe, next to his pistol.

"Most excellent fare," gulped Bear, already busy at the second bottle, then under his breath as Wheatflower left, "At least for a man stomach. Eek, but it would give me heart murmur, or worse, if I tasted this stuff as me." He lost himself a moment, thinking of his snug cave and the great ripe barrels of bark bear honey that awaited his return, and musing on his home, he grew weary, and the prospect of his supper began to lose its promise for him. He tried counting the days he had been gone, wandering about these cold man roads, but somehow the mere counting made him even wearier, and he left his tally at something over eighty days, as Mankind marked it, and wished aloud Wheatflower would hurry back to show him his bed. He'd finished the third bottle, and had gotten halfway through the coffee when the innkeeper came clanking in again, arms full of the same dark brown bottles.

"There should be enough here to keep you, Master, er, I didn't catch the name. Jason Wheatflower, at your service." And bowing low, he placed the new bottles before Bear and picked up the empty ones.

"Bruinlen, friend, and thank you. If you could show me my bed, I'd be grateful. I've been upon the highway now for a good many miles, and would sleep." Bear rose, picking up the bottles. "I'll just take these to my room with me, to ease up a bit."

"Certainly, certainly, Master Bruinlen, come this way, please. I've just put fresh linens in one of my most comfortable rooms, and I'm sure it'll satisfy your fancy."

Wheatflower showed Bear up the stairs, and at the second landing led him into a rather small but cheery room that overlooked the inner courtyard and stables of the inn. Bear thanked his host again, bowed, and placed the honey on the table near the bed. After emptying two more bottles of the heady stuff, he wearily lay back, pulling the thin blanket up to his chin. There was no fire in the room, and he soon grew cold again, so he quickly crossed and checked to make sure his door was bolted, repeated the words and crawled back into bed, more comfortable in his heavy, warm fur body.

"Men," he muttered sleepily. "Not even thick-skinned enough to ward off a simple chill." Almost before he finished his speech, his head was beneath the pillow, paws to his muzzle, and he was snoring, his dream mind filled with the light of the dragon stone and great golden fish that breathed precious jewels.

Below him, in the stables, Wheatflower was waking his stable hand, a knobby-boned gypsy that worked for a scrap of food a day and warm hay to sleep on at night.

"Wake up, you useless lump. We've work to do." Wheatflower directed a vicious kick at the dark head.

Whining, Strap cringed before his master. "No need in cracking my skull. I'll do what you want, just give me time to get the sleep out of my eyes."

Wheatflower handed the man an old, rusty dagger. "We have a guest tonight. I won't expect to see him for breakfast tomorrow. If you do your work well, you'll be justly rewarded. If not, I'll flail the stinking skin off your miserable back."

Strap shuddered.

"Is it another soldier whats you wants me to cut? Does he carry things to hurts me with?" Strap cringed, holding the rusted blade close against him.

"He's unarmed, just like you like them. If he'd carried weapons, I wouldn't have asked a stinking dog of a coward to kill him." Wheatflower aimed a kick at Strap's backside, but the man hurried out before him, still cringing and complaining. He looked up at the dark window of Bear's room, twisting the knife in his hands.

"Use the trapdoor, idiot. And don't wake him, or I'll have seen the last of your likes. He's a big one, this fellow."

Strap entered the dark galley and disappeared. Wheatflower walked slowly back across the courtyard, listening to the hard-packed snow crunch beneath his feet, already counting the other jewels in his mind, the other stones he had seen after his strange half-waking nightmare, when the man had dropped them. He took the small, round, warm thing out of his pocket and held it before his eyes. It caught the silver-white light of snow and stars, holding them in its smooth surface, reflecting back the dark blue sky like a field of glittering, shimmering, brilliant fire.

"At last," he sighed. "After all these years of sweating and starving I have my chance. No more licking boots for my living. I'll be my own master for a change." He laughed, and the stone glowed dimly in his dark eyes, burning his hand and mind with the power it would give him, once he had the others. Then it would be Master Wheatflower, or General Wheatflower, if he wished, and he would be feared and admired by all those scum who had stepped on him as if he were no more than a beetle. Once he possessed all the stones, he, Jason Wheatflower, would step on a few beetles himself.

With these thoughts raging through his fevered brain, he went into the kitchen and sat down at the table to wait.

In Bear's room, a rug shifted a few inches, raising slowly, and Strap peered out of the small slit at the large figure upon the bed. He listened for a few moments, making sure the man was asleep, then slowly raised the trapdoor fully open. Its hinges creaked as he laid it back, and terrified, he froze to the spot, not daring to breathe. The snoring went on unaltered.

Strap fingered the dull blade of his knife, stretched out a foot, and repeating the process, put out the other, slowly, carefully, one after the other, until he stood beside the bed. The man was covered completely by the rag of a blanket, and in the poor light, Strap couldn't be sure where to strike his blow. Holding his breath, he carefully placed his hand out and grasped the edge of the blanket, drawing it slowly down. The pale, dim starlight filtered in across Strap and onto the peacefully sleeping form of Bear. Thinking the figure unlike any other he had ever seen, Strap leaned close to the sleeping muzzle. Bear snored loudly, smacked his lips, and turned over, sprawling one huge forepaw over the edge of the blanket. Strap's knife clattered loudly to the floor, followed by his scream, and he stumbled backward, teetered a moment, then went crashing down into the open trapdoor. Below, Wheatflower gloated, hearing the scream and scuffle, and went out to the stairway to claim his rightful treasure, the jewels that would make his fortune. He was greeted at the landing by a huge, towering dark form that was cloaked from top to bottom in what appeared to be a fur robe. As his foot touched the last step, the booming figure whirled.

"A demon ghost," shrieked Wheatflower, stumbling headfirst down the stairwell, thumping and bumping down to a stunned heap. Bear, thinking something had attacked the man, hurried down to the crumpled form.

"Easy there, easy," he said, patting the man's hand with his paw, and trying to think what he ought to do. "Water, he should have a nice glass of water," he mumbled, and lumbered off in the direction he thought the kitchen to be. In the galley, Strap held a mangled arm to his side, and white with fear, was racing toward the safety of his stable. As he crossed the pantry, Bear's shadowy form filled the room, muttering in his own tongue, trying to find the pump handle to draw up water for the unconscious innkeeper on the stairway. Strap, eyes accustomed now to the dark, fainted away at the sight of this apparition moving purposefully about in the dim kitchen quarters. Bear finally found what he was after, and leaving, looked down and saw the small tin cup clutched in his huge paw. He returned hastily to man form, and hurried out to his stricken host.

Wheatflower sat cowering on the bottom stair, his pistol clutched unsteadily in his hand. Seeing Bear, he tried to steady his aim, but his arm shook, and still weakened and dazed by his fall, his shot went wide, burying itself in the wall beside Bear's head. The report and blinding muzzle flash stopped Bear in his tracks, but before the man could gather himself to fire again, Bear was on him, swatting the firearm away with a heavy, quick blow.

"I'm not your assailant, friend. You'll hurt someone if you're not more careful."

Wheatflower scooted backward up to the next step, eyes wide with fright. All thought of the stones was gone, and all he wanted now was to go on drawing breath.

"I meant no harm, Master Bruinlen. I thought some assassin had attacked you in your sleep. I heard noises and rushed to aid you, but there was a demon monster at your door that set upon me and threw me down the stairs."

Wheatflower's head spun at the strange visions that had come upon him since this odd man's arrival.

First the frightening scene in the common room, then the giant goblin that had appeared to him on the landing.

"I thank you for your attempt to help, friend, but you should be more cautious about waving firearms so recklessly. Your aid came near to settling me for good." Bear helped the man to his feet. "But what's done is done, and I know you meant well. I think your murderer has fled, whoever he was, and frightened out of his wits to boot. I don't think we need fear any further attacks tonight. I'm going to try to finish out my nap, and suggest you do the same. You'll probably have some nasty bruises tomorrow, and a rest is what you need."

"I don't understand at all," muttered Wheatflower. "I run a decent inn. I can't imagine who would do such a thing. I've never had any trouble before."

"Most likely some passing bandit; the roads are full of all sorts these days." Bear stumped heavily up to his door. "I would make sure my gates were double-barred in the future, to avoid such ruckuses as this."

"I shall indeed, Master Bruinlen," he agreed quickly. "I shall do that, for sure." Another dark thought was slowly stirring in his reeling, tortured brain.

At daybreak, Bear awakened to loud voices from the courtyard below.

"That's him, sir, there's the one who did it" Wheatflower's voice was loud and accusing.

Bear went to the window and looked down. Two soldiers had Strap by both arms, one broken and useless, and a third soldier with a single iron bar on his helmet stood beside the innkeeper.

"He made me do it, it's him what's guilty,"

whined Strap, his arm throbbing painfully, bringing tears to his eyes.

"I was kind enough to give this murdering thief a job when he came to my door starving. I've given him shelter and food, and this is how he repays me," Wheatflower said indignantly.

"We'll take care of his likes," growled the officer. "He's not strong enough for a work camp, but he's good enough to make good target practice for my men."

"No, no," screamed Strap, struggling to free himself from the grasp of his captors. "Not Strap, he's done no harm, you can't shoots old Strap."

"Take him away," ordered the officer, and the two soldiers led the gypsy squirming and screaming away.

Wheatflower was pointing up toward Bear's window, explaining something to the officer, who nodded, and the two of them came back toward the house. Whatever they were up to, Bear knew it was of no good tidings to him. At the least, all those unpleasant questions, or at the worst, another delay. He placed two bottles of the honey in his rucksack, pulled it onto his back, and hurried down the stairs.

As he passed the front gate and quietly shut it after him, he heard the galley door slam and the two men clumping loudly up the stairs. A quick look revealed no one about on the dawn streets, and Bear quickly set out toward the edge of the small settlement, trying not to walk too hurriedly, and as he reached the crossroad where the highway met the village, he veered sharply away, heading for the safety of the thin patch of low shrub trees that bordered the open fields around the town. At any moment, he expected to be hailed, but after a tense few minutes, he was under the low-lying branches of the trees, and no one had seen his passing. The sun had broken the chill that lay over the day, and the bright light sparked gaily on the snow. Above, the sky was a clear, high blue, the wind crisp and fresh, a good day for traveling, he thought, and travel he must, and put as many miles beneath his feet as he could, for they would be looking for him soon.

Wheatflower and the officer had agreed to split the gems between them, and put the fellow into the army, or a work camp, and no one would ever know the difference. They had searched the inn and stables thoroughly, and at last, victim gone, the officer, angered at being done out of the treasure he was promised, marched Wheatflower at weapon point to his commander, and enlisted him in a company outbound for a distant front.

The officer then alerted his men to be on the lookout for a deserter, and promised a reward of gold for the man who brought him the big stranger. He did not mention treasure.

And Bear, moving steadily on, reached woods' end by noon, and was safely far beyond their reach by nightfall. He had seen no living thing the entire day, except for the birds chattering in the woods. He spoke to them, inquiring if any of them had seen a small gray otter thereabouts. And one, a dark russet brown field lark, told him of the strange animal with the odd humped back that had passed through their land, going on away toward the mountains. This news heartened Bear greatly, and he doubled his speed, in hopes of overtaking Otter before the little fellow reached the now barely visible lines of low foothills stretched out across the horizon.

Otter and Flewingham roused themselves and broke fast with the remaining food Otter carried, and moved on, ever upward now, across the rolling chain of snow-carpeted hills. They planned to reach a shepherd's camp that Flewingham knew to be safe by nightfall, and with another day's march, to be at General Greymouse's camp.

A VOICE FROM THE PAST

At daybreak, Dwarf was awakened by a chattering, incessant bird voice. It was calling out loudly in a tongue he understood well.

"Wake up, you scoundrel, you crack wing, wake up, I say."

A flutter of dark black wings beat about Dwarf's head. He reached for his sword and began thrashing blindly at the drumming things. The raven flew up out of Dwarf's arm reach and pelted him with a stone he had picked up in his beak.

"Villainous nest robber, I'll have your eyes for my breakfast," cawed the bird in a screeching war whoop, and dived angrily at the stunned dwarf. Just as he fell upon the little man to pluck out an eye viciously, he halted in mid wing-stroke.

"Dwarf! Well, pluck my tailfeathers, if it isn't Master Dwarf." Raven hopped from Dwarf's shoulder to the ground, cawing apologetically.

"I hope I haven't done you serious harm, sir. I mistook you for a thief who has robbed two eggs from my wife's nest. I am sorry, dear old friend. You've been gone so long, I hardly recognized you."

Dwarf picked his hat up and put the sword back into its sheath.

"You've taken a good ten dwarf ages off me, Raven," he huffed. "And quite a good shock of my hair. I should stew you up for my trouble, if I weren't so glad to see you." Dwarf laughed and reached down to Raven, stroking his back feathers twice, as manners demanded. Dwarf was, if hasty and impetuous in some ways, very mannerly and polite in others.

The two sat down to talk while Broco fussed about building a small fire, and Raven related to him the strange events which had preceded the destruction of the valley. He told how he had come upon Otter that far distant morning in September, and Bear surprising him soon after, and the terrible fight and Bear's slaying of the werewolves, and how after that day, they had passed out of his life, and he'd heard nothing of them from then to now. He stared dumbfounded at Dwarf whirling and dancing around, throwing up his hat in a great burst of joy and racing about shouting.

"How long since was that, Raven?" asked Dwarf at length, holding his breath awaiting the answer.

"I make it no more than three full moons ago," said Raven, eyeing Dwarf suspiciously. Then he spotted the simple sack, and hungry after watching Dwarf's antics, hoped it was full of something to eat, as in days of old. "A dwarf cake would do me nicely now," hinted Raven. "All this jabber and frolic has made me hungry, and I still have the missus and kids to think of."

"I haven't had the time to bake," replied Dwarf, "nor the makings of dwarf cakes since I was carted away by those filth. I do have a tin or two of sweet comb that I found in poor Bear's wrecked pantry. You're welcome to share that."

Raven hopped over and studied the opened tin of

bee comb. "Hum, it doesn't look so bad. Did he put it up recently?"

"I think Bear wouldn't keep something about that wasn't fit to eat," Dwarf answered, taking a fingerful and holding it out to the bird. Raven took a small piece in his beak, wiggled his head up and down twice, swallowed, and paused.

"It's not so bad," he said. "Nothing near the pleasures of good corn or wheat bread, and certainly nowhere near the delight of water bug, but under the circumstances, I think it'll do nicely." Raven pecked up a beakload, and mouth full, he added, "I'll just run this back to the family," and was gone, black wings beating noisily over the snow-shrouded ground.

Dwarf finished the honey, and satisfied for the moment, sat down and began making his plans for finding his two friends, while he waited for Raven's return. The gladness of the news that Bear and Otter had indeed not been slain overcame him again, and when Raven flew back, he came upon Dwarf cartwheeling furiously about in the snow, first one way, then the other, making fancy turns in midair, and ending with a double backover dwarf kip that left the little man standing on his head, breathing hard.

Raven cawed twice, shook his head, and tried to talk sensibly to the figure of the bottoms-up dwarf.

"If you plan to overtake Bear and Otter, I would suggest you look first toward the mountains. Neither of them said anything to me of where they were bound, but from the direction they started off in, I would venture to say that's where they were heading. No reason for them to veer away from that course, for from what I've heard from the few strangers that fly over these parts, the only place to find shelter or food lies there. Of course, the whole place is overrun with Mankind down that way, but then that seems to be the lay of things, these days."

Dwarf's mind turned to his cat, Froghorn. Raven had not mentioned the cat.

"What of my Froghorn, Raven? Do you know what's become of him? Did he escape?"

"You mean the wizard Fairingay? You speak of him as if you didn't know." Raven ruffled his feathers up and laughed.

"You mean, my cat, Froghorn, was ..." blurted Dwarf, remembering Greyfax's drawing room, and what he had said about being more closely guarded than he knew. "I've heard of thick-headed dwarfs before, but none that can top me," mused Dwarf, angered at his own blindness which had kept him from seeing through the wizard's disguise. Moving to an upright position, which put Raven more at ease, he recalled how he had thought the eyes gave him the idea for the name of Froghorn. But now he saw that it had been the magician's own sense of humor that had tricked him, so that he gave the wizard his own name. Dwarf chuckled, recalling how they had often fought.

"I think perhaps he must have hated that chore," he started again, laughing. Then his mirth faded, and he yearned for some way to find Fairingay, or Greyfax.

"You didn't by chance discover where he was going, did you, Raven? I have urgent need of his counsel now."

"A great swift steed came and bore him away. To where, I fathom not, yet doubtless he was off to wherever wizards go when they are not off somewhere else," Raven said sagely.

"Where on this side of the River could that possibly be?" complained Dwarf, going over in his thought any mention of places where the two wizards were always going to or coming from. If it were somewhere that could only be reached by the high magical spells of Greyfax, he was lost, but if it were upon some errand among Mankind, he had a slim chance, no more, of finding one of the two, but a slim chance was enough, and Otter and Bear had already gone before him, so they were out there too, somewhere, and with the least particle of dwarf luck at all, he would surely find one or both of them, sooner or later.

This prospect burned brightly within him, and thanking Raven for all he had said, Dwarf gave him one of the last of the tins of honey, stroked his backfeathers courteously, and began once more his long and wandering journey that had brought him so far, across the Great River, into the now destroyed valley where he'd dwelt so long, into the heart of the enemy's camp, and now farther still, ever onward, toward the dim shapes of the distant mountains.

Raven, too flustered to speak by Dwarf's great kindness, cast his eyes downward, unable to meet Broco's gaze as he said his farewell. He was too ashamed to tell Dwarf he had taken the fine, shining bell from the ruins of his house.

IN GENERAL GREYMOUSE'S CAMP

"Stand down, stand down," went up the excited cry. "Make ready to move within the hour." The soldier hurried along the company streets of the sprawling camp, repeating his message over and over, and a great noise of men moving purposefully about greeted Otter and Flewingam as they entered the picket lines of General Greymouse's perimeters. They had been challenged every few miles since entering the mountains, but Flewingam had known one of the men at the first checkpoint they had reached, and found out from him the current password, so they had passed on unhampered until with first light they were in General Greymouse's large war bivouac, listening to the orderlies raise up their loud cry of tidings.

"It looks as if they are preparing for battle," said Flewingam. "They usually don't hold stand down unless a skirmish is close at hand."

Otter, walking by his side, carried the firearm, for the other man's arm was still sore and weak from his wound.

"Here, you two," bellowed a deep, growly voice, "over here and give me a hand with this gun."

The two men walked on.

"Hey, you men, get over here and help me," barked the curt voice, and a hand tapped Otter's shoulder roughly. Seeing Flewingam's wounded arm, the sergeant who had stopped them softened his voice.

"I didn't see you was hurt. Get along then, and have it tended, but you," he said, jerking his thumb toward Otter, "you get over here and give me a hand. You ain't hurt none, are you?"

"I'm helping this fellow along," explained Otter sensibly. "I've got to get him to where he can get his arm fixed."

"Oh, you do now, do you? Well, I'm going to tell you a little secret, soldier. I'm going to fix *your* arm if you don't move it and help me get this piece loaded up." The man glowered dangerously near Otter's startled face.

"Go on and help him, Otter. I'll wait," said Flewingam softly.

Otter handed him the firearm and went with the sergeant to put the gun up on a pack-harnessed mule. Returning presently, he wiped his hand-paws on his trousers and whistled angrily in his own tongue, then added in man speech, "I can see why you gave up this business, friend. Soldiers certainly seem to have a very grumpy sort of meanness to them. I thought Dwarf was bad with his face forever puffed out, but these fellows make that seem like nothing at all." Otter took back the weapon, and they continued on.

"I'll be anxious to meet your Dwarf, if ever I get the chance. From the way you speak of him, he must be a most jolly sort of comrade."

"Well, I wouldn't go so far as jolly, although he

does have a few chuckles in him. When he's not in a huff, or skulking around raving about worrying, he's quite interesting to chat with. And Bear, dear old fellow, is always full of some yarn or other. I do miss them, you know."

Flewingam nodded, and pointed his good hand in the direction of a large tent.

"That'll be the hospital tent. I'll just go in and get this broken wing patched up, then we'll see if we can't see General Greymouse. You come and wait inside so some duty sergeant won't snap you up."

The two friends went inside, and a man in a white apron came out and took Flewingam behind a lowered canvas flap, leaving Otter sitting alone to wait. There was nothing to pass the time with, so he fell to listening to the hurrying, noisy sounds of the army outside, preparing itself for battle. Shouts and curses broke back and forth over the louder clink of weaponry or wagon, and far away, like the promise of a thunderstorm on a hot humid July morning, came the distant thumping of big guns. Otter had heard the noise of bombardments many times on his journey, but this barrage grew louder still, until the very earth trembled from the pounding reply and answer of the huge cannons. Instead of dying away, to be followed by the ragged din of small arms, this bombardment increased its pace. Even the medical orderly who worked at a field desk before Otter halted in his work to listen, whistled, and shook his head.

"I'm glad I'm not over *there* this morning" he mused, half to Otter, half to himself. "But I expect we'll be busy enough ourselves before the day is out," he ended cryptically. His pale, thin features contracted into a smile.

Otter walked to the open flap of the hospital tent and peered out. Platoons and squadrons marched by, singing, and the cold air hung heavy with the white breath of many men. Above the mist cloud raised by the soldiers, Otter could make out a distant, brownish gray pillar of smoke that had billowed upward from away in the direction of the enemy lines. The bombardment continued, and the lines of men thinned as they passed the door where Otter watched. Looking off to his right, he saw an unbroken string of men and equipment winding away over the soiled white snow in the direction where the smoke pall hung. The beginning of the long line was almost out of sight now, and reminded Otter of a dark bluish green snake rippling away into some high meadow grass on a faraway summer when he rested by his quiet stream from play.

A sudden whistling grated across the rust-colored edges of the sky, was silenced, then a tall, towering geyser of debris rose up to a great height, and the earth trembled violently. Otter's ears were buffeted with a deafening, reverberating boom. He regained his balance, and looked out again. Like ants in a disturbed hill, the tiny, faraway figures of men scurried here and there, filling his visions with thousands of crawling small things. Another series of whistle grates, and more muddy brown geysers lifted their heads into the cold morning air. The bursts were still far toward the front of the line of troops, but an occasional explosion fell long, behind the vanguard, ripping apart a tent not half a mile from where Otter watched, an awesome curiosity aroused in him.

A figure raced by Otter, bumping him aside. The medical orderly shouted back over his shoulder at him, "Find cover, you ass. Those are incoming bursts," and so saying, fled away to the safety of a long, zigzagging trench. Loud whooshing whumps rocked the hospital tent. Otter bolted through the drawn flap where the doctor had taken Flewingam.

In his haste, he left the firearm where he had dropped it when the orderly had brushed him aside.

"Friend Flewingam, where are you?" Otter yelled, trying to be heard over the terrible explosions.

Flewingam's head appeared from beneath an iron bedstead.

"Come here, quickly. Get down here with me. It won't stop much, but at least the debris won't get us." The man pulled Otter brusquely down beside him.

"What does all this mean? Are we attacked?" asked Otter breathlessly, trying hard to hold down the ugly fear that had crept over his heart. Waiting for the sky to split open on top of him wasn't a way in which Otter would like to face dangers. There was something so terrible about the idea, his limbs began to tremble, and he felt the strong, steady hand of Flewingam on his own.

"It's all right, Otter. These things aren't very accurate, and they only shoot them over to try to frighten us."

"They're enough to frighten me. And what happens if one of them falls on your head? Does that only frighten you, too?" Otter was beginning to regret bitterly having been led to his destruction by this man.

As quickly as it had begun, it stopped, and the tent flap flew open before six cursing, sweating men. They carried a seventh, covered with dirt and blood, and hastily laid him upon the gleaming white table in the center of the room. Two of the men wore aprons such as the man who had led Flewingam away, and they had white bands tied about their faces.

"Get his shirt off," shouted one of the masked men. "And get lots of water."

An orderly burst out, running hard. "And you, get

my kit, quickly, lad. I'm afraid he's taken a grievous hurt." The masked doctor began quickly arranging a number of gleaming sharp instruments on the table beside where the injured man lay. The orderly, bearing a large caldron of water, returned, and soon the six figures moved silently about the man upon the table, hands going rapidly here and there, opening, closing, swabbing, scrubbing, sewing wounds, until after more than half an hour had passed, the masked figures stood away from the table, sighing wearily.

An elegantly uniformed man with silver markings at the shoulders came in and lingered a moment, still holding the flap in his outstretched hand.

"The general?" he asked hesitantly.

"He's going to make it," replied a doctor

Flewingam flinched as he heard the word. It was General Greymouse who had been wounded. He advanced toward the table where the silent figure lay.

"You, you there, soldier, what are you men doing in here?" snapped an orderly, approaching Otter and Flewingam.

"I was having a hurt mended when the barrage began. We took shelter here."

"Well, get on about your duties. Your wound is bandaged."

Flewingham looked down at the ashen, drawn face of General Greymouse.

"I had intelligence for the general," said Flewingam.

"It'll have to wait," broke in the other doctor, removing his surgical gloves. "The general is in no shape to talk to anyone."

"Come here, trooper," the man with silver embroidered on his trousers ordered. "I'm General Greymouse's next in command. What intelligence do you carry that's so urgent?"

"Sir," said Flewingam, forgetting his injured right arm and wincing with pain at the movement.

"That's all right, soldier, I know you're wounded. What message have you?"

"I had counted on being able to tell the general sir."

"You can see for yourself he's wounded. Come, deliver your message."

Flewingam quickly told all he knew of the numbers and location of the Gorgolac raiding party they had encountered.

"And this fellow carries dire tidings from his homeland, from whence he's been upon the road for almost a hundred days, seeking General Greymouse's counsel."

The colonel looked from Flewingam to Otter. "Are you in the service?" he asked.

"No sir, I'm waterfolk by trade, and come bearing news of a friend of the general's."

"A friend of the general's? How is he called? What army does he command? Is he upon the way to aid us?"

Otter answered each of the questions as best he could.

"He commands no army, sir, or at least none that I know of, and he is called Froghorn Fairingay, and he's not on the way here, or at least if he is, he wasn't when I left him." Otter paused, gathered his breath, and went on. "He sent me to the aid of Mithra, I mean General Greymouse, for some dark power holds our Dwarf hostage, and General Greymouse might be able to help us get him back."

"Dark powers? Dwarfs? What sense is there to that? General Greymouse is battling a great army of heathens, from the northland, and has no time for such blather. Dark forces, indeed," the man snorted.

"It's all exactly as I say, sir. Froghorn Fairingay and Greyfax Grimwald are off on errands at this moment to gather the Circle, and it's most important I be able to speak with General Greymouse upon the matter."

Otter scolded himself for having mentioned the names of the two wizards, but he knew of no other way to convince this man of the urgency of speaking with General Greymouse.

"Grimwald, Grimwald," mused the colonel aloud. "It seems I recall the general mentioning that name before. Where is this man now?"

"I know not, sir."

"Well, at any rate, your news shall have to wait upon the general's recovery." He turned to Flewingam. "Your intelligence, soldier, comes in good time. I'm afraid the raiders you spoke of are gathering to strike a blow upon our flanks in the battle today. But now we shall be ready. We shall have a little, very unpleasant surprise for them." The colonel laughed grimly to himself. "As for you two, you may come with me as runners, where you may be of some use."

"But when shall I be able to speak with General Greymouse, sir?" asked Otter, so close to his quest's end, yet further than if he had still been snug in his faraway holt by the river.

"We'll see, trooper, we'll see. Now we must be off. There's much to do, and you shall need your strength."

The colonel moved away, motioning them after him, and the three made their way along the littered company streets, now pocked and covered with fallen tents and men, and through the busy work of clearing and carrying away the wounded and dead, they marched to the large tent that was the headquarters for General Greymouse. Otter saw one of the walls was torn and shredded from a blast.

Inside, men moved and worked around tables of maps, and mock battle sites, speaking tersely, hand-ing slips of paper back and forth, and as the colonel came in, all stood quickly to attention.

"Carry on, men," snapped the colonel, going on through the bustling room. At the tent flap of his compartment, he halted.

"Denwild, these men are to be used as runners. Give them something to eat, then put them on duty."

"Yes sir," said Denwild.

"And see if you can't round up a decent uniform for this fellow," he added, indicating Otter. "I won't have him going about sloppy." The colonel disappeared behind the flap.

"It looks like you've been drafted," laughed Flewingam.

Otter did not think the matter funny at all, and whistled his disapproval of Flewingam's jest in his own tongue. He wondered what the gruff colonel would say if he knew he now had one furry, gray, very unhappy otter in his service.

"Would probably ask if I were a general," he said aloud, getting into the drab fatigue uniform Denwild had brought him.

"At least it will make an interesting entry in the lore book," he consoled himself, "If I ever get the chance to write it."

At that moment Denwild approached and handed him a sealed brown parcel.

"Take this to the captain of the fifth squadron of field guns. They shouldn't be hard to find. They wear the insignia of a cannon over their left shoulders."

"I'd better go with him to make sure," offered Flewingam.

"All right, but be quick. We've many orders to send out, and will need you back here."

Otter and Flewingam set off at a rapid walk in the direction of the gunnery captain's battery.

From beyond the rim of low hills that ran downward into the valley below, out of sight, came the crashing flurry of many men joined in a heavy fight. The steady popping of rifles swelled to a deafening crescendo, broken occasionally by numerous bumping bursts of grenade or shell.

"At least," Otter offered up a logical answer to the question that troubled his mind, "I'm not there."

In reply, a burst of angry, fiery, buzzing sounds began crackling about his ears.

"Run," shouted Flewingam. "They've broken through somewhere."

Leaning forward, and moving faster than he thought man legs could carry him, he saw away off to his right a line of grotesque soldiers approaching, clad all in black uniforms, firing their weapons steadily at him. He reached the safety of a large rock and fell across Flewingam.

"How do you like the life of a soldier?" he gasped, looking up at Otter's panting form.

Otter had no time for reply, for immediately behind them, they heard the sound of more firing, growing heavier, until at last it was a steady, pulsing roar in their ears.

Raising his head cautiously, Otter watched as the reinforcements sent from their camp fell upon the intruding enemy and forced them slowly into retreat. The air all about them was alive with the crackling, popping sound, and it looked to Otter as if the world were filled with the flying lead darts. Flewingam sat calmly behind the protective arm of the boulder, waiting until they could move on again.

"Enough excitement for you?" laughed Flewingam, gravely.

"I would prefer less of it, friend. Man's amusement appeals little to my sense of adventure. I'd prefer a good frisk of a swimming trip, or at most, a scamper or two in some quick flow of river rapid."

"You speak strangely, Otter. You're as odd a man as ever I've chanced acquaintance with, meaning no harm. All the tales you've told me seem fairy-book stories for children." Flewingam finished, listening a moment, then raised himself. "But come, we'll speak more of that latter. Now we must make a break for it while we have the chance."

The two set off in a crouching run, away from the receding fight behind them.

They found the gunnery captain after a brief search, delivered their message, took his answer, and returned cautiously to the headquarters tent, giving Denwild the brown folder from the captain.

"The colonel wants a word with you," he said, looking sternly at Otter.

"What does he want of me?" he asked, feeling out of place in his strange new clothing.

"He didn't tell me," snapped Denwild.

"More questions, I suppose." Otter resigned himself, and marched smartly into the colonel's private quarters.

The colonel sat at a paper-strewn desk, looking important, and shuffling about a bunch of official documents.

"Come in, and stand at ease. I'll be with you in a moment." His voice took on an air of kind wisdom.

Otter stood fidgeting before the desk, wondering if it would be proper or not to change forms while this man spoke. He wondered what Froghorn would advise him to do if he were here.

"I should imagine he's capering about off somewhere far beyond this mess," he decided gloomily, speaking aloud.

"Who might *he* be?" The colonel took up his unending, annoying habit of speaking only in questions.

"Fairingay, sir," answered Otter.

"I was going to ask you about him and this other man you mentioned. Grimwald, wasn't it?" The colonel rolled a pencil about on the desk top, and Otter, thinking it looked like an amusing game, reached a hand-paw to join, then checked himself quickly. Men were not easy to play with, and hated to share their fun. He forced himself to keep still.

"Yes, Grimwald, sir."

"How is it that these two men knew our whereabouts? And how came you to find us so easily?"

"I came upon my friend wounded, Flewingam, who's outside there, not more than three days ago. He was kind enough to show me where the camp lay."

"Was he alone?"

"Yes sir, alone and wounded, and if I had not chanced upon him, I dare say he would have been done for. If not by his hurt, then by the Gorgolac raiders who discovered us."

The colonel listened intently, and was silent a moment.

"There is enough truth to what you say to lead me to think you're lying," came his harsh, low accusation. "All these tall yarns about men who sent you and having to see General Greymouse doesn't pull the rug over my eyes. I think you've come from the enemy, to scout us out. But you were caught dead to rights, before you could escape back and report." The colonel chuckled triumphantly. "And to think I gave you the perfect means to make your break. What made you come back? You could have gotten away clean if you'd kept on."

"Escape to where, sir? I came to see General Greymouse, and I'll go nowhere until I relate to him the message Froghorn sent him."

"You're right there, spy-tongue, you'll be going nowhere at all, except before the firing squad. After, of course, a fair hearing of the evidence against you." The colonel paused, leering at him. "Denwild," he bellowed, "take him away."

Denwild came in with two other armed men, who grasped Otter firmly, and before he could speak, they pulled him outside, where Flewingam was also captured, standing between two more guards.

"Take them down to the quartermaster's," ordered Denwild. "They have a stout tent there that will hold them."

Flewingam and Otter were marched briskly away, rifle barrels prodding their faltering feet onward.

At the quartermaster's supply tent, they were thrust inside the dark, crate-filled room, and a scowling soldier left at the door to watch them.

Flewingam sighed.

"I guess we're in the soup now," he said sadly. "It was a darker deed than we knew, when General Greymouse was wounded. Our colonel has long aspired to high command, but he never stood a chance as long as General Greymouse was well. Even I, who detest the fighting, hold Greymouse in high esteem. He is a very wise man, except for the fact that he's a general."

"My friend spoke highly of him," offered Otter, "and his judgment of men is far superior to mine." Otter paced toward the door, to be met with the ugly barrel of a rifle poked at him. "As far as I'm concerned, being a superior judge of men is the last thing in the world I seek. All of them appear bent upon their own destruction, and let 'em, I say, for all the good will they have for me." He returned and sat down heavily.

"They won't shoot us," said Flewingam. "At least not while General Greymouse lives. Even our friend the colonel wouldn't run such a risk of displeasing him with that." Flewingam sat down beside him.

"Cheer up, friend, at least we have safe cover, and no need to go about out there, where we might be hurt. And now we have time to pass, and you can spin me more of your odd tales." He smiled warmly at Otter.

Otter agreed that they were, for the moment, out of harm's way, and being heartened at that, he began his tale again, and talked long into the afternoon.

Flewingam did not interrupt him, but at times the noise of the battle drowned his speech, although these harsh sounds seemed to be dying away as Otter drew near the part of his story where he'd met Flewingam in the ruined farmhouse, and as night approached, and the battle ranged farther away, he finished. Flewingam opened his mouth to comment, or question Otter about some point or other, when the tread of marching feet drew up before the door of the tent.

"Prisoners arise and come with us," ordered a gruff voice, and they were escorted away to eat, then to the headquarters tent, where the colonel wished to question them further. There they learned General Greymouse had recovered enough to talk, and after the colonel had told him of the strange capture of the two spies, the general had sternly rebuked him, and ordered him to bring the two men to his bedside.

Otter, at last at journey's end for the moment, was led in to see the great man.

THE DARKNESS BEGINS TO GATHER

"LOC ALLA DULA INDOMINE"

By forced march, Dwarf drew near the first man settlement Otter and Bear had passed through by early evening. Darkness was lingering above the pale last glow of light when he stepped resolutely up to the barred gate and called out loudly.

"Hail, friends, Broco, Lore Master, Lord UnderEarth, seeks to pass into your city."

An alarm went up with a great jangling beat behind the walls, and a rapid volley of shots exploded from the firing posts, sending Broco scuttling to the safety of the ditch that bordered the road.

"That's how you'll pass our gates, scumlick," laughed a cruel, lisping voice.

Dwarf fumed in the snow-filled bottom of his shelter. "Drat and dwarf curse on the bunch of them," he huffed, his hat tumbled down over his eyes. "I'll teach them better manners for it," he mumbled, removing his hat, spinning it on his hand. An old dwarfish rune he remembered from Tubal's lore book came to his mind, and he repeated the words, made the proper motion with his hat, and sat back to wait.

The harsh rasp of a voice called out again. "We're

ready now to welcome you, filthbreath. Come, my comrades and I haven't eaten all day. You'll at least fill half our cooking pot," it sneered. A grinding noise followed, as the great bolt was shot back to open the gate.

Dwarf grew uneasy, trying to remember if he had spoken the entire spell. If he had left something undone, he would be in for it now, for two black-clad, misshapen men, or at least half-men forms, came forward out of the gate toward his hiding place, their firearms ready in their hands.

Before Dwarf could repeat the ritual, they had dragged him roughly from the ditch.

"He don't look more than a mouthful," complained Lakmog, picking Broco up by his ear. Dwarf twisted in pain, but the man-beast's iron-handed fist held him fast.

"We'll use him for dessert," put in Mishgnash, roughly feeling Dwarf's arm. "He seems to be meaty enough."

The two grotesque forms, Gorgolacs, carried Dwarf back through the gates, laughing and poking his ribs, and took him to the lockhouse, behind which other men dressed in black stood watching from the low door of a guard shack.

"Bake him, broil him, clean his bones," they chanted in unison, pounding their firearms against the hard snow-packed ground.

Dwarf, between painful pokes or pinches, tried to recall what exactly it was he had left out of his spell, and as he ran through it all for the third time, he was heaved brusquely into a steel-doored cell and left to himself for the moment. Broco regained his wind, looking about his prison. His captors had taken his sword and pack, and the hunger grew as he raged to himself at his mistake of a spell that had allowed him to be taken again.

"This begins to bore me," he huffed. "If it's not some jawing by an overgrown cur of a wolf, it's these troll apes pinching and dwarfhandling me. Now where is it I went wrong with that infernal business?" Dwarf paced angrily a few steps, and stopped. There in the darkness before him trembled Corporal Cranfallow and Ned Thinvoice, drawn close into small bundles of terror.

"Hullo," said Dwarf, surprised at the quaking men.

"Wh-who are yo-you?" Cranfallow's voice shivered loudly.

"Broco, heir and Dwarflord UnderEarth, Lore Master, Seeker of the Light," Dwarf huffed, puffed into believing these two men terrified of his terrible countenance.

"Do they hold you hostage, too?" asked Thinvoice, more sure of himself as he looked carefully at Dwarf, finding him only half again as large as he had thought him.

"They *think* they hold me, but I've a surprise or two under my hat for the likes of those trolls. Even the Dark Queen herself can't long keep Broco, Dwarflord, prisoner."

Cranfallow was seized with wonder at this small fellow who spoke so boldly, and talked of Dwarflords and Dark Queens. But this was probably another of the long series of misfortunes that had befallen them since the appearance of those other two witches that had caused their ruin and fall. Cranfallow shuddered as he recalled the swift doom that had overtaken them not three days after the bear witch had gone. An enemy force had overrun them, and these half-men, half-beast soldiers had eaten everyone in the village, one by one, until he and Thinvoice, and this new sorcerer, were the only ones left unharmed.

Dwarf paced furiously back and forth, hat far

down over his forehead, thinking. He ignored the gaping stares of the two men.

"Now, In'mun dula dil,
Mot in dun a' brill
Loc Alla Dula Indomine,
Rocco ronco il da fine,"

he chanted slowly, going over it again, then repeating it in reverse.

"That must be it, it simply must. Surely I haven't let it slip my mind so soon."

Dwarf fell into silence, and there came a golden arc of pale light that lighted the room, and down the bridge of the glowing ray came two small, almost invisible figures. Broco, with his back turned, didn't see the light bridge or the figures at once, but Cranfallow and Thinvoice broke in together with their chorus of rattling teeth.

"Eh, what's that?" asked Dwarf, turning. "Upon my beard," he cried, delighted and relieved. "It's about time." He crossed and sat before the pale golden figures, and fell into a tongue the two men could not understand. After what seemed hours, Dwarf got up, the light bridge glowed brightly once, then disappeared, and all was once more left in darkness.

"Well, that settles that. It seems they took so long because I neglected to mention exactly what plane I was on," explained Dwarf to the dumbfounded men.

"Ahhhh," moaned Cranfallow, "have mercy on our souls, another witch. A curse on the day I ever laid eyes on the bunch of them," he sobbed into his hands, teeth beating madly, body twitching. Thinvoice was frozen where he sat.

"Here, here, old fellow. Obviously you can't have anything to do with these brutes out there, so you have nothing to fear. Come, friend, tell me your names, and be of good cheer. We'll be out of this before morning," Dwarf tried to reassure them.

"If we're not had up for supper," groaned Thinvoice. "They seem to have no end to their hunger."

"My little surprise for them may spoil their appetites a bit," laughed Dwarf. "They'll be thinking of other things than food before this night is out." Broco went to the iron-barred window. "Come, one of you, and hoist me up that I might see out."

Neither of the men moved.

"Come," said Dwarf, in a sterner voice. "If you want to keep out of the dinner pot, come and hoist me up."

Cranfallow slowly rose and went to the small figure of Dwarf. Hesitantly he touched him, then convinced he wouldn't be burned or otherwise harmed, he put Dwarf upon his shoulders and stood close up to the window.

"Do you know this place, friend, or are you strangers here too?"

"Corporal Cranfallow, sir, and my friend Ned and I were of the garrison that defended this town, so I know it well enough." Cranfallow, his fear lessening as he spoke, went on, relating to Dwarf how they had been surprised in the darkness by the superior enemy force, and the town devoured, save he and Thinvoice.

"Most likely, all because of the likes of them other two, the bloody bear witch and the one what hexed us all to sleep," he added. "No harm to yourself, sir, and I knows you means none to me, nor my friend. Just seems that anytime you gets into anything unnatural, something dreadful always gets you."

"A bear witch?" Dwarf tumbled quickly from the man's shoulders, landing lightly. "What sort of fellow was he?"

"Well, sir, he comes up in the night, the first one,

and has a bite to eat, and fills our heads with all sorts of strange goings-on, like I never heard before. Then he ups and hexes us all to sleep, and we wakes up the next morning to the commander bringing us another one. I brought food to him right in this very room, and he told me things that stood my hair up straight on end, he did, and while I was standing here, right here, he ups and turns his bloody self into a living, breathing bear."

Dwarf had approached Cranfallow, and took the man's sleeve lightly.

"You mean a real bear, friend? Or were you full of malt?" Dwarf's mind raced. He'd found word of Otter and Bear, he knew, but he couldn't understand the strange tale this man told of their being of man forms. He had no way of knowing of their meeting with Froghorn, or the secret he had given them that enabled them to change their forms at will, but he knew this man was too frightened to lie or try to deceive him, and he knew, too, that from what the man remembered so vividly of the bear witch, it could be none other than his old friend.

"Clever Bear, dear old ass," he laughed as Cranfallow finished his tale of Bear's escape. "I never would have thought it of him."

"I wouldn't have thought it about him neither, if I hadn't seen it with my own two good peepers. I didn't get these stripes of mine by going about spreading kegtales. I has my drop of malt, I'll grant, but not so's you'd be able to tell it on me." Cranfallow sat down on the hard bed. "But who is you, and you all full of those powers too."

"I'm a friend of the fellows you just told me of. I have been held prisoner for quite some space of time by the Dark Queen, but am escaped now, in search of my friends. You're both welcome to come along with me, if you have a mind. If it is as you say, there won't be much to stay in this town for."

"We'd have no more brains than the droppings of swine if we was not to travel on with you. But we ain't out of the woods yet, leastways not to my way of thinking. For one thing, we can't gets out of here," concluded Thinvoice wisely.

"How do you mean to spring us, sir, if it's not too much trouble my asking?" Cranfallow looked down at his feet, ashamed for having fallen in with the lot of a dwarf witch, but more afraid of falling into a chafing pot.

"Keep your eyes and ears unplugged, and you'll see," said Dwarf. "The fun should be about to begin, if my timing's not all off. Lift me up again, good Cranfallow, and I'll see."

Cranfallow stooped low, and Broco slipped onto his shoulders once more. Outside, a loud, ugly rumor of a fight broke the stillness.

"I'll has your head for that, wormslime," came a low, snarling voice. A firearm went off, followed by a grunt and the sound of a heavy body falling.

"Now that's done it, Amogth. What's gotten into your head? He meant no harm." Another guttural snarl.

"He's the one what flung his dagger at me. I didn't start this."

"You has finished it, though, fool. Now we has to answer to Burlag."

"A curse take him and his high speech. I got no use for his likes."

"He commands here, scumbreath, don't forget. And you knows how he treats those what crosses him."

The voices faded, the two Gorgolac soldiers moving away, out of hearing of Dwarf or his companions.

"Good, good," gloated Dwarf. "They've begun. Now they won't be thinking so much of their precious supper."

"One killing ain't going to hold them up long, sir," corrected Cranfallow. "They don't think nothing at all of killing or fighting. As like as not, they'll have him up for supper, too."

"No doubt they will," agreed Dwarf, "but the excitement has only begun. You'd see some real fireworks if only I had my dragon stone." Dwarf bitterly regretted the loss of that precious heirloom, for he'd carried it long, like all his father's fathers before him. It was of mighty powers of old, although not as powerful as the magical powers of the wizards, but on occasion, and performed right, the spells of the dragon stone could dazzle the eye with a bursting, brilliant display to stand any but the wizards themselves in stupefied, wondering amazement.

Many roaring and dreadful-sounding voices raised themselves at the gates of the town, calling loudly their promise of death to the Gorgolac soldiers there.

Their captors rushed back and forth about the compound, shouting and shrieking oaths in their own tongue, and firing their weapons into the air.

Dwarf allowed himself a quick giggle.

"What's happening out there, Cranny?" Thinvoice strained to see over Cranfallow's figure at the window, where Dwarf perched atop his shoulder still.

"It sounds like an army at the gates. A whole bloody army out of nowhere," answered Cranfallow, trying to see more of what was happening beyond the gates. At the other end of town, a brilliant, flaming shadow had begun to move from that direction toward them.

"Have you done all this, sir?" asked Thinvoice respectfully.

"Some of it, although most of it is merely illusions my two friends have conjured up. But our jolly fellows outside there don't know that."

The crash and din of weapons going off grew to a deafening roar. Shouts and cries rose, and as the plunderers of the city set about defending their front, the blazing, molten red-gold flames leapt high and besieged their rear flanks. The fray was shortly over; those that yet lived fled away over the mountains, to be eaten or maimed by the wild dogs there. No enemy had in truth attacked them, but their fear at what they thought was an opposing army had driven them mad with rage and terror, and those who were slain were felled by their comrades in their blind fits. Soon the noise and screams died away, leaving the sudden silence behind heavy and complete.

"Well," said Cranfallow at last. "We's done the bloody lot of them, or they've fled, but here we sits locked up as tight as doomsday, and here we'll sits till then, I wager." He looked reproachfully at Dwarf, who had gotten down and walked to the great, massive steel door.

Dwarf made the sign of the sacred alder, touched the lock, and the door swung loose on its hinges.

"My kin are masters at doors and their secrets," he explained. "And it's a rare door that has runes I can't undo, or at least not upon this world."

Cranfallow and Thinvoice gratefully followed after Dwarf, who was poking about the area, trying to find his gear. Unable to find his own sword, he took a firearm from one of the slain beast soldiers, and began searching for food and a drink of water. Working his dwarf spells always parched his throat, and his lips and tongue felt dry and cracked. Cranfallow guided him to the storeroom and well house, and soon the three sat down to a meager meal of potatoes and cabbage, but to the hungry company it was a feast, and before the meal was through, their three plates had been polished clean, and the supper washed down with cold, pure water.

Cranfallow lowered his water bowl and looked steadily at Dwarf.

"What path draws your feet now, sir? Would you minds if Ned and I tags along? Or at least until we can get back to our army?"

"I'd welcome your company, friends," said Dwarf courteously. "Three together might keep us from harm from the likes of those." He indicated the fallen body of one of the Gorgolacs.

"With magical powers like yours, sir, what use would two fellows like us be?" asked Ned.

Dwarf frowned. "You must never mention my spells to a soul, friend. And your use is that you have a strong back and two good feet, and we'll most likely have need of both before we go too much farther."

"And how far mights that be, sir?" Cranfallow asked.

Dwarf told him he had come upon his home and lands in ruin, and how he had set forth to try to find his old comrades. Beyond finding them again, he had no notion as to what he should do, or which way to steer, except in their footsteps. Now that he knew they had passed this way, he was eager to set out immediately, but his weariness held him until he would be fresh again, and after setting Ned to watch, Dwarf and Cranfallow took their turns at sleep.

With daybreak barely more than a pale band of golden light across the low sky, the three companions set out from the deserted, ravished town, guiding their steps toward the next settlement, a day's march ahead, if they hurried, and Dwarf was anxious to reach there to inquire after his friends, so the pace was set at a rapid walk, and the three strode on all that morning, took an hour's break at noon, and as the sun went down over Atlanton Earth, crossed the bridged river, answered the sentry's challenge, and entered a walled stronghold that Cranfallow knew. The friends found an inn shortly, and tired and hungry, went in to their supper and beds.

The innkeeper, a hawk-nosed man of great age, looked on and marveled at the two strange men, gaunt-looking enough for all that, and their strange traveling companion, Dwarf.

"Whatever is this world coming to?" the man muttered, setting out their plates, shaking his head. As if it wasn't enough a war going on, men taking up with the likes of dwarfs and such.

"Things just isn't right in that order," he grumbled aloud, then stopped just inside the galley door, trying to hear the words of the three strangers, who were talking in low, earnest voices, about something or other he didn't quite catch. He moved closer, bent low, and placed his ear against the door.

DWARF HAS A RIDING LESSON

"What we needs is more arms," argued Ned Thinvoice, flushed from the glasses of thick, dark ale. "If we has more men and weapons, we won't have no trouble."

"I speak against that, Master Ned," said Broco, one pointed-toed shoe resting near the warmth of the open fire, "for where there are many, there is no speed. I have need of great haste now, and have no time to wait upon more feet than my own."

"You can't gets off by yourself, sir. Your safety lies in speed, but also enough strength to turn away an attack. From the way I sees it, these Gorgolac troops are strong enough in these parts. Any what can take a forted village is strong enough to settle a dwarf, sir, no offense, and I knows you has those wonderful powers and all." Cranfallow halted, remembering Dwarf's warning. "Anyhow, you'll needs the two of us for a bit longer."

"I don't doubt but that's true enough, good Cranfallow, and I thank you for your service. But I don't know exactly what it is I am about now, except that I must find my old comrades, and that road is as dark a mystery as any I've laid eyes on. I know they're somewhere, but I don't know to what destination or purpose, and yet that's where I must follow."

"Maybe they've gone seeking aid, thinking you're still held by that Dark Queen, or whoever, you was speaking of. There is still those about who stands up for the true and honest folks, what few there is left in these troubled times. I's heard of a great leader that's away in the mountains, but I can't say for sure whether that's just soldiers' talk or no. There must be some that knows, though, if we was to ask about."

"He goes by the name of Greymouse," offered Ned, feeling important and knowledgeable.

"That's him, General Greymouse. Folks say he's a mighty powerful man," said Cranfallow. Then, lowering his voice to a whisper, he added, "They say *he's* got the powers, too."

Dwarf couldn't recall ever having heard of the man they named but the two seemed struck with wonder when they spoke of him. If that were not his real name, he might indeed be one of the kings of the Circle, disguised as a common man, and too, if that were so, he might have word of the whereabouts of Greyfax or Froghorn, or possibly even Otter and Bear. It wasn't much of a promising plan, he admitted, but it was all he had to keep his hopes up, so he decided then he would set his course for the mountains, and seek this great leader with the odd-sounding name.

"Very well, I shall go in search of this man," said Dwarf. "And if you wish, you may come. I know not what dangers there are awaiting us, and I can't ask you to follow me, but if you will, you're welcome and I thank you. If not, we part friends, and good health and long life." Dwarf drained his coffee mug and called for the innkeeper to fetch them up a refill.

"Well, turn my old bones to salt if I've ever heard the likes," muttered the hawk-nosed proprietor, bursting back through the door where he'd been listening to the three comrades. He took the tankards and withdrew mumbling under his breath.

"I thinks our good host has been at the keyhole," laughed Thinvoice.

"Then I hopes his head is full," replied Cranfallow.

Dwarf looked after the receding figure of the host. "I hope he's up to no mischief. Our way is dark enough without meddling old fools interfering with us."

"He's nosy, but harmless enough," put in Cranfallow. "I's been in his house often enough in the past. Whatever else he is, he's not one to harm anyone purposely."

"An unpurposeful hurt can be as painful as any," said Dwarf, pacing to and fro restlessly before the fire.

Cranfallow fell silent.

Hawknose returned with the ale and coffee, followed by two more men, soldiers with dirty greatcoats and muddy boots. Their gear was that of horsemen, and the pungent smell of horseflesh was heavy upon them. One man carried a leather pouch over his shoulder, and was obviously a dispatch rider of some sort, and as he sat wearily down, he glanced over the companions, eyes finally coming to rest on Dwarf, still pacing before the fire.

"Hail, and well met, strangers. I see by your markings you're in the 3rd Battalion," spoke the first man to Cranfallow and Thinvoice.

"We was, but no more. Our outfit was butchered, and we're the last, escaped from under their noses, with the help of Master Dwarf here," said Cranfallow, moving away from the fire so the newcomers could warm themselves.

The man's eyes widened as he studied Dwarf. "Be you of the Old Square, sir?" he asked politely of Broco.

"Nay, friend, I'm of no army. I come from the western land in search of my comrades, and have only been traveling with these two good fellows for a short time. We escaped together from an enemy-held garrison yestereve, and are trying to decide ourselves what's best to be done."

"We came through the checkpoint late this afternoon. All was deserted and in ruins, and we saw many of the enemy slain. Were you only three that cast that number down?" the second rider, who called himself Cinch, spoke.

"Only three, and luck," said Dwarf. "They fell to fighting among themselves and we escaped in the fray."

The first soldier shook his head in wonder. "I've seen strange things in my time, but this is the first dwarf warrior I've come on. You speak well for yourself, sir. My name is Quickspur, and I serve in the legions of Wentworth."

"Then well met, friend. My good Cranfallow there and Thinvoice and myself are at your service."

Hawknose brought in two mugs of ale for his guests.

"Thank you, kind keep. My bones are frozen to the quick. This will go down quite well," he said, lifting his mug in salute, and the others followed after, with many "good healths" and "long lifes" spoken over cup tops.

After a supper of hot soup and wheat bread, the guests sat once more before the fire, mulling ale and exchanging news.

Quickspur and Cinch, it was learned, were upon the road with urgent messages for a commander that camped in the hills bordering General Greymouse's rear area, and the two men offered to carry the three with them that far.

"Our steeds are strong enough to carry double, if we go carefully, and I doubt your weight to be more than my horse can carry, Master Broco, even with another fellow behind. You may ride before me, and you, Thinvoice, on my cantle." Cinch rose as he spoke, and wiping the flecks of foam from his mustache, yawned and stretched. "And now I shall find my rest. I'm full of the journey, and the ale has made me quite drowsy."

The others rose, and as Quickspur crossed the door, he motioned Dwarf aside.

"We'll be away before full light, sir, so if you would meet us here to breakfast, we'll be on our way the sooner."

"I'll have our host awaken us, then," said Dwarf, thanking the man. "Your offer is kind, and it'll make our journey much easier, for the time. My feet could use the rest of riding awhile, although I dare say I haven't been much about horses."

Quickspur laughed. "Perhaps we can find you mounts at our next camp, to carry you where you will. Going about on foot is a weary and dangerous business these days."

"You speak truth there, friend," said Dwarf, making for the stairs that led to their sleeping quarters.

"Until the morrow, good rest." Quickspur turned away to follow after Cinch, already disappearing into a bedroom.

Dwarf blew out the lamp, listening to his two companions already snoring, and went to the shuttered window. He opened a slat, peering out over the cold snowlight that dimly lit the sleeping village, his eyes following the dark road into the distance, trying to see the invisible outlines of the mountains.

"We shall make up some time tomorrow," he mused aloud, quietly shutting the window slat again, and lying down on the stiffly starched sheets of the bed. Its comfort overcame him, and he fell asleep quickly, warm and snug for the moment, and at last with a clear plan in mind.

At dawn, Hawknose wakened the sleeping trio with the news that a large company had passed through in the night and the threat of a large battle loomed near at hand, and the innkeeper told them of the Gorgolacs and Worlughs who were reported seen no more than ten leagues distant. Their host was shaken by the news, and wrung his hands as he related his unsettling tale.

"I'll sleep easier knowing you three were about to help defend my inn, I would, or those other two who came last night. Your speech shows you to be of a good sort, and not the usual ragtaggle that's been my ruin since these wars began."

"And what speech of ours have you heard that makes you think we won't rob you as quickly as the next fellow?" Dwarf growled, drawing himself up a bit and laying his hand to his firearm. Hawknose stiffened and fell at Dwarf's knees, still being almost as tall as the little man.

"I beg you, spare me, good Master Dwarf," he blubbered, clasping at Broco's shoulders.

"Come, come, old fellow, we mean you no harm. I only meant to scold you for having an ear where it ought not be. Come, I jest, we mean you no harm."

Hawknose rose, thanking the three men profusely. "I'll sees to it your sacks are filled with victuals before you leaves, and throw in a few pieces of dried fruit or two."

"You'll be amply rewarded, friend, for your trouble. Are Quickspur and Cinch up and ready?" asked Dwarf, pulling his hat down firmly onto his head and adjusting his pack straps.

Hawknose started. "I thought I told you," he began, tugging at his chin whiskers. "They were up two hours ago, and gone with the company that passed through. An officer came to the inn and fetched them, but they left this message for you." The host handed Dwarf a sealed parchment envelope, boldly addressed in a thin, high hand.

To Sir Broco, Dwarfmaster:

Good tidings to your travel. We have been called away on dire matters, and supplied with fresh mounts to go on. We ride as I write this, but the good inn master is to deliver this, and the horses which we leave you as a loan. You may deliver them up to the stable sergeant in the village you are bound for. Show him this letter, for he knows my hand. Perhaps he shall be able to give you fresh mounts to continue your quest.

Health and good fortunes,
Sergeant T. Quickspur

P.S.

It is most important that you go quickly, for you must be out of these perimeters by dawn. A battle is close joined even as I write, and you risk being caught up if you are not far out of reach.

The letter was sealed at the bottom, with common tallow, impressed by the man's signet ring.

"The horses are below in the stables. I had my boy saddle them for you, sir," said Hawknose, waiting until Dwarf had finished the letter before speaking.

"You have done most excellent well by us, Master

Hawknose. I would that we had more to pay you with than thanks." Dwarf removed a small, finely wrought ring from his left hand. "Here, take this, old fellow, and may it keep you safe until the end of your days."

The innkeeper stared in wonder at the fine ring, but before he could thank Dwarf, the three of them had gone quickly downstairs and out into the courtyard.

"Can you ride, Cranfallow?" asked Dwarf, hesitant at the thought of going about on the high perch of a horse.

"Yes, I used to do it often as a boy," replied Cranfallow.

"I'm not much of a hand at it," broke in Ned. "But then I guess I'll risks it, seeing as how it's saving my poor feet."

"Good. I'll ride behind you, Cranfallow, but mark me, if you so much as jog me, I'll have you turned into worse than stable chaff," threatened Dwarf, and Ned and Cranfallow helped Dwarf clumsily onto the saddle.

Broco sat awkwardly, holding on tightly to the packstraps. Cranfallow mounted, then Ned, and the three companions moved slowly into the stable yards. The two men raised their hands in farewell to Hawknose, but Dwarf stubbornly clenched his teeth, and held Cranfallow fast about the waist.

"You're choking me," he gasped, turning his head to Dwarf, who only slackened his grip a breath's length.

"Get on with it," Dwarf bellowed, terrified, frightening the horse into a trot, and the trio set out, Cranfallow first, Broco bouncing up and down behind him, promising a string of gloomy ends to everyone, and Thinvoice following, holding back his laughter at the sight of Dwarf, hat jammed down over his ears, short, stout legs flying. And in this order the two horses carried the friends out once more to the road toward the thin, smoke-gray mountains, far ahead.

As they rode on, the ugly rattle of rifle fire erupted from somewhere across the fields behind them, and a gray haze rose up over the brilliant snow-covered farmlands.

Upon hearing this, and reminded of Quickspur's note, Dwarf huffed up all his last remaining courage and urged Cranfallow to hasten his pace.

INTERVIEW WITH THE GENERAL

In the tent where General Greymouse lay, dim candles gave off their weak light. Otter searched the compartment carefully after his eyes readjusted to the shadows. A great many maps hung on three of the walls, and on the fourth, what appeared to Otter to be a star chart of some sort. He had seen a few like it in the books Dwarf had taken from Tubal Hall, but this map was much larger, and looked very important, covered with red and black and white pins with colored flags on the ends. A huge carven desk with golden-scroll-worked legs stood at one wall, before the star chart, and what smelled to Otter of pine resin incense hung thickly in the air.

"Stand still a moment that I may see you," came a low voice from nowhere, "And speak your errand."

Otter, flustered and afraid, began speaking in his own tongue, his words tumbling out over one another, and he went on for a few moments like that, until he realized what he had done.

"I'm sorry, sir," he blurted in common man tongue, "but . . ."

"I understand you well enough, Olther, but you

must slow down. It is long since I have heard that dialect."

As Otter stood before the desk, an outline of a figure cloaked in gray began to form, lighted at first at the edges by the flamelight of the candles, then glowing softly, circled by a pale white reflection. Otter bowed low.

"Master," he said, greeting the wizard in high speech.

"You must quickly tell me of your travels, and all news you carry with you, but come, take a cup and drink first. Our time is not that hurried that we must forget manners."

Mithramuse poured Otter a shining cup of a shimmering liquid, the same he had had long ago before the wizard fire of Greyfax Grimwald. He drank, feeling the cool drink ease away the past weariness and memories of danger.

"I understand little, sir, of such goings-on, but Froghorn Fairingay charged Bear and me to set out in search of you. Some dark power has captured Dwarf, and I left Bear behind, since there was no need of both of us leaving our homes. Froghorn went to seek the lady of the Mountains, and that's about as much of the story as I know. I've lost Bear, and Dwarf is a prisoner somewhere, and I've been traveling about in this clumsy shape for more days than I care to remember." He paused, indicating his man body, sighing wearily.

"You have done well, Olther," spoke Mithramuse. A sound outside the tent flap alerted the wizard. Quickly the soft glow about him passed, and in its place came General Greymouse, slouched and bandaged, in the large chair behind the desk. He motioned for Otter to see who was there, lifting a feeble hand in the direction of the sound. Otter opened the flap quickly, hoping to surprise their eavesdropper, but only the rapidly disappearing figure of the colonel was to be seen.

"I think he's gone, sir. It was the kind colonel who thought we were spies."

"Ah, yes. He's a very ambitious man. Still, he has a part to play, as do all of us, for good or ill." Greymouse paused, putting the cup to his lips again. "Even I can't foresee the end of that," he said. "But come nearer, Master Otter, and I shall try to fill in your story as best I can for you."

A tiny silver ring glowed faintly on the wizard's hand, then its dark stone lightened, revealing a swirling haze that spun and whirled until Otter grew dizzy watching it; then the stone cleared, and there in that small frame, large figures grew. Otter could make out what appeared to be towers, but they were of odd shapes, turtles and swans, and he saw there too a tiny figure of a man standing alone, glancing around as if searching for something, then looking directly up at them from the ring's depth.

"Froghorn," gasped Otter.

"Yes, it is our friend Fairingay. He is in the halls of Cypher."

"Is that far?" asked Otter, always bewildered and delighted at Wizard's work.

"Far?" mused Mithramuse, "Yes, you might say far, although in another sense, no more than what's under your nose is far."

"He's speaking, but I can't hear him," lamented Otter, leaning close and watching the lips of Fairingay move.

"He bids you greetings, and congratulates you on your success."

"Does he know where Dwarf is then? Is he safe? And Bear, where is Bear? Has he left the valley?" shot Otter, a series of whistles and chirruping chittering sounds.

"One at a time, one at a time, I can't answer you until you settle your wit a bit," laughed the wizard, patting Otter's arm.

"Now," he said, making a slight motion with his eyes, and the stone darkened, then cleared again.

A snowlit night slowly focused in the center of the stone, and Otter saw Cranfallow and Thinvoice, strange to him, yet somehow familiar, astride horses, moving rapidly along a winding ribbon of shadowed road.

"What does this mean, sir?" questioned Otter.

"Look closer, Olther."

And there, banging and bumping, and obviously in a battered huff, jostled Dwarf, hat covering his eyes, stout little legs flying with every movement of the horse.

"Then he's freed. But where is he, and how came he to escape? Did Greyfax or Froghorn save him?" Otter's questions burst forth again, and he couldn't contain himself in his excitement from picking up a paperweight from the wizard's desk and rolling it back and forth between his hand-paws.

"He is making his way here, old fellow," said Mithramuse, removing the weight from Otter's grasp and replacing it on top of a sheaf of documents. "He escaped on his own, quite without his knowing how, I'm sure. His singing of the old song was what did it. It is quite a secret that, and very, very powerful. It is one of the Five, which Dwarf carries. He will be with you soon, barring no further misfortunes."

Another cloudy veil passed over the stone, and Bear, in his man form, appeared, curled into his cloak for warmth, asleep beneath the low roof of a small shrub tree in the foothills Otter and Flewingam had just crossed. There was something disturbingly familiar about the manform, but Otter could not decide what.

"There is your friend, no more than a day's march from us," said Mithramuse, smiling at Otter.

"Bear? Why that silly dear old ass, he came along after me anyhow." Otter's delight in knowing Bear was so near vanished. "Why in the name of Weir did he follow me? He could have been safely home looking after our valley. There's no telling what mischief someone wandering in there could do, our holt and houses left unprotected, not to mention the damage those werebeasts might cause, not finding anyone about to protect it." Otter's eyes opened wide with the memory of the wraithwolves, and he smacked a hand to his forehead. "Aieee, I didn't think about those beasts. They've probably been the cause Bear fled. They almost got me, but I escaped by the skin of my teeth. I didn't suppose they would bother anyone as big as Bear." Otter scolded himself silently as Mithramuse rose and walked around the desk.

A dark shadow crossed the deep veil of the stone, and it seemed to make the wizard's hand tremble as a vague image took shape, outlined at first in a dirty red, then greenish yellow light.

In the middle of this flickering, vile glow stood a deeper shadow of the darkness surrounding it. And then there burst into view a terrible wraith of a shape, formless, yet oozing evil and terror as it devoured the light, and it seemed to Otter as if he were being sucked into the terrible maw of this monster.

The stone whirled upon itself, and a brilliant flash of dazzling white sent Otter staggering backward, struggling to shield his eyes from the searing flames.

When he'd recovered and looked again, he saw a lady, very still, gazing into his eyes. It seemed she was not a lady that he felt he would like to know, yet he could not take his eyes off hers, and once more, he felt he was being drawn into the stone of the wizard's ring.

A clap of light flared suddenly in the hidden depths of the shadows, and a small tail of smoke turned from blue to gray, then to a soft gold, and the ring quietened.

As Otter stared, dazed and shaken, he heard the wizard's voice reach him, as if he were listening from far away.

"You have seen the faces of Doraki, and Dorini, and Cakgor, who took Dwarf to the Dark Queen. Those are the forces we are up against here. We are thrown against other creations of hers, these half-man, half-beast soldiers she has fashioned from numbing minds to all but the darkness. They were men once, but after a time, they become more like beasts. Worlughs and Gorgolacs alike, they were living beings once, with hearts and minds, and now they answer only to Dorini."

Greymouse patted Otter gently.

"But for now your friends are upon their way here, so don't worry needlessly about things past, or things of a discomforting nature. We have much left before us, and other, more urgent matters to occupy our thoughts now. You have told me your news, and I have passed on my little bits of interest, so let's make our plans while we may. You and Flewingam may stay in the sleeping quarters next to mine, and later tonight I shall send for you both. At the moment, I'm expecting the surgeons to heal my wounds." Mithramuse laughed lightly, and in the guise of the gravely wounded General Greymouse, led Otter to the door. Otter bowed low, thanked the wizard, and crossed quickly to where Flewingam sat, waiting.

"What did he say? Did he believe you?" Flewingam's questions increased until at last Otter raised his hand for silence.

"One at a time, one at a time," he scolded, then

giggled at the phrase. "Come, let's find a quiet place where we may sit down and talk, and I'll tell you all." Otter reflected to himself, wondering if he should reveal all that was done and said to his companion, then decided he would tell him all he had been told, but not in the manner he had learned it. The old cautiousness and hesitance about speaking of wizards and their doings warned him against revealing General Greymouse's disguise.

"As thick-headed and stubborn as men usually are," Otter said aloud, "there's little doubt in my mind anyone would listen anyhow."

"Listen to what?" asked Flewingam, eager to learn of Otter's interview.

"To a rude fellow always bursting with questions," chided Otter, leading Flewingam into the sleeping tent Mithramuse had instructed him to use.

Over the smoking lantern, Otter carefully related his discoveries.

BEAR MARCHES WITH THE WORLUGHS

Bear, in a wild dream that came to him, saw two figures, one in gray, softly lighted with a pale white glow, and the the other was Otter. They had warned him, and seemed to be speaking to him, although he could not make out the words. Then came a disturbing vision of a great white tower that looked like a marble swan in flight, and Froghorn Fairingay smiled reassuringly down upon him, and after that faded, the chuckling sight of Dwarf riding about on a horse. Bear awakened suddenly, rubbing his stiff, cold limbs into life, and muttering at bumping his head against a low, hard branch of the shrub tree. He looked about dismally, finding himself once more awake, and still lost in the same thicket patch that ran up the side of the low hill, still alone, and a growing hunger rumbling deep inside him, as it had when he laid down to take his nap.

"I don't know what in the crown of Bruinthor it means," he grumbled, "except that here I still sit without my supper, freezing my fool self to the bone in an ill-fitting suit of man skin." He returned to his bear form hurriedly to warm up, having been too weary to remember to do so before he slept.

"Here now, what's this?" he growled, hearing the sound of many heavy steps thudding over the soft fresh blanket of snow somewhere near him. He raised a cautious bear muzzle, testing the wind. An ugly odor filled his mind with the scent of Worlugh soldiers. A large company of them were passing not a hundred paces from where he lay hidden. He waited until the last of the troops had clumped heavily by, scarring and turning the fresh white snow a muddy brown with their passage, and crept quietly away in the early night shadow, pausing at the rim of a low hill to catch his breath and find his bearings.

Below him, the enemy army moved, the pale trine moon glinting at times on dark helmet or rifle barrel, and Bear counted until he grew weary of numbers. This, however many there were, was no small raiding party. Their movement cut off the course he had chosen to take, and he now had either to skirt the foothills that led upward toward the open pass into the highter mountains, or follow along in their muddy wake, a choice he didn't like, for fear of being overtaken from behind by more of their comrades. To leave the foothills and swing around far out of his way didn't suit his fancy either, so he sat down heavily beneath an outcropping boulder, his paws to his muzzle.

"Ummph," he muttered, lamenting his unsettling dilemma.

"Ummph urgh," came the reply. Bear's ears flattened, his hackles bristling.

"No sneaking off, you dung tread," growled a dimly outlined shape, towering menacingly above him. "Gets back to your march." A heavy, coiling pain seared Bear's back as the thick hide of the whip bit deeply.

He leapt forward to quash this new enemy, but

something turned in his mind, and he halted in mid paw blow.

"If I go as one of them," he thought, "I won't have to travel out of my way, and with any luck at all, I'll give them the slip before first light, and be on my way again."

Bear gave out a low, snarling growl, turned, and caught up the trailing end of the long line of Worlughs. He saw in the pale, dim light that he appeared only another misshapen, huge shadow moving quickly along in the darkness. No challenge was offered, and only the panting grunts from the near running beast told him he was seen as he joined the galloping line.

"So the sergeant caughts you," came the grating snarl of laughter. "Ain't no needs in trying to give that scab tongue the slips. He's got a nose that can smells thunder a mile off."

Bear snarled back, moving along in stride with the foul-smelling body beside him. His nostrils filled with the evil scent, but he grew accustomed to it after a time, and held back the strong desire to flee.

Hour after hour passed by, and still the column moved onward at a fierce pace. Bear's limbs began to tire, but there was no halt called, no break in the weary, fast trot that jolted his numbed brain with every stabbing intake of the frozen air.

At last, toward dawn, the column halted and took cover under the surrounding, scraggly, gnarled trees. Bear, falling down exhausted, looked about him, panting hard. If it had not been for the odor of the foul sweating bodies, it would have appeared no one at all was about.

After a few minutes of steady breathing, he sat upright and found he was alone under his tree. He remained motionless for a time, listening, and having only the fast-fading faint cover of night left for his move, he cautiously began edging away from the reeking scent of the Worlugh encampment. Hardly daring to breathe, he moved with every ancient trick of bear cunning he could muster, and after ten minutes had gone by, he found himself overlooking a small stream that lay frozen before him, cutting the hills into two shallow depressions invisible to each other. Bear quickly passed down, trotted noiselessly along the frozen stream bed for a while, made his way up and over another low, snow-covered hillock, looked back, and saw with failing hopes, the broad, deep tracks of his passing growing clear in the rapidly nearing dawn.

"Well, they're there, that's all, but I'll give them a thing or two to turn over in their morning soup," he muttered aloud. At the mention of soup, he groaned, making a terrible face. "But there's nothing for it," he added, sighing, and making the sign, he returned to the body of a man.

"Let the foulbreaths unravel this one," he chuckled, turning to look back at where the huge paw prints ended, then began again in the shape of a booted man's heavy tread.

Bear quickly checked his course, and aiming at a high snow-glistening peak ahead in the general direction he thought would not again cross the progress of the Worlugh column, he set off briskly, away upward into the growing reddish glow of the sun, appearing slowly over the crowns of the lofty peaks.

"I hope those beasts don't travel by day," he muttered wearily, trying to muster his weary body for one last desperate burst of speed to outdistance the Worlugh troop.

At the second hour after full light his legs failed him, and he collapsed, giving himself an hour to rest, then go on. He awakened from a fitful, unhealing sleep as the last dull golden glow passed into night. He jumped up, fearing he had been overtaken, but no sound broke the silent, snow-covered stillness.

Not knowing what a great distance he had covered on the forced march, Bear returned to his natural form, and loped away at a great bear galloping gait. He had gone forward only a short while when the snapping report of a rifle bullet crackled close by over his ears.

"Halt and identify," growled a piercing voice.

Bear's great heart failed him.

"Eek, but I've run myself right back into their grasp." He sat dejectedly down to await his fate, whatever it might be. Two dark shadows approached him, the blunt outlines of firearms pointed menacingly toward him. Remembering his natural form, he decided he would at least make a fight of it. No enemy could slay Bruinlen, Bruinthor's distant descendant, without knowing they were dealing with a mighty warrior bear king from beyond the Great River.

"What seek you at the camp of General Greymouse?" demanded the voice from the darkness. Bear's ears jerked straight up from his head. These were no Worlughs by the sound of them. If only men, there would be another unending line of questions, but at least he would have food and a place to sleep, even if it were another prison cell. He hastily repeated the words, and stood.

The two men searched him, found nothing, and saying no more, they marched him away to their check post, where another sleepy soldier was awakened and ordered to march Bear down into the camp where the officers would be waiting to interrogate him.

Bear marched glumly along, with only the thought of a hot bowl of soup to cheer the dark picture that began with the grueling all-night tramp with the beast army and ended with his capture by these others, less cruel, perhaps, but no less unkind with their forever questioning minds. He vowed under his breath to answer nothing, and after the brave warmth that flowed through him cooled, "At least until after I've had my supper," he said aloud, sternly.

His guard, in reply, poked him roughly in the ribs, urging him hurriedly along.

"GOOD HEALTH AND WELL MET"

Weary soldiers trudged slowly by, the snow beneath their slow feet trampled and ground into a brown, muddy slush. General Greymouse's armies had successfully routed the invaders from the northlands, slaying or capturing many, but a stiff pocket of resistance still held out upon a well-fortified hill, and had informed the officer sent to treat with them that they would never surrender, but fight on until the last man was unable to fire a shot or throw a bomb. The soldiers that slowly wound their way past Otter and Flewingam's tent were the ones who had been relieved in that siege. Heavy guns had filled the early evening with a continuous booming, making the dark sky alive with the red flaming tails of the big shells as they screeched and wailed away toward the enemy-held hill.

"Is this really a victory, friend?" asked Otter of Flewingam, looking at the worn, staring faces of the men as they moved by, oblivious of all about them.

"For bookkeepers, yes," said Flewingam, coming to stand by the tent flap beside his friend. "For those that fought it, no." He sighed.

Otter searched each empty face as it loomed out, shown up by dim light from the lantern behind him, the dull glow flowing past him onto the muddy company street. Two men appeared from the slow-moving column, one supporting the other.

"We gots to get out of here," the wounded man screamed over and over. "They'll kills us all. Run, you fools, run." The man's voice was choked back by a fit of wailing tears. His comrade helped him on, and the cries lingered a moment, then were swallowed in the darkness.

"Were you ever in battles like this?" asked Otter softly.

Flewingam looked across his shoulder, his eyes filled with the same dead light as the eyes of the men marching by outside.

"I have seen my share of them," he said quietly.

Otter placed a hand on the man's shoulder. "I'm sorry, friend. I've reminded you of things better left alone."

The empty stares and lifeless tread had also recalled something to Otter, although he could not remember exactly what. It was a feeling that had something to do with the disquieting visions of the great animal kings he had seen so long ago by the Great River, when Greyfax Grimwald had shown them his wizard's fire, and all the histories there had been. Perhaps in a time before he had crossed Calix Stay, he himself had seen battles such as this. Perhaps that was why he had crossed the River then. He wished aloud he could cross it now.

"Have you ever heard of Calix Stay, friend?" he asked Flewingam.

"Not to my recollection," the man answered, still lost in dream terrors of past battles.

"It's called that in my tongue, but you might know it as the Great River."

"Yes, I have heard of a river called that."

"Across it lies the Meadows of the Sun, and Gilden Tarn, and the Beginen Mountains, where Dwarf dwelled for so long, and my own holt was upon Cheerweir, as nice a pond as any I've ever heard of or read about. Bear of old had his cave there, too." Otter lingered as he recalled all the pleasant hours he had spent swimming and playing.

Flewingam, his mind turned away from the remembered horrors, was taken up by Otter's voice, droning on softly of his strange homeland and travels.

"All this happened, Otter? Or are you daft a bit? Where is this river you speak of?"

"Calix Stay?" Otter repeated, absentmindedly taking out the fine reed pipe he had fashioned for himself from living plants that grew about the banks of Cheerweir. When it was played upon, the music and laughter of growing things filled the air about those who heard it, and the soft dream of lingering summers passed over minds like the cool breezes that were forever playing over the Meadows of the Sun. Otter put the pipe to his lips and played a short swimming tune, then continued on dreamily with his tale.

"Calix Stay is everywhere. Here, too, perhaps, if it wasn't for the wars. I'm not sure, but I rather think everyone *used* to know where it lay."

"I remember tales of some sort about a river that guarded the shores of the underworld," mused Flewingam, the music having made him drowsy.

"Calix Stay guards no underworld. I have heard the story you speak of, but it reeks of man. It is all spoiled that way, for crossing the River is very beautiful." Otter fell silent, remembering each detail anew in his home upon Cheerweir.

A heavy battery of cannons broke in rudely upon Otter's reveries.

"Great Weir of Baccu, don't they ever tire of shooting those things off?" Otter clasped his hands over his ears.

"Not likely," offered Flewingam, leaning back upon his cot. "Come, play me another bar, Otter. The music puts me to an easy sleep."

Otter began a tune about oak trees chuckling deep in the forest, and notes bubbled with merriment and soothing breezes snoring lightly through green leaves. Flewingam began to mumble his thanks, but was asleep before the words passed his lips. Otter finished out the tune, and feeling much better himself from playing the old songs of his homeland, decided to take a short walk before sleeping. He remembered then the soldiers passing outside, went to check, and found the company street now deserted of all save the posted sentries. The sky was a distant, dark velvet blue cloak, sprinkled with many flickering dim star lanterns. Otter saw the pale, shimmering halo of Dracu, mother of Baccu, and just over the high peaks of the mountains before him, he saw the mighty steed of Augia raise a twinkling forefoot, poised to break forth into pursuit of a speeding moon. (These were constellations in the southern skies of Atlanton Earth during the Fourth or Iron Age, of the second cycle.)

Otter walked out onto the deserted street, whistling to himself a tune he had made up about silver-armored water bugs darting about above a dark, fish-sleeping river. He wandered as far as the checkpoint that guarded the edge of the camp's outer perimeter, then turned to go back. He had exchanged greetings with the drowsy sentries, and as he moved away, one of them called out into the darkness.

"Halt and identify."

Otter, without thinking, stopped in his tracks and blurted out his name. Out of the cover of night came another voice.

"Private Kranz, with a prisoner for our intelligence corps."

"Pass in," replied the sentry.

Otter stopped a few paces off the road to see these new arrivals. A rather large, stout fellow came into the dim lantern glow of the guard post, followed by a soldier with his firearm at his captive's back.

"Oww," complained Bear, feeling the sharp bite of the rifle barrel in his now tender ribs. "I'm going on as quickly as I'm able. No need poking me about like that."

There was something curiously familiar about the voice, Otter decided, and fell into step with the guard as he passed.

"Here, stand away. I've got a dangerous spy here," growled the guard.

"He looks harmless enough to me," said Otter, and whistling one of Bear's old songs, he continued on beside the man.

The prisoner stopped dead, and the guard bumped headlong into him.

"Offf, you oaf, I've banged my nose," snarled the guard, and started to give Bear a good nudge with his rifle.

"Otter?" said Bear, squinting closely at the strange man shape of his old friend.

"Bear? Is that you, you silly ass?" giggled Otter, holding down the great urge to fast-nose-scamper between Bear's legs to bowl him over.

"Get on, you," snapped the soldier, raising his weapon, menace growing thick in his voice.

"I can explain everything if you'll hold a moment, friend," said Otter, twirling twice around and repeating the words. The guard looked stupidly down at the small gray creature standing on its hind paws before him, addressing him politely.

"You see," Otter went on, "you have my friend Bear here, held captive, when he's of no mind to harm anyone, and comes only in search of me."

The guard looked up, directly into the great open jaws of the fully upright bear, who was rumble-chuckling low in his broad chest.

The soldier's firearm clattered to the ground at his feet, his eyes wide, mouth pumping furiously open and closed.

"You see, I'm not a spy, but a bear," carefully explained Bear, moving one huge forepaw in a general explanation of his large animal shape.

"And he's found me, and we're together now, and General Greymouse knows all about it, so thank you kindly for escorting my friend here," went on Otter. "And now we've much to mull over and decide on, so we'll leave you with our thanks."

Bear bowed low. "One small courtesy before you return to your duties, friend," said Bear, and he picked the stunned figure of the man up in one great paw, lifted him briskly off the ground, and landed a resounding thwack to the man's backside.

"Our accounts are even, friend," said Bear, depositing the man back on his feet and gingerly rubbing his own sore ribs.

"Now I think you had best return the way you came, friend. Your duty is done," said Otter, placing the weapon back into the man's clenched hands.

Bear and Otter dropped to all fours, and quickly trotted away toward the camp, leaving the numbed guard staring unbelievingly after them.

"Gor," he said, trying to shake away the disturbing nightmare visions. "I'd better get right down to sick call. My mind has got the battle sickness," he said, walking slowly after the now invisible figures of Otter and Bear, dragging his rifle along beside him by the barrel.

Passing quickly the sentries posted at the beginning of the company street, and leaving them startled and wiping their eyes to clear away the standing sleep they had lapsed into, Otter and Bear entered the tent where the sleeping Flewingam lay.

Bear studied the man, growling. "Who's he? Another of the poke-ribs?"

Otter was frolicking about the floor at Bear's feet, turning first one way, then the other, then under the bed. From over the sleeping Flewingam's stomach, Otter's gray-whiskered face popped up.

"He's a friend," chirped Otter, then scampering hard about the entire floor twice, he raced over and gave Bear a quick nip just above the big animal's hind paw.

"Oooch, you little beast," bellowed Bear, trying to catch and hold the scurrying gray creature. Otter giggled from his hiding place under a cot.

"So you followed along, after all," he sniggered. "And where do I find you? Trapped as neatly as a silly ass of a bear could be, with a tin soldier marching you around on a string."

"Otter," growled Bear, swiping away the cot with a quick paw blow. The noise awakened Flewingam, who sat up quickly, thinking a shell had landed close by.

Otter's head appeared from beneath the blanket that had been flung to the floor.

"Hullo, friend. Here's Bear." The head disappeared, leaving Flewingam wide-eyed with astonishment and terror, staring at Bear's huge form.

Otter appeared from behind him, in man form once more.

"No need to worry, friend. He's my comrade of old I was telling you of."

Bear hastily returned to his clumsy man shape. "Bruinlen, friend," he said, forgetting his anger at Otter for the moment and extending a hand-paw out to Flewingam.

"As I live and breathe," gasped Flewingam. "I thought all your stories just tales to cheer me up, Otter." He gingerly took Bear's hand, looking down at what but a moment before had been the huge fur-covered paw of a great animal.

"Well, as I live and breathe," he echoed.

Otter interrupted the two men.

"I'm sure you must be half starved, Bear, and thirsty, so I'll run out and see what I can find for your supper. I think there's still a pot or two of tea about here somewhere, so you two make yourselves acquainted, and I'll be back in a wink." Otter disappeared through the tent flap.

"So he was telling me truly all along," went on Flewingam, watching as Bear carefully searched the tent for the tea Otter had mentioned.

"How came you to know my pesky little comrade, friend?" asked Bear between lifting or lowering anything that might conceal the promised drink.

Flewingam at last rose, put the small kettle on the camp stove, found the tea left over from their own supper, and quickly poured out a cup to the warmly grateful Bear. He related the story of their meeting as he worked about the stove.

"Ah, but that eases my pain a bit," he said, sighing, and feeling the warmth slowly returning to his chilled body. "That's a nasty business," he continued. "Trolls and half-men roaming at will over the countryside. It's a wonder you made it here. I myself brushed into some ugly fellows of that sort not more than a day ago, and only escaped by my wits, with the help of the darkness. I've seen fire and destruction enough in all my travels, though I've never met a friend of any kind. Otter is fortunate to have you for a comrade."

"Thank you, good Master Bear. Otter has spoken many times of you. I'm sure it is *my* good fortune to have the friendship of both of you."

Bear quietly studied the man, who met his gaze evenly, not once looking away, or down, or in short, showing any symptoms or signs at all of an underlying meanness that might be covered over by a mannerly veneer. Bear decided he liked this man, Flewingam, and that perhaps Otter did, after all, have the sense to seek aid from a well-meaning sort. As a rule, Bear trusted no one who went about in the thin skin of a man, but Flewingam had something about him, something different he could not quite put his paw on.

Otter burst into the room, clink-bumping against Bear, his arms laden with a heaping stack of boxes and bottles, and he noisily placed his load upon the floor, spreading out his treasures. There was half a melon, and tinned beans, an almost whole crabapple pie, and three full loaves of freshly baked shortbread. As Otter placed the meal out, Bear sat hastily down bear fashion and attacked the pie, smacking and grunting his approval.

"There, old fellow. Fill yourself, and then we'll catch up on your adventures. Since you're busy, I'll start with my own, first." Otter drew up a camp stool and sat before Bear's feast table, and Flewingam sat back on the bed with a fresh cup of tea he had made.

Starting with the attack of the werewolves, Otter began his long tale, while Bear greedily filled his agonized stomach with the still warm food, and between drafts of milk or tea, or bites of apple pie, he would raise a hand dripping with juice to ask something of Otter, or blow out his full cheeks in surprise, or belch loudly his approval of something or other Otter was saying. As Otter neared his meeting with Flewingam, Bear finished and sat back sighing, satisfied for the moment. He took a long sip from his cup, and nodded as Otter related his near escape with Flewingam from the raiders' war camp.

Bear, his hunger gone, delighted in the two eager listeners as he took his turn at speaking.

Otter, upon hearing what had happened after he had fled the werewolves, chittered quickly.

"You mean you slew them, Bear?" he asked, looking on his old friend in a different light. Here before him was a changed Bear from the cheerful, peace-loving bear he had known in their quiet years in the valley. "I had no idea that you, Bear, of all fellows, would be much good as a warrior."

"I wouldn't have thought it of you either, dear fellow, if I hadn't found you in a battle camp after chasing you from the valley to here until my feet have almost turned to travel dust." Bear smiled, then continued his story, ending with his long forced march with the Worlugh army the previous night.

Flewingam listened in silence as Bear related how he had been caught up by the ugly Worlugh sergeant and lashed into joining the column. He laughed now at what he must have looked like, galloping along with the ugly, misshapen horde.

"If they'd known they were marching a good-sized breakfast along with them, they'd probably be looking for me yet," laughed Bear, the weary unpleasantness of the memory fast fading.

Flewingam stood suddenly up, a hand to his mustache, stroking it.

"They may still be, for all that, Bear. From what you say, it appears help has come to our enemies. General Greymouse must know of this at once." Flewingam looked quickly to Otter.

"Will he receive you, Otter, on short notice?"

"If you think it important, I'm sure I could have a few minutes with him," Otter said, puzzled and worried at Flewingam's grave expression.

"I have to break up your reunion with ill tidings, but this may be dangerous indeed. With the enemy still holding the hill, most of our army will be busy at that, and our flanks left to be overrun like a dam burst. We must be quick."

"Don't leave me behind," muttered Bear, following after them as they rushed from the tent. "You might need me."

"Hurry, Bear," coaxed Otter, impatiently waiting for Bear to catch up to them. The big fellow hurried along, still holding a half-empty bottle of tea.

"Oh, Bear, how can you fill your stomach when we're hanging on the brink of ruin?" Then softening his voice, he reached out and touched the unfamiliar form of his old comrade. "But come, I'm unkind. I'd forgotten you hadn't eaten. Good health, and well met once more, for all of it. What matters is that we shall face any dangers now together."

In the darkness before the tent, Bear gave Otter a quick, strong hug.

"We've gotten this far alone, I don't see what's to part us now that we're united."

"Hurry, we must see Greymouse. I fear the enemy is even now beginning to move. Look yonder." Flewingam pointed back along the road that led downward into the foothills. A thousand or more torches blazed with a flickering, ugly red glow.

As the three companions hurried on toward Mithramuse's tent, an alarm bugle, far away, began blowing wild, high, sharp notes of distress, and all along the besieged rear perimeter, other horns took up the desperate call.

Like a fiery, unstoppable wave of fire, the enemy was sweeping away the few defenders before them, advancing onward toward the sleeping camp, where Otter, Bear, and Flewingam were led into the tent of the wizard king, Mithramuse.

General Greymouse sat, more slouched and haggard than Otter remembered, and with a weary hand, he bade them enter.

Bear's expression betrayed his disappointment at seeing the tired, gray-cloaked old man Froghorn Fairingay had sent them so far to find, and Bear, after all the days he had traveled, and after giving up his own home, and the knowledge of Dwarf's imprisonment, and the dark wars that raged over every realm, grew saddened, and afraid. This kindly-looking wounded old man would not be of much aid, after all, he thought, and finding Otter would come to a bad end with the death of them all.

With those grim thoughts, Bear sat down with his friends before the desk to hear the words the old man was saying.

THE CIRCLE MOVES

"Grimwald," exclaimed Lorini, surprised at her old friends' unannounced entrance into her private study, a long, light-filled room lined with the sacred volumes of the lore of Windameir. "Whatever has come over you?" She softly scolded him as he angrily strode into the room and began pacing furiously up the spinning, light-dazzling carpets, his cloak trailing along behind him, stirring to life the colors and weaves of the most ancient of tapestries fashioned into coverings for Lorini's marble floors.

"Where is he?" demanded Greyfax.

"Where is who, my dear Grimwald? You've burst in upon me while I was speaking with Melodias, and I must say, travel doesn't improve your temper."

Greyfax halted, bowing low. "I'm most sorry for this rude interruption, my lady. I'll retire and await your command. Please forgive me." The gray-cloaked figure bowed once more, moving away toward the high marble-arched door.

"If you're seeking young Master Faragon, you'll find him in the gardens somewhere, with Cybelle." Her voice grew gentler. "And I shall be with you in a moment."

"Thank you, my lady, I shall eagerly await you."

He returned her smile, and went out upon the balconies that ran around the house of Cypher and looked about, trying to find Froghorn. Cybelle's light, tinkling laughter rose upward onto the soft breeze, away beyond the north garden, which overlooked the lands of Atlanton Earth upon the northern borders. Far beyond, the dazzling white halo of lights dimmed as Lorini's realm ended, and beyond that, the black haze of the Dark Queen hung over the world. There, even at the stroke of high noon, the darkness was only a dim shadow of the day, and the one remaining sun appeared there only as a faint, ugly red-orange glow, like a siege lamp burning fiercely above a great battle.

Greyfax heard the light laughter once more, and turning his vision from the dark north, went down into the great courtyard, crossed it, and entered the hedge gate that surrounded the green, lush gardens that bordered all sides of the house.

He saw Froghorn, standing with one booted foot upon a fountain edge, speaking quietly against Cybelle's golden spun hair. She laughed again, but her smile faded when her eyes fell on the grim countenance of Greyfax, who strode quickly to the two.

"Greyfax," began Froghorn, turning.

"Don't Greyfax me, you sideshow magician." Greyfax bowed low and took Cybelle's hand.

"If you'll excuse us, my dearest lady, I have urgent tidings for your Master Fairingay." He placed his lips to her hand.

"Please don't keep him too long away. We've been having the most delightful walk."

"I shan't keep him long, my lady." Greyfax watched Cybelle until she had crossed through the green gate of the garden.

"I don't know what you're in such a state about, Grimwald. I have the Arkenchest here safe."

"Yes, and our delightful lady of Darkness has Dwarf as safe there. How in the name of Windameir did you let yourself get snared that way? Have all our warnings flown in one ear and out the other? Or has the lady Cybelle blinded your eyes to all but her?"

"Don't make jests with her name," warned Froghorn, glowering.

"I haven't had time for jest in three ages, and I shan't for three more if I'm burdened with a stupid lump of a magician that takes more interest in amusing the ladies than seeing to it his task is well done."

Froghorn opened his mouth to speak, but Greyfax raised a hand and went on.

"Don't interrupt me, I must think." He sat down on the edge of the fountain and fell into a deep, far-seeing meditation. Fairingay fidgeted uneasily beside him. At last he rose and turned to the younger man.

"Well, that settles that," he explained, and began to walk toward the gate.

"What settles what, Grimwald?"

"Don't you ever pay attention? Must I forever be explaining things to you?" scolded Greyfax.

"You said nothing," objected Froghorn.

"Of course I *said* nothing. What in the wildest fantasy of Erophin do you think you have a head for? To carry your hat around safely?" Greyfax scowled. "But come, I must closet with the lady Lorini, and perhaps you can manage to keep your mind off one certain young lady long enough to discover the errands we have before us."

"Are we leaving then, so soon?"

"Not soon enough, I fear, if soon is waiting about for a love-sickened whelp to leave his beloved." The gray cloak opened briefly, and the brilliant white glowing robes of Greyfax shone forth for a moment.

"Great dome of Windameir, give me the patience," he began, rolling his clear gray eyes upward, then, knitting his brows down in a piercing, scalding gaze, he spoke. "Yes, we are leaving soon, Master Fairingay, within the hour. I suggest you save your questions for later. Try listening a bit. It might fill your ears with something more than sweet whispers from your lady."

Greyfax stormed away, Froghorn close at his heels.

As the two entered the high east door, an elf in the livery of Cypher approached.

"My lady Lorini will receive you now, Master."

"Thank you. You may tell the lady we are upon our way."

The handsome figure of the elf disappeared before them down the long, sun-filled corridor.

"What have you learned that makes our stay here so short, Greyfax? Have you been with Melodias?"

Greyfax walked silently on.

"As close as ever, I see."

"Not so close, as you shall learn in a moment," corrected Greyfax, entering once more the spacious, airy antechamber of Lorini's study.

"Ah, good, you've found him," came her clear, soft voice. She sat at a large table, set out with three finely wrought cups and a silver pitcher. "Come, let us have a cool drink; then you may begin, my good Greyfax."

After the three had made themselves comfortable and tasted the cool, clear drink, Greyfax spoke.

"If you were speaking to Melodias, my lady, you know that Cephus Starkeeper is with him at this moment, and that I have returned from council with him bearing the gravest news. Erophin of ancient Windameir was there to advise us, and he too was most anxious that we be about our business as quickly as possible."

"You saw the Starkeeper, then," muttered Froghorn aloud. Lorini quietened him with a frown.

"Cephus is with Melodias even as I speak, and I doubt not they will soon be ready to strike. Others of that realm have made their way to Atlanton Earth to offer aid. I have not been abroad yet, to see what state we stand in, but as soon as we have finished here, our patient Master Fairingay and I will be off."

Froghorn had moved away from the table, and stood looking out the high-pillared window that opened onto the gardens and courtyards below.

"Your news comes as no surprise, Grimwald, although I dare say perhaps none too soon. I have counseled with Melodias, as you saw when you interrupted me in your haste before. Cephus Starkeeper and Melodias Starson will move their forces to the very borders of my realms, for my dark sister has begun a siege of my northern realm, and she grows stronger by the hour if none move to check her."

"Things are dark, my lady, but not without hope. Melodias and Starkeeper have contained her before, along with the aid from others of the Circle." Froghorn spoke, still at the window.

"That was ages ago, my dear Faragon. She has waxed strong since her last defeat. And Atlanton Earth lies half in her designs."

"But what victories there are, snatched from the very jaws of destruction, my lady," smiled Greyfax. "And this will indeed be that if we win through."

"Even with that, my dearest old friend, what then? It is an ending and a beginning of us all. Whoever may be victorious, we cannot alter fate."

"Yes," mused Grimwald, sitting back and taking the cup in his hands. "But still I would not like to think of having to continue this business next time."

The room fell silent a moment, and each of the sad, gay faces of the three grew older, as each one thought of the many long ages they had seen, all now drawing to an end. A golden glow from the wind lighted the room in swimming, swirling motions, and a myriad of sounds and visions began, from the farthest memory of a beginning, through each of the countless ages and histories, and at last, the wind smoothed the colors gone, and Greyfax finished his drink.

As Froghorn stood at the windows, a bluish white space opened before his eyes, spreading around him like a flowing azure pool. From far away, the secret sign of his name was made and Mithramuse appeared to him. Froghorn saw the man figure of Otter beside him, bent low over a veiled circle of pale white radiance, looking at him. Froghorn knew at once Otter, at least, had reached his journey's end. He spoke quickly to Mithramuse in High Elvish, and the pool withdrew as the other man bent his thoughts away.

"I've just seen Otter, Grimwald. He's with Mithramuse at the moment."

"What of the others? Did you see any sign of Bear, or of Dwarf?"

"Nay, I saw only Olther."

"What tidings are these, I wonder?" Greyfax began pacing the room. "I must find what fate has fallen upon my small charge, and alter it if I may." He smacked a fist down hard into his open palm. "If only I'd told him what he carried," he cried.

"But it would have fallen into her hands had you told him, Grimwald. At times, I must admit, a close tongue has its part."

"Yet it's my fault he's taken, and close tongue or no, it's my errand to free him if he yet lives."

"I fear we have other more urgent matters to deal with at the moment, my dear Grimwald. I regret as deeply as you the cruel prison of your Dwarf, but if we are to move, we must be swift."

Greyfax nodded reluctant agreement. "I think the Arkenchest as safe here as anywhere, so it shall stay with you, my lady. As for myself, I must find my stirrups and be away."

"Where, this time?" asked Froghorn, coming quickly down the room.

"My wise Master Fairingay, I told you you should use your ears for something more than a well-spring for keeping the voice of your fair lady. Think a moment, and I'm sure you'll discover all the replies you have been missing, standing about the window, mooning like a wounded dove." Greyfax turned and bowed low to Lorini. "My fairest lady, I must bid you farewell once more. You shall hear word soon, I trust, of my errand's end."

"I await your return, old friend. Perhaps next we meet, we shall be able to finish our supper before you would bolt off again."

"I shall do my utmost, my lady."

Greyfax raised his hand to Froghorn, and motioned him to follow. At the stable entrance, he gave his last instructions, mounted, and was gone.

Froghorn went in search of Cybelle to say his farewells once more.

And away beyond the borders of Cypher, upon a dark road in western Atlanton Earth, Dwarf and his two companions came upon an ambush. And yet farther, a great black-shrouded army fell in vicious assault upon the war camp of General Greymouse.

THE CIRCLE OF LIGHT

AMBUSH

Under the cover of darkness, the two horses moved steadily on at a fast trot. The three riders were bone-weary, and sore from the unaccustomed manner of travel. At last they reached a shallow ford of a small stream that crossed the road, and eagerly dismounted to water their steeds and walk about to uncramp their aching limbs.

Dwarf, legs asleep and numb, fell backward into the cold running water, and small floes of ice brushed his back, making him cry loudly in an agonized huff.

"Aieee, I'm stuck with a thousand hot darts," he wailed, struggling futilely, short legs uselessly pumping.

Cranfallow, thinking Dwarf had been struck a blow from some concealed enemy, fired off two shots in rapid succession into an old overhanging willow, laden with a shelf of snow in its bent boughs. The horses shied at the sudden loud reports of the rifle, and while Thinvoice held their wildly rearing heads to calm them, he shouted over his shoulder, "You got 'em, Cranny, I heard 'em fall." The rustling plop of deep snow sliding off the limbs, caused by Cranfallow's bullets, had sounded to him like the noise of a body falling.

Dwarf, witless and half hysterical, darted away, his legs now recovered in his fright, and brushing past Ned, was under the bolting horses before he knew where he was, and almost trampled down under the flashing hooves.

Cranfallow splashed quickly across the stream to investigate his fallen assailant, but found only the willow tree, empty.

"Ooooooh," huffed Dwarf, hat down hard over his eyes, "I shall turn the lot of you inside out," he fumed, then screamed again as a piece of trapped ice slid out of his soaked cloak into the back of his yellow trousers.

"What demon has you, sir?" cried Cranfallow, rushing to the little man's side. Ned was dragged struggling away by the terrified horses. Broco removed a pointed-toed shoe and stood hopping about on one foot to try to dislodge the icy finger that trickled slowly down his leg, then out.

"I'm soaked and frozen, you ass, and almost trummled to my end by those infernal beasts, and now you stand there asking what's amiss?" sputtered Dwarf, drawing a quick gasp of breath as the freezing wet cloak fell solidly against his back.

"I thoughts you was attacked by some enemy, sir," apologized Cranfallow, laying his rifle aside and trying to help Dwarf stand while he replaced his soggy boot.

"Where has that ninny Ned gotten off to? Are we left afoot?" glowered Dwarf. "Well, don't stand there with your jaw in your shoes, do something. Start a fire, or find me dry clothing."

"Yes sir, yes sir," moaned Cranfallow, sure of his horrible doom at the hands of the dwarf witch. "But I don't thinks we should tarry here to builds our fire, I don't. We's only gone a few leagues or so, so we'd best waits to warm you out at the next settlement, sir, if that's not too much my saying."

Ned returned with the snoring horses.

"What's been at us, Cranny?" he asked, eyes wide with fear.

"Nothing's been at us but your lame-headed friend here," grumped Dwarf. "Now help me back up on that beast and let's find a fire to dry me."

"Yes sir," said Cranfallow, and they helped Dwarf back onto the high back of the near horse. Feeling weight again, and still shying, the animal broke away at a fast gallop, the flying figure of Broco clinging madly to the beast's mane and neck, shrieking horrible dwarfish oaths that scalded the ears of Cranfellow and Ned Thinvoice.

The horse's crazed flight was taking Dwarf back exactly in the direction they had come, and for an hour or more since dark, the three companions had heard, and seen, the heavy battle lighting up the dark fields behind them.

"Ride after him, Cranny, or he's done for sure," wailed Ned.

Cranfallow, terrified of being caught up in a battle, but more afraid of what would come upon him from the dwarf witchs anger, mounted quickly and spurred his horse after the wildly galloping Dwarf.

Broco's mount grew more crazed still, hearing the Dwarf's frightened oaths and feeling the terror-gripped hands upon his neck and the bouncing weight on his back. Nostrils flared, eyes starting, he put on more speed to throw off this thing upon him, and the two, horse and Dwarf, raced onward toward the evil, red-glowing darkness before them.

Cranfallow, not much of a rider, but desperate now, finally began overtaking the runaway, and just at the moment he was reaching an outstretched hand over to grasp the bridle of the fear-crazed animal that bore Dwarf, his own mount stumbled over the sprawling corpse of a fallen horse directly in the middle of the road. As his horse struggled to keep his feet, Dwarf's mount reared once, shuddered, and snorted a long, blowing, rushing breath, and stood frozen. Cranfallow kept his seat by releasing the reins and clutching blindly at the horse's neck. After a few more stumbling near falls, the horse regained his footing, and standing at rest, quivered, lowered his head, and shook his mane.

Cranfallow dismounted, and leading the tired beast, rushed to where Dwarf still clung wildly to the runaway's neck.

"Is you all right, sir? No bones broken?" Cranfallow reached up a hand to help Broco dismount.

The ugly, mean click of a safety being let off startled Cranfallow into looking down into the ditch near his feet, only a few paces away from the corpse of the dead animal.

"Who's there?" snapped Cranfallow, peering into the dark confines of the ditch.

"I might ask you the same," gasped a thick voice. "Before I blow your black life back to where it came from." An unsteady, reeling shadow rose from the edge of the ditch. "But I'll take the use of one of your mounts first," it croaked, and the stumbling shadow figure approached nearer.

"Quickspur," said Dwarf and Cranfallow in chorus.

"What's happened, man, what hurt have you taken? It's Broco who's found you."

"Master Dwarf," gasped Quickspur. "You've come too late, I fear, for my wound bleeds badly, but at least I'll die in the presence of friends, instead of at the hands of those cowardly dogs." The man, gravely wounded by a bullet through his ribs, collapsed before the two.

"What's happened, sir?" asked Dwarf, trying to cushion the man's head with his soaked cloak.

"They laid for us in ambush, and Cinch was slain before he could escape. All the others taken too. The filth," he gasped, coughing. "But you must fly," he said, opening his eyes again. "Leave me, and save yourselves. They can't be too far behind. I would have been gone clean, but the first volley got my mount, and he only could run this far before he died."

"Quickly, Cranfallow, help me get him to the horse," said Dwarf, and the two men placed Quickspur upon the runaway.

"Is you strong enough to sits, sir?" asked Cranfallow.

"I was born to saddle, so I just as easily may die in one," gasped Quickspur. "But you should leave me, now. I'll only slow your escape."

"Nonsense, old fellow," broke in Dwarf. "We'll have you away from here in no time at all."

Cranfallow mounted and Dwarf jumped up behind him, holding the reins of the horse that Quickspur was upon. Riding slowly away in this fashion, to keep from jostling the wounded man, they at last made their way back to Thinvoice, who was crouched low behind the shelter of the willow tree.

"Ned," Cranfallow called. "Is you there?"

"I thought the bloody bunch had you for sure," he said, coming out upon the road. He stopped short, seeing the slumped figure of Quickspur riding behind.

"Who in bloody blazes is that?" he asked, approaching the injured man.

"Sergeant Quickspur," said Dwarf, tumbling down from behind Cranfallow. "We found him wounded on the road back there. His friend and he were set upon from ambush, and Cinch and the others slain or taken."

Quickspur lay unconscious upon the saddle.

"We must get aid, and quickly," said Dwarf. "How far is it until we reach the next settlement, Ned?"

"A two-hour ride, if we was hurrying." Looking up at the wounded man, he went on. "Four, if we has to go easy."

"Then you mount and hold him, Ned, and I shall go on behind Cranfallow. We'd best be off now, if we've so far to go. I fear he has a grievous hurt." Dwarf struggled up to his perch once more. "Don't spare me, my good Cranfallow. Go as quickly as you can. I take no pleasure in this battering you give me, but we must make all haste."

"We'll has him there safe, just you wait, sir," said Cranfallow, relieved that the dwarf's anger was turned by the discovery and rescue of the wounded Quickspur.

Occasional groans from Quickspur told them he yet lived, and the miles ran on until Broco thought they would never reach their end, but at last, after a time he could not count, they neared the crest of a rolling low hill and looked down on the other side at the distant glow sent up by a great army camp around a small village. He made out the outlines of many tents by the fires that burned about them, and hoping it was the camp Quickspur had been making for, the four wound away downward toward the flickering fires.

Soon a challenge was given, and after advancing so they could be seen, the four were passed on, and after another mile's ride were in the teeming heart of the war camp. A sentry directed them to the hospital tent, where medical orderlies helped to take the unconscious Quickspur inside to a well-lighted, clean operating room.

"Will he be all right?" asked Dwarf anxiously of the grim-faced doctor that had gone in to examine him.

"Your friend is still unconscious, and has lost much blood. He was lucky, in a way, though, for the bullet passed through clean. He's a strong fellow. He has an even chance of recovery."

The doctor walked quickly away, leaving Dwarf pacing about in front of the tent.

"Gribbit," muttered Dwarf. "Ask a simple thing like is it day or night, and all you get is, 'well, perhaps,' or 'that's still a question.' "

"He's a big one," said Ned, trying to reassure Dwarf. "He's as stout as an oak, and it would takes more than whats *they* could do to him to slay him."

"We'll makes for the inn in the village, and gets our supper, and you dried off, sir, and come again in the morning. We won't be able to learns anything tonight if the fellow you just spoke with is any sign of whats they're like."

Dwarf paced a moment more, halting to look at the closed flap a moment, trying to see inside to where his friend lay.

"He's shown us great kindness, this fellow, and I shall long lament it if we can do nothing for him."

"You has done bravely, sir," said Ned. "Why, we carried him all this way for help. If them what's in the white coats can't mend him, no power in heaven could."

"I guess you're right, Ned." Dwarf looked around at his two companions. "And I've forgotten my two loyal friends are hungry and cold and tired, too. Food and sleep is the aid we need, if we're going to be of any further use to our friend in there."

Dwarf mounted once more behind Cranfallow and

Ned followed wearily behind, and saddened and afraid for their wounded friend, the three made their way slowly to the small inn that bordered the camp's edge and was the single structure in that dark village that still showed lights in its windows, a warm and welcome sight to the three travelers.

From the sentry that guarded the checkpoint on the road to town, they had learned of the looming battle, and that dread phantom of thought hung heavily over the pleasures of fire and food and a warm, dry change of clothes.

BESIEGED

"This indeed, my friends, is a dark tide running. My army is split upon two fronts, and the enemy has fresh troops to throw up for battle. I little doubt they are guided by the foul hand of the dark lieutenant. I mention not his name for his nearness is everywhere." Mithramuse spoke clearly, without emotion, as if he were quietly away in a study, gazing at stars. "Still, I shall be able to do something to check the assault, although I am far too weak to hold long, alone. If the aid I have summoned reaches us in time, we may hold. If not . . ." The old gray-cloaked figure stooped.

"What aid might that be, sir?" asked Flewingam. "I know of no other armies closer than a day's march. By then, all they shall find is our charred bones."

"I speak of a much swifter army, my good fellow. One you would perhaps find most startling."

"You mean witchcraft," said Flewingam, looking steadily into the wizard's eyes.

The old man looked to Otter, who sat blushing to his ears, then back to Flewingam.

"Yes," Mithramuse laughed, the clear gray eyes twinkling from unfathomable depths, "witchcraft, although it is called by another name."

"My two companions gave me a brief display of their powers earlier," explained Flewingam, his desire to see more of the wizard's work growing.

"Ah yes, that. A simple device known to all of lesser powers. Mere child's play when you know what you're about."

A great roar filled the air with hideous screams, and the heavy rattle of many firearms exploded through the night.

"Whatever you have in mind, sir," broke in Otter, "I fear it must be quick. The battle closes nearer."

"Yes, my little friend, too near, it seems. We must set to our work." Mithramuse moved from behind the desk, once more in the guise of Greymouse, general of the army. "Olther, and you, stout Bruinlth, and you, my faithful Flewingam, shall serve as my personal guard. If all looks as grave as it sounds, I pray you serve me well."

"To the end of the worlds, and farther," said Flewingam, bowing.

"Greymouse, Greymouse," chorused Bear and Otter, raising the clumsy firearms.

"Then let's set our plan to action," said Mithramuse, and the four men went out into the red-glowing darkness, toward the advancing lines of the black-covered enemy. Running soldiers hurried about, shouting orders and curses, and a mud-splattered, exhausted captain passed closely by Mithramuse and his three guards.

"Sir," cried the captain, "we're hard pressed at the perimeter. I've sent for a battery of cannons to use, but they take too long. We may have to give up the line and retreat farther back to hold them."

"Very good, sir. Then carry on. Help is coming." Greymouse touched the weary man's shoulder. "Stout heart and steady hand, Captain. We must not fall."

"The men are so tired, sir. They've fought all day,

and have had no sleep. The villains have us to advantage there."

"Fight on, sir. We shall do what we can." General Greymouse smiled grimly at the man, and the captain saluted smartly and was gone, swallowed up in the throngs of soldiers hastily deploying to strengthen the faltering defenders of the outer perimeter.

Great, low clouds skidded over the mountains, and a storm announced its approach with a renewed icy wind. Mithramuse looked long at the ugly grayish undersides of the clouds as they caught and reflected the glow of the battle fires below.

"It looks not of nature to me," he said aloud, and repeating a quick rhyme in stanzas of three, a single, swift-flying shadow of pale, shimmering fire shot upward from the wizard's hand. As it neared the cloud, it grew, and soon covered the entire sky above where the armies of General Greymouse battled for their lives. As the shadow light reached a great height, it burst into a brilliant pale blue shower of arrows, raining down among the enemy like a deadly torrent of screaming, fiery hailstones. A great wail went up among the Worlugh ranks, and many fell back, dropping their weapons and cowering before this sheet of bluish terror. The defenders, equally amazed and terrified, soon took the advantage to fight forward a few moments, but soon the sky darkened once more, and a fresh wave of enemy flowed over the field, sweeping their comrades in front back into the fray, and they joined battle once more, howling fiercely. The thinning line of defense crumbled, fell back, and regrouped, held, then fell back again. The fighting grew heavier upon the enemy hill to the front, and soon they, too, advanced down the slopes, eyes blazing, and shrieking over the volleys of rifle fire. The siege troops, now the besieged, staunched the tide after a time, but their supplies were low and their relief as sorely pressed as they, so no aid came, and they began slowly retreating back toward the inner defenses of their camp.

Doraki, astride the great black steed Brugnath, circled the battle in the cloak of the snowstorm, maddening all those who saw him, and the tall, powerful, iron-crowned servant who was in the form of a horse demon to bear down Doraki from the World Between Time breathed out choking grayish poisoned gases over the field, deadening men's minds and hopes. These were the visions Mithramuse had seen when he studied the sky and storm.

"We are set upon by no less than her second-in-command," he thought aloud. "They must indeed want this victory." A great golden, humming dome appeared about the slouched gray figure, spiraling away upward into the disturbed slumber of night. The wizard called upon the sacred numbers of Windameir and spelled out the name of the Circle in the high tongue of the ancients, and a dazzling line of high golden hills appeared upon the battlefield, and a tall, fair man appeared, amored in silver mithra, with a huge five-colored shield emblazoned with the coat of arms of Cephus Starkeeper. At the man's side hung a long, double-handed sword that glistened with a harsh steel fire, and at his lips a curved horn that blew forth over the din of battle. Long and unbroken the horn winded, and the sound unbearable to hear. Otter and Bear held their hands over their ears, and Flewingam beat madly at the air with clenched fists. The thick, brown-hided Worlugh and Gorgolac soldiers fell stunned and whining before the terrible notes this prince of the Circle had blown.

Doraki, hearing the horn, sent Brugnath wheeling down to do battle with this new and powerful foe, and bellowing black flames and greenish-yellow spears of light, the two towering visions joined battle above the field, where all eyes turned upward to watch the haze-shrouded phantoms locked closely in combat.

Up one cloud mountain, then crashing down another, the phantom warriors struggled, the prince Na'tone afoot, Doraki mounted, and loud thunder clapped and rolled across western Atlanton Earth, and great geysers of fire and lightning rolled and flashed, lighting the darkness until it was as bright as full day. Time and again, the tide turned first one way, then the other, as Na'tone and Doraki fought. The black-clad armies below howled and sent up a great cry as they saw Doraki throw the white prince down, and Brugnath reared to smash the hated figure with his coal-black forehooves. The dark army swarmed enraged over the hopeless defenders, and on the small open hill where Mithramuse stood with the three friends, the air grew thick with whistling, crackling darts, and the enemy still came on, hordes of the Gorgolacs sweeping by them, around the hill, on into the very heart of the camp. Lines were breached, and the army of General Greymouse was forced to fight in small, surrounded, desperate groups. Belching black smoke, the camp was aflame, and the enemy that had come down the hill now advanced quickly upon the leaderless and broken, weary troops.

The onslaught was once again held fast, as Na'tone regained his feet and hurled the dark lord from his saddle. A last spark of desperate hope blazed in the hearts of the weary defenders, and they surged back bravely into the hordes of dark soldiers, stemming the tide once more.

Mithramuse looked on anxiously at the fierce struggle in the cloud. Na'tone at last had touched Doraki with the scalding white blade of the flashing sword, and horse and rider vanished in a great explosion of crimson black light, and the thunder rolled one last time, deafening all those who heard, and the grayish clouds burst wide, and thick, blood-red snowflakes began falling over the battle raging below. The golden mountains dimmed, then vanished, and the tall warrior Na'tone glimmered faintly once, then was gone.

"Did the white warrior slay him?" asked Otter, eyes wide in fear and awe.

Mithramuse did not answer for a moment, so deeply lost in his far mind he did not hear Otter.

"I don't think whatever it was was slain, Otter," said Flewingam. "But look at the snow." Flewingam held out a hand and caught a few of the driftng flakes. They showed up a deep crimson against the pallor of his hand.

Bear held out a hand, and looked also. "It's the strangest thing I've ever seen. Red snow? What new disaster awaits us now?"

Mithramuse returned from where his thought had touched Na'tone's.

"He is safe, where no trick of the other can harm him. He touched that unliving flesh with the Sword of Light from the White Flame of the Starkeeper. He cannot be slain by that, but he has returned to his Dark Queen's realms for a space. Perhaps in that time, we may win through here. Her armies will be without will now, although they still greatly outnumber us."

Otter looked around, and it was true. All around them the battle still raged, more fiercely now, for the dark armies were vicious and cruel, and knowing not bravery, they yet knew bitterness, and all about they fought on.

"Can't you do something more, sir?" asked Bear, hoping his renewed faith in the slouching gray figure of the old man would not be deflated again.

"I grow tired, Bruinlth. I called Na'tone from a

sphere far removed from ours, and the cost to me to do so was dear. I must rest first."

"Watch out," cried Flewingam, casting Mithramuse to the ground as a flurry of rifle fire burst over their heads.

"They've seen us. Quick, Bear, you hold that side, and Otter, stand closer there that you may cover the approach." Flewingam crawled over the general and began firing rapidly down the slope of the hill. Otter, trying to find which end of the man weapon the lead darts came out, looked downward and saw the running, crouched black shapes below him. They fired as they ran, and were coming straight for him. Behind him, he heard Bear's rumble-growl as he fussed with his own unfamiliar man weapon, then a loud report, and Bear's stunned cry of pain. Otter pumped the trigger of the rifle twice, and felt the sharp blow against his chest as the thing jumped alive in his hands. Bear had had the butt of his rifle against his jaw, and the sharp blow it had given him stunned him for a second.

"I'd rather use my own paws," he mumbled over the din. "No chance of losing your teeth from them banging in your face."

Otter looked over to where Flewingam lay, and trying to copy the way he held the weapon, he began firing jerkily again. After a few terrifying moments, the hill was clear of attackers. Otter looked down at two fallen black shapes that lay sprawled at the bottom of his side of the hill.

"You've done well," said Flewingam, crawling over to him. "For waterfolk, you do passing well as a soldier." Then laughing grimly, he touched Otter's shoulder. "Don't think about it, friend. And don't look at them if you can help it." He crawled back to his position.

It was too much for Otter's whirling mind to associate his firing the jumping thing in his hand to the dead Worlughs below, so he simply lay, waiting, and hoping Mithramuse would be rested enough for another magical trick to help them escape the noise and fury of the battle.

Bear turned, and moving slowly, crawled beside Otter.

"This man thing has broken my jaw, I know it," he complained, putting a hand gingerly to feel the swelling lump on the side of his face.

Otter looked at it, then moved his own hand over the swelling to see if he could feel a break.

"It's just a bruise, Bear."

"I know it's broken, I tell you. How in the name of Bruinthor will I be able to eat? If I can't chew, I'll be forever sucking mush through my front teeth to stay alive. Eek, but what a sad fate, starved to death." Bear groaned, thinking of the still unfinished loaf in Otter's tent. He groaned again when he saw the whole camp burning below, and knew the food lost forever, burned to a blackened char.

A great volley of heavy firing and shouts broke out farther away, toward where the road led into the main camp. They all strained to see what new aid or assailants the noisy stir brought, but it was too far away to make out plainly any more than two horsemen galloping through an angry swarm of dark-clad soldiers, passing through the great glow of the fires out of sight.

Above, the snow had stopped, and the sky began to lighten faintly, with a pale, teardrop-shaped glimmering light that appeared to be approaching swiftly from away over the high peaks of the mountains.

"What new deviltry is this?" said Mithramuse aloud, rising and turning to face this new threat wearily.

AN UNQUIET PEACE

By far the most dangerous of the enemy armies—more deadly and cruel than the Gorgolac half-man beasts, or the thick-hided Worlugh soldiers—Dorini had fashioned in her grim halls were the tall, well-shaped, handsome men of the northern realms who had fallen into her treacherous web of destruction. Once they had been a proud race, seafarers and horse-men, and the now darkening lands where they dwelled still showed the beauty and strength their hands had once wrought before they turned to warring and slaying the neighboring inhabitants that yet lived in peace. The Urinine, as they were called, were promised wealth and great power by Doraki, who after a time drew the once wise ruler of the strong race into his malignant plan, and Dorini, as she had promised, bestowed great wealth and power upon all those of the Urinine and their minds were filled with greed and lust, and all other thoughts were lost under long years of disuse. As their treasures grew, their minds sought still more, and the handsome dark heads of Urinine warrior clans turned from their sea and their pastures to destruction and chaos upon others of Atlanton Earth, and they ranged far and wide, pillaging and burning, forever in search of gold or jewels to fill their coffers.

It was a small troop of these Urinine that Cranfallow, with Dwarf behind and Thinvoice following, broke through in their mad flight to enter the general's heavily besieged camp. A moment before, the three had looked down upon the great battle from the confines of a tree-sheltered hill, and Dwarf at last had spoken.

"There's no use going back, for they do battle there, too, and if we ride on, what shall we find beyond? This is no small skirmish by the looks of it. We either fight through, and hope to win out, or perish. Our choices are none too pleasant, but all we have."

Thinvoice looked up from where the burning camp lay, covered with a thick shroud of black smoke.

"If this Greymouse has them powers too, why isn't he after using them? It don't looks so good, to my way of thinking. I gets out of one stew pot, and rides until my backsides is blistered well enough to suit the taste of one of those filth, just to get off my horse and jumps into another one."

"It looks bad," said Cranfallow, "but what fight don't? We can't sees nothing for sure, until we knows how they stands. We might as well tries to go on, like Master Dwarf says."

"I don't likes it, I says, but I don't wants to go back neither. My good sense says run, but my bottom says no, so I guess we might as well gets on with it. At least in a fight, I can gets off this bouncing nag." Thinvoice paused, and gravely held a hand out to Dwarf and Cranfallow. "If we doesn't shoot through, then well met, and we parts as friends."

"We'll do it, Ned. Just hang on tight, and I'll see

if I can't stir up a spell or two to help us along." Dwarf shook Thinvoice's trembling hand.

"Can you makes us invisible, sir?" asked Cranfallow, having second thoughts about riding down through the whining, flying storm below.

"No, my good Cranny, I can't do that, or at least I could if I remembered the verses, but they're long, and we'd most likely as not be here all night while I tried to remember them."

"Well, that suits my fancy fine, sir," said Ned, hopefully.

"No, we can't wait. I'll see what I can do with this one, then be ready to ride like you've never ridden before, Cranfallow, and don't worry about losing me, I've got a grip like a good vise."

"I knows that, sir," replied Cranfallow. "But if the bullets don't do me, I'll be squished clean, sure."

Dwarf laughed. "That's a worry I shouldn't entertain, good Cranfallow. A dwarf hug is strong, but I don't think it's fatal."

"If all your kind is as strong of hand as you is, sir, you never needs to fret over dropping your supper plates, I'll says that, and no harm meant, sir."

"I'll see about that the next supper I have, Cranfallow, and we'll continue our talk about a warm fire. Now we must move. It seems to grow quieter down there."

Dwarf removed his hat, spun it, called the secret sign forth of that ancient dwarfish king Brion Brandagore, and set forth before them a great horde of pale, glimmering figures of dwarfs with great bladed battle-axes, and helms with the fierce masks of griffin heads upon them, causing their horses to rear and shy from the ghastly, shimmering vision.

"Ride on, stout Cranfallow. On, Ned. Brion Brandagore," bellowed Dwarf, and the crazed horses flew headlong through the glowing images of the advancing dwarfish army, onward, until the reeling lines of Gorgolacs before them parted, panic burning in their half-lidded yellow eyes, onward still until the three had crashed past all alike, defenders and enemies fleeing aside from the terrible vision of the swarthy dwarfs with the flame-gleaming great axes and death-filled eyes. The two horses neighed and pulled up suddenly near a cavalry troop that seemed to be standing by in reserve of the battle.

"Hail, comrades," shouted Cranfallow, addressing the man who seemed to be in command, a tall, clear-featured man with a handsome roan horse that paced about, eager to join the struggle that raged all about them.

"Who be you?" questioned the tall, dark-haired man, his cloak thrown back to reveal a solid black tunic, with two faintly flowing dark disks upon his epaulets, the insignia of the Dark Queen's armies. The man cruelly spurred his horse toward the three companions, brandishing a pistol with a long, glistening black barrel.

Dwarf quickly removed his hat and twirled it twice around, and the grisly figures of the dwarfish army broke through the smoke, their ancient war cry chilling the frozen air with a bloodcurdling, booming thunder.

"Fly, fly," shrieked Dwarf, and Cranfallow lashed the animal, but the beast reared and Broco fell stunned to the ground beneath the flying hooves of many riders. Cranfallow jumped to help Dwarf, and the explosions of rifles fired at close quarters rattled harshly in their ears. Ned fell, a bullet lodged in his elbow, but with his good arm he raised his weapon and shot down a closing dark rider from his saddle. Dwarf, having regained his breath, and Cranfallow beside him, pulled Ned into the low cover of an overturned and burning wagon.

"Bloody traitors, murdering scum," bellowed Cranfallow, aiming and firing at a madly galloping Urinine horseman. "Bloody missed 'im," he said, firing again.

The Urinine cavalry troop galloped around the burning wagon, singing their dreadful war song.

Black death rides, we are
The Urinine,
We come in darkness
Bearing doom,
We are the Urinine,
Bloody, heartless Urinine.

and their rifles sent volley after volley of crackling bullets all about the three desperate comrades.

Broco's spell had worn away, leaving the three friends hopelessly surrounded by the circling black-cloaked cavalry. The smoke grew a dark blood-red from the crimson reflections of the burning camp, and Dwarf, having no time to reach for his hat, which had been blasted away by a bullet passing close enough to his large head to stun him for a moment, dropped to his knees and began wildly firing the man weapon at the gradually closing circle of horsemen. Ned Thinvoice fell back, stricken for the second time, and soon Cranfallow was holding a bloody leg with a clenched fist, trying to staunch the flowing wound, and Dwarf, in a voice he did not recognize as his own, was crying in a terrible hoarse voice, "Brandagore, Greyfax, Brandagore, Fairingay," firing the bucking man weapon into the smoke until darkness overcame him, and he remembered no more.

Bear, at Otter's side, was tying a piece of his torn jacket about his friend's arm. After they had watched the two horsemen disappear, they had been set upon by a platoon of howling Worlughs, who cut all escape by encircling the hill. They were too hard pressed to see Dwarf, who had been upon one of the horses, but so small as to go unnoticed, or the desperate stand he was making only a short distance from their embattled hill. Otter flinched as he tried to move back to his position near Flewingam, who was also wounded, and bandaged about the head with another piece of ripped clothing. Bear's own huge left hand was numb and useless from a bomb that had landed near him and he had to hold the clumsy, noisy man weapon with his remaining good arm, which caused the bumping thing to bang repeatedly against his sore jaw, making him groan bitterly with every jarring report. The whirling, fire-smothered night around him at last began to grow dim, and weakened from his wound, he slumped, falling away into a soundless black cloak that covered him heavily, pressing him spiraling away into a dreamless sleep.

Around the four figures, the firing grew more intense, and a billowing pall of grayish red smoke covered them. Mithramuse looked upward, trying to see the sky, and to detect what this new threat was that had been approaching for the past explosive minutes of the battle. He could see nothing at first, so thickly clung the evil haze, but he at last broke through the dark mists, and there before him, flying down the rearmost ranks of enemy soldiers, was Froghorn Fairingay, son of Fairenaus, leading a great host of shining, grim-faced elfin warriors. They swept away all before them like a blazing white tide, and winding the ancient battle horn of Fairenaus, king and Elder of the Fourth Age, the raging brilliant light of the Elfin host rampaged nearer, slaying great numbers of Worlughs and Gorgolacs, and falling upon the terrified but grimly holding Urinine.

With a sudden fit of uncontained joy, General Greymouse, Mithramuse, lifted the hems of his gray, mud-spattered, bloodied cloak, and danced a quick jig upon the beleaguered hill. He had not had time to look about him at the wounded, unconscious figures of his three faithful guards. With a jubilant cry, and revived somewhat, he sent soaring skyward green and blue rocket bursts, which turned blazing in midair to a fine, gold-hued dust that fashioned the glittering letters, "HURRAH, FARAGON FAIRINGAY," then all gleamed a deadly crimson, and turning and whirling ever downward, flowed into the forms of a thousand exploding shells that burst savagely among the crazed, fleeing enemy ranks.

Froghorn, engaged fiercely by two grimly struggling Urinine, spied the fallen mud-covered bright-green-brimmed dwarf hat, and with deadly skill long unused in battle, he cleaved a head and split a helm with a vicious two-handed stroke of the bright blazing elfin blade his father had carried long ages before him upon Atlanton Earth in the Wars of the Dragon Hordes. He dismounted and knelt beside the wagon, and his clear gray-blue eyes clouded with a terrible, burning wrath. He reached out tenderly and touched Broco's brow.

"Thank the breath of Starkeeper, he yet lives," he said aloud, and quickly moved the little man and carried him to his great steed, Pe'lon.

"We must find Mithramuse quickly, my friend. I fear our Dwarf has taken grievous wounds."

"I shall go as softly as wind across shadow," replied Pe'lon as Froghorn mounted, holding the limp figure of the little man closely to his body, and Pe'lon moved gently away toward the hill where the now shining figure of Mithramuse stood outlined against the raging, fiery bier of his camp.

Mithramuse sobered from his wild elation as Froghorn neared, bearing Dwarf.

"What dark news mars this hour?" asked

Mithramuse. "Are we to celebrate a victory with the funeral fires of our brave Dwarf?"

"He yet lives, Master, but we must find healing for him quickly," said Froghorn, looking down at the gentle calm settling across Dwarf's face.

"I have Bear and Otter here with me. These three, I think, must come with us to Cypher, for the halls of Lorini have healed many hurts more grave than these."

"Are we allowed that without our lady's word?" asked Froghorn, surprised at the older wizard's suggestion.

"I shall answer to her, although I think she will not find it amiss, for these three have been her faithful followers and have borne up their parts most gallantly. She will deem it an honor to be able to reward them with a stay in Cypher."

"Then what of the crossing? Shall we be able to hold them safe?"

"With prudence and good timing," replied Mithramuse. "But we must be quick. Come, carry Dwarf here, and let Pe'lon return as he will."

Froghorn dismounted, and the great horse neighed once, bowed, and was gone.

"Come nearer here, and help me call the Watcher. He shall carry us safely over." the older man, gray cloak covering the halo glow of light, stooped low and began his chant. Froghorn joined, and soon all sky and earth reversed, and the distant glimmer of stars shone through the hazy pall of smoke, and a shimmering, golden ship came riding upon the breath of wind from the last outer meadows of Windameir's realms, and across that deep, silent beginning and end of time bore back the two wizard kings, Faragon, elder of Fairingay, and Mithramuse Cairngarme, ageless of the ageless Circle of Light, servants of Cephus Starkeeper, and the unnamable holy name, and also among them were the three unknowing figures of they who had set out from beyond Calix Stay, Great Water that guarded the nether realms, and on and beyond time they flew, and on and beyond sight or vision of mortal eyes that yet lived upon Atlanton Earth, and Dwarf, and Bear, and Otter passed there into Lorini's halls for a time.

And behind, across the darkened borders of Northerland, Melodias Starson and Greyfax Grimwald moved with their white shining hosts against the foes that threatened Lorini's borders.

For a time, an unquiet peace settled over the waning twilight of the world of Atlanton Earth.